Beyond Night

Eric. S. Brown
and
Steven L. Shrewsbury

Let the world know:
#IGotMyCLPBook!

Crystal Lake Publishing
www.CrystalLakePub.com

ISBN: 978-1-64255-860-9

Cover Art:
Ben Baldwin—www.benbaldwin.co.uk

Layout:
Lori Michelle—www.theauthorsalley.com

Edited by:
Monique Snyman

Proofread by:
Tere Fredericks
Jan Strydom
Sue Jackson

Welcome to another Crystal Lake Publishing creation.

Thank you for supporting independent publishing and small presses. You rock, and hopefully you'll quickly realize why we've become one of the world's leading publishers of Dark and Speculative Fiction. We have some of the world's best fans for a reason, and hopefully we'll be able to add you to that list really soon. Be sure to sign up for our newsletter to receive two free eBooks, as well as info on new releases, special offers, and so much more.

Welcome to Crystal Lake Publishing—Tales from the Darkest Depths.

Other novels by Crystal Lake Publishing

The Third Twin: A Dark Psychological Thriller by Darren Speegle

Blackwater Val by William Gorman

Where the Dead Go to Die by Aaron Dries and Mark Allan Gunnells

Beatrice Beecham's Cryptic Crypt by Dave Jeffery

Aletheia: A Supernatural Thriller by J.S. Breukelaar

Sarah Killian: Serial Killer (For Hire!) by Mark Sheldon

The Final Cut by Jasper Bark

Pretty Little Dead Girls: A Novel of Murder and Whimsy by Mercedes M. Yardley

Or check out other Crystal Lake Publishing books for more Tales from the Darkest Depths.

Other titles by Eric S. Brown

Monster Hunt

Mecha

Kaiju Wars

Kraken

Other titles by Steven L. Shrewsbury

Philistine

Born of Swords

King of the Bastards (with Brian Keene)

Last Man Screaming

"In their castle beyond night
Gather the Gods in Darkness,
With darkness to pattern man's fate.

The colors of darkness are no monotonous hue—
For the blackness of Evil knows various shades,
Full many as Evil has names."

Karl Edward Wagner

Preface

Blood across the stone slab, blood flying in the air, August saw nothing righteous in this place of worship.

Dismemberment didn't evoke nightmares in August Arminius, Decurion of the Ninth Roman Legion. As a youth, he'd seen tribal leaders in his Germanic homeland chopped to pieces, either in clan warfare or by the encroaching Roman forces from afar. Once, in Iberia, he witnessed an attempt to pull a man apart using four horses, but that operation came off hitched when one animal failed to run at an equal speed to his kindred. Never, though, had August watched an arm being ripped loose from a living man. Sliced off with a sword at the mid-bicep or chopped crudely free with an axe, yes. The sight of one of his auxiliaries shoved against a standing slab in the stone circle, pinned at the waist by the huge foot of a monstrous shape and then having his sword arm torn out of the socket would stick in August's mind for all time.

August found that he couldn't blink, couldn't move, nor even shout and alert the others in the scouting party near the border of Caledonia. Though the soldier being mutilated raised his shield in defense, a swiping blow by the figure in the murky time before twilight downed this action. August's mind struggled to reconcile what his eyes told him: That a shape taller than any man, even a warrior from his native lands, bearing a halo-like outline of white haze, dominated the scout before him. Froiz was that scout's name—or Flores as they called him back in his Spanish homeland that the Romans absorbed him from.

Just a kid, August thought as the young fighter struggled on and bled badly. *Barely twenty years old. How does a twenty-year-old bleed well?*

The shape towering over young Froiz—a being from a nightmare, surely not a man—gave the auxiliary soldier a roundhouse shot to the face with the dismembered arm. That blow sent Froiz's helmet flying and it bounced off a nearby stone pillar. August saw a host of birds, blacker than night, fly from this stone as the helm flew. As the cloud of birds separated, they revealed two human forms behind them in the woods. The dying cries of Froiz didn't make these grim folk of the woods smile. August named them as Picts, having the skin and reddish black hair of a breed of savages that lurked by the thousands in Caledonia. One was a tall man, his hairline far receded, and a flowing white robe about his shoulders that seemed to mate up with his long ivory beard. Beside him stood a boy of just a shade over ten years of age, clad in a robe similar to the old man, but brown in color. They watched the further dying throes of Froiz as he staggered and fell over a vertically laid stone slab. The blood of the Iberian pooled for a moment just before Froiz fell off it. August thought he slipped, but soon noted the bearded man's hand ran red in the moonlight, and that his touch had guided him to the earth. These two figures showed no fear at the sight of the hairy monster in the deep night.

Again, August couldn't warn the two soldiers that rode up to the stone circle on horses. He wanted to scream that a monster skulked amongst the stones and that the robed boy from the woods had retrieved Froiz's cover and flung it almost playfully their way. The two soldiers halted as the helm came to rest before them. August could only watch as the creature, certainly a hellish beast belonging in a fireside tale to scare children, charged howling at the two men from August's cavalry group. Arms out like a bird ready for flight, the massive thing went after the horses and slammed its forearms into their necks, up under their heads. August heard the sickening pops as bones broke, but his eyes held amazement as the horses reared back, toppled by the strength of the beast, and sent the two men out of their secured positions.

He wanted to fight, wanted to draw his gladius, wanted to call on the spearmen and archers to move in and aid their brothers in arms, but he couldn't.

As the creature attacked the two prone men, August saw the foul form clearer in the diffuse morning light. The miasma that surrounded the thing wasn't anything supernatural nor endowed by the gods with spirit. The white haze was fur.

One soldier's helm had rolled off him. He'd probably undid his chin strap and been lazy as he rode in the night. It cost him dearly as a falling white furred paw sent him to see if there were any gods out there or not. The helm of the other soldier didn't help him, though, as the beast used both hands to slap either side of his head and render the Legion short one more man. Once the clubbing blows of the ivory beast pulped each soldier's head, the fright on two legs turned to look in his direction. August came to understand why he couldn't act. When the blue eyes of the creature focused on him, pupils growing smaller, August tore his look from that scene back to where the two men from the forest stood by the stone slabs.

His heart ached as the two savages froze in place like the world ceased to let time go by. Their features flattened like they took on the attributes of a two dimensional sketch . . . and they dissipated like a thousand leaves shaking loose from a tree. In moments, the two figures were no more, but in their stead, further back in the woods, like true lingering shadows of these men stood two more shapes. However, these two were female in profile, but akin to the others of the woods in that they wore robes and one was an aged woman with a girl in tow who looked over ten years old.

The beast howled and August sat up at last.

"Dreams, damn them."

He reclined on his bedmat in the morning trying to make sense of it all. Within his tent amongst the encamped Ninth Roman Legion, August sucked his breath in fast. Head throbbing, sweat soaking his face, the big man clutched the sides of his head as the images swum fast within. He breathed deep once, then several times shallow.

"Just a dream," the words fell out, but louder than he planned when his mouth opened. Though a warm summer morning, chills tremored across his body. "But Froiz rode out with the scouts, didn't he? Damn."

He thought of the men that went north the previous day to scout, and wondered why he'd dreamed such a wild thing. To fear those priests of the oaks—yes, that came naturally after what they'd all seen of the Celts in the south and heard yarns about for ages. Often, he and others spotted the ones they named Druids in the forests, watching and holding branches, staring . . . and seeming to disappear back into the green. August didn't think it magick, just good placement, but he'd not have wanted to ride in after one of those wizards, either.

"Decurion?" a voice called out from outside his tent flaps. "Sir?"

"It's all right, Rufus," August croaked, measuring his breaths again, his body calming from the nightmare that felt so real he could smell the beast inside it. That dank odor curled inside his nose for some time afterwards, like a rude fecal scent mingled with heavy sweat.

Still, the head of the slave not yet fifteen years old poked through the flap. "Sir? You were trying to cry out in your rest. What ails you?"

August faced the young man, his servant, a boy enslaved by the Romans from southern Britain since he could toddle, and said, "Was I loud?"

"Just once," Rufus grinned, and shook his head of curly red locks that were cut tight to his head. "Do the gods confound you in your sleep?"

"Perhaps," August coughed and rubbed his eyes again.

"I was taught as a child such things happen when you sleep on a land full of gods not used to your presence."

"Conceivably," August answered, eyes scanning the interior of his tent as if the answer would be written there. *Damn Celts*, he mused about Rufus. *They had a god in everything*.

Rufus took a knee, but stayed out of the tent for the most part. "There are bad, old gods the closer we get to the Pictland border, sir. They are different from the gods of my Celtic peoples and certainly of yours from Rome."

"I'm not from Rome," August muttered and winked, getting to his knees, head still shaky from the nightmare.

Rufus smiled back. "I know. It isn't uncommon for the gods of a foreign land to haunt the dreams of a stranger."

"Oh?" August stepped out of his tent and stood, naked as the day he was born in afar off Germania, and took in the new day. "How rude of them to visit."

"Then again, we have entered their free land of tribes with swords and shields, not flowers and compost, sir."

"I knew we forgot the daisies and manure." August stretched and yawned. "Rufus, fetch me some water."

The youth held up a basin and a pitcher from behind the tent, then set them on a tiny table he'd erected by the dwelling.

August nodded, glad for Rufus' efficiency. "Very good." He looked to the forest, far off from where their portion of the group bivouacked, and saw dozens of servants emerge from the forest at once. Though startled, August saw them all carrying sacks or animals foraged from the woods. Two fair haired youths, twins, not slaves but soldiers, waved to August. "I see the brothers Crispinus and Decimus have bagged their share of rabbits."

Rufus only glanced over at the twins, who carried sets of arrows with four rabbits apiece strung through them. "The archers are excellent at their trade, though their morning desire to slum with us servants is curious."

August frowned at him. "Don't be that way."

Rufus shrugged. "There is game aplenty in our forests."

Our. The Celt boy chaffed a bit at his servitude even if August treated him well.

"Have the scouts returned from yesterday?"

Rufus turned abruptly. "Amusing that you ask, sir. There is great distress among the ranks that they have not."

Amusing? Water cupped in his hands and sloshed over his face, August trembled. "And you listen well to the ranks?"

"Of course. While the higher ranks stay silent, the centurions gossip like women at a party or Senators at a bathhouse."

"Yeah?"

Rufus' eyes rolled to the sky. "Or so I hear."

Again, he splashed his face and then gripped the sides of the tiny table and allowed the drops to fall into the basin. "But the scouts are not back, no word from up that way?"

"No. sir."

He wanted to write it all off as a silly dream, and wanted to pray for answers, but all he could do was say the name of the one he secretly prayed to. "Jesus Christ."

Chapter I

General Malitus didn't care for how his day began. He had been roused from a drunken sleep due to the arrival of a frantic messenger. The rider, sliding down from the frothy horse like he'd been born to perform the act, announced himself from the scouting party, one dispatched ahead of Malitus' Legion at Eboracum.

The General sat on a folding bench and frowned as he listened to the report. The messenger, a young man of barely eighteen by the look of him, wasn't familiar to Malitus. His breaths came out hurried, and the youth spoke so quick Malitus reprimanded him twice with sharp words. Head still full of wine, the General tried to even out his thoughts. His mouth dry, Malitus reached for some morning wine. His head throbbed as a dire fear swam in the messenger's eyes beyond the uneasiness of one so low ranked reporting to a General. That fright ran deeper and more primal, Malitus mused, as if the hounds of Tartartus themselves chewed at the puppy's heels during the long journey back to Briton territory. The city of Eboracum, where Malitus' quartered the Legion for the time being, sat near the border of the land of Caledonia where the wild Picts roamed.

"Enough boy," Malitus ordered, weary of the broken attempts to speak and cursing his own swimming mind. "Am I to understand the cause of all your spirited words this morning is that one of the scouting parties has met a rather untoward end?"

The youth nodded vigorously, looking from the General to the two other military men emerging to flank him in the large tent. "Yes, sir. Decurion Arminius requests you come see yourself at once."

Malitus bit down his anger and sipped the wine. His face contorted at the sour nature of it, but this beverage ran typical of what the soldiery drank.

"August," he said aloud and rubbed his brow with his thumb and index fingers.

"August Arminius," said the taller of the two officers, "for all his faults, truly acts as the best cavalry commander and judge of advanced scouts we have at our disposal."

Malitus muttered, "Thank you, Ralta, I know who he is." He turned to the shorter officer on his right and muttered, "A bad end? Are there men dead up there, Quintus?"

The officer shrugged and waved at the messenger.

The youth nodded again, fast.

Malitus sighed loud. "I assigned Arminius to use his men in order to avoid these kinds of problems."

Quintus' brow furrowed, but his look grew intense. "Arminius is a veteran, even if he's a mutt German. He's the best horseman we have and his instincts are better than a hound's."

"Scouts sometimes die, sir," the taller man to his left offered and rolled his eyes at Quintus words.

Malitus turned, glaring at the taller man. "Mind

your attitude, Ralta. August has served under me for several years now, and very well." Though he didn't extol the fact, the General understood August and he had never become high-quality friends, but he did hold the cavalry auxiliary leader in high regard when it came to the man's abilities.

Ralta made a fake bow at Quintus. "Forgive me greatly, Quintus Pilate."

Quintus' look at Ralta soured. "Arminius' job was a simple one. He and his detachment were to travel ahead of the Legion proper, out of Eboracum, and serve as not only its advance eyes but also to attack as bait for any locals in the region who were brave enough to go up against Roman might. His auxiliary force in the forward position must be compromised."

Malitus sipped more wine and sighed. "I hadn't actually thought there would be any who were foolish enough to try to oppose them, but the Picts of Caledonia are an unpredictable lot."

Ralta seemed unable to stop smiling as he stated, "The 9th Legion, a battle hardened one, strides to action composed of veterans and men who know death well. I think a few of them have Death nicknamed."

The General declared, "The 9th prepares to march out of our base here at Eboracum soon to head north again and I won't have it delayed long. Certainly not by what was more likely the work of a lucky group of bandits than any real military threat. I shall hear what happened to our forces beyond August's camp."

The messenger nodded and wanted to back out of the tent, but he stayed put.

Quintus said, "The 9th had better get on the move

or they would never reach their intended destination in the time allotted by the emperor."

Ralta pursed his lips. "Do you think Hadrian will really visit this Isle in the next year? Such a trip for him seems based in words, not actuality."

Malitus spat a curse, and a mouthful of wine, before saying, "It's too early to talk wretched politics."

He quickly moved to the door and left his quarters in the Scamnum Legatorum. His eyes beheld what his ears had heard before, that a bulk of the 9th assembled in the heart of the city, preparing for review, to be told when to march. Quintus Pilate and Ralta flanked him again in the yard of the Praetentura. They were officers upon whom he knew he could depend. The messenger was still present, and Malitus chose to ignore him.

Malitus turned to Quintus. "Ready my personal guard and a small group of your best cavalrymen."

"Are you sure that is wise sir?" Ralta challenged him, his humor faded. "We haven't heard what happened out there yet. If there is a large force of Picts afoot . . . "

Malitus glared at Ralta. "When I want your opinion, I will ask for it. I am neither so old nor feeble that I cannot ride or wield a sword."

The General heard Quintus snicker at the good natured, if edged, rebuke he gave Ralta. If they were not all familiar with each other, then one could almost describe the relationship between Ralta and Quintus as that of blood enemies. Such was often the relationship between leaders of infantry and cavalry. Ralta believed Quintus a pompous showman and Quintus thought Ralta to be a simpleton. Their affections for one another did nothing to interfere with the effectiveness of the 9th's operations, however, so Malitus tolerated it. The two men were soldiers and had spilt blood together.

Beyond that, they were brothers, though one could not judge them so by their appearances. Ralta, a tall, hard man, his shoulders wide and his jaw sat firmly as if carved in stone. The skin of his arms stretched tight around the masses of muscles underneath it, while Quintus had the appearance of a pampered scribe. He was thin and much shorter than his brother. Anyone meeting his gaze could see the fierce intellect that dwelt within him. He relied on speed and guile whereas Ralta was nothing short of a powerhouse of brute strength and determination.

As Quintus departed, Malitus returned his attention to Ralta, shaking a finger at the giant. "And no, you're not coming with us either."

Ralta's expression was a tightly drawn rictus of rage but Malitus knew the big man would challenge him no further. "As you wish, sir."

"I need you here to get the Legion moving. We are already behind and cannot afford more delays. The emperor is expecting progress with quelling the Pict threats into Briton since the last trip up north. I'll not have our reputation tarnished. Channel that fury within you toward the men. It will surely motivate them to move all the more quickly."

Ralta's scowl slid into a wicked smile. "I imagine it will sir. I imagine it will."

"Good," Malitus laughed, slapping Ralta's shoulder. "I will not be coming back to comfortable quarters soon. I expect you and the greater part of the

Legion to catch up to us on the road to this place within a few days. Do I make myself clear?"

"As a sunny day, sir," Ralta acknowledged the command, looking across the sky at two dark birds lazily flying across the open sky. "Severus?" He called out to a centurion nearby, standing at the ready, lance in hand.

"Yes, sir?" Severus answered, still at attention.

Malitus followed in the direction Quintus had headed, but turned his head to hear Ralta ask, "Is it ordinary for ravens to fly in pairs?"

Severus said something about thinking the animals Ralta saw were crows, but the General ignored the rest.

By the time General Malitus and his detachment reached Arminius' forward camp, the sun had already peaked in the sky and begun its descent. August awaited them by the assembled horses and rushed to meet them as they climbed down from their mounts at the camp's edge.

"General Malitus," August saluted him, standing straight. "I had not expected you to come yourself, sir."

"You send a messenger who babbles on out of crazed fear as if the whole of the region had risen in arms against us and you didn't expect me to come personally?" He put his right fist across his chest to salute and smiled. "Perhaps, you're slipping Arminius."

August's face remained rigid, betraying no anger or embarrassment. That the General would only travel with the bulk of the Legion wasn't a bad assumption.

"All this fuss and bother, overtaken by a few

barbarians in the night?" Quintus chuckled as he walked along with the General. "Just how many men did you lose August?"

"Nine, sir, veterans to a man. Valintien commanded them," August answered, head up, chest firm, hands at his sides. "They weren't all auxiliaries."

Quintus' smug tone departed his voice. "Valintien? You jest with me! That big animal is dead? He's about as mean as that Porcius beast in your troop." He gestured with his right hand over at the thuggish cavalryman, Porcius, who checked the hooves of his mount, cleaning them out with a fine rod usually used for scouring teeth. Porcius' black eyes, typical of a man from Greece, drilled into Quintus, but went back to his labor presently.

"My, my," Malitus said, eyebrows raised as he glanced from Porcius to August. "There were few men in the Legion that would give Quintus or his brother, for that matter, pause. Valintien was one of them."

"That is a reason for concern, sir. He was one of my best," August replied.

"You of Germanic blood are known for a berserker rage, no?"

August blinked. "Some of our kind are very much so inspired in battle, but we are all Romans now."

Malitus smiled at his self-correction. "True. Very true."

Quintus looked to the forest off to their right and said, "I had once seen Valintien carve a path through the ranks of a barbarian horde, leaving a trail of hairy bodies in his wake. A true loss to us all indeed."

August agreed. "No one knew for sure, but Gaius our scribe of the dead, claimed Valintien had killed over three dozen of the enemy on his own, the last two with only his teeth and bare hands as he had lost his sword toward the end of the battle." August expected no less of his countryman, but didn't say that in front of these hailing from Rome proper. Though all the world soon would be Roman, most were still considered adopted children by those from the Empire.

Quintus turned his gaze to August. "All of your scouts died further up the road?"

"The entire squad of them, sir . . . but it's how they were killed that's the cause of my summoning you, for messaging you about it all." August admitted. "I can't give words on the matter, so I felt it best that someone of higher rank saw it for themselves."

"Well, here we are August," Malitus addressed him, using his first name. "Lead on then and let us see what horrors you've stumbled onto."

August figured the General knew his tone retained a mocking lilt but doubted he cared. It didn't take August long to understand Malitus' ire came when faced with the possibility of the incident causing a delay in the 9th's long march that lay ahead.

August climbed on his horse and Porcius joined him. Malitus and Quintus accepted fresh mounts from the group and followed along the road. A dozen more men on horseback joined them, but stayed mostly meandering near the General.

As they rode along, Porcius shot August a sideways glance. "So, we're marching to the North Sea to plant a flag for Rome?"

Eyes on the road, August replied, "Looks like."

Porcius grunted and breathed a few times before

he wondered, "And all of those tribes of Picts are just going to kiss our asses as we pass?"

Still emotionless, August replied, "Oh, certainly."

Porcius burst into laughter and August even cracked a grin.

Quintus shouted up to them, "Care to share the hilarity, gentlemen?"

August called back, "You'd have to comprehend Grecian temple practices to appreciate his jokes about the locals worshipping trees. It's rude humor, sir."

Glad for their silence, and for that of Porcius, August studied the forests as they rode. He thought of those in his dreams who watched from there. He shivered and wished more of the Legions were about him, and not just for fear of those workers of magick in the woods.

After they'd gone over a mile, Porcius said, "I wish Ralta had come up."

"Shut up, will you?" August admonished him, not wanting to hear punitive words from the commanders again.

Porcius yawned and shifted his great girth in the saddle. "He's a strong guy for a proper dandy, that one. I respect that no matter what his loves in life are."

August shot him a look that conveyed his desire to nail Porcius lips closed.

Grinning, Porcius drew his fist over his chest in a mock salute to August. "I'll just be over here dreaming of being a Spartan, sir."

The afternoon wore on as the cavalry detachment, guided by August, reached the site. Like many stone circles they'd all seen in Briton, this one held a particular pattern of jagged rocks and a few longer slabs not unlike what stood taller out on Salisbury plain, but to nowhere near that scale of breathtaking design.

"Here's where the massacre happened," August said, pointing from his mounted position. "In the stone circle."

Malitus looked at the village up the road, a mere dot on the horizon, then turned his focus on the site.

"Massacre?" Quintus looked around, his face stunned at the term, but his way soon softened. He squinted and mumbled, "No other word to describe this scene, is there?"

The grass and earth, tainted red from the dried blood, were accented with the entrails of the squad's men strewn about with insane abandon. Insects had formed on the men, but August had left the scene as it lay.

Malitus murmured, "You didn't alter it much, aye? Wonder the animals didn't scavenge from the bodies. Look, there's guts dangling from a lone tree that bends into the circle."

August said, "I wanted someone to see this as it was left. The men have guarded it in shifts to keep animals out."

Quintus blinked many times. "Thank you so much."

The four dismounted and moved about in the waning light to inspect the carnage. Behind them, the others waited with notched bows and drawn swords.

An arm with jagged, torn flesh lay in the dirt, its fingers clutched, blue, around the sword it held.

Malitus commented, "Some of the men tried to fight back against whatever had swept upon them."

And sweep upon them it had.

Right hand firm on the pommel of his gladius, August waved his left arm about. "Whatever had slain these men had done so with frightening speed from the look of things. The men hadn't had time to form up into any sort of rank. They had been slaughtered where they stood when the battle began, or as close to such as not to matter."

Quintus picked up a piece of a shattered shield. "By the gods, what could have the strength to do this? This shield appears to have been broken by a single blow."

Malitus stared at the terrified expression upon the face of a head that rested only a few steps from where he stood as August spoke up again.

"Do you see now why I called you here?" he asked. "This . . . " He struggled for a name for the violence around them but settled instead for another sweeping gesture of his hand, "This was not done by men."

Malitus' look slowly turned to August, but no derision or insults followed. He knelt by the man and said the name, "Valentien."

Quintus, though, had no such quizzical looks about him. "Oh come now, Arminius! I know you're not a proper Roman, but surely you aren't suggesting this was the work of some supernatural force?" Quintus spat literally on the nearest stone slab. "Yes, this is horrific and needlessly brutal but have we not seen the like before from the barbarians of these parts? These savages are animals, capable of almost anything."

Before August could respond, something moved in the shadows of the woods nearby. His head cranked toward the movement, and many behind them faced that way, too.

Malitus' finger stabbed towards the running figure. "Stop that man and make sure he's taken alive!"

They heard the twang of bow strings as guards fired arrows. The missiles flew through the night and the figure in the distance cried out as arrows pierced flesh. The archers and men on horseback dismounted and moved to the edge of the forest, hesitating to enter after the crying man they'd shot.

Swords drawn, the four went to join them. As the officers drew near, the regular soldiers dived in the grim forest. They rushed after the man who now lay, rolling about at the edge of the woods, shouting curses amid his cries of pain.

They closed around the man, who made no attempt to do anything but strive in vain to tear the arrow from his leg.

"He's a druid," August announced. "Not a Celt, though. He's a Pict."

Malitus wondered, "Because he's pale of skin and red haired?"

August shrugged as the archers trained fresh arrows on the figure. "That and the tattoos colored on him."

"I don't care if he's a damned Egyptian," Quintus cut in. "Get that arrow out of him so he'll shut up, and drag him back to camp with us. If he saw what happened here . . . "

"Agreed," Malitus nodded. "We need to know."

Quintus glared at August. "Anyone here speak their tongue?"

August nodded. "My servant Rufus speaks all dialects of Britannia, including the savages of the Caledonii tribes."

"Good," Quintus grunted as he turned away. "You choose your servants well. It is proper to have a useful slave about, correct?"

While the group had come up to the small stone circle to witness the carnage, August's troop had moved their camp up the road slowly. The soldiers, who hauled the druid out of the trees, dragged him back to August's new camp that camped at the mouth of the village. Even though he'd been staked down spread eagle on the ground, the Pict made no sound.

Quintus walked up, sighed loud to show his displeasure at Rufus' progress in questioning the Pict and asked August, "Where are the locals? I figured they'd be out and watching this like the gawking pigs they are."

Rufus grimaced at his words but August stated, "The village is empty. I thought you'd heard the report I sent along."

Quintus' look intensified on August. "I must've missed that part."

The General walked over to where Rufus sat on the ground beside the prone Pict. "He still won't talk?" Malitus asked the servant.

Rufus bowed his head. "No, sir. This one is rather tight lipped."

"He understands you?"

Rufus took a breath. "I know he does. He doesn't respond in any emotional way to a tongue save for his own. He knows, but refuses to speak."

Quintus raged and swore, but Malitus asked Rufus gently, "What would you surmise about him by his age, appearance and all that? Is this here red haired savage a druid?"

Rufus breathed lightly before saying. "That's a simple term, druid, and is not native to this land of ours. But he truly is of a secretive priest caste, judging by the tats and woad markings on his skin. He's not elevated to a full priest, by the looks of him."

Quintus grumbled, "What was he doing in the woods?"

Arms folded across his chest, August offered, "They pray to trees. Maybe he was worshiping and we disturbed him. It's his home, anyway."

Unamused by August's jeering, Quintus asked Rufus, "Could he have been spying on us? Ask him again."

Rufus wrung his hands together. "That'd be a good guess, sir. I doubt the high priests would go themselves to scout or spy."

Malitus stretched. "Agreed. Still, his silence is infuriating."

Quintus huffed. "You should have listened to me an hour ago and we would have our answers already. Crucify him." His hands balled into fists and he glared at the Pict. "It works each damn time it's tried."

"Have your men do it, Arminius," Malitus ordered with a soft voice. "We can't wait any longer to get some answers. Use one of the trees the druids love so much for it. The 9th should be ready to march at day break, off to the south of us. I want to know what killed those men before Ralta and the rest of the Legion arrive on the morrow."

August took his leave to oversee the crucifixion. Rufus sprang up to shadow him. The sun had set by then. Legionaries dragged the Pict forth to a tree at the edge of the village, presenting him like a prize stag just killed, then dropped him to the ground in a slam meant to stunt him further. Others made ready the means of the crucifixion itself, fetching hammers and nails.

"I know you speak our tongue," Rufus pleaded with the man. "Please, now, tell us what killed our brothers."

August said to two of the soldiers, "Flavius, Mathew, help him stand."

Flavius, a plain faced soldier sporting hair so blonde it ran white, armed up the Pict and held him under his armpits. The other soldier, Mathew, an olive skinned man with black hair, aided him, but remained quiet.

"Careful," August cautioned them at their rough tactics, but felt silly asking his men to be gentle with one they were about to crucify.

Flavius said, "Sir, the medics say the arrow shattered the bone of this fool's right leg. It was a wonder he hadn't bled out."

Seeing they had patched up the leg so he didn't in fact bleed out, August said in a low voice, "Only the grace of God has kept the man alive so far." August could see the man was weak but his will to survive boiled strong.

The Pict then spat at August, missing by a good distance. He did speak.

Frowning, hands to his hips, August asked Rufus, "What did he say?"

Rufus translated, "*I'll tell you nothing, Roman.*"

August shook his head sadly, and thought that he wasn't much of a Roman.

He waved for his men to begin their gross work. The prisoner's hands were bound to the outstretched arms of the tree, his feet next. August saw the hatred burning in the young man's eyes as Mathew squatted over his bound feet and readied the nail that would be driven through them. Flavius stepped back and let Mathew have that duty. August wasn't surprised by this, as Flavius came from highborn stock in the northern reaches of Italy, while Mathew was the son of dispersed inhabitants from Judea, a few generations removed from the destruction of their temple under Titus. For Mathew, the Legion meant a life. For Flavius, it was a portion of a resume.

"Roman or not," the man rasped, suddenly speaking in Latin, "You will die. All of you will die! Adelaido will crush you all."

The thunk of a hammer striking the head of the spike in the Legionnaire's hand turned the man's warnings into nothing more than screams. The spike drove downward through his flesh, separating the bones of the man's feet as it pierced them. Mathew continued to hammer it in. Two other Legionaries went to work on the man's hands. Flavius held the Pict's chest against the tree and let the others do the hammering in fast.

Flavius said to them, "Get his wrists, Lucius, or hold him in place while Porcius drives them home."

Lucius, a thinner soldier, but far older than the rest, pinned the Pict's right arm in place with a cross body move as Porcius, a stocky, shorter man drove the nail in fast. Porcius possessed arms like a man's thighs and made quick work of the nailing.

August shut out the man's screams. Though not a

weakling who couldn't stomach the act, August preferred not to dwell on it. What had to be done, had to be done. A few moments later, the man's body sagged, but the nails held him up fast.

Flavius made a quick bow to August as the men assembled in a line behind him. The three men all stared at him.

Flavius asked, "Sir?"

"Break his legs." August said, looking in the dark forest as the night enveloped it.

Flavius bowed again as Porcius brought out a larger war hammer, a gigantic version of a mallet not used in combat, but liberated from a Celt tribe on Anglesey years ago. It served the purpose Porcius planned for.

August said, "No, Porcius . . . wait."

All eyes went to him.

"Flavius, you do it."

Flavius' mouth dropped and Porcius grinned for a few heartbeats, then hid his smile.

"Yes, sir," Flavius answered, not protesting, but with no strength in his voice.

Unlike the powerfully built Greek, Flavius had a spot of trouble picking up the huge hammer. Not to look weak, he held it off the earth, firm and nodded for the men to hold the Pict in place. He swung the hammer, smashed it into the good shin of the Pict, and while the man screamed once more, the leg showed no damage.

Porcius said, "Come along, Flavius. Swing harder. That didn't make a bruise. Put some balls into it."

Hands about the handle of the long hammer, Flavius swung again, this time connecting with the knee cap of the Pict and by the bones that stuck out and twist in the joint, shattered it.

"Good," Porcius grunted in approval. "Hit 'em again. Lower."

As the cracks and screams sounded out in the night, August decided the work complete enough. He spun about and headed back into the camp.

Porcius voice echoed out, "C'mon, yer not man enough to do the other knee the same way. My wine flask says you choke!"

Flavius and Mathew were both laughing at the jeering.

The woods taunted August and he fully expected to see the shapes of people within to turn to leaves if he stared hard. To cure this fear, he decided not to look at the woods, though every bit of wind, crack of a branch or night bird call made his skin blister with gooseflesh.

Malitus and Quintus shared a late meal. A small fire burned in the center of the circle the officers' tents made in the main avenue of the abandoned village. August nodded at the grim faced sentries of the General's personal guard as he passed them.

"It is done," August announced, walking about the two officers. He noted they didn't dine on the hard tack, vegetables and vinegary wine of the soldiers, but what smelled like dried venison and better wine.

Quintus inclined his head in his direction as August took a seat across the fire from him and the General.

"And?" Quintus demanded, but his indignation ran low.

"Nothing," August said. "He has said nothing yet, but Rufus and the men are with him."

Quintus blinked in surprise though he recovered from it quickly. "Give it time."

"He can speak Latin. He's fooling us."

Malitus chewed, swallowed and stated, "He'll be speaking Greek soon." He cleared his throat. "This venison is exceptional."

"Deer are as plentiful as Picts hereabouts." Quintus wiped his mouth. "These priests, these druids, I know they are outlawed by Rome and rightly so, but how are they so bright as to know so many languages? I thought we stomped them out over a century ago."

August took a cup of wine offered by Malitus and said, "They are a learned class, sir. They write nothing down. It's all in the mind. That's impressive in itself. Their own masters are cruel in their initiation so he's probably a hardened man."

Quintus rose, stretched and said, "The cross will loosen his tongue in time. I trust in the cross. The tree is just as good and more fitting in this case."

The words burned unto August's soul, he drank of the cup and closed his eyes.

Long after Malitus and Quintus had retired in assembled tents, August remained at the waning fire. He saw no reason to enter his small tent Rufus had made up. Sleep would not come for him. His blood felt too stirred by the recent events.

Stretching his legs, August rose from the fireside and began to walk about the camp. Again and again, he replayed the dire dream in his mind. Had it been a sign from God? There could be no other answer as he saw the pieces and the deaths exactly as they happened without being present. Was there meaning to it or was it merely what it seemed . . . a dream to warn him? He prayed, silently, for understanding and guidance. He also wondered just who *Adelaido* was whom the Pict named in his threat.

When he came to a stop, August discovered he had walked to the camp's edge where the prisoner hung; struggling for each of his labored and pained breaths. The man saw him, straining to lift himself on the tree once more. As his body reached the peak of the height the man could hoist himself to, he gave an animal-like howl at August. Somewhere in the night, overhead, August heard the squawk of a bird, a crow perhaps, maybe two.

"You want to know?" The man wailed. "I will tell you! I will tell you all!"

August listened to the man's words as he spoke so furiously, spittle flew from between cracked lips in Latin. Rufus had fallen asleep at the feet of the opposite side of the tree, but awoke and joined August as the Pict spewed the words. August stepped backwards, reeling when the man's tale was concluded. The man on the cross started to laugh.

A crowd of soldiers had gathered behind August in the night, roused from their slumber by the loud declarations. As August noticed them, only then did he realize the man had been shouting, his words carrying throughout the nearby section of the camp, bouncing off the empty domiciles. Many of the Legionaries were pale at the words. Others appeared on the edge of confusion by their open mouths. There were those who shouted back at the dying man, mocking him pointedly with barbed sayings, but they were few in number.

Quintus emerged from the ranks of the crowd, shoving his way through them.

"You!" Quintus barked at one the Legionaries closest to the cross. "Cut out that man's tongue! I will hear no more of this superstitious dung."

Flavius didn't move, he only stared at Quintus in shock and disbelief.

"I said cut out that man's tongue. Now!" Quintus ordered again.

At this, Flavius leaped into motion. He scrambled over to the tree and drew his dagger. His right hand shot out, grasping the front of the crucified man's garments, using them to pull him downward. The man cried out as the nails in his hands shredded his flesh further. Flavius, using the man's own body, climbed up, trying desperately to reach the man's mouth. A blow from the Legionnaire's dagger sent teeth flying from the shot before he was able to clutch the man's jaws. The dagger's blade slashed the man's lips as Flavius drove it inside rough.

Say what one wanted to about being highborn, August thought, *Flavius doesn't screw around in his tasks*. He hadn't let the high class soldier shirk his duties, and Flavius dutifully performed what he had to, but by his expression, he'd rather be fishing.

August felt some revulsion as he watched Flavius, unable to get directly in at the man's tongue from his position, twist the fine blade about wildly within the man's cheeks. The blade plunged through the rear portion of the man's cheek before he finally stopped struggling. His voice, half gagged, half muffled by

Flavius' hold on him turned to harsh cries and then a continued stream of low moans. Blood flowed freely from the mangled remains of his mouth as he tried to suck air in, the man's head dropping onto his chest.

Like a child seeking affirmation from his father, Flavius whirled about to face Quintus, his job done in full.

Quintus gave a nod of approval and disappeared back through the crowd, heading back into the camp.

Flavius' smile faded and he gaped at the bloody tongue, unsure what to do with it.

August watched Quintus go. The group of soldiers began to disperse as well. There was nothing more to see and certainly no more words to hear. August lingered long after they were gone, though. At last, he drew his sword and approached the moaning figure on the tree. He eased the sword's blade up and through the man's short ribs. The man's body gave a final jerk and then collapsed to hang limply upon the tree.

As they did most nights about the campfire before retiring, Porcius and few of the fellows were getting drunk. When August approached and meted out stern looks, a few peeled off the pack and yawned, deciding to retire. Porcius, however, sounding moderately drunk on his sour ration of soldier wine, still laughed.

August wondered, "You find humor in this adventure?"

Porcius quickly retorted, "I find humor in everything, save for my dreams."

"You have bad dreams?"

After a shrug, Porcius stabbed at the fire with his spear tip. "I ain't the only one, huh?"

"Why do you say that?"

"I sleep not far from you. I hear you in the night. It happens."

"Thank you for sharing."

Porcius swigged down the last of his wine and stood, belching loud. "I dream crazy things lately, too."

"What about?"

Porcius shook his head fast as if trying to expel the images from his ears. "I dream of women. A lot."

"That's scary? Hah. I didn't think you were that sort of Greek."

"Piss off and die badly, sir," Porcius shot back. "No, of women in the night, women in the woods."

"I see monsters in the woods. I'll trade you dreams."

"You wish. No, they come to me a lot, images of man older gal with reddish gray hair, all kinky and long, gotta lil gal with her, 'bout half her size."

"You don't say?"

Porcius nodded. "They raised a woman from the dead last night."

August near to choked on his flask of wine. "What?"

"Yeah, these two gals prayed and chanted over this big ol' pupil thing, a cocoon like a butterfly, and it burst open, oozing blood and guts . . . and out rolls this beautiful woman, pale and red haired . . . nicely built too."

"Wonder why you'd dream that?'

"I dunno, really. I can't say I ever think about such things, or hear about them . . . well, once I heard a story as a kid about an evil queen that promised to return from the dead for her people. I'm sure it's a folk tale retold lots of times."

"And something brought it up now?"

"Bloody curious, huh?"

August agreed and gave Porcius his flask. The Greek born man proudly sucked it dry and smacked his lips together.

"Better?"

Porcius burped again. "Much. We'll see if the wine keeps the spirits away tonight."

After he lay down, August wished that was possible.

Chapter II

August's men and the cavalry detachment, brought up by the General, rose with the sun. Trumpets sounded out as the men were called to assemble and prepare themselves to move out.

In a low voice, August noted to Quintus, "Thought the original plan was for us to wait for the rest of the Legion here, the General has decided to move on?"

Quintus replied in a quiet voice, "Not far. Just a few miles north to the town of Rutland that lies beyond the empty village."

"It's the closest town," Malitus explained, mindful of their talk even if he, Quintus, and August rode at the front of the column of advancing troops. "That druid had to come from somewhere close. The populace there may know something about what happened to your scouts and this empty village. Send a runner back to the Legion and inform them to start their advance."

"Their deaths should not go unavenged," Quintus added, eying the forest about their road. "Besides, we still need to know what happened to them. If there are dangers on the path that lies ahead of the 9th, it will be better to discover them now than the hard way later on."

"I thought we could afford no delays General,"

August reminded Malitus, also scanning the trees and keeping a tight hold on his reins.

"There will be no delay," Malitus smiled, not taking malice in the slight rebuke. "The town of Rutland lies in the direction we would be marching even if the rest of the 9th had caught up to us already. They will find us."

"Fear not Arminius." Quintus grinned, using his proper name. "Not everyone in the next town will be as tight lipped as that druid spy."

"I recall him telling us quite a bit, Quintus." August frowned, his eyes full of the story they had heard in the end.

Quintus gave a dismissive wave of his hand. "What? That manure he spouted while nailed on the tree? Really?"

"Quite a tale to spin as you are dying, sir."

Quintus guffawed. "Are you really such a fool as to believe a story like that?"

August stiffened in his saddle, the fingers of his hand brushing the pommel of his sword in its scabbard. "I'd have rested easier in the night if he'd have pleaded for grace from his gods instead of deciding to tell such a crazed yarn."

"Quintus," Malitus warned, though the cautionary tone was actually meant for August. "We are all men of Rome here, in one fashion or another. Let us show each other the courtesy of civilized respect in our duty."

August moved his hand away from his sword, forcing away the anger he felt. The day would come when Quintus would push him too far but that day was not today.

Rutland proved to be another small town not too different from the abandoned spot. August hoped for it having a more defensible layout in such environs. Most towns did, even in such a primitive place. Not this one however, even if it appeared Romanized at one point due to the gravel streets and grid pattern of homes. A cluster of randomly placed hovels had been added to the more structured Roman lines of tiny buildings. Celts built fine abodes, but some of these hovels lacked the architectural skill that typically accompanied the mindful Celt carpenter. One glance at the place made it clear that the town was a dying one. Several of its structures were badly neglected and on the verge of collapsing inward on themselves. There was no chance of it providing shelter to an entire Legion once the 9th caught up with them and even the baths in the middle of town had been filled with weeds.

"What a dive," Porcius murmured. "There aren't even enough thatched roofs to shelter many more than the current cavalry detachment and scouts."

"We camp again then," August snapped. He noticed the dark clouds rolling in from the south and sighed. "The last thing we need for the next night is rain."

Rufus galloped up to August and offered him a full canteen of water. "I think the rain and storm may miss us. I know the skies."

August drank deep and nodded to him. "Thanks. The short march hasn't been a bad one but it ate up some of the morning."

Head bowed, Rufus soon eyed the other officers and then rolled his eyes to August.

Quintus kept busy, ordering the men to dig in and make a camp about Rutland.

Thinking, Quintus Pilate the master of understatement yet again, August rode up to where the General waited with a cluster of cavalry men. Malitus gestured at the crowd of townsfolk who had gathered together in the town's center. August could almost smell the fear coming off them; they shook at the very sight of the armed soldiers. They were primitive folk by Roman standards, nothing more than simple farmers. The sight of so many armed Romans had surely turned their day into a bad one. These were not the savage Picts of the northern territories, but merely domesticated farmers, trying to reach up the ladder to the next level of civilization.

"Let us go meet the locals," General Malitus smiled at his officers. "Hard to accept such a people could produce an army of brutal bastards to challenge us."

The General, the members of his personal guard, and August rode to where the villagers waited. August noticed at once the burly man, with the appearance of a blacksmith by his apron and the pincers in his belt, who stood at the head of the cluster of villagers. Though he held no weapon, his back stretched up firm and his stance was one of defiance despite the Romans' numbers. August prayed the man wouldn't try anything foolish in defense of his people. One crucifixion on this journey was one too many already.

"I am General Malitus, commander of Rome's 9th Legion. My troops and I mean you no harm. We seek only a place to camp until the morrow, and information."

That last bit only served to put the townsfolk

further on edge. They whispered amongst themselves in a tongue he couldn't put a finger on. He almost spoke up, but it wasn't August's place to question Malitus at every turn. He kept his mouth shut and let the General play things as he wanted.

The big man rubbed a meaty hand in his beard and jutted his chin at the General. No words came out, just a look of boredom radiated from his eyes. August half smiled at the man's pluck, but again, he stayed silent.

"A Roman scout party was attacked not far from here by a group of your druids."

The big man said, "Druids?" like it was an alien word to him.

Malitus carried on. "My men will be questioning each of you as the location of that group. I highly suggest that you be forthcoming with them."

"Huh, druids . . . " the blacksmith said again, a smile probably buried in that huge beard, but from August's angle it came tough to find.

Malitus let his words hang in the air over the townsfolk like the approaching rain clouds, dark and ominous.

"We shall begin with your mayor or village elder. Whoever is in charge here."

"That would be me," the blacksmith said in Latin, stepping further from the group. He ground his hands together furiously as if he were crushing a Roman skull between them. In his eyes danced fire and he made no effort to hush it.

"Good," Malitus smirked. "I applaud your honesty, sir." The General turned to his guardsmen. "Bring him. That man and I have much to discuss."

As they all moved, August turned to see Rufus

again, offering the canteen of water at a distance. August smirked and pointed to the flask dangling from the slaves' waist belt. It was time for a good belt of weak wine.

In about thirty minutes, after they had chosen camping territories and drank their ration of wine, August and Quintus joined their leader. They flanked Malitus as he sat inside the hut he'd claimed as his own for the duration of the detachment's stay in the village. Two soldiers led the blacksmith to the hut's entrance and shoved him inside.

General Malitus sipped at a cup of wine as the blacksmith righted himself and stood, tall and proud before him. "What is your name?"

"I am called Fagan," the burly man growled. "Your Roman courtesy isn't a lie, I see. But I and many others know your tongue for generations, for common trade purposes and well, for the fact that you are here."

"Well, Fagan," Malitus leaned forward. "Since you say you are in charge here, I hold you responsible for the massacre of a scouting party of *my* men."

"I know of no such thing."

"The Roman Empire does not take the murder of her troops lightly, I assure you."

Fagan's lips twisted into an angry snarl. "We had nothing to do with that."

Malitus chuckled and waved a hand dismissively. "Oh, I don't doubt that . . . but those who did almost certainly passed through your village."

"You assume much."

"I need to know who they are and what their purpose is. Do you understand me?"

Fagan looked at the other officers and his nose

flared a little. "I understand, Roman, that you and yours believe you are the greatest power in this world. You are *not,* at least not here."

Malitus smiled. "Go on, you significantly amuse me. Tell on!"

"You are far from home." Fagan's voice fell grave. "And have no idea what you are facing."

"Then enlighten me," Malitus grinned, sipping more wine. "Am I to fear Druid magick? Will you send enchantments from the woods to strike me down?"

Fagan glared at the General but remained silent.

"I could have you tortured, you know that, Fagan? Did you not hear the druid crying in the night, crucified?"

Fagan said nothing but his eyes screamed many things to August. He wondered what the blacksmith understood about it all and how the General missed the clues.

Malitus said, "However I do not think that you are the sort of man who would yield to such tactics. Your people are your life and I appreciate that. Your every word and action bespeaks that resolution. You would die to save them, aye?"

Fagan's expression grew dour in the middle of his hairy face, his features drooping low, but still he said not a word.

"Do not make me order my men to slaughter your folk and burn your homes to the ground, all right?"

Fagan spoke at last. "What do you want of me, Roman?"

August thought he spoke the name like a curse word.

"Only what I have asked to you this very day,"

Malitus reminded him. "Tell me who murdered my men."

"There are a great many Picts in these parts, General," Fagan said as if those simple words explained all.

"And? You are of a Celtic stripe I can see, but live on their border. Picts." Malitus pressed. "Are they involved with the Druids?"

Fagan gave a loud laugh. "You prove your ignorance, great General."

Lucius, one of the two soldiers guarding Fagan, stepped forward, striking him between his shoulder blades with the pommel of his sword. Fagan grunted in pain and slumped forward down to his knees.

August worried that Fagan would do something rash but the man only craned his head about to give the soldier who struck him a look that promised death. Blacksmith's were always bigger men, August pondered, as the Celtic folks brought such men more portions of food and drink. One didn't want the maker of your sword to be a weakling.

"You forget yourself, little man," Quintus warned, and August came near to smiling, as the smithy was bigger than him. "You are speaking to a commander of the Roman army!"

"Enough!" Malitus ordered, flinging his half-finished wine to the dirt floor. "Tell me more of these Picts."

"What is to tell great General?" Fagan spat the word *great*, making it an insult. "They have fought your kind before and your Legions have gone north before. You ask me to taunt me. They are an ancient and dark people. Their ways are not yours or ours.

They are in touch with things beyond the ken of normal men."

"Superstitious nonsense," Quintus raged and looked at the spilled wine like it was a dead pet. "Is that all you have to offer us?"

Malitus gestured Quintus to silence once more. "Let him speak."

"There is more in this world, darker, fouler things, than those like you can begin to imagine," Fagan said as he stood up. "The Picts didn't kill your men, great General, of that I am sure. More likely it was the work of the beasts."

August spoke up. "We found strange tracks amid the bodies of men, tracks that no man could have left. The druid spoke of such beasts."

The heads of Quintus and Malitus turned to glance at August.

"See?" Fagan smiled in pure and open defiance, "You know already what you face but refuse to accept its reality."

Malitus had grown weary of the interrogation as it was proving most frustrating and yielding little fruit. "This man's presence sickens me," he commented with a fake yawn. "Have him taken away and flogged for his disrespect."

The two guards closed in on Fagan, taking hold of him. He shook himself loose from their hands. "And what of my people?" Fagan demanded.

"I did not come here to claim this land for Rome," Malitus sniped dismissively. "It already belongs to Rome. Despite your insolence, I will not punish them for it. We will leave on the morrow, when the rest of my men arrive, and go forth to the wild lands beyond."

Fagan nodded at Malitus and allowed himself to be led outside.

"General," Quintus urged emphatically. "Should we not teach these savages proper respect? I think they deserve some."

"Still your thirst for blood, Quintus," Malitus answered, giving his body servant a motion for more wine. "We have no time for such petty matters. There are far greater things that our efforts should be focused on, savvy?"

August felt relief wash over him at that moment. He had no love of Fagan and his shoddy kinsfolk but neither did he have the love of violence that Quintus possessed. The villagers were no threat to the Legion. If his instincts were true, there would be plenty enough blood ahead of them without adding Fagan's folk to it. The Picts loomed large in his mind and he dreaded their willingness to die to meet their gods.

Noticing that Malitus' attention was now focused on him, August did his best to conceal his respite.

"What do you make of all those, August?" Malitus asked as he unrolled a scroll and then threw it to one side. "Do you believe these wild tales of monsters that roam the night, and the dark magicks of these Picts?" His perturbed look probably wasn't angst to August, but that his servant hadn't brought him wine yet.

August was caught off guard. "I truly do not know what to think, sir," he answered honestly. "I do know that *something* killed those scouts."

"*Something?*" Quintus challenged, shaking his head, hands flat on the table suddenly like a slap. "It was the Picts or those bloody druids of theirs."

"I want to accept that, sir."

Malitus smiled. “Good to know. There are no such things as monsters, August. Any civilized man knows that.”

“I am not Roman . . . ” August stated with confidence but ready for his speech. “ . . . by birth.” He turned to the other officer. “Perhaps there is more to these wild tales of the dying man than you give credit to, Quintus. Perhaps not. All I know is that we have a long road ahead of us and it is proving to be a dangerous one. We should be on our guard.”

“On that I can agree wholeheartedly,” Malitus nodded, a smile appearing as his servant returned with the wine “Keep the men alert, Quintus. I want us to be in a great state of ready if trouble should find us here.”

“Yes, sir,” Quintus gave the General a half bow. “Now if you will excuse me, I have a flogging to oversee.”

Malitus sighed as Quintus departed from the hut. “Sometimes I believe that man was put on this Earth for the singular reason of spilling blood.”

August watched the General slug down more wine and said, “Then perhaps we should consider ourselves blessed that he is on our side.”

“Indeed.”

The Romans easily adapted to the environs of Rutland. Their private tents were quickly assembled, and each soldier went about a task August laid out for him. Be it a patrol to scout the area, or to forage for fresh food, the men performed their assigned tasks to fill out the day.

August mounted his horse, planning to ride the perimeter of the town.

Checking in the opposite direction of the circle August decided to head off on, Lucius commented, “I’ll be glad when the rest of the Legion gets to us.”

Porcius scanned the trees all around and adjusted his helmet strap under his thick chin. “Yeah, true words there.”

After a double take, August saw Lucius look long at Porcius. “What is it? You see something in the forest?”

“Naw, more of a smell. My ol’ nose knows.”

August smiled and titled his head back, testing the air with himself. “Your senses rival mine, young man.”

Porcius coughed and heeled his mount about, then winked at him. “Not a surprise, sir, least not to me anyhow.”

Lucius looked all about and frowned asked, “What is it you smell?”

Porcius shook his head. “It’s more of a feeling, like the trees are going to melt together and walk out after us.”

Both August and Lucius looked into the greenery and then at each other, dumbfounded.

“Well, let’s hope it doesn’t come to that,” August said,

As the men parted, the twin archers appeared from the edge of the forest, Decimus already holding a small hare skewered through with an arrow over his shoulder. August thought how the twins had a lot of guts to go near those forests when he noted Crispinus waving him to ride over.

Once he arrived at the twins’ location, they gave salutes and both pointed to the north east at the same time, one with his bow, the other with a dead rabbit on an arrow.

"Sir," Crispinus said. "There's another stone circle up there a ways."

August looked where they pointed, but couldn't see anything but trees. "Not surprising. Everywhere these locals pray they set up a bunch of rocks in circles. They seem to like killing horses as a part of their ceremonies. I don't know why."

Decimus stepped closer to August. "But sir, it is much more elaborate than the previous one we saw there."

Crispinus added, "Worth seeing, sir. I find them quite amazing, what it would've taken to make such things."

August nodded. "Ever been to Egypt or Greece?"

The twins shook their heads as one.

August explained, "Though in ruins, their stone structures are something to behold."

Decimus adjusted a dead rabbit on his makeshift carrying spit and said, "We've all heard stories about the pyramids. Are you saying they are real, sir?"

August nodded once again and looked north of Rutland. "Can't believe they are possible until you see them, but yes they are."

Crispinus turned his nose up in revulsion but not at what his brother did. "I don't believe in such things until I see them. I want to touch the pyramids. They are fairy stories to keep people marching to the edge of the world."

Decimus nodded in agreement, and August laughed. "You have to be joking with me."

Both looked up at him as one but Decimus spoke. "Why believe such things are real or that the paintings of such grandiose objects are not an artist's dream?

Look where we are here this day, marching to the north, to the supposed end of the natural world. It is nonsense for truth. I think it's all a story to get us to be better soldiers."

"I suggest you twins go there some day and see them. They are real."

Decimus responded, "What difference does it make if they are there or not? I still have to get up and eat the next day here."

August sat back in the saddle and didn't feel much like debating such things. These two weren't slaves, ever. "You two are from Italy, yes?"

Both sets of eyes stared at him. Crispinus deadpanned, "From the same place there, yes sir, Tusculum."

Decimus threw out, "Our General Malitus was born in Pisa, but hails from Verona."

August wore a broad smile at their jests and information as he moved his horse ahead and the two followed, now talking to each other.

Crispinus said, "I've heard that. I also heard his mother dropped him there on her way away from Verona."

His brother gave him a sideways look. "That's an interesting trip."

Crispinus shrugged. "I heard she ran away but the childbirth slowed her down."

"It often does."

August fought down laughter, but didn't say anything.

Crispinus added, "Perhaps that's why Malitus seems to want to keep moving and not be happy in one spot."

Decimus chuckled, "That he rumbled from the womb early and thus, keeps wanting to walk on all over the world?"

"Yes."

"You're drunk."

Crispinus frowned. "Not so."

Decimus sighed loudly. "If I had to be cut from my mother's belly, would I be overcome by the urge to leave a house by climbing out the window each day? You're drunk."

When August and the twins drew near to the stone circle, Decimus' head jerked, facing the forest. Crispinus, his mirror image, repeated the look as if a tether connected the two.

"What?" Crispinus asked, though, confused by why his sibling looked away.

Bow tip pointed into the greenery, Decimus said, "There."

August jeered the soldier, asking, "More game?"

Decimus gave his superior an indignant look, one his brother aped in a moment. "In the woods, sir. Look yourself."

August climbed off his horse and stared into the trees. "What is it?"

"Not Diana herself." Decimus took a few steps forward, but his brother hung back, more cautious. "In the gap, like a bench or reclining couch, but not so much."

Crispinus wondered, "Is that a trick of the light in the moss?"

August looked overhead as the sun had crested at mid-day and started to move west, avoiding the dark clouds. The sun did filter into the forest like shafts that extended to the sky. "An eye not so keen may have missed that."

Decimus wore a snide look. "A man not keen to the wonders of loving Diana above would've overlooked it."

When August started toward the forest, sword drawn, the twins fell in behind him, arrows notched. Slowly, they stepped into the edge of the tree line and ventured through a few brambles toward the object. His sword extended, August jabbed at the flat object and he chuckled.

Deflated somewhat, Decimus said, "I thought it was a fallen tree but it's flat."

August rooted his sword in the covering over the bench-like structure. "What is that? It isn't heavy moss or . . . " All three moved back when the blade pulled back and crimson oozed out of the green moss in the sunlight.

Crispinus whispered, "Is it blood?"

August affirmed, "Looks to be that, but perhaps it's a trick of the light or Diana is screwing with us all now."

Taking the barb to his goddess in stride, Decimus went forward and squatted, but wouldn't touch the bloody moss. "What plant bleeds?"

His sword swiped again, this time a loud screech echoed in the trees. "That's stone, like in the circle, yes?"

The twins nodded together. "Same shape, too. Long rectangle," Crispinus said, "Why did they put the stone slab on two blocks out here?"

August wondered after his use of the word blocks, as the two leggings under the slab weren't wood, but also stone.

"Whoever made the circle probably made this as well," August ruminated, word patting his thigh. "Lots of flies buzzing around beyond it, hmmm."

The twins, like spooked dogs, both looked about themselves at the trees in a slight panic, weapons aimed at everything.

August looked away from the bloody moss. "What is with your two?"

Decimus said, "We could be in a sacred nemeton."

Unconcerned, August prodded at the slab again. "So what? You suddenly fear a religion or faith not your own? So much for your faith in Diana."

Crispinus said, "Diana wouldn't go in a nemeton of these barbarians either. It is said a great curse hangs on one that takes anything out of a nemeton."

Decimus nodded fast in agreement with his brother. "I heard tell of a Roman soldier who found a torque offering a Celt threw in one of these near Wales and died the next day. It is a great curse to take anything out in any way."

August grunted and stood up straight. "Then leave empty handed."

Crispinus grabbed his brother's arm tight and pointed with his bow. "Look, the necklace of wolves' teeth!"

August spotted the object he spoke of, half hanging on a low branch of a tree, and his heart skipped a little.

"That scares you two?" August sighed out hard and a few birds flew at his vulgar exhalation. "I see a stone altar covered in blood and moss before me, and you are afraid of a few damned bones?"

Both brothers exchanged a look and stood at attention, trying to wear a face of concern for the altar. "Any thoughts on that, then?" They said in unison.

August opened his mouth to answer, but he looked back beyond the altar and gagged. "Good Lord, what is that?"

The twins fell in on either side of him as August stepped up and they all took it in clear.

Decimus offered, speaking rapidly, "It's like a giant green gourd, broken apart from within and oozing."

August said, "That's a hell of a gourd, look at the size of it."

Crispinus backed away and said, "No, no, not a gourd. It looks like . . . an egg."

While his twin joined him in retreat, August sighed again, walked about the altar and gave the gourd a kick. It bent in, but didn't break. "Doesn't feel like an egg."

"Get away from it, sir!" both shouted and more birds flew.

August walked with them and they hurriedly departed from the trees, back into the open air near the stone circle. "What could hatch out of that thing?"

While Crispinus shook all over and faced away from the trees, his brother did turn back, and quickly raised his bow and fired.

"What?" August asked, curious to his action.

The guttural roar from the woods told August that Decimus' arrow found its mark. It took but a few moments, and a string of angry words for August to understand what Decimus shot drew breath as a simple man.

Crispinus drew and fired as Decimus shot again into the cluster of trees. More brash shouts and what August took as curses by their pointed drops in an unknown tongue, echoed into the warm summer's air.

In the breech that held the altar they saw a thick figure, and the shine of sweat off his bare skin, though a mane of hair billowed from his head. The man didn't shout, swear or run. After a croaked rush of breath, the big man fell backwards, showing three arrows in his chest as he pitched to the ground. As he fell, two figures were revealed beyond the altar, both with long hair, but one being a taller woman clad in a long one-piece robe, seconded by a smaller version of herself.

Just as the man fell, Lucius and Porcius rode around the western edge of the stone circle, instantly drawing swords when they saw the archers at the ready. From the direction of Rutland ran in three slaves, Rufus leading them. In a moment Rufus stood at August's side.

All stared at the women in the distance. No one made a move.

When the tomahawk flew from the woods, one of the servants became easy pickings. Though aiming for Lucius who dismounted, the tomahawk nailed the servant boy, splitting his skull.

Porcius cursed loudly as he charged the woods, making August shout for him to stop fast. A figure moved quick across the opening in the woods, but no clear definition could be had. Porcius didn't hesitate and drew back, throwing his gladius like a knife, sending it end over end at his target.

"Damn," August mumbled as a groan cut into the air. "He hit him!"

Everyone ran to the tree line, where a burly Pict warrior sprawled in the brambles not two yards from a mirror image of himself. Tattooed, covered in sweat, scars and blood as the gladius had skewered him in the kidneys and passed clear through the edge of him. He sucked air in and struggled to stand, but couldn't.

Porcius went at him, reaching for the pommel of his sword. The twins covered him with their bows, arrows notched and ready.

August saw what would play out, and dreaded Porcius' questions as he turned the handle and Rufus interpretations of the Pict. Nonetheless, the Pict raised his left hand as if to get their attention for a second. Porcius held up, watching the Pict draw out a dagger . . . and insert it into his own sweating throat. The Pict's eyes went desolate for a moment as he ripped his own throat out, and then his eyes registered nothing.

"Curse him," Lucius said, face resolute with frustration.

August, not content to stow his gladius just yet, said, "Go figure, huh? He'd rather die than face the cross."

Porcius put a sandal on the Pict's backside, fisted his pommel and pulled his weapon free of the Pict. "Rome's reputation precedes us."

"Weaver," Rufus mumbled, his right hand extended, pointing far beyond the breech in the trees. His hand shook.

All looked at him, then to where he pointed.

As if they suddenly traveled a quarter mile, the woman and her tiny shadow stood far beyond the other side of the forest, in an open field. Behind them stood a horse, a great red steed, but it appeared motionless like a statue

August didn't take his gaze from them. "You know them?"

Rufus licked his lips a few times. "Know of her, the

older woman with the horse behind her, look. She grows faint in the weeds."

The tall grasses seemed to envelope the one he called Weaver and the girl, to the point they almost vanished from sight, as if they were sinking or drawing back from the plain. Their image stretched, like it bent. Gradually, Weaver and the girl faded away in the tall grasses. The outline of the horse lingered a bit longer, but soon disappeared as well.

Porcius stared at Rufus. "Who is that?"

The slave swallowed hard and loud. "Weaver is the mistress of the oaks, far beyond our territory, meaning the Celtic folk."

August turned him from his gaping look to the weeds to face Rufus. "You know of this? How can you be so sure?"

Rufus blinked and tears sprang from his eyes. "I've heard of her in oral tradition since my birth, like Drust, famous the master of the oaks to the north. Her hair, her figure, I see them in my mind, my heart and soul. I know who she was . . . is."

Porcius wiped his blade clean on the deerskin kilt of the dead Pict. "And is scares your innards all to hades? Wonderful as a dead dog. And you are from here." Porcius laughed once, but held no humor in his manner. "Wondrous, indeed."

Lucius glared at Porcius with intensity. "Would you ever want to face one of your famous oracles in Greece?"

With a reflective nod and a belch, Porcius headed out of the woods. "Ya got me there. I'd stay away from the shadows of those folks for true."

"What does she want with us? What is this slab, the blood and the gourd?" August asked Rufus.

Rufus took a few short breaths before saying, “We are entering into their realm, sir, their land, their place of everyday life. What would you do if an army made an excursion over the Alps and started down into Italy?”

August gritted his teeth but said nothing.

Rufus wasn’t done. “Or Germania?”

Turning away from the woods, August recalled just what his folk did when the Romans stabbed forth into Germania. Warring tribes, feuding factions and blood oaths were suspended to try and combat a common foe. Even their priests came out to pray together and curse the Romans. Would the Picts do no less?

Lucius spat on the grass as they entered the open fields again. “The Legions have marched through here before, but never with our intent of reaching the North Sea.”

Porcius chuckled as they walked onward, “The savages couldn’t know what we have in mind. That’s crazy talk.”

Yawning, Lucius quipped, “Hope you are correct.”

“Oh, I am. I hope.”

Rufus returned to the fallen slave boy, gently touching the area broken apart by the tomahawk. “We all die for Rome, be we Celt, Pict or from Ethiopia.”

Due to his skin color, August understood the dead servant as from the Dark Continent, but couldn’t recall his name. “We’ll send others back to help get him.”

Rufus looked at the soldiers and said, “Since the other servant fled, I will do fine.” He took off his tunic and wrapped it about the ruined head of the slave. Though skinny and small, Rufus pulled the dead slave up and maneuvered him over his shoulder, Lucius helping a little, but Rufus insisted he carry the corpse back alone.

Up in the saddle again, August looked back to the gap in the woods. His mind turning, his heart beating hard. He tried to not concentrate on things he couldn't fathom, but failed.

Porcius' mount danced near August and the Greek cussed the horse.

"Can't you control him?" August snapped.

Lucius' horse and then August's started to prance.

"They sense something." Porcius gripped the reins to lead the horse away from the circle and the woods.

Lucius laughed. "They are brighter than us, wanting to leave."

August, though, still looked back to the woods.

Porcius sighed loud enough to make August face him again. "Do you see something or are you obsessed?"

"Just curious."

"Huh, better not be curious. Gonna end up dead going into those woods. They are full of devils. Look at that simple walk in, will ya? Altar and offerings, bloody eggs hatched . . . "

"Egg, huh?"

Porcius shrugged. "Looks like one to me."

August turned and they rode a little ways before he said, "A bloody egg in the woods on a druid altar? That is terrifying then."

Porcius pondered aloud, "Yeah, 'cause what comes from an egg like that?"

When they neared Rutland, August stopped and so did the rest. Rufus, who carried the slave by himself the whole way back to Rutland, hurried to catch up.

"You should've put the dead kid on your horse," Porcius said to August.

August sniffed. "Guess I'm an officer after all, huh?"

Lucius and Porcius grinned at his line.

"Do you two know where Malitus was born?"

Lucius shrugged and put out, "Rome, I always thought."

Porcius asked, "I know he's native to Italy, but why do you ask?"

"Just curious. We all have motivations in life. I wonder where his lie."

Uncapping a flask, Porcius drank deeply and replied, "I hear his medicine for dealing with life comes out of one of these, same as us rotten ol' foot soldiers, but in better quality and quantity. I don't think I needed an oracle to know that, though."

Lucius fished out his flask and so did August. They raised their wine and drank, sharing a hoot in a place far from where any of them came from.

Slowly, Rufus caught up with them. He kept looking to the ground, but August saw him peek at him, once or twice.

August drank again and wondered why the kid would be smiling.

Chapter III

August dreamt of his youth. The snowy steppes of his home in Germania before the Romans came were a lovely landscape not all could excel in creating. His peoples were toughened by the climate, a thick skin that served him his entire life, not just to the warm humidity of Rome, but on the road across Iberia, Gaul, and now Britannia, where many natives of Italy in the Legion shuddered at the slightest drop in temperature.

What interrupted his pleasant dreams wasn't the cold, although the temperature had fallen during the summer night. The putrid odor in the air made his dream of snowy romps with his childhood friends change to them finding rotten deer. The dream quickly stopped and he awoke, nostrils filled with a stench he couldn't quite place. He mused at the humor that reality seeped into his imaginings and changed what he dreamed.

He heard an unsociable commotion all about his tent. As he rose, Rufus opened his tent with a fast flourish.

"Sir, something moves in the night beyond our eyes." Rufus' face shone in the near to full moonlight, and August read fear.

"Is the camp being roused?" He felt silly after the words tumbled from his mouth.

"Yes, sir."

As August hurriedly donned his clothes, and pulled on his sandals, he asked, "What is that damnable smell?"

"That's a matter of some debate among the servants, sir," Rufus quipped sharply, eyes scanning the exterior of the tent. "It's not from within the camp or the village, like a smell that moves in a cloud or a swarm."

"We'll set up a defensive perimeter, fast," August explained as he grabbed his gladius. "Have the watchmen spotted anything out there?"

Both of them turned their heads and stopped in their actions as a brutal scream cut through the deep night.

Rufus looked at his master. "I would venture to guess they have just now discovered something, sir."

Throwing on his helm, August asked, "Have the villagers panicked?"

Rufus shrugged. "I haven't seen any of them out, sir."

August glanced about the village and saw no signs of the populace.

As he trudged on to the middle of the camp, August met Quintus, who also struggled to get his sword secured in place. "What in Hades was that?" His nostrils flared wide as he cursed more. "What is going on around here?"

Other soldiers joined them as the sounds echoed around the group. To August it sounded like the noise bounced off the trees and rattled all about them in a loop. The appalling scent in the air strengthened and guttural grunts flowed in the air.

Helmet already on, but his legates forgotten in the hasty call up, Flavius stood with them and attested, "That isn't good."

Quintus frowned at him but August said, "Thank you! Your grasp of the obvious is well defined, young man."

August then barked orders to the rising soldiers to set up a perimeter, shields up, to expand out in a flare move and find the watchmen. The twin archers kept near August, ready to strike at anything beyond the veil of darkness, which was only pierced by moonlight.

As the men fell into a formation, Malitus appeared, hardly dressed and unarmed. "What madness is this?" he demanded, eyes fluttering, sweating wine.

Quintus looked him over. "Might I suggest you get prepared, General?"

"For what?" Malitus shot back.

Quintus drew his gladius. "War."

August felt that same thing Quintus had in his mind; they all felt the sensation of the air leaving, of walls closing in tight. "We're surrounded," he said lowly.

Swallowing hard, Quintus agreed. "Yes. We have our asses hanging out here."

"We need to get to the horses and get out of here, or at least that will give us a fighting chance," August said.

Quintus nodded but Malitus hissed, "What? What are you saying to me and who is out there? And where are the bloody, forsaken villagers? Answer me! Did they all slink away into the darkness? Is it they that play at the game of war?"

August realized with a start that Quintus noticed the lack of village folk as well. The villagers were gone to a man. A few of the slave boys soon confirmed with shouts that none of the native folk were anywhere to be seen. Had whatever was out there in the night taken the villagers already? Or had they fled, having knowledge he and the others didn't possess? Regardless, it was something to worry about later. Right now, there were larger issues at hand.

"General," August pointed with his gladius at the darkness, woods, and the direction of the growls and stench. "Be it a pack of rabid wolves or the Picts trying to scare us, we are vulnerable here. If the villagers have disappeared surely they know something."

As Malitus' servant started to get him better dressed and armed, the crazed bleating from the forest cut into the night, causing all of the men to take a step back. Many crashed into each other and felt inane for doing so.

August and Quintus exchanged a look, both aware of what had just died. "Rufus," August shouted. "Have the horses brought to us here. Something is at them."

The youth blinked and didn't move. He was no fool, August mused, as he understood the sound they just heard as a horse bleating in death.

August looked to Quintus and then his other soldiers. "To the horses. If they get at them we'll be in a sorry shape."

"They?" Quintus questioned, but nodded in agreement.

Porcius, clad in his armor and hardly anything else, staggered from his tent to join them, reeking of wine and breaking wind loud. His sword out, his feet planted, steady. Armed but naked hanging out of his armor, earning him a few pointed chortles, but after he bowed, they all got in line. The Greek was prepared to fight and die, clothes or no.

All had brandished weapons as they started to move toward the place where many horses were tethered. The Romans had expanded the meager stables of the village and used a series of logs and makeshift hitching posts.

"Like we are in the arena," Porcius snarled, clearer in mind and voice than August thought possible.

Malitus shot Porcius a look. "What say you thus?"

"I've fought blindfolded, surrounded by beasts at first," he confessed as the loud shrieks near the improvised horse paddock ceased. "I know the smell of beasts and their ways well."

August saw a few of the horses, legs broken and ripped apart, just as Rufus asked Porcius, "How did you fight them blindfolded?"

"I took off the blindfold after I got a hand free."

Still not understanding the love of such gory sport by the masses in Rome, August stopped short of the three slain horses. Flavius brandished a torch at the sickening display and wretched. He took the torch out of the way, depriving them of the scene, mercifully. The dead horses hadn't simply been torn apart—they had been ravaged in long straight lines . . . as if gnawed on.

Quintus turned very pale. "What is this madness?"

Porcius pointed his sword. "Some of the carcasses have been *chewed* upon, if my eyes are good and they are."

Lucius appeared, having roused others from their

sleep. The full two dozen men stood around them, long shields at the ready, many holding their gladius to fight, but unsure of where to direct their attack or defense.

Fuming, but eyes now clear, Malitus said, "Surrounded, aye?"

August locked eyes with Quintus. "Feels like it. What do you think?"

Quickly, Crispinus and Decimus went back to back a few times, spinning, searching, then parted, like they were a single weapon themselves; ready to revolve on the hidden enemy.

More horses screamed at the opposite end of the village and Quintus ordered, "More of our mounts are in the center of the town. Surround the General and move there. Whatever is out there is working up its courage to attack."

August thought that wishful thinking as they moved.

The troops fell into formation around Malitus and the commanders, except Quintus and a few who mounted some of the dancing horses left at hand.

August said, "Might I suggest that we do the same in finding the courage to attack."

"What?" Quintus snapped from the back of his horse, not looking in August's direction,

"We need to make a choice to go, but go as a unit. Strike forth on the road, north or south, but I suggest south as the Legion will be approaching us that way."

Walking rapidly with the group, Malitus chuckled. "Courage and insanity in the same idea. What a night!"

August affirmed, "If we take up a dug in posture to fight out of we'll be as dead as those in this village."

Quintus swore and then said, "You think that fool on the tree told the truth?"

August flared his nostrils. "Smells like he did to me."

Bitterness in his puffy face, Malitus said, "Argue that point if we all survive. August, your suggestion?"

"Burn this town to the ground," answered August. "We'll get no shelter here and if they are beasts out there, perhaps they fear fire. Most do, right? When the town goes up, we may see what is attacking us, but we also may get the break we need to get away."

Flavius stammered, "The Legion will not arrive in time to save us this night."

Quintus nodded and addressed the men about them. "Strike flints, burn every house, every stable. Get the horses alive near to us and get ready."

Though he ordered the soldiers into this task, Rufus, the servants, the twins and August all helped out as well. None dared to be alone as they ran the immediate avenue of the town, setting blazes, moving as a collective force.

As the first homes started to vaguely flicker with flame, Rufus elbowed August's ribs and pointed to the southern avenue of the town—the place they wanted to flee through to meet the Legion the next day. In the moonlight several large forms started to move into view. They weren't running out to display themselves nor howling and beating the ground as it had sounded earlier. If anything, they moved slow, looking at the flames and assembling across the avenue. Perhaps monsters or wild beasts, they formed an effective wall against them leaving that way.

August and Rufus kept moving about, setting fire

to the dry thatched roofs and to the hay bales stacked against certain domiciles.

"By Mars!" August heard a soldier scream.

The fires were spreading quickly across the entire village now. Their light was as bright as day in the heart of the village. It wasn't the fires that made the soldier cry out, but what the man saw emerging from the trees. August saw it, too. Three giant creatures, unlike anything August had ever even heard in legends, emerged from the forest. Each of the monsters stood between nine and twelve feet tall. Their entire bodies were covered head to toe in thick, matted hair. The hair did nothing to disguise the layers of muscle beneath as the things moved, though.

August did not doubt the monsters' strength. From the looks of the things, their bare hands would be more than formidable weapons. He knew at once they needed to drive the monsters back.

"Lancers, forward!" August bellowed as he saw Quintus and a group of mounted cavalry men come into view. He swung himself onto one of the nearby horses, joining the men who'd already mounted and were ready for combat. "Archers! Fix arrows!" The twins were ready to fight and had missiles notched. A few others with bows joined them at the ready, but they shook in the revelation of what they faced.

The soldiers raised their lances as they galloped, hard and fast, towards the humanoid-shaped creatures. To their credit, the monsters didn't run. The things held their ground against the charge. The quickest of the beasts, dodged the tip of a lance aimed at its wide chest and moved around it. One of its massive hands grabbed the lance from the side and crushed it as easily as a man would crush an egg. Its other hand lashed out, knocking the mounted soldier the lance belonged to from his saddle with such force, August thought he heard the man's ribs shatter, despite his armor. The soldier thudded to the ground, spraying bright red, like a stream of vomit, from his mouth.

The second of the beasts met the first rider by charging it head on. It snapped the neck of the man's horse effortlessly with a two handed chop to either side of the neck, sending its rider flying from its back. Another rider came upon them, his lance digging deep into the beast's side. The beast roared in pain and anger, lashing out wildly. A backhanded blow shattered the skull of the horse belonging to the soldier who had struck it. The horse's corpse careened sideways into the path of two other cavalry men, causing them to stop short of their intended target.

August's own lance hammered into the flesh of the third beast as he bore down hard in his attack. Though it pierced the white haired thing, the blow fell odd, like charging into the side of a mountain. The beast barely staggered as August and the horse carried forward. The giant beast yanked August's lance from his grasp, cast it aside, and nearly broke his wrist in the process. When the creature flailed at him, he turned his horse about, avoiding the swipe, pushing off another monster with his shield. August ignored the pain in his wrist and drew his sword as the beast closed in on him. It advanced in swift movements, confident in its attack. August delivered a wicked slash to its face, the blade of his weapon slicing a deep wound through its nose and cheeks, stopping the beast in its tracks. Blood flowed from the thing's wound as it howled its fury into the night.

Another thunderous cry arose from the woods, and the beast facing August whirled about before it bounded off into the darkness. Only then did August have time to bear witness to the carnage around him. Three of the men who had charged the beasts at his side were no more. They lay on the ground, broken and twisted bodies where blood pooled around their crumpled forms. They weren't cut open nor stabbed, crushed, pummeled and rent would be more accurate. His mind swirled at the sight.

He kept seeing arrows appear in the monsters, but had not noted the twins launching volley after volley until that moment. They kept their back to each other, turning, firing, like a wheel in the water, processing the river current but never tiring nor running short of arrows.

The entire village churned bright, though, blazing wildly behind August and his men.

Rufus rushed forward, snatching up August's fallen lance. He offered August the end of the lance that had been thrust into the monster. The spearhead bore a scarlet fluid, shining wet in the firelight.

Rufus smiled.

Quintus was with them, smiling at the sight of the lance's tip. "Thank the gods, they bleed!"

August and Porcius both gaped at him.

"Then they can die," Quintus completed his thought as he turned to the two dozen men who brought their shields up and surrounded the officers.

August murmured to Porcius, "I didn't see him get that excited at the avenue of prostitutes in outer Naples."

The skirmish became a full battle as more of the creatures emerged from the trees surrounding the village. August and Quintus were forced to abandon their horses when the animals panicked. Trained warhorses they might be, but the smell and feral cries of the beasts filled them with fear. There weren't enough horses present to carry the battle anyway.

"Form up as infantry," Quintus yelled as the archers tried to pick targets in the blazing night. Decimus took a knee and his twin stood tall, firing over him. "Our sole hope rests in making this an infantry battle against the beasts."

Malitus shouted, "Here, I concur. No force in the known world could stand against the Roman infantry."

August didn't care for their bravado and wished he dreamed it all, as what happened next didn't pass for reality.

The avenue filled with huge shapes, hairy creatures like the rest he'd just fought. August wished it all away as a nightmare. The appalling stench of the beasts seemed to increase and their huffing throaty roars grew louder as they approached.

All of the men felt this reality of doom fall on them at once. Nonetheless, they reacted as they'd been trained.

Though many of those standing with shields were cavalry men deprived of their mounts, they still sported the long shield of the Legionnaires. They quickly rowed up and formed into the testudo formation, or turtle maneuver as many liked to call it. A line of troops took a knee and interlocked their long shields with their fellow soldiers nearby. Then men behind them held up their shields, balanced well overhead like a sturdy roof. Men behind them, and on the sides sealed off this defensive structure to perfection.

None inside said what all thought, that they prayed it'd hold in such a wild attack.

It took no more than a few moments to find out.

The heavy blows of the beasts rained down, denting shields and surely breaking bones on hairy fists as they screamed. They persisted but were repelled, thudding loud but ultimately bouncing back from the resolve of these veterans who held the beasts at bay with the science of the interlocked shields.

August understood the balance of the shields, and the strength of the men would be enough to ward them off at first, if only barely and by the grace of God, but the next part of the testudo would be tested fast.

Once the initial attack by the creatures proved unsuccessful, they tried again, but through the cracks against the fires of the village. The Roman army watched the beast men step back.

"*Impetus! Lay on, lay on! Attack!*" Quintus shouted.

The wall shoved forward into the line of perplexed giant men, though one could hardly claim it moved the beasts by any means other than shock. They were simply too massive and too strong. The Roman's shields and lances came out, striking low and ripping hair covered flesh. The shields stabbed down, chopping into the tops of the creatures' large feet, and the swords curled on hooking moves, slicing into muscle and knees.

August's sword stabbed into an ivory haired calf of one of the beasts and Porcius' lance impaled the long foot of the same creature into the dirt road. The beasts were being pushed back now, slowly. Quintus was still screaming for blood as if a madness born of the excitement of battle and fear had claimed him. He was in his element and better for it, not holding back as he became one with his shield and threw it up high, smashing a jaw of a beast up and throwing its head back, stunned and blood spitting from the lips.

The twins stabbed through the cracks in the crowded turtle, jabbing with swords what they could, forcing the maneuver to break up.

The Roman formation then crumbled as a beast, far larger than the others, roared its way into their ranks. Its strength seemed beyond all reason as his arms dropped and shattered two shields and flung men aside as if they were nothing, opening them to the others behind it.

As the formation dissolved, Quintus dove into the path of one of the beasts. His sword slashed fiercely with expert skill. Its blade sliced the throat of a beast towering over him, showering him with its blood, as he laughed madly. There was no berserker rage within Quintus, only the enjoyment of a man who loves dealing death and has a natural talent for it.

August watched another grey monster come at him from his side but Quintus whirled, meeting it well. He drove his blade upwards, through the monster's ribs, into its heart. The beast died instantly, breath choking out, its huge form sagging, before it toppled on top of Quintus, burying him beneath its great weight.

August could hear Quintus' furious cries but had no time for stopping them. One of the beasts was upon him. August swung his sword in a desperate defense against the monster's outreached hand, thinking the shot to the heart a good move but tough to execute. The blade buried itself between the beast's fingers, cutting deep. The beast loosed a howl and drew its wounded hand back. August lost his grasp on his sword as it was jerked away. He backpedaled fast, his eyes on the creature, and drew the dagger sheathed on his belt. Truly a poor weapon at the moment, he knew, but also his only hope of surviving the following seconds. The beast lunged forward again. August moved to sidestep its attack, half falling in the process. That stumble saved his life as the monster shot passed him. He smacked hard down into the ground with a sudden grunt, his breath leaving his lungs in an almighty *whoosh*.

"Regroup!" he heard the General shout. "Regroup and hold!"

Not all of the detachment had formed the turtle and those in absence were returning, casting darts and spears as they ran to join the battle. Two darts sunk into the chest of the beast August had dodged. Blood leaked from its wounds but it did not fall. It ripped one of the darts free, a fresh spurt of crimson erupting from its chest. It leaned its head back and rumbled like thunder that seemed to shake the very ground where August lay.

August rolled to his feet and leaped onto the beast, one arm curled about and legs clinging like a wrestler. It tried vainly to swat August from its back as he stabbed it time and again with the small blade he clutched in a white knuckled grip. Finally, the dagger found its spine and plunged deep into it. The beast jerked twice, then collapsed. August jumped off its carcass, his eyes already scanning for the next foe. He spotted the giant beast, so much larger than the others. It had left a trail of carnage in its wake as it moved across the avenue of the village, an unstoppable juggernaut, better suited to the realm of gods than that of man. The hair of that creature was black, not white.

The arrival of the other troops of the detachment had surprised the beasts, though, and their disorganized, savage attack came to a halt as suddenly as it had begun. The beasts were not retreating, August saw, merely pulling back for a moment. Still, their doing so bought the Romans time to regroup and fall back as well.

As August and Porcius worked their way up the flaming west side of the village, he spotted Flavius and Lucius double teaming one of the creatures. August half laughed, watching the well trained, but experienced Lucius stabbing, dodging, parrying and using fletch moves with his shield like the monster used a sword not his limbs to counter. The beast didn't move too much on Lucius as Flavius performed a similar duty on the creature's back side, stabbing at his hindquarters with a lance and swiping at its knees with his shield. No quarter seemed to be gained in this exchange, which looked stylized in the face of all the brute carnage about them.

August didn't call out to the men, not wanting to break their concentration and thus, let the monster beat their brains in fast. He did move up and dance about the opposite side of the creature's reach. When it swiped out at him with his left hand—a move that would have surely turned his brain to dust if it connected with his head—August shouted to Porcius to raise his shield.

Porcius pulled the rectangular shield up, far above his head, striking the wrist of the huge creature. Annoyed, the beast gripped the top of the shield and shoved it back to the ground. It focused on the Greek for a moment, but it was all August needed to swing his gladius down and chop at the wrist—open to him as it held the shield in place. The blade chopped nearly through the beast, taking it through the bone. The creature howled in a quick burst, pulling back his arm, its hand swinging down from the wrist joint, flopping. The appendage was held in place by a tiny piece of skin and muscle, spewing blood and marrow over the shield.

Shuffling with its big feet, the monster pushed past Lucius and slapped his shield with the flat of its good hand, knocking the soldier down. The beast didn't attack him, but fled away down the avenue to the north of the village.

As Lucius picked himself up and Flavius sucked in air, August joined them and barked, "Where are the others, dead?"

Flavius shook his head violently. "I think they went back by the barns beyond the village. They may have died there or they are pinned down."

Lucius helped Porcius to his feet, adding, "I knew you two lived when I heard Porcius cussing on the wind a few moments ago."

August grinned as he motioned for them to follow him. Porcius, the Greco-mutt of the troop, frequently sang bawdy songs and used fowl words in battle, more than was necessary. "Let's get gone and rejoin the others."

Though they ran with him, Flavius scanned the few soldiers about the General. "There are so few of us left." As if on cue, the twins emerged from the darkness and ran along with the group.

As Rufus and other body servants joined them, August mumbled, "We should've gone back south to the Legion."

They rounded the corner at the end of the village. Two homes there seethed in flames more than the others. August thought these the residence and adjoining shop of a barrel maker as the skeletons of such objects stood in the flames. The cut timbers of the buildings went up fast in the night. He still saw no people from the village anywhere.

Out past these flaming homes sat a series of small stables, not much different in design than the homes, however, the sides weren't packed with mud and no attempt at brick work was made. Beyond these places, built into the side of the sloping landscape were a series of openings, almost like hatches on a ship but built into the side of a hill.

August mumbled, "Fogou."

Rufus nodded fast. "Maybe the creatures hide in them?"

"Fogou?" Flavius asked as he followed along.

Rufus stated, "Subterranean spot to store food. Same as in Gaul."

Lucius said, "We've seen them before, you just don't care to recall them."

Flavius slowed. "Would the monsters be in there? Stop at once Porcius!" But the man was faster than them despite his girth, and ripped open the hatch to the slope storage area and went inside. "You'd be mad to go in there to look."

August shook his head as he jogged a bit closer to these places. past the burning stables. He heard a string of profanity. “Sounds like someone was in there.” He then noted one of the creatures in the dirt by these hatches on the Fogous, on his all fours, holding his hands together. At first, August thought this to be the creature they’d just maimed badly, ran off to weep here. However, this creature held its right hand with its left.

“Kill it,” August ordered his men as they started to approach the Fogou.

Before they could strike, one of the hatches burst forward and Porcius leapt out, somersaulted forward, ass over elbows. He flopped on the ground just past the creature, and turned to strike it at the left temple with a small hatchet. The weapon sank in the beast’s skull a few inches and stayed there as the monster rose up. When it stood, they all beheld that several fingers were missing from its right hand. It tried to pull the hatchet out and couldn’t quite get its huge feet planted.

“Lay on!” August ordered, causing Flavius and Lucius to jab at the beast with their swords, full on. The thing left its belly exposed and both men inserted their gladius’ in a few inches. The twins added four arrows into the chest a couple of seconds later.

August grabbed each man like he hugged them from the behind, forcing his weight onto their insertions. The blades of the men delved in deeper, pushing on through the beast. Blood and urine spurted out as a blade destroyed a kidney. The other blade stopped at the spine, causing the creature to flail its arms out and then tremble all over.

Porcius got to his feet as the men retrieved their

swords and let the beast drop to its knees. Quickly, Porcius grabbed the hatchet out of its head and drew back. He nailed the thing in the head again, this time losing the hatchet in the center of his skull. He let go of the farmer's device as the beast fell backwards, dying and gasping its last breath.

August laughed at Porcius as he shook off the dust of the earth. "You either have guts or no brains running in there."

"Seemed like the thing to do, sir. Damn things reached in and I grabbed what I could, chopped off its fingers."

They all stared down at the thing as it died. Lucius asked, "What is it?"

The rest of the survivors from the troops filtered out of the town as the flames raged, and approached when they saw August and the rest of their kin.

Flavius sighed at the sight of Malitus, Quintus and a few more soldiers. "Damn us all. Is that all there is left?"

August said, "Five of us, a dozen counting them and their two servants."

They weren't greeted with derision but looks of terror in the faces of the General.

August pointed at the Fogou entrance.

Quintus squinted at these and then glared at him. "You can't be serious."

August tilted his head to the left and looked back at the town. "They seem to be dispersing or running, but would you feel better running across country or in the woods this night?"

Quintus never answered, but Malitus said, "We'd be trapped like rats, but no chance on the outside."

Porcius offered, "There are two ways out beyond this series of hatches here, one a murder hole, an escape route probably made for floods. The other leads into the earth, I didn't follow it. Either way, better than rubbing organs with them out in the woods, uh, sir?"

Malitus faced August. "Then into the caves."

While Fogou meant *cave*, these structures were manmade food storages that stretched deep below the surface, to keep various cured items cold, but it felt like a real cave to August.

The dozen went inside and August closed the hatch behind them, peering through the slats at the village as it burned.

He saw a few of the beasts lurking in the night, but they stayed well away from the flames and did not come their way either. August also beheld a human form out there amongst them and his heart raced, but soon fell. He'd thought this man a stray soldier they'd lost, or a villager out running in his heavy over cloak, but neither theory proved accurate. This man stood very tall, but not as big as the hairy giants. He wore a more stylized robe, not a brown woven garment, but a single piece, draped over him—ivory white in color save for the profile of the ebony raven head on its back. The man turned, a long branch in one hand and a deer antler in the other. Two ravens came to land on either forearm, and a boy appeared by his side in the night. The youth also wore a mantle, but of a different color—brown, woven tighter.

You are from my dreams, August screamed inside his head, trying to deal with the madness gripping his self.

Both chanted and sang while a huge creature

emerged from the smoke. This beast stood a bit bigger than the others, and was the one sporting black fur. Two of the grey creatures brought him gory bits of Roman soldiers. One held a leg, the thigh end glistening in the moonlight. The other tossed a head up and down in its hands like a child playing with a ball. The black haired creature snatched the head from the grey monster's grasp, and bit into it like a man would an apple, and threw it to the ground. The big thing smacked its lips so loud those in hiding could hear it.

While the big creature back handed the leg, like it displeased him, he did nod as they brought him another prize. He readily took up what looked like a small bundle from the Fogou. The form was that of a small figure and the biggest of the monsters ripped it apart, opening the head that was already ruined, and scooped out the brains inside. It then licked its fingers like a child enjoying sticky cakes. Then, it laughed.

Rufus cussed under his breath and August frowned at him. He understood Rufus' angst, though. The big monster ate the brains of the small slave boy Rufus had carried back to town, and it was disconcerting on so many levels to August that he could only imagine the emotions Rufus might have felt.

"Stay quiet," August whispered, and Rufus nodded.

None of the creatures molested the man in the white robe or the child who chanted.

August grabbed Rufus by the elbow and pulled him to the slats of the Fogou door. "What is he saying? I hear names, like *Tancorix*, I've heard of her in legends of the Isle folk."

At that name, Tancorix, Porcius head spun to meet August's gaze. "Huh? What did you say just now?"

Once his initial terror left him, Rufus listened intently to the chants. The tall man and his tiny boy shadow moved away, slinking into the darkness by the woods nearby.

"I can't understand much of it, but he has mentioned Tancorix and he keeps talking to and about Adelaido."

"Adelaido?" Quintus groaned. "Who?"

Porcius pushed them aside and looked out, then retreated, gritting his teeth.

Malitus barked, "And who is Adelaido? I hate to sound obtuse but really, this is getting odder by the moment."

Rufus pointed out and pulled his finger back in like it'd be eaten if he didn't. "The King of the Beastmen."

Malitus' jaw went slack, but no words came out. He moved up to the door and squinted out into the night.

August looked out at the towering creature with black fur, which didn't look their way, as Rufus slowly mouthed the words, "He is."

Chapter IV

While fear ran amok amongst most of the men secluded in the Fogou, time cured many of their mental ailments. The soldiers kept moving, restless, not wanting to betray fear to their superiors, few as they were, but the feeling of being backed in a corner ran wild. The couple servants shook in primal fear. Rufus, however, held his usual placid demeanor. The soldiers all muttered of taking to the caves below them as an escape, but others wondered what lurked in those tunnels, and the fear returned.

The General, who sat against a sack of wheat, wore a tart look, and chided the servants and soldiers to calm down.

"They will, in time," August told him, but didn't know if that was true. "They've seen the manifestation of a hundred childhood tales and fears."

Malitus scowled. "They are soldiers."

"Sir, they aren't trained to fight those things. The slaves, well, they have not that nerve or ability to fall back." August gestured at the soldiers. "Even they tremble, trying to forget." He didn't know if he'd ever erase that image of the black haired beast eating the brains of that poor, dead slave.

Quintus sat not far from Malitus, his face barely visible in the dim light of the meager candles struck by Flavius. “This is madness. I don’t think we are safe here.” He breathed deep, trying to recover from his battles. He searched in his robes and cursed the fact that he had no small flask most soldiers kept at the ready.

Porcius coughed and laughed, then tried to put on a respectful face.

Quintus’ focus sharpened and he snapped, “You find humor in my words?”

“Yeah, sir, I do.” Porcius cleared his throat, rubbed his thigh, massaging a huge bruise. “Ya ever gonna feel safe again, anywhere?” A grin played on his lips, and his sweaty face showed the heavy shadow of his unshaven chin.

Very deliberately, Quintus leaned back on the mud wall, pondering these words, taking slow, deep breaths.

Porcius reached down to his right and picked up a tiny ceramic jar. Quintus eyed him as he broken the waxen seal and sipped it. Porcius then handed it to Quintus.

“What is it?”

“Something close to whiskey. It’s powerful, but wet, so watch it.”

Cautiously, Quintus looked into the brew. “What if it’s poison?”

Porcius held up a different jar, one already open, and took a long draw on it, showing it was partially empty. “I ain’t dead yet.”

Quintus tasted it, made a face, but took another sip. “Strong, indeed.”

Porcius nodded with vigor. "These people invented whiskey, these Celtic bastards . . . Water of life they call it. How ironic is that, huh? I bet my ass to odd high that if ya drank enough it'd kill yer ass dead in an hour."

Malitus looked to August, who sat by the door with Rufus. "Are they gone?"

"A few stragglers out running about, sir, but the big one with black hair is gone. That's something."

"What did they call him?"

"Adelaido," Rufus said. "Sir."

After a fatigued sigh, Malitus said. "I don't think I feel keen on protocol at the moment, boy. August, can such things have names?"

Eyes on the exterior of the Fogou still, August replied, "I take it that one does, sir. The people with them spark my interest, though."

"Quite, I saw them, too." Malitus frowned. "Was he named by the one crucified? Was he a Druid priest?"

"Drust," Rufus muttered. He peeked up at the General then looked down. "The master of the oaks is called Drust, sir. It has to be him for this region."

August and Malitus stared at him. The General asked, "How would you come by such information?"

"Yes, how?" August demanded.

His eyes not rising to meet theirs, Rufus stated, "Every one of my kindred knows of the master of the oaks this far north, the Pict great wizard as you would call him. Drust, the eternal."

Porcius cackled loud at that and many were disturbed by his drunken giggles, but Quintus' look grew angry at Rufus. "Eternal? You don't say?"

As Malitus opened his mouth to ask, Rufus

answered, "His name is known and feared among all who breathe on this isle. Our true lords of the wood are gone in the south, but Drust endures. He always will, I think."

Sarcastic, Malitus asked, "Because he is eternal and lives forever?"

Rufus nodded slowly.

"Nonsense," said Malitus, hands gripping to fists. "I won't debate your silly ideas of religion, slave boy. You think that old man with the monsters was this druid master Drust you hear of?"

Again, the youth nodded.

August wondered, "Who was the boy with him? His apprentice?"

"Perhaps his vessel, I don't know." Rufus shrugged. "Such things are done amongst the Picts like our own folk."

Malitus grimaced. "Would this Drust person name the beastmen? Are they his pets? Are they his to command?"

August turned away from the door and took a deep breath. "They didn't seem worried about him. Not one came near. They killed us and ripped the town apart to find more of us, but wouldn't go near Drust, as Rufus calls him, or that kid shadowing him."

"The men of the wood command these beast men?" Malitus asked.

August said, "Could be."

"I've not heard of such monsters under his command, sir. Honest." Rufus shook badly.

"You all right?" August asked, earnestly concerned.

"No, not really," Rufus whispered to August, "What about Tancorix?"

After August shushed him, Quintus and Porcius both perked up to face them. Quintus said, "Tancorix, yes, I've heard that name. Isn't she the subject of many ballads?"

Malitus gave a feeble laugh. "Now who is the fool? You confess to listening to the tales of slaves, who lament their long lost Queens and Kings?"

Undaunted, Quintus said, "The nights here are as dull as a Sumerian artist's imagination. I've heard that name during my service in this land, yes. Why would this Drust invoke it so? What did he say about Tancorix, boy?"

Rufus answered meekly, "He didn't talk of her in legend or the past tense, as you all say about the Queen of the ashes."

August closed his eyes, aware of what Drust had said, but didn't share with the crowd. He didn't want to face it.

Quintus wondered, "How did he speak of her?"

Oddly enough, Porcius listened with some intensity, still sipping the powerful water of life.

Rufus swallowed and said, "Like he'd speak to her today, like she was alive. Right now this day in Caledonia. He didn't talk of her in legend, a story or a saga, no. Master Drust spoke of her in terms like he knew of her today."

"Mind your mouth, boy. Your master is August not Durst." Malitus sat forward. "Tancorix? The Pict Queen of lore, alive?"

Rufus kept looking down. "That's how he acted."

The General roared with laughter and sat back. "Rubbish."

The boy sank back into the shadows as August said,

"Perhaps we need to listen to words we all write off as madness, sir. Just think how crazy we thought the Pict we crucified was at his revelations about the beastmen"

While Malitus closed his eyes and didn't answer, Quintus spoke up again. "What else did that raving fool say?"

Rufus cleared his throat. "That Adelaido would kill us all and mate with our women."

These words drew some laughs amongst the men.

Porcius spoke up. "Flavius, watch your ass. You're the closest thing we have to a lady on this mission."

Then men traded insults as the mood lightened up. In time, they hunkered down to try and get some rest.

August found himself looking out the cracks again to the village, which quickly turned to rubble as the fires died. He wondered where the villagers were . . .

When dawn shone through the door of the Fogou, August snapped awake, stunned that he'd slept much at all. He gazed about the inner chambers of the Fogou and noted that all who'd survived the night, slept. Most snored. True, their fear had been high upon entering the underground chamber, but their bodies—so exhausted from battle and the struggles of the mind to cope with it all—had given out.

"Are they gone?" Malitus voice called out, sober and soft in manner August hadn't heard before then. He did have a tinge of the brew Porcius had found on him, though. Desperate times calls for desperate measures, he supposed.

"Looks like it, sir, but we'll have to see the hard

way. I doubt they are afraid to come out in the full light."

"Why did they come out at all?"

"Perhaps they have better eyes at night, but I don't know. I'm just guessing." August looked outside again, hungry to find something to report on. "If I had to speculate, I'd say the man Drust encouraged them."

Malitus fell quiet then said, "Wonderful."

"I'll rouse the men and be ready to flee at the slightest sign of trouble."

Quintus yawned. "Why do we need to do that now? Perhaps staying in here until the Legion arrives is best."

August opened the door and drew his gladius. "Rutland was a Romanized town, partially in the past, so they will pass on through the other one we left behind in theory."

They all soon filed out of the Fogou, arms at the ready, but found the silent summer morning quiet, save for birdsong.

Quintus stretched and yawned loud. "Too bad the baths in the middle of town are overgrown. I could use one."

Porcius smirked, saying to Quintus, "I think I have some oil back there at the encampment if the damn beasts didn't stomp it to nothing. Dose yourself in that and scrape it off if you have a spare strigil in your gear."

"My bathing strigil is amongst my effects and they were on one of the horses slaughtered by the beast men," Quintus ruminated. "Damn them all."

August and Porcius smiled at one another, took the point for the group, and led them into the main avenue.

Porcius whispered, "We almost got our asses handed to us, and he's worried about cleaning up and lounging into a nice caldarium."

"The warm room of the bathhouse sounds good, but silly to think on it."

Porcius reached to his crotch and winked at August. "I could use my mornin' flow and make him a salty tepidarium to rinse in though."

Fighting off a smile, August said, "Mind on the tasks, soldier."

"Yes, sir, right away, sir," Porcius said, but paused a moment to relieve himself out in the open. As Porcius went, he asked, "Where are they all, sir?"

"The villagers?"

"Yes, but where are the bodies of the beasts we slew? Can't see any around."

"Wotan's ass," August mumbled and quickly said, "By god, you are right."

Porcius winked as he stowed his manhood. "Stop saying those German names or they'll nail you up proper."

"They are gone." August looked down the avenue, took a little run on the gravel and stopped, turning about to face Porcius and the rest of them walking up slow. "I don't see any of our brothers here, either. Not all of them, anyhow." He waved at a few grisly pieces and limbs strewn about.

Flavius moved up by then and stuttered a bit before saying, "We . . . hid in the ground and they took them all away, all of our men?"

"Strong heart, soldier. They are beyond hurting now." August chided him.

After a more extensive search of the old camp and

burnt out buildings, they could find no bodies, human or otherwise.

Porcius walked back up from the plain where the Fogous were. "I can't even find the fingers of that one I hit."

"Sir," Lucius called out, pointing to the east of town. "See in the morning light? See how the sun rises over the stone circle beyond those woods."

All crowded in to see where he pointed, while Rufus and two of the servants watched horses wandering south of town and went to get them.

"They build those stone circles we have found all over this Isle to line up with the sun, moon or stars," Quintus said.

August shaded his hand from the rising sun and agreed. "That's true. It wasn't visible in the woods in regular daylight yesterday. We just avoided it when we patrolled and found the bloody altar in the woods."

"More druid magick?" Malitus jeered.

"Sloppy scouting more like," August grunted and shook his head. "But all of my good scouts are dead now."

Rufus and the servants brought over the four horses, smiling at their prize.

Malitus' smile faded as Quintus stepped closer to August, who touched the muzzle of the horse offered to him. "I didn't fight my way across half the rough world to die here. We need to be more apt at things."

"And you were the only one to do that?" August replied, his jaw tight, not hiding his contempt for his superior officer.

Quintus' mouth fell open, but it was Malitus who stepped closer to August to speak. "Have a true care,

Decurion. Our numbers are so very few here, and our manners have gone relaxed, but don't forget to show respect."

August raised the horse's head and said, "He's been drinking water. I'm sure there's some around." He then faced the men. "Flavius, Lucius and Porcius, mount up and come with me. We'll check out that stone circle as the light has gifted it to us." He climbed into the saddle of the horse offered to Quintus and looked down at Malitus. "Oh, I always respect authority, sir. However, a great deal of Quintus' guile is supported by the Legion, which is not here to give his back steel. Respect is a two way avenue, remember that."

Quintus' eyes narrowed at August as the men mounted up. "I'll remember your insubordination, Decurion."

"If we live through this, have me flogged like you did that poor blacksmith." August wheeled his horse about and the four of them set off trotting over the grasses toward the woods. Rufus jogged along by his master.

Once over a ridge that he had scouted himself the day before, August saw the paths between the level ground, where crops had been laid. Barley, wheat and turnips in small areas, he saw many of these lands extend out far to the north and they were free of weeds.

Lucius pointed out, "Looks like the crops are doing well. Harvest is getting closer."

August shrugged. "Certain vegetables are already in, but yes. I think it is near."

Rufus caught up to them as they spoke on harvest. He glanced over the lands and said, "Lughnasadh draws close. They call that Lammas in some places."

Porcius chuckled loud. "Another festival where the savages get together and screw in the moonlight to thank the gods for good crops? Hot damn, that sounds like a time! I'm praying to the wrong gods, I am."

"Let's head over to the circle, and be on your guard," August ordered.

Porcius wondered, "Want to check that altar in the woods for more eggs?"

"Not especially," August answered. "I am curious, though, to see if the Picts we left for dead are still there."

Flavius wiped his brow with the back of his left hand. "Do you think that is why the beastmen attacked?"

August shook his head. "If they had that sort of command of them, why do it now? And over two guys? I doubt it."

The four rode around the lip of the woods and the stone circle spread out before them on a level plain, nestled in by another set of woods, and beyond these by the village. The circle was filled with stone monoliths, more grim single sentinels not built atop each other like the henge they'd seen before. Though the outer pattern wasn't apparent, the main circle obviously held an inner spot of worship or purpose. They stopped and looked things over, but as Rufus arrived behind them, he pointed near the edge of the other woods and cried out.

August, Flavius, Lucius and Porcius dismounted fast and drew their swords. With caution, they approached the gap at the edge of the stone circle. The stone pattern looped out, nearly touching the nearby woods. By the edge of the coppice, they all exchanged looks as they spotted the single stone slab that lay prostrate. On that slab were a series of wadded up articles, a few looked to be linens the soldiers used for clothes or washing.

A few steps later, they all stopped for any one could see that the objects on the slab were the grisly bits of human bodies. August swallowed hard as Lucius receded back from the scene. He spotted the partially ruined heart, and what he thought a tiny bowl but was really a crushed skull still pooled with gray matter that could only be brains.

Flavius pushed up between August and Porcius to get a good look. From the way he gripped their tunics and shook, August guessed they looked anything but good. Flavius moved back slow, seemed to recall his great dignity and didn't move back very far, but still leaned on the nearest erect slab and started to vomit.

They exchanged a look and August said, "Terrible."

After a grunt, Porcius said, "Something's been at those pieces."

"You mean like a wolf or a beast?"

Eyebrows arched, Porcius rapped his knuckles on his own helmet and shook his head. "Naw, look." He pointed with the hand he hit himself with, and then drew his hands together, cracking knuckles. "The bites are round, not canine in the pieces."

August nodded, feeling his stomach turn. "I thought it a sacrifice stone, like a few we've seen in the off-the-beaten-path places."

Porcius turned and faced Lucius, who stood gaping

at them but not the grisly stone. "An offering to the gods, like a bracelet or torque thrown into a sacred grove over there. The desire is luck or appeasement of their gods."

August understood. "Yes."

Head still shaking, but not in revulsion or disgust, but recognition, Porcius put forth, "That was no sacrifice, laid out neat and defiled by forestry animals. It'd be sloppier if it was. Naw, that was a meal and those are the leftovers."

August watched Lucius turn, hand on his thin gut and joined Flavius in throwing up his morning rations, scavenged in the Fogou.

Porcius undid the strap and pulled the helmet from his head. Unlike the clean shaven Flavius, Porcius' skin didn't run pale or smooth. He had a deeper tan, sported an incoming beard, and a network of scars. No shame touched Porcius' manner. In fact, he swaggered more and held his head up too high, as if parading his scars. August had seen many hide in shame after they'd been wounded or disfigured. Porcius, however, seemed awfully proud of his scars.

"They'll learn," he said softly, surprising August, and not taking anger at Flavius and Lucius for vomiting their guts onto the stone slab nearby the pieces of their friends. "One gets used to innards after a while. Ya'd think Lucius would have a stronger gut at his age."

August smiled and turned from the gory scene himself. "Does one?"

Porcius shrugged and rubbed the knuckles of his index fingers in his eyes. "Yeah, but some take longer. I remember the first time I saw guts up close, ones I set outside a man by my own hand. Well, check that, in the arena anyway."

"In Rome?"

"Naw, some craphole prelim spot near where Pompeii used to be. I gutted the guy and he practically shot his own innards at me. By the ghost of Leonidas, I got sick too."

"I reckon so."

Porcius coughed and looked at the sky as if seeing the scene again. "Puked all over him. Kinda added to his end, I suppose. The crowd cheered, but they were drunk and full of inbreeds. His buddy hit me in the gut with a knee and woulda killed me right fast, but I puked all over his pommel. The jackass stared at his wrist too long."

"You got him?"

Porcius grinned, still looking at the sky. "Yeah. Upper cut swipe with my broken gladius. Split his jaw up to his nose."

"All right," August admonished him, trying to quiet the story that would surely go on and on if he didn't.

Porcius stretched his thick frame. "Hungry? I am."

Damned Greeks, August cursed the race. Then again, Porcius, while born a Roman citizen at Ephesus, thought himself descended from long gone Spartans. August didn't need to hear another version of that family history, or why he wished he was born centuries before, during that glorious time.

Flavius, son of senator—well, the fifth son of a senator. The others had easier jobs, but Flavius craved adventure and didn't tend to his studies, but he did not have the body for it. He did not have the mind for politics or the arts, nor civil service, at least not yet.

August didn't think him a bad man, but not as ready to wade in gore as Porcius. Flavius wasn't timid, though. He fought well, but did so by the numbers, which was why he rode as a horseman and not in the front line with the Legion. By his look of shame at getting sick, August knew he'd spent too much time indoors.

Porcius followed August into the stone circle and away from their ill brothers. "I bet the life of a civil servant seems pretty nice now to that kid."

Eyes scanning the circle of systemically laid out stone slabs, August answered, "Military service will aide you or inspire a man."

"If we ever see the Appian Way again," Porcius coughed, tossing his helmet in the air a few inches and spun it around in his hands.

"You fear we will meet our end out here?"

"In Britannia or this arm pit of the Picts?"

"Either or."

"A few days ago, I'd guess the Picts may rise up and go to war, thus giving us a fight and a chance to die in battle with the full support of the Legion at our backs. However, the danged buggerman will get us now."

August frowned and glared at him as they walked the stone circle. "That's enough of that talk."

Porcius shrugged. "You heard that Pict dyin' on the cross just like I did. Why lie at such a time? He called it all as such and we saw them monsters of his yarn."

"To deceive us greatly once more."

Porcius gave out a laugh that echoed in his thick gut. "He sounded real to me, as a suffering man at the end, but what do I know?" He walked over and sat down on one of the slabs laid across two smaller rocks, like a bench.

August's eyes rested on him. "You've seen so many men die up close, so I accept you as a wise man at consul."

"Doesn't matter if you do, sir. I'm with you till the end."

August half smiled. "You fear not sitting on that altar?"

Looking down at where he rested, Porcius asked, "Is that what I'm on?"

"Looks like."

"So I'm angering the gods?"

"Of this place, yes."

"Good." Porcius lifted up his right buttock and broke wind loud, just as Flavius walked into the stone circle. "Ready for breakfast, Flavius?"

The blonde youth shook his head, but meandered into the stone circle. "Amazing this place. Another site like this?"

"Yeah," August threw out, waving a hand about. "Aligned in a perfect order, like every other we see in this land."

Lucius emerged, wiping his mouth with the back of his left hand. "There are circles and sites similar in Gaul, but not on such scales as here."

Porcius snorted and spat. "If you kids travel more, the world is littered with rocks the ancients decided to throw up on each other. I've been to Babylon, to Ur, Egypt, and Judea. There are amazing things all over this world. This isn't so impressive."

August thought of his fatherland, of the Germanic places he saw as a child, memories growing dim, but still there. He closed his eyes and remembered his grandfather showing him the Degernau Menhir or

Bühlhölzle Menhir stone, a standing slab bigger than those in this circle. He felt sad that he couldn't recall what it was for or to whom. He did remember the Goseck circle in his homeland, but it wasn't made of great stones, but more of mounds, ditches and alignments dug in the earth and propped up with many walls of logs.

Eyes open, August saw Porcius sipping from his canteen, and Lucius walking the perimeter of the circle. Lucius squinted at one slab after the other.

Porcius taunted him. "You won't be able to read any of that etched markings."

"I know," Lucius replied, not making eye contact with him.

Porcius continued, "Ever see anything like that by the mouth of Ostia?"

"No," Lucius admitted.

"Ah Ostia," Porcius lamented like he loved the port to the sea. "The bottom end of the toilet bowl that is Mare Nostrum. That musta been fun growing up in that smelly place."

Offense taken by the stern look in his dark eyes, Lucius retorted, "Was it much better at Ephesus?"

Porcius belched and put his canteen away. "The great sea port was not a port like Ostia, where the Tiber River pukes out the waste of the Roman sewers into the ocean. It was a nice place, even after the crazy emperor made my family outlaws."

August spoke up and asked, "I'd heard something of that, but never asked you."

"Not much of a story. My father refused to acknowledge Caesar as a god, so he was sent off to Patmos to turn bigger rocks into smaller rocks. His family was dispersed, sold off as chattel, my sisters and I were sent into slavery, until I grew tough enough to fight and be a gladiator. My dad has his beliefs but he wasn't thinking of us when he took a stand."

August nodded, thinking of his father, who died fighting the Romans with a horde of barbarians at his side. "Did he die on Patmos?"

"Probably did, most do, unless you're a magic man that can live on forever. I heard they had one there once that did that trick, but that is another story." He rose up and stretched. "Lucius, what brought you to Britannia to die?"

Again, Lucius gave him a heated look. "Curse you. My father was a Centurion, as was his before him, and so on."

"Not smart enough for a real job either, huh?"

"Shut up."

Porcius chuckled, walked over by a stone pillar and voided his bladder again, all over it. His head cocked as he heard a crowing in the woods. He taunted the squawking birds to come closer with waves of his stream.

"Doesn't matter where we are from," August said in a low voice, not far from Porcius as he himself answered natures call. "If Flavius has old Gaulish blood in his Roman line somewhere, enough to give him blonde hair, is irrelevant. I don't think the beasts of this forest or the magic workers who inspire them care. We are all one race to them."

Porcius yawned and asked, "You think the Pict shamans control the monsters we saw? Was Drust in charge for real?"

"That's my idea," August said low, still so only

Porcius could hear, eying Rufus as he wandered the circle. “That dying Pict seemed to shriek along those lines.” He turned to see Rufus stop and gaze into the woods. “You all right, Rufus?”

The curly haired youth nodded, but didn’t look at his master. “Yes, sir.”

“Don’t wander off on me,” August smiled and turned away from Rufus. “He’s a good kid, that one there.”

“You don’t have him in a heavy collar or anything, just a light chain, like a necklace. Nice of you, really.”

They walked to the other end of the stone circle and kept talking. “I trust Rufus and appreciate him very much. I love him like a son. He’d never betray me.”

Rufus hated August’s guts.

The words he heard from him made his stomach churn, but he held his manner in check. That horrid language of the Romans he learned as a child even made him ill compared to their native tongues. Eyes shut tight, he wept inwardly knowing he should be a druid, as the Roman invaders called them, one with such a memory to chronicle his people and their faith. No, now he served the piglets from Italy and he could barely keep it all inside.

The linens of Roman life clung to his sweaty body and Rufus longed to throw them off and run naked into the woods. August was a fine man and a good master, true, better than the devils he served with, but Rufus still hated him and all Romans for what they did to his earth, to his homeland. He couldn’t fathom any of their loyalty to mother Rome. August own words told of the Romans encroaching into Germania and slaying his folk, and yet, he served them. The Romans destroyed the Celts of the south and Rufus was a slave to them, simple as that, but he still felt the pangs of his heart or as his grandmother had called, the call of the blood.

In the woods, he saw the outline of dead branches sway just slightly. He knew that in this time of year such branches wouldn't exist unless the tree they were attached to had died long before. He saw the antlers and walking sticks of those of the wood, as they watched him and the Romans. Rufus saw the patterns of the branches and that they created a form, a figure, and how the wood weaved to create the lady Weaver.

Rufus said nothing. He turned his back on the woods and returned to August's side.

"We're here, good men!" Ralta snarled from the head of the massive column of armed soldiers as they marched into Rutland. "Best we be about setting up!"

An aged, but fit man not wearing armor, but simple togs, drew near to Ralta and looked at a scroll he carried. "How long do we stay? To rest or encamp?"

Ralta slapped the older man on the back. "Well, Gaius, I don't know how long the General would have us tarry. I feel it is always better to dig in as if you faced the fight of your life than not. We are in a strange land and unwelcome here."

A bored look on his face, Gaius replied, "Looks like they have the dead in pieces, or what is left of them. That will make them difficult to name."

Ralta's boisterous grin faded. "My dear. Well, do your work and see if you can tell who is who."

Gaius left the Legion and set about to chronicle the dead, but they were only fragments.

The men of the 9th tore into their duties with determination, despite their token protests. They were all veteran enough to realize that the work might save their lives in the long run.

Ralta, as many of the men, could tell a great battle had transpired in this place. "They burned the place to the earth. Fascinating," he said to any close enough to hear, while they assessed what had happened.

Any simple soldier could see that the village had been burnt to the ground by the hands of men.

They had arrived early and the sun still climbed into the sky. In its early light, the blood stains upon the avenues of the village, and the grounds surrounding it, called out. There were no bodies of common folk, though. Not a single intact corpse left for the animals and birds to feast on, only crude leftovers of a slaughter.

It was an odd thing and struck Ralta bitterly. The General and his detachment *should've* been here waiting on their arrival. Yet, there was no one. Not even the poor souls to whom this place must have belonged. The men were not concerned to the point of questioning him, so Ralta figured he had time to figure things out. Whoever attacked this village had decimated it and apparently driven off the General and the men.

Ralta ordered a strict defense of the burnt out village's perimeter, assigning numerous squads of men as sentries, while the others worked at making camp.

He put others to work salvaging what huts and structures they could, reinforcing them and making those that had survived viable places for some of the men to stay. Others he put to work on clearing out the village's baths. Ralta knew the less time the men had to dwell on what might have transpired here, the better.

Finding the General and those with him was the top priority.

Normally, August would have been in charge of such a thing but he was among those missing as well.

Ralta unfastened the strap of his helmet and removed it. The day's slight breeze felt good as it blew over his sweaty, matted hair. He ran his fingers through the damp mass and shook his head like a dog, slinging sweat in every direction. He knew this season was what passed for summer here, and the gods knew its days were hot, but the temperature sometimes dropped fiendishly cold at night by Roman standards.

Ralta dismounted his horse and moved about the men of the 9th, watching them as they worked. His stomach grumbled, demanding to be fed soon, but Ralta ignored it. Such was part of life in the Legion and he enjoyed it.

A commotion erupted from a group of sentries he had posted nearby. Ralta rushed towards their position. As he approached, he saw a cluster of men approaching from outside the camp's borders. A smile split his lips as he recognized the newcomers.

General Malitus, at the center of the approaching men, matched his beam.

"Well met, Ralta," the General praised.

"Sir!" Ralta snapped to attention, standing to his full height, shoulders wide with pride.

August, Porcius, Lucius, Flavius, and Quintus, among others were with him.

"You missed quite the fight, Ralta," Flavius teased. "You'll need to march the men faster if you want your share of blood next time."

Ralta stared at the younger man, unsure how to respond.

"And an epic one it was," Quintus taunted, his tone far from serious. "If you have a desire to stand face-to-face with abominations that shouldn't exist but does."

Ralta's expression grew even more confused.

"Ignore them," General Malitus said. "We shall soon talk of what happened, but first some food and wine." Malitus' gaze swept over the hundreds of busy Legionaries. "Ah, I see you have the men clearing the baths. Join us there when they are done. I think they are fed by wells nearby."

Ralta nodded, burying away the flood of questions that washed into his mind.

August eased himself into the waters of the bath. They were not warm but neither unbearable as he took a seat. Quintus, Malitus, and Ralta were already waiting on him. He noted Porcius, Lucius and Flavius meandering about the inner edges of the bath house

"By the gods, it's damned cold in here," Quintus complained, stretching his still aching left arm.

August said nothing.

"Aye, did you expect warm waters filtered from their deep wells, brother?" Ralta asked. "So cold your manly bits, be they as small as they are, may shrink up inside you Quintus, never to be seen again. A blessing or a shame?"

Anger flashed over Quintus' features but August knew Ralta and Quintus well enough to know the two brothers would not come to blows over such insults. Their respect for one another as Legionaries and officers kept them in line, even if the brothers loved to beat each other senseless.

"General," Ralta said. "You said you would tell me of what happened?"

"We were attacked," Malitus replied simply. "Routed by beings straight out of the legends of the primitive folk who tend these lands."

"Big, hairy creatures, Ralta," Quintus snickered and washed himself down. "Uglier than even you on your worst day."

"You jest Quintus, but the beasts are not to be trifled with," Malitus warned with graveness in his tone. "They tore through us as we might a horde of the barbarians here."

"They are fast *and* strong," August added, taking a container of oil from a servant and pouring it across his chest. "A combination that no real soldier cares to meet on the battlefield."

Ralta watched August scrape off the oil from his chest and looked to the regular soldiers. "Tell me of this, you all."

"I saw one of the things snap the necks of two horses at once, as if the act were nothing to it," Flavius spoke up with the fever of youth.

Porcius nodded. "They tore through our shield wall as if we, we of the 9th, were nothing more than weakling farmers playing at war. The turtle held on a few minutes, but in time we were wore down like fools."

To August, Ralta appeared a man who was unsure if a great jest was being played upon him. His eyes, wide, doubted them.

"It's true," Malitus confessed. "We are all that remains of the detachment that departed ahead of the 9th."

Ralta shook his head. "How can that be? Surely you are—"

"Quiet Ralta," the General commanded. "All is as we have said it to be. The 9th is in great danger here. Be that as it may, we still have a mission to carry out. The emperor awaits word of us pushing back for forces of Pictdom."

August dipped deeper in the water and looked toward Porcius. "Tell them what you have discovered."

Clearing his throat, the stocky man moved forward a step and said, "While we were clearing some of the burnt out homes when we discovered hatches in the ground, under the hovels, not unlike those on the Fogous. We thought them cellars of canneries, but when I stuck my head in them, and dropped in light, I realized they were entryways to tunnels."

Malitus leaned forward in the water. "Tunnels?"

Quintus asked, "Them?"

"Yeah, uh, sirs." Porcius added. "There are many openings, one in each home. Probably tunnels all about under this place."

"That explains much," Ralta splashed idly at the water's surface as he spoke. "I confess, I don't know what to make of that. Perhaps they belong to these creatures you speak of."

Porcius snorted and they all faced him. "Um, I doubt it."

Ralta grinned. "Why so?"

"I doubt my big ass can fit in one of those dark tunnels, much less one of those giant things we fought last night. They gotta be for the villagers to exit and come back if they so decide. I for one would love to get a hold of a few of them for letting us get our pricks out in the open for these monsters to bite off."

August nodded but had no chance to speak.

"This village is not safe then." Quintus splashed the water like he would slap a servant down. "Not that I ever claimed it was."

"We'll be on the move soon enough, Quintus," Malitus told them. "I have no intention of lingering here beyond this night. The forces of the Legion will protect us as we fight as one."

"But sir," August leaned forward, "We need to explore those tunnels as well as the woods surrounding this place. The more we know about these monsters we face, the better prepared we'll be next time. If we are going forward into Caledonia in search of the barbarians, we'll surely see these things again."

"Are you so sure there will be a next time?" Quintus challenged. "We escaped them yes? And there has been no sign of them since last night."

"Don't be a fool Quintus," August spat. "You know as well as I that these lands we are passing through belong to them. Whether those priests are controlling them or not, they will come at us again. That's as sure as the rains in this region."

Quintus, for once, ignored August's jab. "Those things attacked a simple detachment, August. They will not raise themselves against a full Legion. The druids would be mad to direct them to do so. The very notion of something of the sort is insane!"

"Is it Quintus?" August went on. "We know not about what they are or their true motives. Worse, we have no idea of their numbers. How many of those things do you think it would take to challenge the 9th as a whole?"

"How many of those things could there be?" Quintus demanded. "You speak as if there is an army of the foul beasts. There are thousands of us now."

"And we don't know that there isn't," August said again. "We know next to nothing about them. That is my point."

"Perhaps we should head back to the fort," Ralta suggested, "Let all this blow over before we press forward? If these beasts are connected to the savages of these parts, they might see this as a chance to move against us as well."

"Cowards!" Quintus scowled, his hands stabbing into the water so hard water splashed over the General's face. "I am in the company of cowards!"

"Remember who you share this bath with, Quintus Pilate," Malitus said firmly. "You need to curb your anger."

"Forgive me, General," Quintus lowered his tone. "But are we not Romans? Are they all not dirty assed monsters and savages?"

August had to laugh then. "Do you think that mattered to the men we watched get torn limb from limb last night, Quintus?"

"There is something to be said about the healthier part of bravery here," Porcius agreed with an awkward belch.

"We cannot go back until we know more and until we engage the Picts for the emperor," General Malitus stated in a way that told them all, on that point, there would be no further argument on it. "We press ahead."

Ralta merely nodded as Quintus stretched his arms upon the rim of the bath and grinned like a cat that had caught its rat. Flavius appeared unsure of himself and the decision that had been reached. Porcius accepted the General's words stoically, as a man who knew his rank and was content with whatever might lay ahead.

August rose up and took a towel from the servant. "But General, again, we should take the time to learn more about these beasts before we press on. Doing so might give us an understanding of their motives. Right now, we don't even know what they are, much less why they seem to be after us."

"There is wisdom in what you say, August," Malitus admitted. "But we have little time. We all agreed that this village is not safe and our mission demands we be on the move as soon as we are able." Malitus paused, thinking. "You have until dawn when the 9th departs this blighted region to search the tunnels and woods if that is truly how you wish to spend your afternoon and evening. Take whatever men you need, no more than a few squads, though. The rest will be needed here should another attack come. Learn what you can."

"Thank you very much, General," August bowed his head in respect, grateful for the granting of his request. "Some of the men I will need are here now," he gestured his left hand at Porcius and Flavius.

"Well, that's all fine and lovely then." Ralta changed the subject abruptly and sighed loud.

Malitus grinned. "Very true."

Ralta lay back and smiled. "Cold or not, this bath was sourly needed. I do so adore a bath. It is a shame the rest of the world so adores their dirt."

"Brilliant thoughts worthy of grand philosophers of olden times."

Ralta belly laughed. "Does it not feel good to have the trail dirt or dried blood wash from your skins?"

At this, they all chuckled except Quintus who continued to glare at August.

Chapter V

Suited up in fresh togs and light armor, August walked from one burnt out home to another looking at the openings discovered underneath. Rufus followed his master, and Porcius and Flavius soon joined them in their quest.

August peered back at the hunk of the Legion that joined them, numbering in the thousands scattering across the village grounds, and asked, "Where's Lucius?"

Flavius replied, "Helping them set up a good perimeter and stabling the cavalry for the night."

August's eyes scanned what used to be the town of Rutland, and saw a mini version of the Roman fort assembled up fast. Tents, tiny and for individual dwellings, peppered the street and surrounding country, all tightly knit together. Larger tents also sprang up, all laid out in the usual manner of a Legion on the move. When he saw one of the slingers try and hit a raven that perched on one of the carts, he suddenly felt ill. They missed.

Porcius chewed on something and wiped his right hand on a cloth near his waist. "What? The foragers bagged some nice venison on their trip in the night. Go liberate yourself some from the mess, but it's a trifle fresh even for my taste."

A good hundred men stood guard facing out into the wilds of Caledonia, to the east alone. Hundreds more performed basic tasks of maintenance and settling in for the afternoon and night, but each kept an eye on the forest.

"This isn't the entire Legion," Rufus noted, looking the men over, not the forest.

"Naw," Porcius said, mouth full of deer. "All the bigger pieces of artillery and machines are slower to reach us. Thousands stayed for that deliberate trek. A boring assed walk for true, but better than quick time marches any day."

Rufus asked his master, "Will the beasts come again tonight?"

All eyes went to August, "The leaders seem to think that they won't, confident that the numbers of this portion of the Legion will scare them away."

"I heard that talk too, huh!" Grinning, Porcius wondered aloud and smacked his lips, "Is that what you think?"

August knelt by one of the hatches in a burnt out domicile and flipped it open. "I think they haven't been right yet, so I'm sort of on guard."

He kicked the hatch with a sandaled foot.

"August, what do you think is the deal with the tunnels around here? Back home, I knew an old man who said a flock of Strix lived in such deep places." Flavius asked.

August rolled his eyes. "Vampiric birds? Please."

Porcius knelt with him and said, "I think they are just what they look like, escape routes. All of those pricks took flight, but not over land."

To his knees, August peered into the opening

further. "We set the place on fire and the town escaped unseen?"

"Ingenious," Flavius commented, still standing, shying away from the hole.

Rufus offered, "But that's wrong thinking. It was really quiet before that. They departed or hid beforehand a long while." Rufus looked back to the south. "I wonder if the abandoned town south of here was really as such or if they were all hiding from us in rabbit holes."

Head tilted to the side for a moment in reflection, Porcius said lowly, "Not a bad idea, I guess. We went by and didn't flog or burn anything."

Flavius' jaw hung open for a moment, before he said, "We didn't do a search for hatches in those homes."

August hopped down into the opening, narrowly fitting in the spot. "I don't think we have to worry about the creatures popping out of these in the night. I can barely fit within." He shrunk down to his haunches and looked down the rectangular shaped tunnel. "Someone really understood what they were doing when they made these."

Porcius offered, "They are reinforced with tiny rocks, all along the sides and top. I couldn't get far enough into see much, but that."

"That's some project." Flavius then asked, "Do you think these people made the tunnels hereabouts?"

August looked out at him. "Why do you say that?"

"I doubt they made the stone circles here or elsewhere, these locals here anyhow." Flavius pointed all around and then gestured at the stone walls of the tunnels that interlocked very close together. "I bet these people built this village atop that network of tunnels. Whoever came before and made such circles and things were far brighter than these Pict peasants."

After a belch, Porcius held his gut and stood. "Take guts or no brains to crawl through that and see what ya can see. These people are scared of the things in the earth, right kid?" He reached out and slapped Rufus on the shoulder. "Aren't you afraid of such things?"

Rufus stepped away from him, and said, "The children of the night could dwell down there. They are tiny."

Porcius laughed. "I'd fear some Karkinos, big ol' crabs. They pop out of tunnels in Greece not even near the sea."

Flavius jeered him, saying, "Probably at the rooms of temple prostitutes."

With a wink, Porcius admitted, "It happens."

August hunkered down into the tunnel and stared up at Rufus. "Stand watch for me, Rufus. Flavius, go to the Fogou and await me there by the tunnel we saw. I suspect it will connect with this one, but I cannot be certain."

Rufus nodded and Porcius stepped away, looking away from them.

Flavius blinked several times. "Sir?"

August's look hardened at him. "Unless you have decided not to obey orders, do as you are bidden by me."

"Sir," Flavius said, glancing at the woods and then back to him. "What you are doing is not . . . advisable."

"But I am doing it," August said and cleared his throat. "I'm not making you do it. The might of the Legion is all around us. Have comfort in that, remember?"

As August squatted down, Flavius called in, "Sir, how shall you see?"

"There is a dull green glow deep down in here. I'm not sure what it is, but I think it is similar to such things I've seen in caves in my homeland, deep in the earth. I've never seen such a thing so close to the surface or anywhere else in the world."

He heard the men speak a few things as he moved into the tunnel. Porcius mentioned a patrol and being summoned to join it. Flavius cursed as his voice ebbed away. Rufus said nothing and August focused ahead.

As a youth in Germania, he had climbed about in caves and even crept into deeper recesses seen by no one of adult size, or at least he figured as much. These tunnels, while not too far below the surface, reminded him of that dank place, yet, were assuredly manmade. The walls, while not dirt or all clay, had been piecemeal covered by rocks, like walls dividing fields in the isle of Erin, north of the druid stronghold at Anglesey. His mind twisted at the task, how these tunnels were painstakingly reinforced with such rocks, and yet they didn't perfectly fit together. Surely, this was the work of a previous group than these evolving savages.

In the seams, though, he saw the greenish glow seep out, like it was ready to drip. August stopped and used his dagger to pry one of the rocks loose. That took some doing, but he saw the glow in its more natural state, like veins of the arm in a spidery network. He couldn't fathom why this glowed such a way in the darkness, but felt thankful for its light.

His heart descended a little when the tunnel did likewise, dipping gradually the more he crawled. He did fear a dead end in his future, but the air in the tunnel path felt fresh on his stubble face. The hairs on his body stood up all over as he moved onward, fearing rats, bugs or some ghoulish beast worse than the ones hiding in the woods. He doubted the giant beastmen were here, as he barely fit in and he was larger than most males. Porcius truly was too thick to slide through, and he didn't recall the thuggish soldier arguing that idea or offering to try beyond his initial look.

In his mind's eye, August figured he journeyed beyond the edge of the town, toward the Fogou. Excited at making this simple progress, mind alight with memories of his youth cave exploring in Germania, August failed to note the abrupt drop in front of him. Suddenly, he pitched headlong forward. His momentum came as such that at the sharp incline he flipped over and started to slide at the steep angle. The glow hadn't shown him anything more than more tunnels ahead, and when he crashed a few yards down, he looked up to see a path about the gap he fell in. This was probably known to the villagers or whoever traveled the tunnel. Indeed, the tunnel carried on to the other side of this great hole or whatever he fell into.

On his backside, sore from the fall, August closed his eyes and prayed to the white Christ he'd found many years ago, amongst the slaves in Italy.

"Lord God, deliver me from this place of darkness."

He stood and reached up, unable to get a good hold of the sides, but suddenly aware in front and back of him was another tunnel, or trench . . . a gap in the earth, this time natural and big enough to walk in, and also illuminated by the green glow.

"Lord, your grasp of the comedic element is fierce today."

Rufus stiffened when Severus rode up with another centurion. The pair of horses stopped and the soldiers looked at the slave boy waiting by the hole. They then told Porcius, "Find a mount and come with us. We need to skirt these woods and patrol."

Porcius gave them a rough salute. "I haven't had my rations this afternoon."

"Didn't I see you scarfing deer a bit ago?" Severus frowned, and then spat to his left. "You're tough enough to wait a little more."

His feet not moving, Porcius stated, "I'm a better man with food in my gut."

The other centurion looked at Severus and shrugged. "We have some daylight left and the General is set to drinking already."

Severus' manner softened. "We have entrenched here. All right, then." He faced Rufus. "Boy, Lucius is over by the south end of the accursed woods. Please go and locate him, and take rations along this instant."

Rufus never spoke and departed from them.

They followed as Porcius called out to the soldiers to get him a horse ready, and then went to the newly assembled mess.

Rufus walked to the mess tent before all of them, sandaled feet stabbing at the earth like it belonged to Severus' neck. He honestly hated these men more than they could fathom. Yes, he admired August but still wanted them all dead, and off his Isle. He looked to the woods and tried to hide his smile. He could feel it, the natural way of things coming around, and his gut yearned for greater things to fall, wild things like he'd seen the night before. Granted, the beasts of the forest may just bring his death as well, but in a way that was a sort of freedom.

He closed his eyes, felt the faint wind on his face, and could smell the beastmen nearing. When he looked about at the hundreds of soldiers making camp, none seemed to care or note the odor in the air. Then again, he reasoned, many perfumed their bodies or put on oils after baths. He reasoned that this alone would mute their senses enough to not get what lurked near.

"Something funny?" a soldier named Mathew asked, but didn't stop to make any trouble with the slave.

Once Mathew had moved along, Rufus licked his lips and studied the woods again. "Yes, something is very funny."

Dutifully, like any slave, Rufus quickly did as he was told by the centurion. He took a pouch from the mess full of hard tack and grabbed a small canteen of wine. The cook slipped him an extra portion with a nod, knowing the slave would feast on the same as he went. Rufus nodded back and bit into the hard tack before setting off for the woods. He would find Lucius soon, but couldn't quit staring at the woods. Oddly, he didn't feel afraid or thought his death loomed near.

The goblet in his hand was empty once more, so Malitus reached for the bottle and poured the last of the wine into it. He sat alone in his large tent. The bath of the day hadn't left him feeling clean and renewed, it had left him feeling desperate and not much else. This troubled him, so Malitus retreated to where he usually found solace. His mind alight with things, he tried to focus and understand it all. The future of the 9th Legion lay bound up in darkness, completely entangled by forces he had no experience dealing with much less had the ability to understand. There were no means of escaping it, at least not that he could see.

He raised a toast to himself. "A great General," he said and sipped anew. Would he be remembered as such? What did that serve him in the here and now? When the orders came to march into Caledonia and discover its secrets on the way to the North Sea, he had not shirked in his duty. The 9th Legion remained one of the best fighting forces in the world, if not the best in his own mind. His leaders even told him so, thus he accepted it. "I've ridden the back and barbarians rise in the ranks, and those from not too great stock," Malitus said to no one, drinking more.

He thought of his grandfather's humble farm in Italy, a man he called 'father' his entire life, as his real father had run off, thus not branding him an orphan or bastard. His rank and rising had paid for that accomplishment in blood not his own. Malitus' fought so many battles on so many fields he could scarcely remember them all. So many victories were his. He knew he should be filled with confidence and pride but all he felt was the blackness of death's approach. She was coming. Of that there was no doubt. She came for every man, the poor worker in the fields, the royal noble in his grand bed, and even great warriors came to an end after their time of war was finished.

Downing the remainder of the wine in a single long

gulp, Malitus cast the goblet aside. He tried to stand but the edging folds of the tent spun around him. He could not maintain a perfect balance, and collapsed back into his chair. Shame struck him like a blow to the gut. He was a General, and his men were counting upon him to see them through this journey as he had so many times before. Yet, they were deep into a dire enemy territory, danger all around them, perhaps even beneath their very feet, and the best he could do was leave the work to his officers and get so drunk he couldn't even stand up properly.

The beastmen, or whatever they were, terrified him beyond all reason. Any human foe he could meet on equal terms and there was honor to be found in the spilling of blood. These creatures were not human, though. They were stronger, faster, and cunning. Monsters stepped forth from the worst of nightmares to walk the earth. They shouldn't—couldn't—be real, but they were, both more and less than man. He could never show this fear to anyone.

August Arminius understood these things on some level, or he appeared to. What that said about the man also left Malitus disturbed. He questioned if he were allowing August too free a hand. Quintus certainly thought so, but what else could he do? The young officer showed promise and the entire 9th needed such a man guiding it. Besides, he rather liked August. He reminded Malitus of himself in better times. What the 9th faced in Caledonia was not what he was trained for, but August had cunning in reacting, which he liked. It was more than simply leading men in a clash of arms. The trade of death was what he excelled at, but these things, these monsters in the night were far better at it, ferocious and brutal. They ate the flesh of man, living or dead.

With a shout, Malitus called for the guards outside his tent to fetch him more wine. They delivered it hastily, fleeing his presence as quickly as they could. He wondered if they could see the fear within him. If so, all was lost already. Any army was only as good as its commander, and this time, in this place, Malitus was sourly finding himself wanting.

Chugging half the new bottle of wine, he slumped where he sat, his eyes closing, seeking peace, an answer of some kind, in his dreams.

Panic didn't grab August for the air didn't smell stale, and the rut he trod in under the earth ran dry. When it occurred to him that in this larger, rather trough-shaped passage one of the beastmen could easily fit, his mouth grew dry. He paused, licked his lips and swallowed hard. The veins of green light still showed him a way to travel, so he carried on.

August kept searching for a way to get back up to the level he traveled on before, in hopes to reach the Fogou. He moved away from that area in his mind's eye, going to the east, more toward the murky woods. The cleft in the earth dipped lower gradually sending him further down. The temperature dropped and August shuddered.

Time went by as did strange etchings on the walls amidst the green lines. Many appeared like cave drawings he'd seen in the caves in Gaul. The pictures drawn with a substance were fading and very dim, but the images carved remained. August thought he saw images flying in the sky, and several figures beneath them. He then noticed there were winged beings on the ground. The longer the drawing went the smaller figures appeared flanked by larger ones with no wings. As he crept further, August saw many diagonal lines and figures cut in half . . . no . . . drowning in waters. Then, a large tubular raft.

Again, his distracted attention caused August minor trouble. His feet shifted and he slipped. He reached out as the wall ran out but nothing existed to hold on to. His heart racing, he thought himself falling into eternity, but that only lasted a few moments. He crashed into what felt like a series of thin branches, some of which broke as his backside crashed and his body flipped over. August twisted on his sheathed gladius, and swore, then begged his God for forgiveness for his outburst. Hands flexing, August thought he swam in piles of leaves, but soon he gripped tight on something solid. In each hand he raised up a similar object.

"Bones," August said to no one and almost jumped at the echo of his own voice. "Lots of bones." He stared at the long bones in his hands and then down at the array about him. He'd fallen and rolled into a vast chamber full of skeletons.

He turned, squinting, seeing that it was more than just a depositary of bones. Over and over there were skeletons. Huge skeletons. A majority of them were quite massive and bearing skulls more apish than those of men.

Understanding that he stood in a weird graveyard, August figured there was some compliance between the locals and these stinking beasts. That didn't mean much at the time, as he heard voices from down the way, ahead of him. Barely able to see in the grim light, he flattened against the wall of bones between him and the cave wall, wishing he could climb out, balance on the ledge and go back the way he came. August thought that with some time he might be able to scale out, but the people coming near him were his primary concern.

August suddenly felt the fool, holding the two long bones in his clutches instead of proper weapons. He couldn't drop them and unsheathe even his knife, though, as the voices grew very close. A peculiar odor hung in the air, striking his senses, and August grimaced as the first figure moved into the shadows—a burly man with thick hair and a beard.

Fagan, the blacksmith, his own damn self!

He talked in low tones to a man behind him, a slender figure swathed in a hooded robe not unlike he saw the one they'd assumed was Drust earlier. August dismissed the figure as not Drust, because this person stood much shorter and groaned over the parcel he carried.

With no more time to deliberate it, August struck. He brained Fagan on the top of his head, drilling the bone in his right hand into the mop of the blacksmith's hair. August's strike caused an immediate reaction as the thick man dropped the bag he carried. Not content that he subdued the stumbling man, August used the bone in his left hand in a sideways swipe, nailing the rear of Fagan's skull. The man fell forward, half coughing, half swearing in shock.

August spun to drive a knee into the robed figure's midsection, before he swung the right bone again, smashing it into the hidden face. This thin figure dropped the bag he lugged along, allowing a loud sound to echo about them. August thought it sounded the same as when he fell into the pile of bones. Unconcerned about that for the moment, August saw the smaller figure tumble back into the bones more to the left and cry out loud, like a voice not so mature. The squeal was a higher pitch than August expected. Seeing that shape fall flat in the bones, August turned back to Fagan, who got to his knees, shaking his head. Since he reckoned Fagan had been hit before in his lifetime, and was one of those kinds of men who could take an ass whipping, August recognized the fight wasn't over.

He dropped the bones and unsheathed his gladius. "You better be ready to talk, Fagan, or the scrounging you got before will seem like the tongue of a whore by comparison."

Fagan turned about, still down on his knees, blinking many times and suddenly focusing on August. He grinned. It came as tough to discern in the glow, but the big man smiled. That expression didn't fill August with joy.

Fully prepared to kill Fagan, August primed to dismember him slow as the opening portion of his interrogation.

Behind August, the soft moans of the robed figure moved into coughs. August glanced back, seeing the hood fall, and that he'd struck a woman sporting strawberry blonde hair, who struggled to even get her footing and rise under the bones.

Fagan's grin, though, came due to what lurked beyond the tunnel they traveled from. August saw the shadow in the dim light as it moved into the chamber of bones. The light shone enough for him to see that the shape belonged to one of the beasts, albeit a very small one, perhaps a child. The youth of the creature didn't stop the stench of the thing from assaulting August's nostrils.

Fagan started to chuckle.

August didn't.

Rufus didn't care for Lucius, either.

While he served August as his direct master, at least the German came from his same background—an oppressed tribe made slaves by the imperial Roman ways. August inspired him, showing him that he could be more. However, that didn't sit well with him either.

Jogging beside the mounted Lucius, Rufus stifled an outburst of laughter as he pondered that. A life of advancement being a slave under their yoke, never earning freedom back. Oh joy! How privileged he was to get such a prize, that of being a soldier, like August . . . angry all the time, but not starving and not a slave with chains on. Or he could be Porcius, a tough thug, who had a mouth so strong he fought his way through death mills and arenas to be, again, a soldier, killing and oppressing others like himself.

Lucius? A genuine Roman from Italy? Rufus smiled as he jogged, knowing he only watched out for him in case they encountered natives, and so he could have his supper rations delivered to him, which he didn't share. He utterly despised Lucius and prayed to Lugh to send a shining spear to spite the olive-skinned man and take him away from slavery. Though not overly cruel, Lucius had served longer than most and neared an end to his career.

As they rounded the southern lip of the woods, Lugh's aim proved to be off just a little. Only an instant passed when the object swung out of the forest and struck the horse Lucius rode. Decapitated at the torso, the horse trotted on a few paces, unaware its head had been swiped off by the long limb bearing white fur.

Rufus felt glad he jogged on the left side of Lucius, but that only made sense. If the Roman was to be attacked, it would be from the woods on the right. The Roman, arrogant and erudite, never questioned Rufus' moves.

Lucius stayed in the saddle as the horse began to shake. The horse stopped and collapsed, sending Lucius headfirst over the empty neck and head, which lay in the long grasses not far from where Rufus had stopped running.

From out of the forest emerged one of the beastmen, close to twice as tall as even August. The beast ignored Rufus and stepped closer to Lucius, kicking the horse over and approaching the Roman on the ground. The monster reached down and grabbed Lucius by the legs.

Lucius squealed like a woman, Rufus thought, and even managed to get his dagger out, but that didn't stop the monster from putting a foot between his legs and dislocating both limbs from their ball joints. Lucius screamed so loud Rufus felt someone was bound to hear it in the camp.

Rufus was about to run back the way they came, around the edge of the woods, but another gray giant stood in his way. He twisted, about to flee, wagering he could elude them in the dense forest. He turned and saw that the first gray monster had Lucius up and under his arm like a parcel. When he looked back, in Rufus' path stood a tall man in a hooded robe.

"Pleasant afternoon, child of the south," The deep voice of the hooded man washed over Rufus' face. "I am Drust. There is a favor I must ask of you, child."

The lips of master Drust's mouth were not moving.

After their time in the baths, Quintus and Ralta did take a long rest, then a light meal of common rations, enjoying a supposed or perceived commonality amongst the troops. Soon, though, they decided to exercise, to practice their skills.

For Ralta, the exercise was a daily habit.

"I believe in staying sharp," Ralta declared, making sure all the common soldiers lounging could hear his words. He then said softly to his brother, "It keeps one alive as an infantry man."

Quintus leapt at his brother's offer to join him, because he needed to unleash some of the anger burning within him. Though, he would have rather been gutting August Arminius, slowly and with something dull, he figured pummeling his brother was the next best thing. Quintus fully believed the German become Roman had grown too comfortable in treating his superiors with a growing lack of respect. He had told General Malitus that many times in private, but Malitus disagreed. He also shared this with his brother.

"Oh, nonsense," Ralta yawned, faking to show his lack of interest in Quintus' hate of August. "The

General likes officers who take the initiative, relying on their own brains and experience as much as the orders they were given."

Quintus' nose flared as if he could clear it on August, so far away, after a crazed duty searching tunnels. To Malitus, August was a rising star in the ranks of the 9th, and as much as it pained Quintus, Malitus was willing to give the young officer room to grow.

Perhaps slapping his brother around would clear his mind.

Quintus remained so lost in his thoughts that he almost didn't see Ralta's thick, wooden blade arcing towards his face. Only the speed he was so well known for saved him from having his nose reduced to a black and blue, swollen mass of broken bone. At the last second, he managed to bring his own blade up to block Ralta's. Even so, he was forced several steps back in retreat from the sheer force of his brother's swing. Ralta's advantages were in his strength, reach, and weight. He was a far larger and more muscled man, but Quintus was far from helpless. He watched Ralta recover from his failed swing and ready himself once more.

"Best get your head where it belongs, brother," Ralta laughed. "I nearly took it from your shoulders that time, even in playtime."

Quintus sneered at Ralta's words. "If that's the best you can do, may the gods have mercy on you."

The two paced about, staring at each other, each searching for a good moment to strike. Quintus was perfectly happy to wait for his brother to come at him again. Though rage burned within him at August—and now Ralta as well—he was no idiot. He bided his time and prepared to show his brother just how dangerous he could be.

Ralta grew weary of their dance, and with a roar, charged forward. His heavier blade lashed out. Quintus ducked, darting under it, his blade thrusting outward to score a hit against his brother's ribs. Ralta staggered from the pain as Quintus pressed his attack, hammering Ralta with a flurry of blows that would have sent most other men to their knees.

Dropping his sword, Ralta grabbed Quintus' blade, jerking it from his grasp. Ralta cast the practice weapon aside with a snarl of fury.

"What's wrong with you man?" Ralta bellowed. "This is just simple practice, not a battle to the death."

Quintus fumed, adrenaline continuing to rush through his veins. He delivered a well-placed kick to the inner side of Ralta's right leg. With a howl, Ralta fell. Quintus met his collapsing, gigantic frame with a knee to his chest that sent Ralta sprawling onto his back.

Standing over his brother, Quintus glared down at him. "You asked me for a fight, I gave you one. What have you to complain about?"

The soldiers watching gave out faint, somewhat cloying applause.

Ralta's hands snaked out, grabbing Quintus' legs and yanking him off balance. Quintus toppled, and as he fell Ralta was there to meet him. He swept Quintus into a wrestling move that pinned his slender brother beneath his weight. Ralta held Quintus' arms in an unbreakable hold that applied pressure to them, nearly to breaking point.

The applauding remained scattered, but stronger as Quintus went down.

His face in the dirt, Quintus spat, grimacing at the sudden pain, "Fine! Fine! You win, brother. Release me, now!"

Ralta did so and Quintus scrambled to his feet, wiping at the mud and only spreading it further.

"You let your temper get the better of you again, Quintus," Ralta said, not breathing with any difficulty. "There is more to a fight than passion and wits."

"So says the infantry man," Quintus made sure his remark sounded the insult it was meant to be. "In a cavalry charge, passion matters more than you think."

"August bothers you," Ralta commented softly, "Any fool can see that. But I ask you this, what have you to prove to the likes of him?"

"Shut up."

"Yes, he is a superior soldier out there where it counts and perhaps one of the best scout leaders I have ever known, but he isn't a true Roman like us, Quintus. When all is said and done, your future lies in Rome, whereas he and I will still be in the field." When Quintus said nothing, Ralta continued, "You are a Roman, Quintus Pilate. A noble one at that. Isn't it time you acted like one?"

"My dear brother," Quintus answered, sardonically. "There are many kinds of Romans and not all are as forgiving as you and our General. A man should know his place in the scheme of things and this Arminius does not."

"And you should be the one to teach it to him?" Ralta shook his head, cracking the knuckles on one hand then the other. "Admit it Quintus, no matter what August has done, he isn't really what's bothering you, is he?"

"Tread carefully brother," Quintus cautioned, eyes aimed past the men and at the forest. "You walk on the backs of vipers."

"These beastmen, whatever they are, have you spooked, do they not?" Ralta braved Quintus' fury. "You're afraid we will never see Rome again and your future will be lost. If that's the reason for all this, you are not alone. Most of the men feel the same. It's almost as if they can feel the cold of the earth covering them already."

"But the earth won't cover us," Quintus pointed out. "We will be in the stomachs of those . . . those *things*."

Quintus and Ralta had moved away from the village's center for their practice. They were at the very edge of the Roman perimeter and there were no guards stationed nearby. Both men turned their gaze towards the trees when a loud, well patterned hammering emerged from the woods. It sounded as if a dozen Hercules' had ripped trees from the ground and used them to bash those still standing.

"What in Hades is that?" Quintus stammered.

"Frankly, I don't know," Ralta shrugged, concern on his face. "But I am sure it's not a good omen."

Beneath the rhythm of the crashing noises of wood on wood could be heard a chorus of bestial growls.

"Should we go in and see what all the ruckus is about?" Quintus asked, looking sheepish as he even uttered the words.

"Into those trees? Alone?" Ralta shook his head. "Don't be a mule. Our father made us warriors, not fools."

Ralta walked over to where he had left his real sword and drew it from its scabbard. “Go tell the General what’s happening here,” he ordered Quintus. “I’ll keep watch until you return.”

Quintus nodded and raced towards the heart of the Roman camp, but the rest of the soldiers had already arisen, also on alert.

Chapter VI

Near sunset, Porcius had mounted his steed, and rode along with a two others as they did a patrol. They rode to the stone circle they'd visited before, but found no one about. Porcius rode alone over to the lip of the forest, to where they'd seen the altar and where the Picts had died. After a few moments of looking for the slain men, Porcius turned back.

"Huh, not a fly, nothing."

"What lies beyond these woods, down about the side of this great leg of the forest?" one asked Porcius.

He sipped from his wine flask and shrugged. "I've been wondering the same thing, Severus, but I really don't want to be caught there after dark. I figure when the Legion marches as one, we'll discover it together, aye?"

The two exchanged a glance before Severus stated, "You must not comprehend the purpose of recon and patrol?"

After a swig, Porcius replied, "I understand just fine, but getting my ass killed for foolish curiosity isn't in the handbook, is it?"

Severus said smartly, "We'll ride along to the left, over where the natural road path moves out of Rutland

and into the outlying areas. If you want to circle about the woods, have a care, but watch the skies. It'll be dark in an hour."

Glad to be rid of them soon and the mystical place sooner, Porcius rode out of the stone circle with them and raised his hand toward the lowering sun. Severus had it about right, Porcius wagered, and headed to the right, keeping near to the edge of the woods.

He rode about several minutes before a lower valley spread out ahead of him, picturesque if plain, green and full of tall grasses of the late summer. A small creek snaked through this open land not defiled by crops or homes. He noted that a few tiny bogs peppered the landscape and figured easily why this area wasn't good for planting.

The woods rose steeply, and Porcius spied a couple of small huts, one barely large enough for a man to stand up in.

Probably a storage spot, he mused.

The other one was basic, though, merely a shelter.

When he drew closer to the huts, he saw a round, tall bin hidden behind the small structures. From the see through rounded walls and wound up open top, Porcius calculated this bin placed here to dress deer, not to store grain. He climbed down, peered inside the bin and nodded at his correct assumption. Grain didn't need metal holdings hanging from the ceiling or other tools glinting about the interior.

Still dismounted, he cautiously walked to the first of the other huts, and tried the door. It opened inward, revealing a cot and a crude stone hearth—more for warmth than for cooking anything large. Nearby, a heavy iron bar leaned against the wall by the door, to barricade the door, perhaps?

Porcius closed the door with no real force and walked over to the tiny hut, where the door was also left unlocked. Within the hut were housed a series of implements, hoes, hooks on staffs, a scythe and various other articles for farming presented themselves. He reached down and picked up a sickle, and tapped it on the poles of the hut. All items were well crafted but he expected no less from this isle.

Something caught his eye, and he knelt down to get a better look. Behind the farming tools sat a pyramid shaped object, swathed in a deerskin cover. He reached in and grabbed the cover of deerskin, squeezed the package and felt a series on metal cylinders beneath. He pulled the deerskin back and the bag fell over. Frustrated that he didn't have easy access, Porcius turned the bag over and fumbled with the drawstrings on the package. Once he opened it, he carefully pulled out a series of slender blades used in gutting fish or larger game.

Porcius exited the small hut, turned about and took a deep breath. He looked around for the sunset, which was sure to be blocked by the trees, but instead saw a young woman. She stood near the edge of the forest not far from the bin he'd seen earlier. At first, he thought his eyes betrayed him. If he would concoct a great dream to walk up on two legs, this would be the kind of thing he'd create, though.

Her hair, blood red and tips flecked with orange and black, shimmered in the waning light of day. This coloring inspired Porcius deep in his loins. From her pale skin and tattoos evident on her lower leg and breasts, which was barely contained by loose fitting one-piece tunic, Porcius figured her a Pict if he were a Greek in Roman clothing. The Celtic women were taller, broader and frankly, had hairier legs. This one, her legs almost glistened and while that aroused heat in Porcius' chest and lower regions, he only gave her a friendly wave. Really, what else could he do? Running over to tackle her and have great heat or just asking for her hand to walk fell out of the question.

The woman, barely no longer a girl if he guessed ages correctly, tilted her head but didn't wave back. Her green eyes glowed bright as they looked him up and down, mostly focusing on his lance, and then moving to scrutinize his rough face.

Porcius comprehended little of their native tongue and cursed the fact that Rufus or another servant of local blood wasn't nearby. He also figured if he took a step she'd run, but there wasn't much he could do about that. Frustrated that he'd be unlikely to catch her running in the shape he was in, Porcius waved her off and started to walk toward the big bin again.

She didn't move at his actions and watched him intently as he went to the door of the bin.

He flipped the latch and pulled the bin door open. Porcius looked up at the roof and saw the exposed sky through a small opening. The bin's roof wound up like an inverted funnel, ending in a small hole up at the apex. The straps near the top testified of the station to slaughter deer. Along the well-proportioned walls, several benches fit in snug. Porcius wagered these were intended for quartering and dividing up the meat & innards.

When he stepped out, the girl stood a yard from

him. Amused that she'd moved up closer, Porcius froze, save to nod at the bin and smile.

The corners of her mouth drew up, but she showed no teeth in her expression and looked in at the bin as well. Her eyes widened but her face betrayed no other emotion besides scant wonder.

After leaning his lance on the doorway, Porcius took his index fingers and made playful antlers beside either side of his helmet, feigning a deer with wide eyes.

The girl smiled wide, showing a set of perfect white teeth, and then she laughed.

She stood close enough to grab, but he didn't. The girl was so near he could smell her, a very earthy scent, not perfumed in the slightest, but not stinking vile as some barbarous women he'd been near. Her eyes appeared a shade of emerald he couldn't readily name, and almost swirled like mixing jelly. The teeth, whiter than anyone's he'd seen, bothered him. That sank in his mind as truly unnatural.

Though he had many questions for her and no way to ask them, Porcius figured he might have to seize her, tie her up, and have Rufus question her later. Still, he hesitated doing this. Something about her numbed his senses to such a rude act. The rational part of his mind suddenly registered danger . . . that she was a decoy to fool him. Cursing his male senses that fogged his logical mind, Porcius stepped back and glanced about the bin, not smelling another and also not making a sudden move to frighten her off, even if he gripped his lance again.

She gently stepped back and made a beckoning move for him to follow her with her left hand. The girl took a few more steps backwards and pointed to her chest.

"Tavia," she said and nodded a few times. "Tavia."

He smirked, ready to bust a gut that she thought him too dim to understand her.

"Porcius," he thumbed his barrel chest with his free hand.

Her green eyes squinted a moment. "Pork?'

"Porcius."

With affirmation, she nodded. "Pork."

Tavia clearly wanted Pork to follow her.

Intrigued and still grinning, Porcius stepped after her toward the woods. Under his breath he muttered, "Careful Pork, or your ass is on the ground."

Tavia motioned quickly with her left hand again to follow her into the woods, and stepped in a few yards.

He stopped at the edge of the trees, looked around, took a breath and stepped in. He shifted his lance to his left hand and drew his sword, not afraid if she'd run.

Tavia didn't. She kept looking back and stepping lightly in the woods.

He saw then that Tavia wore a deerskin cover on her feet, not a sole bearing shoe or sandal, but a cover typical of primitives.

They snaked through the woods and Porcius feared that he was being led to a butchering. Since the dense woods soon thinned out and the waning daylight spilled in brighter, Porcius convinced himself he would be all right. Still hearing the voice of his trainers in his head, scrounging him and telling him he acted like a fool, Porcius pressed on.

Tavia stood at the open edge of the woods and pointed, saying, "Pork?"

He stood beside her and she didn't flinch as his bare forearm brushed her bicep. Porcius looked at the open area and saw what she talked about.

"Not pork," he mumbled. "But smells like its cooking."

In the lower depression, on the other side of the forest, a small creek snaked lazily through the greenery. The tall grasses that tapered off near the bank didn't hide what Tavia wanted him to see. Trussed up on a makeshift set of iron poles hung the outline of a man, what was left of one, anyhow. It appeared to Porcius like any man, leaning, with long arms over a set of poles. The man's head drooped down, but the rest of him—his torso and legs—were gone. A spinal column hung from the shoulders, but no guts and other bones. Under this grotesque display a fire smoldered, dying, but enough strength in it to tell him it'd burned well earlier, but not too long before. He hadn't smelt it up beyond the woods, seeing as the wind carried the scent and smoke away down the waters.

At first, he thought this a botched crucifixion by some of his fellow soldiers, but couldn't comprehend them doing it in such a way. His mind then went to the hairy beasts, the creatures, but figured they wouldn't half cook the body or set it on fire for any reason. No, this contemptible act was performed by human hands.

Brilliant, he told his deductive self.

After another step closer, Porcius spotted another body, similar to the one in its position on stakes, but saw that its body still remained uncooked, but sported no head. This form, though, wasn't a broad shouldered Pict but sported skin of a more olive color, like one of the Italians he knew. Porcius drew closer, saw the man nude, but had no easily identifiable marks.

Porcius pointed with his lance and shook his head at her. "Who did this, Tavia? My people didn't." He felt silly as she couldn't understand him.

A look of dull recognition lit in her eyes and she shrugged. Then turned to point at something else in the weeds. She walked over and pointed down at it.

Porcius followed her, still looking about cautiously, watching the long orange hair of the man on the poles wave in the breeze. In the distance, he heard the woods rattle further away. The trees trembled like a great wind blew through them.

He stared at what she pointed at, and blinked.

The tiny object almost obscured by waving weeds resembled one of the mighty structures at a henge near the Sorviodunum fort or the one in the woods not far away. Two smaller stone blocks held up a longer, oblong one. Though it resembled a crude bench, Porcius guessed it to be more significant considering the runic symbols that covered it in finely etched rows.

Tavia pointed at the stone bench emphatically and then at the man hanging in pieces. She looked into his eyes and said, "Drust."

"Crap," Porcius stated, head turning a little as the trees rattled on in the distance. "Like we didn't have enough to worry about. I thought the druids were your priests."

Tavia shook her head, not understanding.

"Maybe you guys fight over gods and who is best, too." He stepped away from her, and his face twisted. The rank scent of something foul entered his nostrils. Panic seized his limbs.

Unaffected by this, Tavia motioned him to walk over to an area in the higher grasses.

Dutifully, he followed her and watched as she stopped, smiled and pointed down again. “Pork? Greyman.”

He walked over and froze as he saw she pointed in the tall grasses at the huge, hairy form. For a moment, he prayed that the thing lay there dead, but saw its chest rise and fall. Those few moments he took to look the giant thing over, to see the white fur all about the massive creature Porcius wasted. He was about to drive his lance into the thing’s heart when it sat up.

His hesitation and the sudden realization of the creature she called Greyman had saved the beast. Porcius did make a rough stab at the thing, his aim adjusted from its torso to its head, but the shot went out awkward, especially when the Greyman’s left hand flew up and quickly grabbed the shaft of the lance.

They stared, eye-to-eye, Porcius and the Greyman, as the left hand snapped the lance head off like it was a dead branch.

All the days he spent in the arena seized him. Porcius swung his gladius over from his right side, wanting to split the Greyman’s head in two pieces.

Greyman moved, seeing the danger, but couldn’t stop his arcing shot from striking his head. The blade, sharp and true, cut loose the left ear of the Greyman and it roared in response. Blood poured onto the white fur of its head and the powerful left arm swiped, smacking Porcius in the thigh, sending him tumbling over into the grass.

Almost dropping his sword, Porcius rolled to his knees, but quickly went up on his all fours and got into a lower stance. Leg throbbing, but body surging, he snapped into place.

The Greyman clutched the side of its head, angry at the wound, and went up to its knees. Easily taller than Porcius, even from that angle, it shook its head and cried out again.

"Run," Porcius barked at Tavia, but didn't stay in that pose longer to see if she obeyed. The soldier charged, gladius again at the ready, prepared to cut the Greyman's head off or at least make a dent in its neck.

Greyman raised its right arm, but jabbed down fast at Porcius' legs.

Porcius did anticipate this reactive move. The action did stop his kill shot to the head he had planned with a right swinging slash. Porcius tried to roll with the shot to his calf. He swung the sword out and down, lazily grazing the Greyman's right bicep, but did not even cut fur loose. The blow sent Porcius turning back into the creature. Smashing into his opponent, Porcius pushed off, feeling the hairy limbs of the Greyman reaching out to envelope him, but failing.

Porcius fell to the grasses again, and spun to his knees, much lower than the beast that started to rise up. As Greyman rose in full, Porcius planned his move and darted forward. The long arms of Greyman slammed the grass Porcius just occupied. The Roman dove between Greyman's legs. Seeing the creature was indeed a male, Porcius elbowed up as he rolled, striking the Greyman's groin with his left elbow guard. True to his nature as a man, the white furred beast's legs trembled and his body shuddered.

Porcius was to his knees again, gladius back in

attack position. Oh, how he wished he had his shield to smash into the dangling bits of the Greyman.

Porcius attacked.

Since Greyman turned to the right a little, stabbing him in the groin and ruining him forever wasn't an option. Porcius did leap off the ground like he fought that huge man in the arena from Tubal, though. Then he had a shield and a spiked bludgeon, but the application remained the same. His left hand grabbed the pit of Greyman's back, and his gladius soared down in an attempt to chop into or through the right bicep. Greyman didn't cooperate, though, and twisted just as the blade fell, which caused Porcius to break the skin but not savagely ruin the muscle. Greyman's movement made Porcius crash into him more and he bounced off, tumbling back into the grass.

Greyman turned and set his feet firm.

Porcius didn't have time to roll and set himself yet. He briefly cursed his thick body, knowing this slight delay would be his undoing someday. However, he didn't count on Tavia screaming and hopping up and down to distract the creature.

Greyman turned his head, watched her scream and then didn't attack Porcius. He took a staggered step after Tavia as she ran back toward the woods.

How little he cares about me, Porcius thought quickly as the Greyman set out to loping after Tavia, who streaked fast toward the grim woods they had come from.

He rose and took a few steps, his head clearing. In the tall grasses his sandal hit something. Not wanting to lose the two runners, he hurriedly reached down and pulled the object up. It was a round shield, not Celtic but similar to their circular design. He thrust his left forearm through the bucklers on the back of the shield, figuring it belonged to the dead Pict on the poles behind him. The design reminded him of old Greek or Spartan shields he'd seen as a child.

As he saw Tavia disappear into the woods and dodge the long swipes by Greyman, two ideas made Porcius smile. One, he wished he had three hundred Spartans with him to form a phalanx against these creatures. Two, he hoped the Pict shield, mostly wood, leather and trimmed in bronze, held up for two seconds in a good battle.

Grinning, Porcius followed them into the woods.

It occurred to August that his eyes might betray him, but he stabbed forth with his gladius at the childlike beastman anyway. When he struck frontward, the creature took a confused step backwards, and that saved its life. The gladius nudged into though-flesh as August probed on, then ripped to the right, hoping to carve out a section of the beastman. The idea of the monster being a child couldn't be proved nor fretted upon, he reasoned, but the thing stood near to his height so that was August's guess. The horrid howl that soon filled up the cavern also told him that he had injured it. Nevertheless, it moved away from him and into a section of tunnel not illuminated by the usual green lines. August held no desire to go in there and turned to face Fagan.

Still grinning, Fagan did wear a sudden look of shock in the shadowy light. He wanted to put his dagger in Fagan's shoulder and twist it, to ask him questions, but understood this may not be possible.

So he swung the gladius down fast, and it lodged in Fagan's right knee just as he tried to rise up and strike.

Fagan's screamed almost rivalled the youthful beastman.

August didn't know if he tore the kneecap loose because of the darkness. However, he saw the big man wobble and fall down, unable to rise. He listened to his continuous cries. August didn't hesitate, figuring he took Fagan out of the fight. When he turned to swing the blade again, this time slashing at the legs of the figure in the robe. He struck something in the folds of the clothing and indeed a female voice whimpered, but August didn't think he broke skin.

Before he had time to draw back, the young creature arrived there again, attacking him. It draped over August like a wet blanket, arms about his limbs, body thudding into him, pushing the German into the wall of bones. The face mashed near to his, lips to his cheek, closer than a lover. Fear grabbed August, but didn't rule him. Afraid his arms pinned, he reacted back before the creature could do him harm. The lips of the creature, fully housing a trap of teeth, were a parting horror he'd not soon get out of his dreams, but he fought back even in his mind, vowing to tear into the animalistic horror.

August bit the beastman youth. Hard. His teeth drove into the flesh of the creature, sinking into the warm skin, filling his mouth with a musky, musty taste that made the venison in his stomach heave and demand release. August didn't vomit, though, but bit harder and pushed back.

Pain of a different sort gripped the young beast,

and it pushed away from him with great force, abandoning any attack, screaming loud and running back into the grim tunnel it'd come from.

August spit repeatedly. The scream of the wounded creature down the tunnel told him it was long gone. On his breastplate he felt blood, but understood it not to be his own. Glad the thing bled like the others, he returned the gladius to its scabbard and drew out his knife. He thought of questioning the girl who must be a druid of some sort, but wondered if she even spoke his language. He wanted to run so badly, back to where he entered the tunnels, but he first turned to Fagan.

"Quite a confederacy you have running out here in the wilds, huh, big man?" August barked at Fagan, kicking him in his injured leg.

Fagan cried out again, eyes shut tight, tears streaming down his face.

August went on. "You fool us, aye? You play games with Rome? Do you realize who you toy with, big man?"

Fagan choked, "Caledonia is not your home, damn you all down to fire. Caledonia is not Roman territory."

August reared back and planted his dagger in Fagan's left shoulder. He turned the grip and Fagan cried earsplitting again. Up to his face in a moment, August hissed, "The entire world is Roman territory."

"Is that all you want?" Fagan shuddered, spit running from his lips. "More dirt for Hadrian? Is that what makes you smile?"

"It isn't about what I want," August grumbled low. "What are these creatures? How do you control them?"

Fagan heaved, coughed . . . no, laughed at August. "Throw a line into the sky and piss up that rope, Roman. Then start climbing."

August drew the dagger out of Fagan's shoulder joint and spat on him. He wiped the dagger on the folds of the druid girl's robe and stepped on her shoulder to boost himself to the narrow ledge about the chamber of bones. She screamed out once, but the shout came out guttural like he punched her lower. That sort of confused him, but he moved on. He hugged the wall and moved back the way he came, ignoring Fagan's laughs and gasps for air.

Eyes shut half the time, August felt thrilled to be on the side of the cavern beyond the spot he fell into. Breathing fast he grew so excited, he edged along the side of the wall for a long time until he came to the open tunnel opposite the side he fell through. August didn't look back as he climbed in the passageway, joyful to be on his way, silently cursing himself for not just going back to the camp where he started. He wasn't thinking clearly, and hoped this wasn't a fatal mistake.

Rufus awoke in the place where he met Drust and the beastmen. Mind spinning, he tried to recall what had happened to him. His forehead felt ice cold, the same way it'd felt when Drust placed his hands upon his head.

But that wasn't here. He looked around at his surroundings. Rufus rubbed his eyes and then closed them. Still, the hands of Drust remained on his head as if he passed on something into his mind, heart, and spirit.

Rufus saw through Drust's eyes, a wise man, a man of many years, centuries he'd lived, so clever was he with the trees and woods that he aged much alike them. He grinned at the idea of Drust chopped in half to count the rings of his life.

Drust's mouth never moved as he looked into Rufus' eyes, but the voice in his head came in clear and alien. The voice wasn't unlike the masters and women of the wood he'd known as a babe. Though, judged not pure stock for their priesthood—not a bad thing in Celtic lore by his father's words—Rufus still held those of the wood in great reverence. Even the warriors sought after their blessings and approval.

As the many prodigious words washed through the canals of his mind, he smelt the sacrifice they'd made to appease the many gods of the ground and sky. Over to his side, Rufus had seen a Pict man trussed up against a pole, ripped to pieces, his body bleeding for the gods. The orange hair of the Pict waved in the air but slower than reality should go. He swallowed with difficulty and it felt like he dropped into a pond of water.

"You think of your father and that is good," Drust said into his mind. "Recall the face of your father now, and on your dying day. I see his life and I see his death. He fell to these aliens on our isle. His name . . . Briac, yes, he fell under their swords rather than submit. You were too young to fight them, but able to walk, reason, and remember."

Tears flooded his eyes, but Rufus couldn't speak.

"The aliens from Rome are not our folk, and we are your cousins, like it or not. You know the ways of the wood and hear my words in your very soul. When we cannot fight enough of our own, we will use the magicks of the earth, and call upon her other children to aide us in this our dire hour."

Drust's hands moved to Rufus' cheeks and wiped his tears away. He then threw off the tears like he wiped off snot. Drust deposited them into a tiny burning brazier near the orange haired man. Rufus noted another body there, headless, but not ripped apart more than that. He looked up at Drust, the mighty priest of impossible age and then felt his dry lips on his forehead.

"Your father fights on in you, Rufus Mac Briac. Your oaths and orders from your new masters are nothing to those made to your own blood. Do you understand me?"

Rufus nodded.

The middle fingers of the priest slowly entered into the ears of the boy and Rufus flinched many times.

"You are one with us again, like always. You are one of us, not them. Carry on my message to their General. Tell him my words. Tell him his fate."

Rufus nodded, tears stopping, and a warm feeling flooded his chest. He then noted the boy with Drust, hands behind his back, watching, unafraid.

He blinked many times, trying to will it all away. He found himself back by the southern edge of the woods in the evening light. Rufus wept again, for he'd thought so little of his father as of late until Drust brought the image back. He'd been a puppy tossed in with the wolves, and had started to act like one of them. He'd forgotten much. Drust made him remember.

Rufus recalled what he had to do. He heard the woods nearby them shake and the howls within echo. He got to his knees and remembered his message to the General from Drust. He also recalled his last statement.

"I am your father now."

He nodded to Drust again, even though he was not there. Rufus then looked over and saw Lucius.

"Not alone after all, huh?" he asked Lucius.

Lucius didn't answer.

While Ralta waited for his brother to return with more of the men from the 9th, he watched the trees and their deepening shadows. The cries of the beasts were out there somewhere among the greenery. The screams continued to echo on the wind. The fingers of Ralta's hand grew tighter about the hilt of his real sword. He almost laughed at the idea of rushing into face such monsters with his practice wooden sword. He'd been in enough battles to sense one was coming, to feel the heat of battle just beyond his reach. He could almost smell the blood drifting on the wind, alongside the screams.

Wishing August was with them, Ralta held his ground despite his growing uneasiness. From the sound of the beasts, it would take far more than a single man to stop the things when they tired of the game they played and emerged from the trees.

Without warning, one of the beasts came charging out of the shadows.

Covered in white fur, it stood at least eight feet tall, eyes blazing yellow. Its lips twisted in an animal-like snarl of rage. The men near Ralta cried out, but he stayed firm.

Ralta raised his sword but made no other move until the beast nearly stood on top of him. Only then did he move to meet it. As he took a couple of steps forward, his sword flashed through the air. Its first swing drew blood, slicing a long gash in the beast's arm. It roared as he struck again, ducking under its clumsy counterattack. In a flurry, his blade parted the flesh of the beast's side, twice, digging deep between its ribs on its backswing.

The beastman staggered, raising its hands above its head in bestial anger. Ralta dove forward, thrusting his blade upwards and into the monster's armpit. He felt the metal of his blade quiver and bounce as it struck bone. Ralta let go of the sword's hilt and spun away from the beast. The creature lurched over, pawning at its wounds, its roar becoming a whine of pain.

As the men came forward to assist him, broken from their frozen pose at last, Ralta's hands drew the matching daggers sheathed upon his hips. Ralta gave a roar of his own. Lunging at the wounded monster, his daggers sunk into the sides of its throat. Its yellow eyes bugged in shock as the thing realized it could no longer breathe.

Ralta twisted the blades and small rivers of blood poured over his hands and wrists. With a wicked heave, he jerked the daggers free and let the monster's great bulk fall. With some grace, Ralta leapt away from the falling mass of the beastman, and landed on the ground with the elegance of a dancer. He took a small bow and the men released nervous laughter.

Ralta's gaze flew towards the trees but no more of the beasts had emerged yet. The cries of the monsters were louder now, hidden deep in the darkness.

The one he had just slain must have been a test, he figured, but to what purpose? Only a fool would believe the monsters weren't on the verge of attacking.

"Ralta," he heard Quintus call to him as he retrieved his sword.

He spun in the direction the 9th current encampment. Quintus had indeed returned and brought well over one hundred fellow soldiers with him. That wasn't all he had brought along, though. While the bulk of the men with Quintus rushed forward, forming a wall of shields facing the forest, the other few dozen heaved several ballistas and even two onagars into place.

"Artillery, very sexy," Ralta said. "I count myself aroused at the sight of the implements."

Quintus read the look on his brother's face because he said, "Better to be prepared than not."

"I do so adore the giant working of the heavier artillery, but we will have to make do, correct?"

Suddenly the men in the wall of shields began shouting and pointing at something that charged out of the trees.

Ralta focused on where they pointed and loosed a string of curses. "What good was artillery if they had no time to set it up?" He sprinted to peer through the linked shields of the soldiers who had formed up and blinked in disbelief at what he saw. "By the ass of Apollo."

Rufus emerged from the greenery slowly. He walked calmly towards the shield wall, carrying something in his hands. Behind him, the forest shuddered and the beasts growled, yet, there he was, walking out unscathed.

"In the evening, the eyes of God never close," the boy bellowed in a voice louder than Ralta would have thought possible.

The brothers exchanged a concerned look.

Rufus walked closer, and many in the shield wall murmured as to what he carried. A few named who he carried.

Ralta grimaced. "Now, boy," he said quietly, knowing the child couldn't hear him and would not respond in a favored way. "Where on earth did you come by that thing?"

The boy tossed the thing he carried up in the air, caught it and then playfully spun it about. As he walked, he kept throwing it into the air and dropped it, once. The object hit the ground, flinging red wetness into the grass, as it bounced along.

"By the very gods themselves," Ralta heard Quintus whisper as he took his place at his side. "That's Lucius' head!"

More men from the 9th, a detachment of archers led by the twins, had moved up. Ralta yelled for them to hold their fire as he left the ranks of the shield wall and approached Rufus.

"Boy," he greeted Rufus, tussling his hair, "The choice you have made here will break August's heart."

Rufus spat out with great tenor in his small self, "August is my master. You think I did such a thing as this? I am bringing him to the General for review."

Ralta eyed Rufus close, reading his eyes.

Quintus joined his brother with the slave. "What happened to you?"

Ralta murmured, "I've never seen this boy before."

After a chuckle, Quintus glared at his brother. "What are you saying? It's August's Celtic slave, you fool."

Head shaking slowly, Ralta observed, "You miss

my meaning, brother. Look into his eyes, Quintus. There's something wrong."

Quintus agreed. "There's something missing there, like he's vacant."

Ralta's usually jovial face screwed up in anger. "No, you are incorrect. Something is there that wasn't present before."

Rufus looked at the thickened blood on his hands and smeared it on his face like he applied woad markings.

A few of the men drew back at this act, but the brothers stayed firm. Rufus looked up at Ralta and asked, "Are you going to take me to that prick that leads all of you or not? My life is running out and I don't have much of it left."

"Sure boy." Eyebrow raised, Ralta smiled as Rufus went over and picked up Lucius' head by the hair. "Sure."

Ralta turned to Quintus and the others. "Hold here, hear me? Let nothing pass and get the pieces ready to fire. They will have plenty of targets here in no time. Call up more to reinforce the line. I'll return when I can."

Quintus looked back at the forest. "Why do they wait?"

"I aim to find out, but a bludgeon will not get it free from this one, not this time."

Leading Rufus along behind him, Ralta headed for Malitus' command tent.

The two of them found the General passed out in its corner, empty decanters of wine scattered about him.

In a fit of anger, Ralta stabbed his blade into the

ground, snatched up a wash bowl of stagnate water and drenched Malitus' face in it.

Malitus came awake with a start, jumping to his feet, his sword drawn sloppily. "Keep back, all of you now!" Malitus wailed at the two of them, before his gaze focused. "Ralta? Can that be you again at this time?" The General gasped, suddenly ashamed of his foolish ravings. "What is the meaning of this?"

"This boy has returned from the woods beyond Rutland with a message for you," Ralta said in disgust. His drunkenness was shameful, but he held his tongue tight.

Malitus shook his head as if to clear it further. "Speak then, boy. You have met with the beasts? Surely you cannot speak to them."

Ralta's eyes rolled heavenward.

Even Rufus grimaced at such words.

Malitus held his head once with both hands as if to adjust his mind. "Picts? I don't understand you at all this minute. Tell me of the message you bring then." He then raised his eyes and saw what the boy carried. "Lucius?"

Rufus dropped the head by the foot of Malitus bunk. "I've been with father Drust, master of the wood for all time."

"Durst?" Malitus wiped his face with a small towel, his mind snapping into focus a little. "Have you now, on this day?"

"Master Drust says that you and your kind do not belong here in these lands," Rufus said far too calmly for one who stood in the presence of such men as Ralta and the General.

"Oh, has he now?" Malitus sneered and looked at

Ralta. "See how these savages are? Pick them up, clean them off, teach them to wipe their asses, and five minutes with a druid in the forest and they are a servant to him."

Arms folded over his chest, Ralta said nothing.

Malitus stared at his fellow Roman for a long time before he goaded him, "Funny, aye? Lighten up, Ralta."

Ralta remained focused on the boy, no humor in his manner. "Hilarious, sir."

With some anger that Ralta didn't join him in his hilarity, Malitus faced Rufus again. "So tell me slave, is master Drust a real person?"

"Very much so."

"Is he a druid?"

Rufus blinked. "Those terms are your words, not ours."

After he stopped laughing, Malitus smiled. "Ours? Ours?" His smile faded and he pointed at Rufus' chest. "*You* are ours, understand?"

The boy remained silent.

"You think yourself different or special? I can kill you now, strangle your life out and go find another slave boy for August," Malitus said. "This master of the woods, Drust, he wants us to leave?"

"No," Rufus responded blankly. "He wants you to die."

Chapter VII

Porcius charged into the forest, still in pursuit of Tavia. The white furred thing wouldn't be tough to track, he wagered. The beast bounced off this tree and that, breathing branches and swiping things aside. Porcius kept at them, quickly following the path laid in its wake.

His mind spun at how he'd kill the thing, but Porcius felt confident he could as he dodged the wiry trees about him. In his mind Porcius traced out a plan on how he'd do it, too. His plans seldom played out perfectly in real battle, and this was against a monster. Of course, Porcius reasoned, he could just run like hell and let the demons take that girl. Still, he had not once shrunk from a fight, as a kid, as an adult, as a slave or a soldier.

But it breathed, it bled, he'd cut its fool ear off. That gave him confidence. He knew they could perish, and he hungered to take its life.

Of course, that thing his teacher called cowardice lurked in the rear of his head, telling him to just go on, run away and leave this woman to die. He didn't especially seek to kill the Greyman out of any chivalrous attitude, but his own ego burned . . . one that told him this thing had to die and he was better than it. He'd fought so many men in his life, dying to such a great beast would be a respectable death.

That said, whatever boiled inside of him as a Spartan wanted to see it gone, or worse.

As the Greyman loped through the woods, the thing reached up to touch his head where Porcius had wounded him. The beastman turned and glanced back, seeing that Porcius pursued it. Greyman twisted back and continued its course through the woods.

That's right, Porcius thought, *I'm coming for you, you damned son of a devil.*

Porcius' ankles hurt as he ran through the woods, but his body surged with primal fire. The battle lust settled in and he grew hungry to draw blood once more.

As they reached the clearance of trees near the huts, Porcius closed in on the monster. He plotted how he'd stab at its calves and try to shatter its knee with the newfound shield.

The beast suddenly turned sideways, pivoted out of Porcius' way and reached down. With an almighty swiped of its hand, it slapped at Porcius' head as he went passed. If the creature had any tangible grace, that swipe would've taken Porcius head off. In this case, the fingers of the Greyman barely tagged his helm, but it was enough to send him flying face first into the wild grasses.

Sure his doom loomed just behind him, Porcius flipped to his left and came up in a defensive crouch.

The Greyman dropped both fists into the earth right where the soldier had just been. Still on one knee, Porcius' gaze met those yellow orbs in the Greyman's skull. The look didn't last long, but in that instant he felt hot fear grow. Instead of fleeing, however, he jabbed his gladius into the Greyman's left shoulder, twisted, causing the beast to reel, start to roar and pull back. As he did so, Porcius drove his weight in, wishing the shot landed in its torso. The gladius struck bone and slipped off, veering into a fleshy area. Porcius came near to crashing into the beast with his body. The round shield up, he aimed the edge at the creature's face. He did impact on the Greyman, but the rising monster threw him back before any damage was inflicted.

Porcius lay back, wishing he could just let it all go for just a moment, and then he rose again. He saw the beastman stand up in full, left arm shuddering as blood seeped onto its gray fur. Greyman touched his own face with his right hand, long fingers tenderly probing the spot where Porcius nailed him with the shield. More blood appeared and started to bathe the beastman's face, running from the diagonal angle cut across Greyman's nose.

Porcius grinned as he brandished his weapons.

"Come on then," Porcius hissed.

Suddenly, the beast threw both arms at him faster than he thought feasible. Porcius waved the blows off, but he felt the full might of the Greyman's strength as a wrist slammed awkwardly into his shield. In his mind's eyes, Porcius felt driven in the ground like a tent spike, but he was just knocked to his backside, legs collapsing under the capacity of the monster.

Looking up at the Greyman, Porcius knew he'd erred trying to battle it out into the open as an equal.

What he thought a fatal mistake changed when Tavia whistled loud.

The Greyman turned to see her and paused.

Porcius flipped over and scurried away from his attention. The beastman's awareness refocused on him fast and he pursued Porcius, howling, striking out again, this time clipping his right arm. The shot felt like a round house punch from a normal man, but he figured the thing just grazed him with a stroppy chop. The shot was enough to make Porcius drop the bloody gladius. He couldn't lament it then and kept running.

Porcius dodged the creature and headed for the small hut, praying for the materials in there. He did not see Tavia as he sprinted.

But he hadn't taken into account the long strides of Greyman, and he almost stopped breathing when the creature leapt and tackled him. To his advantage, the beastman had no inkling of tactics and they both tumbled into the small implement hut by the cabin. The entire cone shaped structure collapsed on top of them, while they rolled in the debris.

Porcius kicked and flailed with all of his members.

The creature growled loud in frustration, angry that he couldn't get a good grip of death on Porcius. His own bleeding body proved too slick to get a firm grip land when he tried to embrace the human.

With a shout of gladness Porcius seized the dagger in his belt and stabbed blindly at Greyman. The tip of the blade scraping against fur, but the right hand of the big thing took hold of Porcius' wrist, pinning his dagger back to the piles of poles and sod that made up the walls of the hut. Missing no time, Porcius swiped with the shield again, striking Greyman in the side of the head. When the creature's only good ear became mashed in bad, the Greyman leapt to his feet and cried out. It straddled the scene as it cradled its aching head, but had presence of mind to stomp on the round shield, pinning it to the ground.

Porcius let the shield go and groped in the debris, praying to any god that would hear him for a weapon. Deliverance came in the shape of a small sickle and he leapt up, left hand balanced on Greyman's right knee and chopped madly at the inner thigh of the monster. Yes, he went for the beastman's groin but missed. Instead, he struck the inner right thigh and cut a foot-long piece of hide loose. Unfortunately, he did not break into the deep flesh proper.

Abandoning his hold on his ear, Greyman reached down and grabbed Porcius by the helmet.

Porcius felt his sandals rise off the ground, felt pressure on his head, and immediately ripped his chinstrap loose. He fell to the mound of the hut's remains, while the creature raised the helmet to eye level, like he'd plucked the Roman's head loose.

Kicking at the poles, Porcius reached into the debris and seized the big full sickle. Hands became fists on the handles, and he stepped back as the helmet dropped down. The Greyman roared.

The impossible speed Porcius hadn't counted on earlier wouldn't fool him twice.

Greyman rushed at him, defending itself with hands low to strike. Porcius spun about as the fast explosion of movements, and used the force of the Greyman against itself. He quickly sliced with the huge sickle, low, clipping the lower portion of the beastman's ankle. After only a step, Greyman became confused that he couldn't run properly. His right leg wobbled, and not from the blood of his inner thigh wound. Something was wrong down by the ankle, something important to let a person stabilize.

Porcius understood that tendon and thanked Celt or Pict craftsmanship that the sickle sliced right through Greyman's flesh. When the monster tried to rise up and run, Greyman stumbled. He did move forward after him, but failed to accurately strike his opponent.

With the elegance of a bad comedian, Porcius twisted about and struck higher up, trying to sever the beast's hamstring. He failed, gouging a few bloody rips in the fur on either thigh until Greyman slapped his hands together on the blade of the scythe. Porcius wasn't about to fight him for it and ran back towards the hut's remains.

He never made it.

Greyman leapt forward, well enough to half tackle Porcius.

Wrestling briefly in the remnants of the hut again, Porcius kicked and punched, rolling up and on top of the Greyman.

Blinking fast, stunned that his shoulders touched the earth for a moment, Porcius fought on. Greyman lost no real momentum in his rage. While the injured left arm lolled back to the earth, Porcius seized the creature's other limb and held on, desperate to stop his doom.

If Tavia hadn't dumped over the rain barrel at that very moment and washed the beastman's face with several gallons of water, Porcius would've died there, tore limb from torso.

Released, doused in water himself, Porcius scrambled away and headed to the slaughter lodge. He looked back to see Greyman climb up and swing at Tavia, who ran away from the barrel as it shattered into a hundred shards. The bleeding creature focused on her, just on his knees, angry.

Porcius shouted out, "Hey, I'm over here, ass-head."

He entered the round lodge and closed the door; Porcius grabbed one of the benches used to quarter deer, and pulled it in front of the door. Porcius climbed atop the bench just as the creature grabbed the door and tore it off its hinges. Porcius leapt, grabbing the ropes hanging from the funnel opening in the ceiling and started to scale his way up.

Greyman charged in and stumbled over the bench as Porcius had planned. Greyman could hardly walk, but tried to adapt to his new condition as best he could.

Up on the ropes, Porcius only cursed himself for his excessive weight that slowed his climb down. Still, hand over hand, legs to the ropes, Porcius climbed like a good slave being taught to be a murderer in the arena.

Greyman made a punch at him, but cried out in pain.

Porcius reached the rope's pulley at the top, and laughed. He had initially thought he wouldn't fit through the hole, but the hole was just big enough for him to squeeze through. Before he could make his daring escape, however, he heard Tavia's voice below. He looked down to find her looking up at Greyman, talking in a tongue he couldn't fathom.

The creature tilted its head, gaping down at her.

That's when Porcius hatched his plan.

Porcius armed up a goodly amount of

under his arm and jumped down, landing on Greyman's shoulders. In a moment he'd looped the access rope around the creature's neck.

Tavia pulled his gladius from behind her and drove the blade through Greyman's left foot, piercing it clean through and pinning the monster to the floor.

Greyman howled and threw his arms out and the girl disappeared outside.

Porcius jumped off the creature's back and started working on the ropes, tightening the slack. After brief work, the rope snapped taut and the Greyman was trapped, his body stretched by the weight of the Roman hanging off the pulley, throttling him.

All of Porcius' prayers couldn't get the Greyman's neck to break under his weight. But rather he hung, face to face with the strangling beastman, wishing he could spell its doom. The Greyman's eyes flared and it cried out with the little air left in its lungs.

Porcius looked down to see the Pict girl stabbing up with his gladius, slicing open the lower abdomen of the stunned Greyman. A deep roar came out, but not from the beast. Tavia gave a cry Porcius was certain the Spartans would get randy over. She twisted the blade and cut deep fast, and like a gutted fish, the Greyman's intestines unloaded. Unfortunately for the girl, they spewed all over her, covering the redheaded girl and flopping her to the floor of the slaughter lodge.

Not wanting to let go of the line, Porcius swung to avoid the final clumsy death strikes of Greyman. Finally he let go, and searched for his gladius in the pile of muck that spewed out of the beastman. At last, he gripped the pommel of his gladius just as Greyman fell to his knees on the floor of the lodge. Dead.

Porcius, exhausted after the battle, took a minute to regain his breath before he headed out of the slaughter lodge. He found Tavia standing outside, only it didn't entirely seem like her.

As the guts and muck fell from her person, Tavia took on a different form, or rather her skin no longer had that chalky tinge to it, but sported a more fleshy hue. Her tattoos seemed more vivid and raw, not as refined. Her hair, so wet and matted by the innards of the beastman, no longer held the bright red color either, rather more of an obsidian purple on a blood red canvas.

"Tavia?" Porcius wondered, knowing something was wrong, knowing his battle may not yet be over.

"Tavia is no more, Greek, or Spartan," her voice didn't come from her full lips but from inside Porcius head. "I thank you for helping me along into this reality. My own folks did the proper sacrifices, allowing me to inhabit the body of little Tavia. Bow before the Queen of all Pictdom! For Tancorix walks the Earth again."

He swallowed with difficulty. His mind raced, not comprehending any of it. This was a woman, arrogant in her stance, dangerous in her way, naked as the day she was born. There she stood, Tavia no more. She was older and infinitely wiser in the eyes. Queen Tancorix as she called herself, emerged from guts like a butterfly a cocoon.

"Queen Tancorix? All right. Yeah, I've heard of you in songs."

"That is a wonder, really, only me?"

Unsure who else she wondered after in ballads, He half smiled. "What do you want from me?" Porcius asked with simple words, feeling quite silly as he did so.

"You?" Her left eyebrow arched. Her hips shifted and his blood surged as Tancorix replied, "I wish your Legion would destroy these squalid animals."

He squinted, surprised at just how different her features were from the girl, but her eyes remained mostly the same. "Aren't the druids your folk? I thought your kind controlled these things?" Porcius waved his left hand back at the gutted Greyman.

Her eyebrows, so fine and thin he thought them penned in place, both raised slightly and his blood boiled more.

"There are countless Picts that will adore their Queen who've returned from the dead. Why would I need monsters?"

Teeth grinding, Porcius soon questioned, "What are these men around with this Drust and the beasts then?"

"Did Sparta always agree with Greece?"

Slowly, Porcius shook his head, understanding she read his thoughts. "So we are marching into a civil war?"

Tancorix whipped her long locks back and laughed. "You entertain me, Spartan. I hope you endure this combat. I'd adore you at my feet forever."

His hands curling to fists, Porcius muttered, "I'm no slave, not anymore."

Her manner calmed and her eyes narrowed at him. "Search your mind, Spartan. You know that is not accurate at all. See? Look around in those dusty halls of your mind, the same place where you hide lyrics of songs about me. You've swapped your rusty chains for metal of a different manner. You serve the slave masters that put a road through your sacred homeland and for what? Kisses to all the pretty politicians."

Feet shifting, Porcius smirked. "Well, ya got me there, sister, or Queen, if that's what ya really are now that yer here."

She took a few steps closer to him. The woods rattled with sound. Neither made much motion to worry on that.

"Do I look like a Queen? What does your heart tell you?"

"You move like a cat, stalking her easy prey, not a Queen of the palace."

Tancorix raised her arms as if to embrace the world. "I'm in my palace, Spartan."

He nodded once, all the tales talked about the Queen of the savage Prytens . . . Picts . . . and how she reveled in the limitless forests that used to cover this land. "I believe you, there."

Tancorix stepped closer to him and his ire rose, but Porcius didn't back up. She reached up and touched his cheek, now a shadowy beard. "I favor you, Pork. I really do. If you were much taller, you'd actually remind me of a warrior I once favored."

"Yeah?"

She licked her bottom lip with a long tongue. "Come along with me, Spartan."

He looked past her toward Rutland. "Where to? I can't do any such thing. My duty is to my men, my group, my Legion."

"They are dead already. Come with me."

Porcius then licked his lips. Damn, but he needed a drink. About a gallon's worth. "Where will you take me?"

"To the north, to be among the army of Pictdom that gathers beyond night. To the north even farther lies the end of the world."

"Yeah?"

"Many more miles away is the northern sea that lies between here and the land of Thule, the great realm of ice and snow, home of my lover-man in ages past, Thule, the land that goes on, forever."

He heard the crash of branches and the howls of beastmen.

Porcius stared into her eyes for a long time.

August trudged through the tunnel, his mind on fire with all he'd seen down below. He couldn't let himself get caught up in the terror that such things implied, though. August simply wanted to taste the open air again.

He wanted to run up the narrow tunnel, but had to settle for his muted way of treading up the grade. When warmer air hit him, August's elation washed over him. The excitement wouldn't last, though, so he fought his emotions down. Seeing the smaller version of the beastmen only taught him nowhere was safe.

The green glowing veins on the walls started to recede and the tunnel darkened. His desperate eyes registered a dull light up ahead, one that didn't move. It was the end of the line. Finally!

More glee filled his long body as August arrived at the end of the passage and saw Flavius sitting with his back near the opening, looking away from him. Unable to resist what would happen next, August reached out and grabbed his left shoulder.

Flavius screamed like a surprised woman and rolled away, fumbling for his dagger and sword.

Laughter filled the lower parts of the Fogou as August tumbled out of the tunnel and smiled at Flavius, who in turn cursed him, his family and his mother for giving birth to such a delinquent.

Once he calmed down some, Flavius smiled too. "I am glad to see you, sir."

"Glad to be here," August mumbled roughly and stood up, unable to stretch in full due to the lower ceilings of the Fogou. "I've seen a few things I wasn't counting on down there in the dark. Sorry you missed it."

Flavius looked him over. "You've been in a scrape?"

August relayed the delay of his journey. "There's something more down there, off to the east. I could feel a rush of wind, air, and the scent of those things."

"The tales of creatures from underground are always of tiny monsters that are like moles or worms."

August headed to the door of the Fogou. "Yes, well, not this time. Maybe they got their stories wrong, huh?"

"Maybe."

The evening upon them, August stretched and they both turned toward the crashing in the forest nearby. He focused on Flavius, who couldn't seem to find anything to do with his hands but wring them together.

"What's your problem?"

Flavius shook his head. "I can't stop shaking."

August nodded and looked to the forest. "You're afraid."

"No . . . "

"Yes, you are. Not a sin to be afraid."

Flavius shook his head. "Speak to me of sin?"

"Wasn't planning on it."

"You jest with me to use such a word. Our people have made a business of ignoring what the primitive minds call sin or vice."

"Don't get mouthy. It doesn't make you feel warm all over to be godless and sinful at the hour of your death?"

Flavius frowned. "Your words don't help."

"They are meant to instruct, but I don't think we have much time to ponder sin and life any longer, soldier."

Swords drawn, the soldiers headed out toward the gap between Rutland and the forest. In the grim moonlight they could perceive a wall of Legionnaires with their shields interlocked, a hundred or more, forming a wall.

August stated, "Looks like the celebration started without us."

"Celebration? You're mad."

"Come along, you want to meet God with a frown?"

"There are no gods or goddesses, only the weakness of men. I really don't think there are such things above or below."

As the beastmen became visible, but oblivious to them, August said to him, "The longer I live, the more I believe in God and His great sense of humor."

Quintus found himself in command of the 9th that stood at the edge of the village. The artillery and men were ready, stoically staring, courage screwed in tight. The Sagittarii moved up behind the kneeling centurions, their bows at the ready. The cone-like helmets and chainmail armor gave their unit a distinct look in the night.

Quintus thought the forest dimmed in density, like the very trees themselves mated with the beastmen, making it tougher to discern where wood stopped and hairy flesh began. When the creatures at last brought their attack forward on the Romans, the rush came without a grand warning or sign, not even a howl. The things came out fast, bounding from the trees at the Roman lines.

No fear in his eyes or voice, Quintus ordered, "Fire!"

The onagars let loose their flaming loads first. The rocks, drenched in burning pitch, released. Quite a few of these flaming loads crashed into the trees, but they illuminated the night all the same. A few of the onagar shots struck home. The fire spread rapidly as they hit running beasts, fire splashing all about.

The ballistas went off next. Their shafts flew low and just cleared the wall of kneeling Roman soldiers. Fired from the huge crossbow-like devices on wheels, the giant shafts caused confusion, knocking a few beasts aside. Few, however, were nailed clean through. A couple up front were, and that sight of an impaled beast, giant shaft through its waist, staggering, unsure what to do next, made the soldiers give a grunting cheer.

More flaming rocks from the onagars caused the creatures' uneven ranks of to stagger. They broke bones and knocked the monsters from their feet, setting fur ablaze and filling the air with infernal howls.

The night sky filled with arrows at Quintus' command. Once one line had fired, they took a knee, reloaded and let a second line arise and fire, repeating the action.

Iron headed arrows pierced hairy hides, digging into the terse flesh beneath. One creature lumbered about, turning back for the trees, nearly a half dozen arrow shafts protruding from its body. Other lay dead, stuck full of arrows, their blood pooling around them.

Despite the impressive display of firepower, the beasts were not deterred in their advance. No more than several dozen of the things were wounded or outright killed in the great release of missiles. The rest surged onward with renewed determination.

They crashed into the Roman shield wall with such force some of the men were flung from their positions and sent flying backwards, only to land on their rears sporting broken shields, arms, and in some cases even legs. A couple who held the line cried out, stunned that their formation broke, tempted to run, and thus ruin it all.

"Hold!" Quintus ordered, his voice so loud it broke, drawing his gladius. "We must hold them here!"

The Romans surged forward in a counterstrike, pushing with their shields, hacking away at the beasts. They were a well-trained force of red death, through the shifting open areas of the wall. One centurion boldly drove his blade into one of the beasts' skulls as it towered over the top of the shield wall. It died instantly, but during its death throes it tossed several men aside.

Another beastman picked up speed as it rammed into the wall of shields. The monster tore through the wall as though it consisted of parchment, shoving men from its path violently. One of the thing's massive hands closed around the helmet of a soldier. Metal folded inward, and the man's head popped like a cracking egg. Two soldiers slashed madly at the beast as it let the man's corpse drop the ground. It backhanded one of them with a blow that separated the man's head from his shoulders. His body, a volcano of blood erupting from his headless neck, slid into to block and another Roman was impaled upon his blade.

Quintus hadn't been able to get a good count of the beasts in the chaos, but he guessed they numbered in the hundreds.

A glance in the direction of the village told him more of the 9th would soon arrive to stand against the monsters. Dozens of men of the cavalry rode in fast, followed by divisions of spearmen. All he had to do was hold until they arrived, and they would turn the tide of the battle.

"Hold them!" Quintus emptied his lungs of breath once again as a beast came directly at him. He sidestepped the thing's wild lunge and struck out with his blade, hacking deep into the bones of its spine where its head met its body. The creature gargled as it slammed into the dirt. It did not get up. Quintus stepped to it, stabbing the thing again to make sure it would be staying down.

As the shield wall crumbled completely, the Sagittarii retreated, scattered and reformed like ants disturbed from their hill. The beasts rushed on towards the village, through the surviving centurions, and met the second wave of soldiers from the 9th.

Quintus didn't get the chance to see what

happened with that clash. His own position had been overrun and he was too busy fighting for his life to worry about the other regiments. The beasts were all around him. The cavalry's horses bleat in the throes of death. Quintus' legs pumped as he pushed his body to its limits. Breaking free of the mass of beasts and reaching the newly forming second line of the 9th was his only chance.

A beast appeared in his path, swiveling out like a door closing in front of him. Quintus slashed his blade along the backside of the thing's legs. Howling, the beast toppled forward. He leapt onto the thing's back and scampered over it to hit the ground beyond, still running. Quintus felt more than saw the thing's desperate grab at him. Its thick fingers brushed the skin of his ankle but failed to lock onto it.

Then, at last, he was free of the beasts. The startled look on the soldiers reminded him just how much of a miracle his getaway was. But he hadn't really escaped anything. He dove through the reformed shield wall of retreating men as it parted for him, spinning about to add his strength to it as the beasts in his wake plowed into the obstacle. Quintus had no shield by then, only his sword, to which he clung until his muscles strained.

The screams of dying men rang out all along the length of the shield wall but it held enough.

Again, Quintus watched as the men of the 9th heaved back against the encroaching beasts and struck with their swords. Many beasts cried out their last bellows but the number of human screams far outweighed them.

He half laughed as Quintus heard singing. He knew it was the crazy bastards of the spearmen class, a unit of a hundred thuggish men bred on the northern edge of the African continent, all blood brothers in their own peculiar creed, all singing in a language no one knew but them. They lowered their spears and marched into the beastmen, singing tunes that may have been about their mothers for all Quintus knew.

Quintus learned how the beastmen fought. The monsters relied upon their strength and no shield wall would hold them forever in a great mass. The shots from the spearmen outside, though, made the glut of beastmen bend in a different direction. Mere humans couldn't stand in the face of such creatures and hope to press them back, no matter how vulgar their tunes. But they certainly made a dent, killing and dropping many more than the tactics his men had deployed. No, the answer to their defeat lay elsewhere, and Quintus believed he had stumbled upon it.

He turned his back fast on the wavering line and raced away from it towards yet another group of soldiers rushing from the village to join the battle.

"Stop!" Quintus shouted at them. "Archers, dartmen and slingers, forward on my words. Form a line there."

The order was an odd one, given that the beastmen were making short work of the shield wall not far from where they'd been ordered to form up. Still, the men complied. They eyed the spearmen's work, making the creatures deflect off the shield wall and move to another point where they didn't plan on going.

"Bows and darts at the ready," Quintus commanded in a booming voice. "When they break through, I want you to greet them properly." His smile was like a devil's. This new line contained almost all of the leftover Sagittarii archers and throwers, who'd retreated and reformed in the back. The twins, Crispinus and Decimus still fought, bows at the ready. Quintus gushed in glee. It was as if the gods had sent to him what he needed to stop the beastmen in their tracks.

"We cannot wait until our brothers are passed us," Quintus continued shouting. "As soon as that shield wall falters and the beasts pour through, we're going to give them all we have. Any man who does not throw or loose as many arrows as he can will answer to me!"

The men Quintus had left behind in the shield wall retreated and parted as the beasts tore through them. The singing spearmen group had pushed them onward, not breaking themselves outright, but inadvertently pushing the crazed beasts over the new shield wall as a means of escape. If this had been fought in daylight, Quintus mused as more horses died and the cavalry retreated, that shield wall and the spearmen would've fought together better. Quintus waited until the beasts were well in range and allowing as many of the men who survived to remove themselves from the field of fire. As he stared into the sea of yellow eyes and snarling faces sprinting towards his position, he knew he could wait no longer.

"Fire!" Quintus screamed.

As one, every archer on the line loosed their bowstrings. A black mass of arrows flew forward into the beastmen as the javelin and dart throwers added to the storm of flying death. The beastmen were struck with a barrage so thick it sent them reeling.

The entire frontline of beasts became pin cushions, half a dozen to a dozen arrows protruding from the flesh of each and every one. They stumbled and fell only to be stomped by the beasts behind them. The ones struck by the throwers' heavy darts and javelins fared even worse. Some of those died outright by lucky or well-aimed throws. One beast took a dart to the soft flesh between its chin and chest, gargling and spinning about, a river of red staining its thick ivory body. It was far from alone in this act. Another took a dart to one of its eyes and fell dead instantly. Yet another received two javelins that sunk through its ribs, one of them surely piercing the thing's lungs.

The beastmen's momentum was finally brought to a halt, but the fight wasn't finished. The archers continued firing as the throwers, their weapons already cast, stepped back behind their ranks. Volley after volley of arrows hammered the beasts in such force the remaining monsters had no choice but to flee.

The battle was over.

A terrible sigh resounded across the battlefield; victory went to the Romans.

"Reload and stand ready," Quintus bellowed, studying the carnage.

The victory had come at a high cost indeed.

The mangled and broken Roman dead outnumbered the corpses of the beastmen by a margin of three to one.

Chapter VIII

Rufus sat on General Malitus' folding chair, inside the Roman's tent. The commander didn't need it at the moment. His frenzy of movement ran, too busy outside trying to direct which of his men of the veteran caste died next. The boy thought of the tent around him, made of a canvas fabric foreign to Britannia, or at least it was before these red crested pricks showed up. They changed most things with their arrival. Even the trails from town to town had rougher, flatter surfaces . . . better to wheel their cargoes of death with. This was called progress and civilization to them. In all of their technical brilliance, they marveled at the stone henges and couldn't fathom how such primitives transported the slabs without good roads. Such was their folly.

He pondered the simple tents of his people, ones they used on hunting trips or camped in after quickly fought battles. They were of the earth, hides mostly, common and warm, sewn to perfection by nimble fingers. These tents folded and could be reassembled like drapes or sheets, also materials once odd in his homeland.

All in the name of progress, all in the name of civilization, all in the name of Rome.

Rufus recalled how some sacred places no longer existed, but the Roman fools couldn't topple the great henges. Sometimes, the Romans built a fort around such a place, but always with a mind for war or control. They erected walls and declared peace. Rufus looked at the canvas of the tent, and smiled. He hated walls. He hated fences. All a fence did was keep animals inside. Rufus bristled at that idea, and understood he was no animal.

Eyes closed, he could recal Drust's voice clearly. The tone and the image Drust made Rufus feel like as a wee lad, back to a time when his grandfather still lived. A wise man, his grandsire never grew as old as Drust or others of the woods. The Romans saw to that. If one didn't conform, they died. There was no way to polish that turd of civilization. Intellectual advancement and a grand society meant death, Rufus understood. The woods, barbarism and no walls meant real freedom . . . and life.

He wished himself a grown man, a big one like the horseman August, a true barbarian in fancy clean Roman clothes. August could kill anyone and Rufus respected that. He wished he moved like that mean assed Porcius, too. If he had their hands, he could slay them all. Rufus smelt the General in this tent, his sweat, his ass, all of him. He wanted to kill the commander. He'd die himself to kill Malitus. But he was just a lad, Rufus lamented. What could he do?

Eyes closed again, he recalled the voice of Drust. Rufus nodded. It came to him clearly. He could do much. His size meant nothing. It was all about heart and spirit.

Rufus looked over at Lucius' head. It lay on its side,

peering toward the flap of the tent and the chaos outside. The boy's smile widened, though his teeth weren't perfect. He stood, walked over to the head, and knelt. Rufus tried to right it, to stand it up on its base but Lucius refused, falling to the side again.

"Fools," Rufus said to the absent Romans. "You've missed the point as always." He walked over to the General's counter and saw a cup away from the rest of his personal articles. He raised it, sniffed, and his face soured at the scent of stale wine. Rufus reached out and picked up the decanter nearby and shook it about. He opened the container and took a careful swig of the fresher wine. He nodded, and drank some more. Rufus turned, walked over to the head, and poured the rest of the wine over Lucius' face.

"Silly Romans, they are so damned blind. You can't see what I did for you all? I brought you back his soul," he said quietly, almost jumping at the crashing and shouts outside. "And you leave it like an afterthought."

Rufus stepped back several paces and ran forward before kicking the side of Lucius head. The object flipped over, but didn't roll. He then repeated the action on the head, the very soul of a man, as the Celts believed. Over and over again.

Porcius stood between two trees, a yard into the woods located not far from Rutland. He could hear the crazed sounds of battle, of beasts and men dying. All of his training and passions for glory screamed at him to rush headlong into the fray and start bloodletting. And yet, there he stood, naked, hands out on the trees, resting on their bark, listening.

His eyes closed, he could feel his own heartbeat, the texture of the tree bark like a wooden snake . . . and smell Tancorix nearby. Somehow, disobeying his orders, disregarding his men and doing acts usually saved for matrimony seemed correct at the moment.

"What do you know of me?" Tancorix had asked him earlier when they receded back into the darkness of the woods.

He lied. Men usually did to naked women. "I've heard the name Tancorix on the lips of drunken balladeers across the lands, even in Greece. The name stuck in my head at the time, but so many more did as well." In actuality, he recalled hearing of her in a few drunken songs, but not in such an abundance that'd make one believe the common folk across Europe knew of Tancorix. Still, he lifted her ego and that always distracted a woman from reality.

She'd laughed for a good long time, saying it flattered her that men still remembered her after all this time.

Porcius hid any note that he achieved his desire through obsequious words. He wondered about that, how she could be here, alive, reborn in this time from one so far away. Something crazy in his mind recalled that green egg shaped object, full of blood. Porcius could imagine her popping out of that thing and again, he fought down an overt reaction. He didn't tell her the tales men sang. Porcius was bright enough to share only the valiant battle hymns, and not the other ones jesters and poets reeled off, many with their lips curled back.

"Tell me a tale of how Tancorix cheated death
Sing to me of how she twice took back her breath
Laud me with yarns over how she made men's heart fall,
Teach me how she was imprisoned in the heart of Gorias La Gaul."

Porcius found himself intrigued by her, the words and desires for her land, far more than the ballads that bubbled in his brain. He couldn't recall all of them cleanly, but a few lines returned to him.

"On the slab of stone, in the rite of copulation, Tancorix cried;
Her and her chosen lover, in torrid passion, both at once died.
In the circle of life, death loomed fast on her shade.
Until her ashes soul be fed, bled and reborn in a loving maid."

He told himself since they didn't go to the stone circle and do it on a slab, it would be all right. So what did he have to worry about? Still, Porcius quickly realized, he wasn't there with her in the woods, naked, to be sacrificed for her life. Something or someone else had given theirs to let her live again, and the guts of the beastman had prodded her out further from whatever maiden had been unlucky enough to be chosen as her vessel. She wanted something else from him.

"Perhaps your men are all dead."

Porcius didn't look back to see her as she spoke. "No, I can't accept that one, sister. I can hear the artillery. They won't go down without taking an army of them things with them."

"For a slave, you sound as if you admire them."

"I am one of them . . . " he said, doubting his words as they came out. "Besides, there's a damned good reason when a few thousand Romans can beat ten thousand barbarians back on their asses. It's tactics, training and high smarts. That may be an army of giant beastmen, sister, but my odds are on the Romans. There are always more of them to call up and fit in place."

She chuckled, her voice echoing a bit more than Porcius thought possible in a forest. "You doubt the resolve of Drust."

"Prolly not, sister."

"How many of those things do you think he will call up from the belly of the earth so that his plans are not interfered with?"

Hands off the trees and cupped together, Porcius breathed. "What are his plans? Do you worry on them for the sake of your own folks?"

"Certainly not for the sake of Romans." Her voice grew nearer to him, but he couldn't feel her breath on his bare skin. As close as the voice was, he felt he ought to be able to. "Drust and his apprentice must be stopped in their desire."

"Yeah?"

Her breath washed over his shoulders and down his sweaty spine. "You can do it. I will tell you a secret."

Porcius turned and faced her again. The moonlight cast a loving light on her creamy skin. He didn't much care for the tattoos and paints that appeared on her flesh as if by magick, but he wasn't taking her for a wife any time soon.

Into his ear she whispered things. Her nails dug into his scalp, then his back, until she drew blood. A lot. Again and again, they screamed into the woods. The din of battle covered both of their cries in the coming night.

Morning brought only a clearer view of the night's devastation, as well as the arrival of the final columns of the 9th Legion.

Ralta ordered the columns arriving to reinforce the perimeter around the town. A force of nearly four thousand could easily hold it, he figured. The horrified faces of the new arrivals at the crushed bodies told the tale. Their shock at seeing the dead Greymen made Ralta hope that they could find their testes while they stood guard and rested.

Auxiliary troops, centurions, doctors, and slaves joined together in the gruesome task of lining up the bodies of those who'd been slain. Decurion August stood there, too, directing many to scavenge the bodies of the dead horses for meat.

Ralta smiled. "Good soldier," he said to no one, watching the scribes writing down the identities of troopers in order to inform their families and evenly distribute their pay set aside for their burials. "No time for a farewell meal, party, proper dress clothes and coffin, be it readied for a tomb, dirt or pyre." Ralta stretched and looked to the western edge of town, to an open clearing where the bodies were being assembled within their set boundary. He understood there would be a pyre, but nothing too fancy.

The morning crept on by as the bodies were laid

out in orderly sectors, with their assigned units as best as could be determined. This practice was followed by the scribes as well, recording the soldiers as best they could too when identifiable. The entire company of the Legion assembled soon after and Ralta did the honors of reading the roll of sticks. He held a small lathe stick with each name on it of each soldier of the Legion. Ralta called out loud a roll of all men they couldn't find. Those that didn't answer were dead to them.

An older scribe, a man called Gaius, took Ralta's stand out sticks and sat at a table, comparing them with a list of dead men he could find. As the bodies were divested of weapons and things to be saved for their families, Gaius' brow furrowed at the pages, his hand repeatedly going for his flask.

"What ails you?" Ralta asked the old man with a soft voice. "A temptingly silly question, to be sure."

Gaius rubbed his chin of gray stubble hair. "I'd say good day, Ralta, but we all know better than that. Well, let us see now. I've got them for the most part . . . "

"Most part? Are some missing?"

Gaius looked up at him. "About a dozen."

Ralta nodded. "We'll go through it again."

The scribe shook his head. "Well, I don't know about that. Sir, can I stop this now and share a sight from the darkness?"

Ralta turned back to him, smiling. "Do tell, sir." He said the *sir* as a slight mock, but he'd known the scribe for over a decade. The old one didn't delight in bad tales.

"When the creatures retreated, I know I saw a few of them carrying bodies with them."

"Why on earth would they do that?"

Gaius sat back and rubbed his eyes. "It is in the height of night, not morning, but these creatures are smart and think a bit ahead. Maybe they were hungry."

"Gods . . . " Ralta gasped and shook his head.

Back to his figures, Gaius suggested, "You'd best get a proper move on with that pyre, Ralta."

Though Ralta pondered his meaning, he turned away from the scribe with speed and did just that.

Porcius stepped lightly in the grass, dodging bloody smears, wearing no sandals, and naught else as he walked up to the camp, nodding to the pickets. The guards lowered their lances, and in their exhaustion from the night's battle, had little left in them to jeer the warrior about his appearance, but did give him a mock salute as he passed.

Quintus stepped away from the men a few paces and snapped at him, "Where in all of Hades have you been?"

General Malitus emerged from the officers and raged, "You have missed the fight. We could've used your sword!"

Ralta walked up and smiled at the others and pointed at Porcius. "I doubt he'd have killed his share with only the sword he's carrying."

Porcius walked past Quintus, yawned and nodded to the General, giving him a half salute as he strolled into the open flaps of the tent. He went to the table, picked up an empty decanter of wine and shook it. With a sigh he threw it down and reached for another. He found it full, cleared his throat and uncapped it.

While August and Flavius exchanged looks,

Quintus wheeled about, fists on his hips. "Have you taken leave of you sense? Are you injured?"

"He looks tired," Flavius said to August, but all heard.

Ralta winked at August. "He smells tired, very tired indeed."

Malitus gave them all a frustrated look as Porcius drank from the decanter, wine leaking out to run across his sweaty, rough beard. The General waited a few moments before asking, "You mind sharing what you are about, soldier?"

Container down, Porcius wiped his mouth with his left forearm, and then snapped his hand down, letting the excess wine hit the ground. He looked over and saw the head of Lucius near the door and belched.

August said, "Yes . . . "

Porcius took another draw of wine.

Flavius added, "He's seen better mornings."

Quintus charged up to Porcius, but when he arrived to grab or strike him, he relented. Something made Quintus step back.

There was no challenge, no ire, nothing in Porcius that would mean he readied himself for a blow or to be accosted. He drank more and yawned. "I had a rough night, not as rough as ol' Lucius by the look of him."

August said steadily, "His head came back via Rufus, who has met with Drust, wizard of the druids or whatever they are."

Porcius looked over at the Celtic youth, sitting on the ground on the opposite side of the tent. "Yeah? Drust sent the soul of one of us back, huh?"

Quintus eyes narrowed. "Soul?"

Ralta nodded. "Dear boy, read or listen a bit more

closely, will you? These savages think the soul resides in the head." He looked at Rufus. "Am I right, boy?"

Rufus nodded and looked at the ground, but his eyes kept returning to the Greek.

Porcius went on to say, "The Celt warriors would shrink the heads of their enemies and put them on the bridles of their horses. Keeping the souls of one's enemies was a powerful magick, a great form of domination." Porcius drank again. "In that way, they even best the Romans with such thoughts of supremacy."

Quintus raged. "How so?"

"All we do is take your land and your life. The Celts? They crush your soul on top of it." He drank again and nearly gagged. "That'd hurt more, I'd think."

Malitus drew close to him. "What is it you are on about?"

Porcius didn't answer right off, and stared at the General acutely.

"He was off on patrol, right?" August said with great haste, trying to cover for Porcius absence and save him a scourging. "Down by that slaughter shed and hunter's cabin?"

Porcius nodded. "Yeah. That's how it started off."

Looking him over, up and down, Ralta commented, "Looks as if you have seen a fair share of slaughter and wounds, soldier."

Porcius stated, "I ran into a young lady there, a local, and a big assed gray monster—a Greyman the girl called him."

Quintus looked him over as well. "You fought this thing?"

"Yeah, I did, sir." Again, he drank. "I killed it, but it took a while."

Right eyebrow raised, Malitus asked, "That happened then? Were you brained by this Greyman and slept it off in the woods?"

The container empty, he sat it down on the folding chair, not trying to conceal his manhood and stared into the face of his General. "Sure, why not?"

Malitus' eyes widened and Quintus again almost moved to strike the naked soldier, but Ralta intervened. "Get yourself some clothes on, soldier. We need every able bodied man now."

"Yes, sir."

Ralta added, "And get to the baths. You smell like a brothel."

Porcius yawned and saluted Ralta before walking out of the tent. He stopped, passed wind and looked about at the carnage in the burnt out village. "I hope to crap on your dinner plate, ya need men. By the gods . . . "

Eyes wide as his smile, Ralta noted, "Those scratches look a trifle rude, don't they?"

After the Legion had come up and surrounded Rutland in full, Quintus cursed the body of one of the beasts laid out on the ground. He walked around it, swearing and kicking the corpse.

August sat with Rufus nearby, both munching hard tack and berries. "That's why I'm not that high up in the chain of command," August commented.

Rufus tried not to watch the officer spitting on the corpse of one of the beastmen "Your background?"

"No. I'm not crazy enough."

The boy half smiled.

August asked him, “Are you worried for your life?”

Rufus shrugged. “It’s not much of a life that I have anymore, is it? I live at the leisure of Rome, don’t I?”

After giving him a sideways glance and then setting eyes on Porcius who sat several yards from them, he said, “Still shook up over the encounter in the woods with Durst?”

Rufus watched Porcius pull sandals and leggings from a dead soldier and put them on himself. “I don’t know what you call it.”

“You aren’t the same anymore, not really. You can deceive these idiots here, but I know you better, always have.”

Rufus looked at the ground and bit into the hard tack. “I’ve been out of touch with my people for some time. Seeing Drust reminded me of a time long ago.”

“We had chieftains and priests back in Germania, well, not like Drust, but near enough. I know. I respect them still. They were wrong.”

“Because you choose to believe in a different god?’

August winked at him as he watched Porcius getting clothes and armor from another dead man. “No, I just found the right one.”

“So you say.”

“I’m not going to argue about the gods of these folk, Rufus. People are the problem with this world. The earth is fine. The people are fools. There are bad men amongst all types, so be careful who you trust.”

The child looked into his face. “I can trust you?”

“Why not? I’ve never treated you unfairly, have I?”

“No.”

"Someday, you can have your freedom."

Rufus again looked down. His chin touched the thin chain about his neck, other collared slaves resented and teased him for having the chain. .

August explained, "How can I give you that now? You are better off with me than wandering the woods or being a slave under some tyrant Roman leader back down south."

Rufus didn't answer.

August stood, stretched, and yawned as Ralta and Malitus approached. "I think the order of the day is obvious, though."

Ralta also yawned, but the General looked a little clearer than earlier. "Greetings, August," Ralta smiled. "You need a respite like the rest of us?"

"Thoughts to nap at a time like this?" August said with a smile.

Ralta scoffed and grinned. "On the contrary, General Malitus just had a great nap, and look, it did him the world of good!"

Malitus shot daggers at Ralta, but soon faced Rufus. "Are you still alive?"

August was going to speak, but Ralta interceded. "Sir, don't be angry with the child because he came from the woods and is of the woods. Killing this boy would do us no good. One cannot slay the forest by killing a child."

The General's eyes burned at Rufus. "Perhaps we can chip the bark a bit?"

Ralta sighed and threw up his big arms. "What shall I ever do with you? We need to discuss what happens next."

At these words August stepped forward and

saluted. "I concur, sirs. We need to get out of this dreadful town."

Quintus walked up, sipping from a canteen of water. "At last, I agree with August."

General Malitus walked to the pile of bodies. "And what do I tell my superiors in Rome?"

Ralta said, "That chronicle will be written by who walks out fastest, sir."

"What? That we ventured north and were attacked by monsters, lost hundreds of men, so we are slinking back home, tails between our legs?"

"Surely, sir, you cannot mean to press on forward after such a bloodletting?" Ralta said.

"We are at full strength now. If we'd had the complete compliment of men last night would've been different."

"No Quintus, we are not," August butted in. "As you just said yourself, sir, we lost hundreds of men," August pointed at the mound of bodies. "All of those men are dead and not killed by other men or natives. How *will* you explain any of it?"

Malitus was silent. Quintus, however, was not. "We still have more than enough men to deal with those beasts, August. Don't be a fool now. We know how to fight them now without taking such heavy losses."

"We got lucky," August corrected him. "That's all. If there had been more of those things, who knows whether we could have driven them off or not?"

All conversation stopped as Porcius made a great cry, liberating a few weapons from the dead that hadn't been yet scavenged by the armaments men.

Ralta lowered his voice to say, "Is he slightly mad?

I worry for him. Whatever really happened to him out there?"

August muttered, "He's always been a little off. He's Greek, after all."

They all nodded like that explained it, but Ralta said, "Something wicked happened to him in the forest, I think."

"He hasn't said what exactly," August answered.

Ralta faced Malitus. "And you want us to go on forth into the open country beyond these woods? To what end? To find an explanation for why this has happened?"

Quintus roughly stated, "They are a bunch of beasts and we have come into their abode, thus they attack us. That part is easy to understand."

Malitus nodded and looked at Rufus again. "You, boy, listen to me. This Drust exhibits control over them, the creatures and thus gives a mind to these things. I would slit Drust's throat if I knew where he lay at night."

"Perhaps that is the answer," August offered.

All looked at him.

"If we could kill Drust then the aggression in the beastmen would be gone, no?"

Quintus blinked. "I'm all for killing the damned druids, but I don't know if we can stake everything on that. Besides, how can we even find this man?"

August said, "I'm not sure, but if he controls them, he must fall. I've never heard tell of monsters fighting in mass in such a way. They must have a leader, must have a purpose."

Ralta agreed. "True. We all hear legends of creatures in the night, but none of this sort. We've all thought of wee beasts out in the night when camping in these alien territories."

Quintus snorted, "Wee beasts. I'd kill to fight a wee beast."

Malitus pondered this. "If we believe that this Drust does control these beasts, then the question becomes how?"

Ralta shrugged. "Bugger me if I know. Don't see how any man could."

"Perhaps, he raised them and his wife suckled them at her breast," Quintus laughed then turned serious. "This Drust can't control them any more than we can. They are just dumbass animals walking upright. Nothing more, nothing less. As I said, we have entered their domain and they hunt us for it. Any creature capable of it will go to war to defend its own home. This Drust is using them, not controlling them. He knows their ways and plays us into their hands so they will come at us."

Ralta shook his head. "Druid, wizard, or whatever, it has to be more than that. If it wasn't, they would be attacking Drust and any of his kin that entered their domain as well."

"Magic," Malitus spat the word. "Are we truly going to resort to that to explain what is happening here? We are Romans and soldiers, not simpletons and dopes."

"You have a better explanation?" August ventured. "Magic or not, this Drust does appear as a regulator on the beasts."

"There he goes again . . . " Quintus sighed. "It's all dung I tell you! Kill enough of these things and they will break off and leave us be."

"Can you be so sure of that Quintus?" Malitus

asked. "How many did you see die today? How many are enough to drive them away? By the gods, man, for all we know there are thousands of the things roaming this place."

"If there are thousands then it doesn't matter, does it? We're dead any way you look at it, unless Drust *is* the key," August said.

"Regardless of what the truth is, killing Drust needs to be priority," Ralta told them all.

Everyone nodded in agreement even Quintus.

Ralta made a fist and shook it in the air. "He dies then, for Rome."

August looked out into the woods. "I wonder why Drust made a stand here, not further into Caledonia."

"What are you saying?" Quintus eyed him harshly.

"Why not draw the Legion in further, really stretch us out, and then strike." August's voice sounded full of calm reason. "Why here? Why Rutland? Why now when we were close to reinforcements?"

Ralta joined August and looking into the woods. "Fascinating idea."

"As I said in my report," August said. "There's a huge graveyard of bones under the earth not far from the tiny tunnels. Maybe this land is near a sacred place to them."

Malitus grimaced. "To who? The beasts or the druids?"

"Maybe both?" August sighed.

"If the theory is that Drust is using the beasts," Ralta offered. "That he may be playing them as he has played us, then it makes perfect sense for him to want to lead us deeper into their lands," Ralta stretched his arms, flexing them.

“And he’s what? Counting on Roman pride and arrogance to drive us after him?” Quintus chuckled.

“It’s worked so far,” Ralta grunted. “Though I would like to think it’s our orders that drive us onward not foolishness.”

Malitus nodded. “Indeed. This land must be subdued and secured in the name of Rome. We are committed to passing through it.”

Porcius walked up to them and listened for a bit before interjecting, “Even if we can get by the beasts and druids, we have another problem to deal with.”

Malitus asked, “What is that?”

Porcius belched softly and said, “The Picts.”

“What about them?” Quintus said.

“Have you forgot them in all this?” Porcius asked, surprised.

“I forget nothing.” Quintus retorted.

Ralta sighed. “Porcius is correct.”

Clearing his throat, Porcius added, “There are quite a few out there if we do survive these beastman. I saw them coming up.”

“I wonder how many Picts there are?” Ralta asked

“Out there in the woods, beyond the valley over yonder?” Porcius faced the woods then swept his hand across the northern sky. “All of them, I think.”

Chapter IX

At the crest of the valley, the eyes of Tancorix looked over the many tribes of Pictdom. So numerous were the men and women that arrived she couldn't count their numbers. All of them came to the fight, but they celebrated all the way. At the periphery of the great forest of Syn, at the edge of the enormous plain of Kassidee, thousands of them amassed, sharing mirth.

Tancorix stayed back in the dim forest, seated on fallen logs, but let herself be seen many times by the multitude.

"It's good to be seen by them all, but in small numbers. Let their wonder wrap about their minds."

Tancorix heard and understood the words of Weaver, her wizardess of the wood. She read wisdom in her words, but made a curious observation over the diminutive assistant to Weaver, Ragala, and wondered if the elder was wise enough in her ways to comprehend the younger lass wanted her elder's place. *Then again*, Tancorix mused, *that was the natural order of the wood.*

Quite a few chiefs of the Pict tribes brought her their gifts of undying loyalty. She desired no children, no blood, no food, no randy mate . . . just their devotion. Many were happy to walk up, give that oath or promise and go back, inquisitive if this figure really was the Queen of legends. A few were skeptical of her until they beheld their Queen, returned from the dead, standing with the elderess Weaver of clan Makinni and little Ragala. Many muttered their feelings as they departed—that they felt it to be her in the flesh.

The little one spoke and Weaver tried her best to silence the apprentice.

When the tribesman had paid their respects and moved on out of the woods, Tancorix asked, "What does she say?"

Sweeping back her mane of tangled grayish red hair, Weaver's jaw tightened some. "She's a child yet, barely into the blood time." Eyes on the girl, admonishing, Weaver added, "Perhaps she needs to be cut up to little bits, her soul wiped on my backside and a new one assigned to me."

Tancorix laughed at her dire words, hands slapping her bare knees. "No, what did Ragala say? Speak up, child."

The slender girl stepped away from Weaver, asserted her flat chest and declared, "It will not be enough."

"You forget yourself," Weaver replied, adjusting her long robe to stand better. "And what would the point of that be? She needs to learn as do you, no matter how wise the centuries made you in the sleeping beyond night."

"I know."

"She speaks because she observes all things, but she is stupid yet. She needs time," Weaver said. "I lived every year of them, the years of your long sleeping, walking this torrid world. Slaying us and forging on with your own mind for guidance will do no good in the end. To assuage your anger on dead enemies cold for centuries, and nothing more? No, I rather think you won't. You need to catch up with the times."

"You summoned me for more than that, Weaver. Those that bested me are long gone, unless they live on elsewhere."

Ragala asked, "It is true you were bested by a baby?"

Tancorix teeth ground and she looked away, across the valley. She spoke to Weaver and ignored the girl. "In truth, it is Drust with whom you are troubled, not I."

Weaver chuckled deep. "I ignore your slights as I have no mother to talk to in these matters."

Both exchanged a glanced and laughed, but little Ragala did not.

Ragala said in a low voice, "Must we waste time watching soldiers prance about and fawn over you, my Queen?"

Too much pluck for a child, Tancorix thought, looking at the skinny girl where stripes and bruises featured her legs and back, many healed atop older wounds. *Curious, whatever made Ragala burn so hadn't been beaten out of her yet.*

"Before I arrived, they were an unruly bunch, but word of my resurrection has given the confederacy of tribes a purpose. I have gathered them, by rumor alone, to end this Roman intrusion into our lands—" Tancorix started but Ragala interrupted her.

"This too, I understand Queen of the Picts," Ragala nodded, her term for Tancorix almost insulting in its tone. “But the Romans are nothing compared to the threat of the beasts.”

“Really? That is fascinating, child. Tell me what you know of these beasts.”

“I do not know *their* secrets. They come and go at their choosing, venturing into the world of man for a time of blood, only to disappear into the trees once more when their violence is ended. That is the way of beastmen and the order of the Greymen.”

“So this Drust, he didn’t create them?”

Weaver shook her head. “No, he did not. A compulsion of his magic has summoned them here. You seek more answers than I can give you.”

More huge men with orange hair walked up to the Queen and bowed.

Her ears, sharp, heard their skeptical words upon entering and then their astonished praises on leaving her presence. They knew her to be real. They too could feel it in their bones. The supernatural force of her spirit sizzled around them.

She arose, flanked by the mystics, and walked the lines. Tancorix saw them gathering their weapons unhurriedly, preparing to fight in units composed of men and women from their own tribes but to walk as one.

“She’s returned to guide us from across the centuries,” the words filtered to her ears from the mouths of thousands of Picts. “The Queen of legend has risen from the dead.”

“My skin felt like ice near her.”

“Those eyes, they will haunt me forever.”

“Can you see the shape of the horse about her? I can.”

"Speak not the secret name of the goddess!"

"That must be some powerful magic to escape the heart of La Gaul."

Tancorix would be flattered, she thought, if she were herself completely. At the moment, she was Porcius. He felt rather fascinated walking around in the body of a naked warrior Queen, but not having free reign over her mind and abilities. He wondered how she felt walking about as a stocky Greek male in the Roman camp. Still, they'd switched places during their violent copulation ritual and he didn't mind, after a while. He figured his life was almost over anyway and this was a funny part of a sweltering dream.

While she spied on the Romans and what they were up to, Porcius viewed the armies of Pictdom. That bothered him at first, but in the face of the monsters and this giant army surrounding Rutland, it didn't matter. Though not impressed by their ordinance, their sheer numbers shook him to his core. He'd read of enormous numbers of Celts and heard tales of massive army buildups, but not in his lifetime. Here were thousands of Picts, outnumbering his Legion surely five or six to one, if not ten!

She mumbled, "And Quintus worries about the beastmen"

To a fact, so did Tancorix, in her core. Her enemy was Rome this day, not Drust and his wild creatures. Frustrated at that reality, Porcius felt her spirit tormented, yet hid desires from his inquisitive mind.

Was this really Tancorix, who died before the great flood itself? Oh yeah, he thought, all over. This was her, in new flesh. She was mean, too, like a hornet's nest on two legs, and he liked that in a woman.

The Queen of the Picts left them on the hill as she ventured into the valley to give her orders to those that served her. As she went, she heard Weaver instruct Ragala, "Girl, bring out the divination vessel."

Tancorix threw leg over the blanket on the horse and rode along with the leaders of the tribes. They made quite a display, the groups of people who hadn't come to see her up close, riding around on horses and showing off, bringing up the spirits of those not having the courage to venture to the sacred grove on the hill. When she stopped to talk with a few, they heard a screaming cry from the hillside where Tancorix had just reclined back to see them.

The warriors drew their weapons and brandished their axes.

Tancorix sighed again, saying words Porcius couldn't stop himself from saying. "As much as I wish that was her assistant in her final breaths, its naught to worry on."

Still, she rode alone, back to the woods and away from the army, unwilling to see where the cry had come from.

Off the horse, Tancorix ascended the hill and saw the source of the terrible scream. A Roman soldier lay across the fallen tree she'd just used as a makeshift throne. The two big Pict soldiers flanked the women of the wood. Long loops of intestines emerged from a huge gap in the Roman's belly, and rested in Weaver's palms. She studied the grisly loops like someone reading parchment. Ragala, hands behind her back, peered at them, too, listening to the words of the wood Weaver spoke.

"What does the future hold?" Tancorix asked, amused by the ritual.

"I worry for our meeting with master Drust, but this is unclear. I think many of us will die in this venture."

Ragala smirked.

Weaver dropped a handful of guts and grabbed the child by the throat. "It doesn't have to be in war, rotten piglet. You can die today and perhaps I can see a brighter future out of your innards." She then dropped the rest of the guts and turned Ragala about, wiping her hands in the child's long hair.

Ragala ran off towards the creek, screaming.

Weaver yawned, stretched her arms out, and walked over to her Queen.

"That was something . . . "

Head tilted, Weaver half smiled. "How are you doing in there, Roman?"

"If not for the war coming around me," she answered, hands running over her stomach and breasts. "This would be delightful."

Weaver's smile disappeared. "Try to control yourself and not be a swine."

Tancorix winked. "I shall try."

"Try harder," Weaver hissed. She then looked across the forest and pointed with her right index finger. "You think it wise to see Drust in this state? With the Spartan inside you?"

Tancorix rested back on her right hip, hand on her waist, standing like a cubby Greek. "Oh, I'm dying to see him up close."

Cracking her knuckles, Weaver showed her own strength as she faced the direction where Drust must be. "He plays games with me . . . us. We shall see whose magick is stronger."

"I'll try not to let you down," Tancorix promised.

"Smells are a powerful memory trigger," Flavius said as he watched the fire go to work on the pile of bodies.

As they walked on to the northern section of Rutland where the Legion prepared to disembark that afternoon, August grunted in agreement. "Nothing smells quite like human flesh burning, save for wild boar on a wooden spit."

Flavius stopped and so did August and Rufus. "You know, now that you say that . . . " His face flushed.

August smiled weakly. "Sorry to ruin boar for you forever." He closed his eyes and saw many in his tribe being burnt alive by the Romans, a memory he suppressed but the scent jolted it to the front of his mind. "Wood spits are better scented as it is natural over any product of metal roasting an animal."

Flavius shook his head. "The scouts saw the Pict army amassing.

They said it was the largest display of humanity they have ever witnessed."

August shrugged. "Scouts say a lot. They are probably exaggerating because they are scared to death scouting in a forest full of monsters."

"Understood, but aren't we bargaining for trouble?"

"You? Questioning the wisdom of the great General Malitus? That's a first."

"I know you see me as a politician in service . . . However, madness and suicide are not good for anyone's political future."

"I agree. The Legion is a scary thing to see in action and the Picts are indeed barbarians. They will have courage, but subduing them is literally the last thing on the emperor's agenda. The end of the world is to the north and thus, the last fight is here."

"Did the emperor count on the monsters?"

"Of course not. No one did." August shook his head.

Rufus watched August command a dozen soldiers into formation, ready to reenter the Fogou. Standing forgotten to the side, Rufus watched as Quintus approached.

The Legion was going forward, catching up and surviving was August's prime directive.

Like any scouting mission, August assured him they would rejoin the Legion in time, as if the druids and the creatures didn't exist out there.

There he goes, Rufus thought, probably off to his doom at the hands of barbarians or monsters.

Rufus' heart sank fast as he realized he was to stay behind with Quintus. Six soldiers flanked Quintus as he stomped over to him. Eyes focused, his hungry look trained on Rufus.

Quintus stopped in his tracks. He still wore a menacing expression, and slowly reached out to Rufus. His right hand caressed the tufts on Rufus' head, and then his fingers slowly seized a curly strand. He didn't pull hard, but his grip was tight.

"Now then, little slave. You'll take me to where you met with this man Drust. I'd really enjoy meeting him up close."

Rufus swallowed loud.

"Do you understand my order?"

Rufus nodded.

"No words? No warnings? No tales of the fantastic wood masters and all of the prior glories to scare me off?"

"I am at your command," Rufus croaked, his voice dry and body starting to shake.

"What are you thinkin' about?"

"It doesn't matter."

Quintus hand became a fist and tears sprung to the boy's eyes. "Tell me."

Rufus stayed quiet.

"Thinking about dying, are you?"

"I've been thinking about that every day for some time."

Quintus opened his hand and took a step closer, his voice dropping low. "You're more afraid of Drust than me, aren't you?"

"You can only kill me," Rufus answered, head down, tears falling.

Quintus barked a mirthless laugh and then stated like a dramatic play actor, "Only kill you? I'd say that is enough."

"Drust can damn me, take my soul and fling it beyond the stars we see. I don't want to fall for eternity in Hell."

"Hell," Quintus said the word like it was excrement on his lips. "The only Hell there is lies in Britannia and I want to find the gate leading out."

Eyes up to Quintus, Rufus said, "I'll show you where I met with Drust, but I can't promise he is there."

"That's all I ask."

Rufus looked to the smoking pile of burning bodies

and put his head down. "You're only taking six men with us?"

"Probably a dozen. Not enough?"

The Legion isn't enough, Rufus thought.

As they headed to the edge of Rutland, Quintus spied Porcius walking about the body pile, quizzically looking at the assembling Legion like he'd never laid eyes on it before.

"Centurion," Quintus called out to him as another six men joined Rufus and the six originals.

The Greek didn't turn his head, but stared at the siege weapons on the cart and the spokes of the wheels, fascinated.

"Porcius!" Quintus shouted.

He turned, faced the commander and walked over to them.

"Come along with us," Quintus said flatly. "I think you're touched, but I've never known you not to give your all in a fight. Can you still do that?"

With what looked like a suppressed smile, Porcius saluted, and then gripped the pommel of his new found gladius.

Quintus nodded. "Good. If Rufus runs away, break his legs."

Porcius asked, "How can he show us the place if I break his legs?"

Not a look at either of them, Quintus declared, "He can talk, can't he?"

Drust smelt guts. The odor took him back to his youth when his grandmother pledged him to the order of the wood. Her hands oft smelled like excrement and guts.

That smell gave the portents of the future. His grandsire, incredibly old and wise, caressed his cheek as she went to the woods to be the sacrifice. The elder of their race, the wisest of all women of the wood, knew when it was time to die.

As he pulled the intestines from the screaming woman, the pungent odor grew, stifling him in the confines of the cave.

"Too many tell men how to live, Gonar," Drust said to the young man at his side, holding the ruined woman's leg down on the slab. "So few show one how to die."

Gonar said nothing, but held the woman in place until her convulsing stopped.

"I'd been saddened when my grandmother explained to me it was her time," he mused, turning the guts over in his hands, nodding at their revelations. "Death is a hard lesson for a child to accept." He then cast the long ropey intestine back down on the woman and waved for Gonar to step back.

Another smell filled the cavern, a dank, animalistic scent. Two of the Greymen stepped from the honeycomb of grim tunnels took the dead woman from the slab. They carried her off down a passage.

Drust made his way over to read the innards, Gonar following closely.

The lad handed his master a wet cloth and then a dry one.

Drust wrung his hands in these and handed them back to his apprentice.

"She was ill, you know," Drust whispered.

"Yes?"

"My grandmother." Drust smiled at the shrewdness of the lad.

The girl whose intestines they'd just read had been ruined beyond healing after a failed act of copulation with the King of beastmen, Adelaido.

Gonar listened, as all good students do. The child had great wisdom and ambition, but was also prudent enough to hold his tongue. "Perhaps her momentous sacrifice was because she lived in pain and this was a noble way out of it, but alas, she died for us all."

"She is a part of our ballads."

Seeing as they wrote nothing down and all knowledge was oral, Drust complimented the boy in his learnings. "She is a part of the world, forever."

"Forever one with the wood?"

They came out into the night and the summer breeze slapped them in the face. "Yes, but a part of her lives in that wizardess to Tancorix."

"Miss Weaver?"

"Yes, the women of immense talents weaving baskets and a proper web of calamitous magick in the world."

"Master, why do you say such things? How is she inside Weaver some way?"

Durst stopped and turned to face the child. He pointed two fingers toward his eyes. "It's how she looks at me."

Eyes wide, Gonar wondered, "And how is that?"

"Like she's going to scourge me with a crooked switch, like she isn't afraid of me at all. That was the look in my grandmother's eyes when she died, one she wore her entire life. She wasn't afraid of death or of what came next. That is incredible courage to have inside and out. Weaver? She has that." Drust took a breath. "Stay near."

"Yes, master."

It was very late evening when Tancorix stopped her horse and shuddered, crying out and then relaxing.

While Ragala looked at her Queen, afraid, Weaver simply asked, "Is he gone? The Roman?"

Tancorix shuddered. "He is and I am myself again all together."

"Good. Just in time."

As night fell, the two of them rode into a clearing beyond the great forest. In its clear center stood a large tree, a giant and ancient thing, its bark gnarled and twisted like flesh bent under the hands of a supernatural torturer. From the shadows beneath it Drust emerged to greet them.

"Ah, those with courage to ride in the fresh night, I salute you," Drust called out, his arms moving up a little swathed in his robe.

Ragala whispered to Weaver, "This one is dark, mistress. Very dark indeed. His soul is black enough to hide the stars."

Tancorix ignored Ragala, and focused on the tall man Drust. Weaver kept her stern chin up, strong and proud, full of power like lightning frozen in place. Still, Tancorix felt it her place to speak to this mighty man she'd heard tell of since her resurrection.

"You're a Pict yourself, why are we at odds?"

"I am many things, Queen," Drust shrugged, no real malice in his words. "Our desires are not so different this night."

"You are from the dark roots of the wood," Ragala slid from her horse and landed with grace on her feet. "Your kind is not welcome here."

"Ragala," Tancorix called, angered that Weaver didn't keep her apprentice on a leash.

The girl snapped, "He's our enemy."

"Am I your enemy, Queen?" Drust took a step towards them. "The Romans are the invaders here, are they not?"

"What do you want Drust?" Tancorix dismounted, moving to stand near him. "It has been a very long time. Tell me your desire."

"Only my due," he answered, one of his hands pressed to the great tree, as if it gave him power and not balance.

"These beastmen of yours. I hear they threaten the Picts as much as they do these Romans."

"Beasts of mine?" Drust spoke as if he didn't understand her.

"They will kill our men, I hear, and do worse to our women. And the flesh of our children are their meat. Is this a reality? Is this that what happened to the village south of Rutland?"

"They are far more than mere beasts, Queen. They are a force of nature, a tide of death and blood that nothing can hold at bay. This land was theirs long before mankind set foot here."

Weaver spoke at last, saying coldly, "They are not his playthings. I told you what he has said. He plays us for fools this night."

Drust drew back, eyes on Weaver. "Tell me these tales."

With no fear, Weaver said, "You think that you can control nature, the wood itself?"

Drust raised an eyebrow as Weaver dismounted with a slight groan.

Suddenly, Ragala screamed, swinging an arm around herself toward her mistress. Weaver turned, hand up and the girl staggered, not landing a strike to Weaver's back. However, she fell and the blade slammed into Weavers outstretched hand.

Weaver recoiled as the girl fell to the grass. Blood drops rained in the air as Weaver shook her hand several times, then suddenly, grew as stiff as the trees they worshiped. Her left hand reached out with no quickness and casually plucked the blade from the palm of her right hand. Weaver flexed her right hand, made a fist then opened it up again. The wound no longer bled. She turned to Drust and smiled. Her eyes twinkled like candlelight.

"You dare?" Tancorix's hand gripped the pommel of the blade slung to her waist-belt.

Weaver chuckled. "He checks my power, my Queen, not yours. If he really sought us dead, a thousand of the things he inspires from the earth would roll across us, wouldn't they? But he's not that stupid. He knows he'd be my only focus in such an attack."

Drust shook his head and looked away. "I am at one with the wood. Your words are dust. What have I to fear of you?"

Tancorix stated, "A hundred thousand Pict warriors would crush even your army of stinking beastmen."

Drust's eyes still focused on Weaver. "They are not mine."

Tancorix gritted her teeth, but managed to ask, "Then what are you playing at?"

Weaver offered, "He plays with forces outside his capacity."

"Nonsense," Drust answered. "These beastmen and I merely have an understanding, the one you have with the unnamable goddess of the Picts."

"Be silent. You have deceived them then, Drust." Weaver cursed and kicked her writhing apprentice on the ground. "Get up and get your mind right, little girl. You have much more to learn in the coming day." She took a breath and pointed at Drust with her bloody hand. "And they will not be forgiving when the truth is outed."

"I'll ask only once, *Queen*. Will you join me? Help me drive the Romans from the land?"

"It's our land," Tancorix said.

"Nor is it truly yours," Drust countered. "Ours? You just got here. Things are a great deal different than when you last tried to get revenge on your former lover, that legend of renown."

"I have no time for your games, Drust," Tancorix growled. "Keep your damned beasts away from my folk and I'll let you live. We are kin, whatever your game. If so many as a single more of my people die at the hands of those things, it is your blood that will cover the grass of this land red."

Tancorix returned to her horse, preparing to leave. Ragala made no move to leave however.

"We cannot leave him alive!" Ragala shrieked. "It will be bad for us all if we do!"

Drust looked at Weaver, but not the girl. "Rein in your toy, sorceress, or else her blood will be on your hands."

Hands out, fingers wiggling, Weaver smiled. "It usually tends to end up there, anyway."

"It's time we were gone," Tancorix told the women of the wood.

Weaver balled up her fists and turned to Drust.

Drust eyed her, hands at his sides. "Well? Are you gauging your chances?"

"For one so damned wise," Weaver began as she opened her hand and swung her arm outward. Blood flew from her hand and spattered the gnarled bark of the tree. "You talk too much."

Drust put his hands together and nodded, before he slightly bowed.

The horses all reared up when the huge tree faded out in the moonlight, to be replaced with the image of Drust himself in its spot. The Drust they had been speaking to disappeared suddenly.

Weaver returned to her horse and told Ragala, "Stay here if you want, but I'd advise you to come with us. Things are not always what you see."

The girl mounted up fast, muttering words of forgiveness for attacking her mistress under the power of Drust.

Weaver waved off her words but rode alongside her Queen.

They traveled over a hundred yards before Tancorix looked at Weaver. The Queen, though back from the realms of the dead, looked surprised.

"Yes?" Weaver asked, serene in the saddle as they paused.

"That was . . . "

"I'm not frightened of him," Weaver declared and cussed her apprentice. "Don't look back! It's a sign of feebleness." She then faced her Queen.

"You don't fear Drust?"

"I never have. That doesn't mean his command of magick isn't superior to mine. I pulled you out of the caldron of history to stand with your people at this hour."

Tancorix nodded "Yes."

Weaver thumbed a bloody hand over her shoulder. "I wonder what Drust used his gifts on."

Chapter X

August, Flavius and the dozen other soldiers entered the Fogou, armed and trying to act like they were ready for what lay below. Each wore stern faces of courage and honor, but these faded as the darkness crept in near. Again, the anomalous green veins of light in the narrow cavern provided sufficient light, even if the men brought torches to be struck when they reached the burial chamber. Not used to the green glow like August had become, many murmured their fears and tried to screw down their courage.

While Flavius served as a capable enough soldier, August wished that Porcius was at his side instead. Although Porcius would never fit into these narrow tunnels.

The smell of death and decay almost overpowered August, but no one else seemed to react to it. Though his stomach churned, August held on to his meagre rations. Did he imagine it? August and the others reached the breech in the tunnel and he instructed all of the men to hug the wall as they headed left.

The very air pressed down upon them like a tangible force. All of the men held their blades at the ready. If they were to meet death, they would meet it head on as soldiers and men of Rome.

"Be strong, step carefully," August cautioned them

as he led them onward. "This is nothing compared to what may lie ahead."

At last, they stood at the open area August had deemed a graveyard. He instructed the men to strike a few additional torches, before he slid into the chamber of bones.

"They are gone," August said.

Flavius asked, "Who, sir?"

"Those I fought there. They are gone, look!" He pointed as a soldier brought a torch to bear. "See the blood on the bones? It is fresh."

"That's frightening," Flavius acknowledged, with a deadpan voice.

"What is?"

"That you were telling the truth, Decurion."

August grimaced and pointed to the larger shaft. "Come along then, all of you. This way."

The men kept moving, the grade of the rocky surface steadily going lower, daring not to linger too long lest the darkness claim them.

Flavius asked, "How far down are we?"

August didn't turn when he said, "A lot farther than I'd really like. I can't really guess."

Flavius shuddered, so did most of the party, as the temperature dropped. All grew tenser and walked closer together.

After what seemed an eternity of damnation in the eerie green glows and the flickers of torchlight, narrow passage opened into a huge, seemingly endless chamber. A golden light seeped on over the edge of a stone lip that wouldn't denote what lay beyond.

"What . . . what is this place?" Flavius asked, knuckles white around the shaft of his lance.

"I think we found what we were looking for." August shot a look back. "Douse those torches, I see lights up ahead!"

Reaching out to give him a cautious touch, Flavius hissed, "What do you see up there?"

August held up the index finger of his left hand and waved behind himself with his gladius. "Silently. "He then unstrapped and removed his helmet. "Stay low. I'm going take a look."

The men stayed low as August inched forward. He studied the surroundings, turned and sank to his backside, head against the stone lip.

On his knees, Flavius held out his hands, begging for information.

August put his sword across his lap and rubbed his eyes. He blinked, as if trying to wash out what he saw.

"That bad is it? By the gods," Flavius whispered, knuckles on the stone floor.

"Bad enough. I'm not sure what's going on, but thousands of those damn things are sleeping there. And then there's that large, black one, too . . . "

"What's he doing?"

"Eating a woman's head. Chewing her cheek off in big bites." August opened his eyes. "Wish I could take a good painting of this place back to the General. He'd piss himself purple."

A serpent-like hiss resounded through the cavern and the men jumped, even August. He wheeled away from the lip, gladius at the ready, helmet on the floor.

Flavius voice cracked. "What is this? A new horror?"

August looked around. "Strike a torch, just one and give it to me."

One of the soldiers did just that, even though his hands shook.

He took the torch and motioned for them to move back into the constricted tunnel. He then raised the torch to look at the walls where the hissing sound originated.

On either side by the entrance to the abyss lay two deep caves, identical in size like grim cells, each restricted by a series of stone bars. No man could squeeze through the small openings, but the shadowy things inside couldn't get out either. At the middle of each series of stone bars was fixed in a glass object shaped like a pentagram, raised up. August thought the odd objects expensive jewels at first, they felt rubbery like gelatin to his touch of the flat of his sword. He showed great care in the pressure on them, just in case this object was the keyhole to a trap. He put the torch near the bars and quickly turned back to glare at the men. Sword up a little, he slashed his hand over his mouth quickly. A few of the soldiers already registered great horror at what they beheld and had their mouths gaping open.

"Cover them," August whispered. "If they scream we are doomed."

Flavius peered between the stone bars. "By the gods, if those things get out, we are doomed twice over."

August looked across the way and saw an identical creature housed in the stone cave. His teeth gnashed, shaking from side to side.

"What do you say to that?"

Flavius muttered, "What are they? Dragons? Worms? Slugs?"

"I don't know." They looked like long lizards, with four legs, but sported bizarre underbellies like a worm and strange protuberances on their reptilian heads like slugs. "I can't dream of such a thing."

Beyond the lip, something growled and snorted.

August motioned them back. "If they come at us they won't be able to fit in the tunnel. That's why they sent a young'un with the burial squad."

He closed his eyes as the growls grew louder. August quickly prayed not to die in such a place. He also vowed that if he saw the surface, he'd run away from the Legion. Even death by the Picts would be better than this fate.

With the sounds of the Legion marching in their ears, Porcius, Quintus and their dozen men followed Rufus close on foot towards the forest. The route they took was the opposite Porcius traveled when he navigated the woods and found the slaughter hut. It was where Rufus went off with Lucius. They all knew it and felt the danger it implied.

As they walked, Porcius ran his hands down his chest and to his crotch for a moment.

Quintus eyed him and wondered, "Are you well enough for this?"

Porcius nodded. "Yes, sir. I just miss someone."

"You'll be missing your family jewels if you cross me."

Eyes closed, Porcius dreamed of killing Quintus and how fun that fight would be. Quintus would be no easy target, but truly, he'd enjoy battling him to the death. He felt excited at the possibility, even if it was a mere daydream. Seeing the look in that perfumed prick's eyes as he died, that came near to making Porcius as excited as his encounter with Queen Tancorix. Almost.

Darkness started to fall as they slinked around the woods and down the grade. In his mind's eyes Porcius traced the route he traveled the day before and realized they would soon arrive near the creek where he'd seen the trussed up body and the beheaded corpse. Sure enough, when they crossed through a thin tree line, he could hear the creek babbling beyond.

Severus, walking further up ahead, whistled and waved for them to dismount.

Porcius moved up even with him in the tall grasses around the edge of the woods and saw two of the beastmen on their knees, rooting around like pigs in the weeds not far from the creek. He could see the orange hair of the dead Pict over beyond them and guessed the beasts fed on the headless body, probably putrid by then. His hands tightened on the pommel of his gladius when he figured this the body of a man he knew and fought beside, Lucius. While not close comrades, they did share laughs and drank together several times. That bonded men and Lucius, while a perfumed prick of a Roman, didn't deserve that after death.

Quintus arrived beside them and his right fist struck the grasses.

A finger to his lips, Porcius turned, pointed at the twins, Crispinus and Decimus. They came forward with their crossbows and slings at the ready. Porcius eyed Quintus intently.

Quintus read the situation and told Porcius, "Go ahead. Command it."

Porcius ordered them quietly, “Hit them high, close to the head or in the back if you can. They’ll rise up. Hit another volley in the chest when they turn about, hit a lung and make me properly randy about it, you copy? But follow with a sling to their legs. Slow the things down good, and we will be on them.”

They nodded as one and took a knee, notched arrows and looked to Porcius.

Porcius armed up his shield and nodded to the others, making sure they read his meaning. Then dropped his sword at the twins.

The arrows flew.

Both metal tips struck the two beastmen; one in the upper left shoulder blade, the other right in the ear canal. The creature which had been struck in the back twitched as if an offending bug bit him, then he turned, meat falling from his mouth as he sat to his knees. As the ear canal shot one roared and rolled over, the second volley struck the first one. The twins fired at it together, striking its chest in similar strikes just below his nipples. The arrow on the left went in and was quickly broken off by a huge hand, but the other struck out, dancing as he arose.

The Romans sprang up and the brothers reared back and slung their slings, easily wrapping the projectiles about the calves of the rising wounded beast. It took a stride, staggered, broke the lines of the slings, but still fell to the ground. A half dozen sword points stabbed into the beast, all in different spots. Porcius’ chose the kidney area and ripped back, fluid bursting out and the scent of urine joining the odor of blood pouring from the other wounds.

Unfortunately, none was a definitive death strike

and the creature climbed to its knees and swiped its arms out fast, throwing them all back and swiping the jaw from the face of one soldier. The man's helmet flew about, covering the look of horror on his face as he couldn't scream. While the soldiers attacking this beast fell back a step, Quintus went forward to aide them, seeing his opening. He sliced with his shield, knocking the great wrist of the beast that swiped to kill, and with an overhand arc, planted his gladius in the chest of the beastman. Eye to eye with the roaring monster, Quintus twisted the blade, shoving it with great difficulty out the back of the monster. Snot flew from its nose as the eyes, so full of rage and shock, felt the touch of death. It struck out at Quintus, sending him to his rump, and stood one last time. It looked at the sword in its heart, and the blood pouring out of so many wounds. Life departed at last, the thing hobbled on its injured ankle, went to its knees abruptly, and fell to its right side.

Rapidly, the twins notched arrows again, running with Quintus' half dozen. They aimed at the remaining beastman, who had gotten up, but shambled drunkenly. The twins fired, striking the creature in the gut. They cleared out as more of the men moved toward the wounded beast, trying to find a place to strike.

"Go low, go behind," Porcius ordered as he squared off against the unbalanced creature It still held its ear as blood and a gray slime seeped through the fingers in the glowing moonlight. "Come get me, you rotten bastard," Porcius challenged as all of the men encircled the monster.

A soldier went for the back legs, looking to

hamstring the beast, but the creature had enough presence of mind to swing a long arm to backhand the attacker. Sent to the ground, the man rolled over, shaking, confused, and choking. Not fully comprehending that something had snapped down deep in his neck. His legs twitched and he couldn't breathe.

Porcius made a charge and then hit the ground fast, rolling as the thing slapped at him with its free hand, like he still charged at him upright. When he did this move, two other soldiers reached the back legs and sliced. The beast took its last step.

A half dozen men jumped on the beast, stabbing their swords deep in its back and pelvis, over and over. Inspired by their two dying comrades, they stabbed and hacked until the beastman moved no more.

Quintus shook his head at the display and then walked to where the two had been eating. "Lucius?" he said silently and turned away.

Severus motioned for one of the two spearmen in the group to attend to the wounded men, who lay suffering.

Porcius watched the spearman walk to the soldier devoid of a jaw, who gagged and couldn't breathe, and give him the coup de grace to his heart.

A shame, Porcius thought, unable to recall the soldier's name. He did recall the man was an excellent cook and could make a tasty mutton stew, if pressed. When the other flipped over the soldier the creature had brained, he rambled, spoke in other languages and suddenly bled much from his eyes. The spear entered his heart and all was silent, save for the voice of the rolling creek.

"Good work, men," Porcius told the survivors of the group and went to Quintus. "At least these damn things can die. Guess we knew that, but . . . "

"Why did we never see such a thing yet in this Isle?" Quintus fumed, teeth biting down as he spoke. "Why here? Why now?"

Porcius shrugged. "Hell, I don't know, sir, but perhaps this needs to be the end of the world right here, huh?"

"What?"

"Perhaps the emperor might consider this the end of all things, this place, this land, right damned here. The freakin' end of it."

Quintus' guile dropped. "Perhaps you are correct." He then turned to see Rufus, watching, smiling. "But I'm not quite done yet."

Malitus enjoyed walking with the men and chose not to ride on this march in the late evening. He'd felt better in his lifetime, but refused to drink anymore wine or take any medicines for his queasy feelings at all.

Ralta's boisterous way was almost infectious as he marched along beside him, saying, "I love the night air, even if the summer seems a trifle warm here. We are from a place far warmer, aye?"

The troops were looser around Ralta and Malitus understood his popularity with the men, even if they doubted his sanity at times.

Malitus felt glad that this crude road widened out after Rutland, thus allowing the men to march six abreast as they were trained. The columns moved well even on these unpaved roads. They nearly achieved *militari gradu*, or military march cadence of a hundred paces a minute. They did their best to stretch out the troops in expectation of an attack. Normally, they marched on with little fear of molestation.

The infantry enclosed most of the army as it moved, unlike usual days, as they had a readiness for war about them. Their numbers, while depleted by near to a thousand, still marched strong and forward, intent on doing the will of the emperor.

Malitus told himself that, anyway. From what the scouts had said, the army of Pictdom was on the move and tribes were seen streaming from all over the northern lands of Caledonia. Part of him longed for a fight with the Picts, as that enemy he could outwit. Yes, they'd outnumber them by far, but the Picts, like the Celts, had no discipline and would fall to tactics.

Cries arose from the Legion's left flank. Spears flew from among the trees, impaling soldiers before they ever had chance to react. The screams of the wounded and dying men were drowned out by the thunderous shouts of the Picts as they emerged from hiding. Malitus' mouth dropped open in shock. He knew a battle with the Picts lay ahead but he had not expected it this soon. He ran, pushing himself to his limits, towards the sounds of battle where axes hammered Roman shields, and swords cleared their scabbards.

"Wait, sir!" Ralta called to him but Malitus paid the man no mind.

Malitus felt that he had failed the men under his command enough. It was high time to make up for it and prove his worth. Gutting a few Picts seemed a fitting way to do it.

When Ralta saw he had no intention of stopping, the man followed after him, gaining ground quickly with the long strides of his pumping legs.

The Picts spilled out of the trees, attacking the entire left side of the Roman column. They moved as one, looking like a glistening snake rolling over, filing out of the trees and forming up again into one organism.

Malitus took pride in how fast his men formed up to meet the enemy . . . any enemy, but he had seen it all before. Shields joined together, the ranks of Legion shoved the savages back. The Romans moved as if they were one large mechanism, all working together. As the strong wall engaged the savages, Roman blades hacked into their pale flesh. Even so, the attack had come so suddenly and without warning, numerous Picts had gotten into the Roman ranks. Malitus sighted one of them. A man of his same size, with a wild, battle-crazed look in his eyes, gripping his axe tightly as the blood of a slain Roman dripped from its blade. Malitus charged the man, leaving him no time to bring his axe back into play. Malitus' shoulder rammed into the Pict's chest, sending the man staggering backwards with a grunt. The General's blade slashed upwards cutting the man from groin to neck. The Pict wailed like a cat stomped upon by accident, blood running down the sides of his legs from his mangled privates, and collapsed sideways, clearing Malitus' path to get closer to the main battle.

Two more Picts slipped passed the main wall, and moved to engage Malitus. He blocked a wild axe swing from the first with his sword, stepping to the right to dodge the spear thrust of the second man. Malitus brought his blade around and downward onto the shaft of the spear, breaking it into two pieces. He was so impressed by his own speed, Malitus faltered, pausing a moment too long to admire the slicing shot. The first of the two Picts had drawn back his axe from being blocked and now swung it at him again.

Ralta appeared as if he dropped in from the sky, hitting the axe by its handle with his shield just above where the Pict clutched it. The Pict stared at Ralta in shock, not figuring his weapon would be attacked instead of his person. His expression twisted into a grimace of pain as Ralta plunged his sword into the center of the Pict's chest. This barbarian wore a series of bones as armor, a lattice work of a covering, feigning protective covering. Perhaps this was just a jest to his brothers to show his courage, or an uncanny need to show all that his gods really protected him. Either way, he died, unprotected. Ralta withdrew his blade as he kicked the Pict's dying body away from him.

Malitus grew busy with the remaining of the two Picts. With his spear gone, the Pict had drawn a bone dagger from his belt and rushed at the General. His attack went quite clumsy by Roman standards, and too full of fury to be properly carried out, no matter his greater size. Malitus took advantage of his sword's greater reach and danced about the bigger man, slashing open The Pict's side and then finishing him with a second blow that removed the arm above the hand holding the dagger from his body.

"Gods be praised, you still know how to fight, sir." Ralta laughed, spitting out some blood that flew to his lips, "But you really need to get out of here this instant. This is truly no place for a General."

Feeling alive and charged with excitement, Malitus laughed as well. “I’m not that old Ralta. Stick around, you may yet learn a thing or two from me.”

Malitus spun away from Ralta, throwing himself at another Pict. The savage whirled to meet him too late. Malitus’ blade cut through the bridge of the barbarian’s nose and into his head leaving his enemy reeling backwards, his face a mangled mess of torn flesh.

Sucking wind, Malitus glanced over his shoulder to see Ralta drive his sword clean through a Pict warrior just as another came running towards him. As the first Pict toppled over from the strike, Ralta let go of his sword’s hilt, leaving the weapon inside the dying man. The giant Roman focused his attention on his new opponent who drove a spear towards his chest. Ralta shifted, dodging the thrust, to close in on the second Pict. His hands caught hold of the attacker and he lifted him screaming into the air. Ralta tossed his flailing body at another Pict engaged with one of the Legion’s soldiers. Both went down together, a mass of writhing limbs. The soldier didn’t need Ralta to tell him what he needed to do. The young man raced upon the two Picts, bringing his blade down on them time and time again, hacking away like a wood cutter. Blood reeled back in waves and splattered sideways as he did his gruesome work.

Malitus realized his lack of an opponent and swept his head around to take in the bloody scene around him. The shield wall that had formed up on the left flank had done its job, driving back those who hadn’t broken into the column’s ranks in the savages’ first wild surge. All of those who lay dead or so wounded as not to matter about the field. Oh yes, the battle continued to rage on but the tide had turned. The Picts element of surprise was gone and now they were paying the price of electing to attack the 9th.

"Orders, sir?" Ralta barked in his direction.

"Let's finish these bastards," Malitus cried out, blood lust of battle filling his veins.

Nonetheless, a great gust of wind seemed to flow out in the night as the Pict mass of flesh drew back from the wall of Romans. The force of Picts, numerically superior, receded back and stopped in their attempt to roll over the Legion.

"What's going on?" several voices cried out, curious of their sudden lack of an enemy.

Ralta and Malitus both gaped at the Picts mass moving backwards.

"Brace up tight and be ready," Malitus shouted and all commanders rushed in to reinforce the wall.

But another rush didn't come. The Picts drew back into the forest, making almost no noise as they retreated.

Malitus whispered to Ralta and his voice came out as a hiss. "What are they playing at?"

With no attempt to curb his voice, Ralta replied, "I would guess they've had enough. Shall we pursue? I wouldn't advise it in the woods at night."

"No, this round is ours."

In the wake of the sudden battle, Malitus wandered around among the many bodies on the grass and the road, taking in the sight of the dead. Aside from the Picts, many young Romans lay strewn about the area. There were so many of them. Each had paid their duty to the emperor with their lifeblood. Still, it was a fine victory for him. The number of dead Picts outnumbered those of his men by at least three to one. It could have been worse.

Malitus raised his eyes from the dead to see Ralta staring at him.

"General?" the big man asked.

"I'm fine Ralta. Truly," he assured him. "It's just this can't be all of them."

"No, sir, I'd wager it was but a handful given the numbers of the scouts had seen. And yes, that was indeed more Picts than we have Roman soldiers."

"It doesn't make sense," Malitus spat. His throat was dry and burned with thirst for anything liquid. He wiped at the blood smeared upon his face. His hand came away red, leaving his cheek no cleaner for the effort. "They must know their only hope is to come at us in full force. Why do this?"

"I agree, General," Ralta said. "Perhaps this was a rogue element of the savages who could not wait until the rest were ready."

"Likely so, but so many thousands?" Malitus nodded. "Hardly rogues, but who can say with stupid barbarians? Let us hope their brethren fall as easily when the time comes to meet them on the battlefield."

The dead were arranged, taken note of and hastily prepared for a mass pyre. This practice ate up much time in the light of the moon. The night deepened. As they approached the valley, the scouts spoke of in their reports.

Ralta joined Malitus in the front of the Legion. The soldiers had stopped and in the distance, beyond the great valley, something moved in the night.

Malitus wondered, "Ralta, pray tell, is all that

beyond the valley? It looks like a vast caterpillar rolling away."

Ralta put his hand flat across his forehead and peered at the distant sight. "That vast rolling orange creature is the rest of the Picts, General."

"What?"

"There are so many of them it gives the appearance of one giant creature. A stunning effect of the moonlight, no?"

"Stunning, yes." The General thought on them moving back.

"When we saw them just now, the grand mass looked similar but much smaller. That is like a rug being pulled back, no? I've not seen such a mass of humanity before in all my days."

"Why don't they just attack us and move forward? This valley was made for such a tremendous attack."

Ralta replied, "Would you rather fight in the dark or light?"

"Good point," Malitus chuckled. "Good point indeed."

Gonar relieved himself by the edge of the woods before going back into the caverns. Since he understood his master did likewise around a few other trees, he relaxed. Eyes closed, he listened, and not just with his ears. His mind, buzzing and warm, felt the chaos surrounding them. In his mind's eyes, he saw the army of Pictdom, and somehow knew they weren't in that valley. This confused him as the images of the Roman Legion did occupy a corner of the valley.

Flesh questions, Drust always said, *but the wind through the wood knows.*

That summer wind trickled through the woods, telling Gonar many things, that the forest was alive with others. Far beyond it all he smelt the death of many on the wind.

His heard the groan of his master and that troubled him greatly. Drust wasn't a weak man by any means, so Gonar finished his task and pulled close the string on his trousers. With haste, he moved about the trees.

"Master?" he said in a low voice, aware that someone else lurked not far away.

Drust groaned again and leaned against a thick oak tree. Shafts of moonlight struck his master through the branches like the sun at midday. In that faint light, he saw crimson on the leaves and the rag his master threw to the ground.

"Death comes for all, my son," Drust said in a calm voice, straightening his robe and taking a few steps.

Gonar stared at the bloody mess on the ground and on the leaves. "We are not alone, my master."

Drust carefully navigated the darkness in the wood. "I know. They came up nearby while we spoke with the women."

"Why do they not attack?"

Drust didn't look in the direction of the intruders. "They are curious. I am glad that you sensed them."

"Master, I could practically smell them."

Drust smiled weakly and then motioned for him to follow. They walked to the mouth of the cavern, partially hidden by fallen oaks. "We'll show them what they want to see, the gate to another place, and far more this night." Drust reached out to the boy. "Give me your canteen."

The boy quickly handed his crude horn-shaped flask to his master.

Drust uncapped the horn and put it close to his wrinkled lips. He spat in the end and then reached in his robe. He brought out his hand and sprinkled what appeared to be dust in the horn. He closed it and shook it.

"Throw it on the fallen oak here, while I invoke the Caoineag spirit."

Gonar smiled wide and nodded fast as he took his canteen and threw the water about as instructed.

Drust chanted low, signed with his hands to the sky. He then screwed up phlegm in his throat, spat it on the fallen oak where the boy threw the water and indicated with a wave they needed to go down into the cavern.

"Is the Caoineag enough for them, master?"

Drust put his hand on the child's back, guiding him into the cavern. "I don't mean to slay them all, just slow them down a trifling bit. One has to amuse oneself, sometimes. It reminds a man that he is still human, after all."

The horses of Ragala, Tancorix, and Weaver pulled to stop as they beheld the valley in its entirety. Ahead, even in the beaming moonlight, they could see that everything had changed since they last rode through the territory. Ragala's mouth opened but a stern look from her mistress made her hold her tongue.

"Where are my people?" Tancorix fumed, "Did the slightest challenge make them run away from their destiny? My people! Hah! The damned Romans are out there in our place."

"Have a care." Weaver shook her head, hand shielding her eyes from the moonlight, so full, perfect and fat above them. "No, the Romans are starting to bivouac there on the southern brink of the valley. But see, the confederation of Pictdom is beyond the edge of the dell to the north still, far beyond their reach. Their torches litter the night in the forest, can't you see it?"

Tancorix strained her eyes to the north side of the valley and spotted a few fireflies in the night, something she wondered if the Romans could see as well.

The Romans had spread out their numbers to the south, though, digging in for a fight. A few pickets walked out in the bright light of the moon, spears up, scanning the plain. They pointed their spears at the three females, but could do little as they were so far away. Ragala made an obscene gesture with her left hand, but Weaver swiped at her in the air as if she could strike her down. The girl frowned, bit her lip and let her chin drop.

Weaver dropped her hand to her reins and sighed. "We are behind them now, but curse them all."

Tancorix cursed in her own ancient dialect. "If an unpretentious curse could slay them in their tracks, it'd be easier than this war that struts before us."

Her head snapped about and Weaver hissed, "Is that so? What do you think you are, Queen? Tell me now."

Her reddish locks flipped in a similar manner to face the sorceress. "What? What do you say to me? You know my fear of wizards is minimal."

"You think me a fool?"

“Far from it. I miss my attendant wizardess from the past.”

Eyes alight in the night, Weaver snapped, “I did curse the Romans. I cursed the ground they walked on. In my cursing I found breath to pray for a way to defeat them. I then searched out such a way through the ultimate goddess of the Picts we never name.”

Tancorix stared at her, curious. “Oh?”

Weaver spoke the name to Tancorix, whose eyes widened. “You know that name?”

“I heard it in the afterworld after my passing . . . ”

“Drust chose his own maddening ideas to deal with this problem on the land, and I chose you, a voice on the ethereal wind that came into my dreams.” She closed her eyes for a moment and went paler than usual, as if she could hear that voice again.

Tancorix’s mouth opened, but no words emerged. She remained silent as Weaver went on to explain.

“I found your ashes, some of the ones from your dire prison in the sacred heart of renown. It was I that spilled the blood of many to return you to this plain of existence. You, dear Queen, are a living curse upon them. No other could unite the tribes of Pictdom, save for those foolish Epidii tribe. You are the fulfillment of that which I could do in this conflict. The Epidii Picts are mules, though . . . ”

Ragala snorted laughter then mocked a horse neighing.

Weaver rolled her eyes. “Horses heads. Horses asses more like.”

After a few deep breaths, Tancorix cracked her knuckles and said, “I am that, dear wizard woman.

Let's get back to our folks now before these red breasted bastards send out a patrol to stop us soon."

Weaver stated, "I'm not disappointed, Queen."

Tancorix wore a grim look. "That is good to know."

Chapter XI

"Back!" August yelled, not caring a wit if anyone or thing heard him.

From over the stone lip of that cavern, one of the Greymen leapt, bounding like an acrobat toward them, as if summoned.

August didn't need to tell the archers to fire, for they drew back and pegged the Greyman twice, a shaft in his right thigh and another in his belly that burrowed deep into the flesh. Feeling the moment of his death at hand, August faced the wounded, furious Greyman. Blood pounded in his ears. He charged forward, a move the bloodied Greyman didn't expect.

Flavius didn't expect August to turn and charge back, either. He cried out, afraid at the loss of the strong cavalry man. However, he didn't run after August.

August threw himself, rolled over, and swiped across at a low angle like a legless gladiator toward the Greyman's calves.

The creature pivoted on the wounded limb, but that didn't make the gladius cut toward him any different. August's wedge dug in deep and struck bone hard. From his swing and force, August wanted to slice both legs off, and had it been a human he would have.

This time, though, the blade stuck in the first limb. When the creature tried to launch himself away from the pain and attack, he ripped a huge chunk of meat loose of himself. Its head snapped back, and a deafening howl resounded through the cavern. Falling down to all fours, the beast grunted, trying to get its breath through all the agony. The beast raised its head and had its face pierced by two more arrows, one deep in its left eye socket, the other stabbing through its cheek. Instinctively, it swiped the arrow lodged in the jowl loose, and fell over, head shaking, wounded leg stuck out, vibrating and bent at a wicked angle.

August hopped up to his feet, then leapt onto the chest of the overturned beast and stomped the arrow shaft down deep into the eye socket. Though the arms of the creature threw August off with great violence, sending him tumbling into a stone wall near the imprisoned creatures, the beast lost all its verve, the arrow finding whatever passed for a brain housed deep in that huge cranium.

Again, August returned to his feet and twisted to see three more of the Beastmen at the edge of the stone lip, gazing over at him consciously.

“Christ,” he muttered, not making a move either way.

Flavius moved in close then and glared at him. “Who?”

“Never you mind. Get back into the tunnel! There’s no way they can fit in after us.”

The archers fired again as the three creatures hopped over the lip and loped after them. August and Flavius moved back towards the narrow tunnel’s mouth. For a moment, August stopped and slammed his shield into the stone bars by the dragon-like things imprisoned in the walls. His shot didn't crack the bars, but it did make the things in the walls hiss and spit enflamed. The move also made the running beastmen stop in their huge tracks. Their eyes went to the beasts behind the bars and they did not advance a step.

With this extra moment or two, the two soldiers stumbled beyond the barred conclaves and made for the constricted tunnels.

The three creatures stood by the area where the two pseudo-dragons were held and paused, looking at the stone bars. They hesitated again.

"Fire," August hollered, getting down low and pulling Flavius to ground with him. The archers let go volley after volley, riddling the three with shafts.

This action made the beastmen more livid. They stepped back, shaking off the arrows as they cried out in frustration. Behind them, more of their brothers arrived.

Rising, August turned to his men. "Get going before they call their damned kids to get us!"

He felt his feet move a few steps and saw the men turn to flee. He felt the world twist and the stone floor came up to meet him. August's head smashed on down to the stone and his helm bounced, his eyes were full of stars but in a moment, his mind filled with darkness.

Drust called up the descending grade of the cavern to Gonar, "Come along now. They will be here soon enough."

After a step or two, Gonar hesitated. The boy kept looking back up the grade and ducking his head, as if that could hide him from anyone looking down.

Drust turned at the point where the walls on either side of him opened into a series of slim stone beams, almost like bars in a prison. The glow of the walls gave Drust an emerald aura when the boy faced him at last.

"I know you are young, Gonar, and the temptation to watch the Caoineag spirit do its action is high, but come along now."

From out of the mouth of the cavern, the sound of a weeping woman started to echo, starting like the cry of a baby then maturing fast to the cry of a sad woman. Gonar's head twisted, facing the opening to the outside world.

"Sorry," Gonar said, bowing his head, drawing closer to his master, but unable to resist looking back again.

Drust shook his head and leaned on the wall to take several breaths. "I was young once, too, centuries ago."

Gonar joined his master at the place where the walls at their sides were not uniform. The boy looked either way and said, "Should we release the Uilepheists?"

Drust looked either way at the stone bars at their sides. At the breathing inside the stone bars, Drust said, "Just because one can command an enchanted quadruped or evoke a spirit however dreadful, it isn't necessary to do all of the time. Just because one has tangible power in one's soul doesn't mean one has to use it."

"I understand, master."

"See that you do." Drust placed his left hand on Gonar's shoulder. "You want to see the Romans ripped apart by the Uilepheist?"

The boy nodded, but couldn't find a place to put his

hands, and settled at last to clasp them behind his back, tight.

"So do I, but patience. We don't need the Uilepheist for the Romans." He looked at the boy intently and then took his left hand and stabbed at Gonar's forehead with his index finger. "What we did just now doesn't involve them. We already have a means in place for them."

The child followed his master close, but paused to glance into the twin chambers at the two Uilepheists, caged by the stone bars and Drust's magic enchantments. A great horror dawned on him at why his master even called up these two dragons-like things and imprisoned them at the gate of the entrance to the underworld. He soon followed his master into the lower places unseen by many human eyes, and his heart raced.

Drust turned and winked at him. "Breathe, boy. Control. I may be dying, but I understand keeping a straight face in the presence of mine enemies. Be strong. You will learn in time."

"Sorry, master."

"Learn not to be sorry. My mother told me many times to never do a thing to be sorry for and thus, never be sorry."

"That sounds impossible."

Drust glanced at him, a scant smile on his lips. "Once you understand who you are and that you are better and wiser than all others, there is nothing left to be sorry about. Your will is law, your will is right, and your mind is all that matters."

"All right."

"Someday, Gonar, you will find a place of no

sorrow, where you will never have to be sorry again. Understand?"

"I'm trying."

"Good."

They descended into cavities down beneath the ground. The tunnel gave way to a huge cavern. They kept trekking downward on a natural ramp of stone, walking steadily, and no longer alone. The walls, while painted with a greenish few lines, were awash in a golden glow that emerged from deeper in the cave. This radiance cast off gave the creatures sitting there about a peculiar halo on their white furry selves. The way proved easy to follow, well lit by a great light source beyond, and populated by the giant creatures the deeper they traveled. None of the monsters moved toward them as the two Picts toured the cave.

"Enemies?" Gonar hissed to his master as they walked amongst the beasts. Every one of them yawned and appeared sleepy to Gonar. Every one of them sported an ivory coat of fur, save for the largest. Gonar peered over the edge of the walkway at the vast underworld. He eyed the only one of the beastmen covered in black fur, the one they called Adelaido.

"Yes," Drust whispered calmly, not fear in his manner. "Every one of them is as such, above as below." He turned and looked down at Gonar, his lips not moving but his words loud in the boy's mind. "In the end, there will be only you and I alone, child. You are the chosen one, given freely from your parents unto my waiting hands."

In his mind, the boy replied, "I know, master Drust. I have no regrets."

"Yes, indeed. By my true, distant kindred from the

far northern lands, you have been gifted unto me many years ago. You will soon understand what it all means. You will soon comprehend your true purpose in life."

The boy looked over the side again, his face alight by the origin point of the extraordinary glow. A series of pulsing golden orbs situated in a tall, cylindrical stack like a spruce tree . . . with balls glowing on it, descending. In his mind, he said to Drust, "Isn't it all about that? The tree of life? The tree of dragonfire?"

Drust spoke to him in his mind. "That's what they think, that's what the Romans will think, that's what even Tancorix will believe in time. She thinks herself so smart and ready to rule the savage Picts, to fight so hard and kill so many. She thinks this will be her reward. So much so she hides it from her woman, Weaver. They are all wrong."

The boy grinned, and spoke back in his mind, saying, "But we know better, don't we, master?"

Drust winked and turned back to face Adelaido down below, ruining another Pict villager woman with his insanely large manhood. "To be a King, to stand next to such power, and still be a beast," Durst said again in the boy's mind. "It is almost funny, no? He thinks they are balls of light, not anything special or powerful, just to let him see in the dark."

Gonar's heart raced, but he took deep breaths and soon moderated his air as to not let the beastmen smell his fear. He told himself that he was starting to understand his master's grand plan, not fully really, but it was coming to him. He learned. Gonar listened. That is the way of Drust.

That is the way of the wood.

Porcius listened in the night as the tall Druid Drust spoke with the child, a youth serving as his apprentice or servant. In his old way of thinking, he'd have been pondering the correct way to out flank him and chop Drust's knees out from under his tall self before they moved farther. Since his dalliance with Tancorix in the trees and his refocusing on the Spartan portions of his heritage, Porcius sat back and listened to Quintus' ego take over.

"Did you see that?" Quintus hissed to the men lying flat in the woods. "Did you see how the women spoke to the air, talking with the others there on horseback, deceived totally that Drust stood nearby still?"

Severus replied, "How was it we could see him away from them and they couldn't? Wasn't that a wizardess with the Pict Queen?"

Rufus mumbled, "Mistress Weaver."

Quintus' helm rattled as he shook his head. "Drust is powerful, and if we rush him it may not go well." He looked at Porcius. "Agreed?"

Rubbing his stubbled chin, Porcius replied, "Who can say that is really him there now? If we can't trust our senses . . . "

Quintus grunted. "Agreed." That surprised Porcius that he'd show a little sense

Getting up close to them, Severus wondered, "Where did the two of them come from? I didn't see how they came to the surface. Are they playing tricks with our mind, even if they don't know we are here? What sort of power is that to deal with?"

Nostrils flaring, Porcius said hotly, "I didn't see

right off and I don't know. Look. They went to relieve themselves, and now they head to the edge of the rocks."

"There must be the mouth of a cave there," Quintus whispered, stamping his feet in the grass a little, his annoyance boiling. "I don't want to deal with this magical nonsense."

Severus' mouth opened, but his words never emerged. His face was blank and his fear couldn't be hidden. The rest tried to screw in their faith or courage and forge on, or at least give the appearance that they did so.

Porcius thought them poor enough spies but figured they lay far enough away from the two to be discovered. Drust, that tall man of slender build . . . He feared him greatly. If Weaver could resurrect Tancorix from out of time and give her flesh, what could that man do? Granted, the sight of Tancorix made him smile and he tried not to feel like a foolish teen. He enjoyed their touches and even the silly deception she enacted switching bodies, but he truly betrayed his unit and men. Yes, she showed him, well, reminded him of his true birthright and what parasites the Romans were to his folk. Eyes squeezed shut tight for a moment, Porcius pondered that so much of the world was Rome, there was no destroying it as easy as slitting a single throat.

When Drust and the boy went down into the rocky outcropping, Quintus motioned for them to move up closer. Afraid or not, Severus took the point and Porcius not far behind. Porcius looked over his shoulder and saw Quintus grab Rufus by the scalp and haul him along. They were far to the back in the bunch.

Porcius slapped him on the pit of the back. "It's all right, Severus. We'll be getting drunk later and laughing at all this."

Severus muttered with no humor, "Do you believe that?"

Porcius grin could be seen in the moonlight. "Certainly. These damn people have never seen me run when the buggerman is chasing me."

"I'll be in front of you," Severus promised.

"Doubt it. Get going."

Severus moved up toward the opening first, brushing back the low hanging branches. Porcius heard him curse what he called wet dew on the branches that splattered him in the face. Porcius thought that silly as it was not early enough for a heavy dew, but that's then Severus dropped his sword and shield, the loud echo ringing as it struck stone. The solider spun in a circle and gagged loud, certainly giving away their position even more than his fallen weapons, but nothing around reacted to such an action to come get after them.

"What ails him?" Quintus hissed from a few yards off and the words half came out as a shriek in the night.

Porcius moved up to face Severus in the moonlight.

Over his face, Severus sported a blanket of clear gelatin, a thick film moving like rushing water. Eyes and mouth wide open, nostrils flaring, Severus struggled for air, but none came to him as the translucent fluid flowed about his face.

Porcius dropped his sword and shield as well. His hands reached out to get a hold of his fellow soldier, but Severus whirled around, dropping to his knees, body warped in half at the convulsions. Roughly,

Porcius pushed him down and then flipped Severus over. He struggled to get Severus' helm strap free and then to scrape madly at the clear mass flooding all over his face and neck. Porcius wiped a portion away of the jelly, but it swiftly rushed back over Severus' mouth and nose. The part he pulled free squirmed in his palm, like he held a live fish. He snapped his wrist down, throwing the substance away.

"What goes on?" Quintus raged, still pulling Rufus along for the ride to the spot where they struggled.

Porcius moved his fingers and felt the leftover gelatin squirm in his hand. He quickly wiped his hand on the grass and still tried to work the clear substance away from Severus' mouth and nose. Severus made no sound, save for this thrashing on the ground by the brush. Vainly, he struggled and wrestled, but within a few minutes, Severus stopped moving.

"Well?" Quintus demanded, eyes scanning the fallen soldier all about. "What is it?"

Porcius shook his head and threw up his hands, still straddling Severus. "He's stopped breathing. If I didn't know better, I'd say he drowned." He pushed on Severus' chest and pried his lips open, but still, no air or sound came forth.

Quintus released Rufus, and the boy took a few steps away. The Celtic slave laughed a little. Quintus turned about and made a grab at the slave's curly locks again. This time, by sheer bad estimation, Quintus' fingers missed the Celtic boy's scalp. Quintus did move closer, though, and slammed his chest-plate to the youth's face and knocked him down to his backside.

"What is this sorcery?" Quintus demanded of

Rufus, grabbing him by the hair and dragging him to the scene.

Rufus dropped to his knees, released, and looked Severus over again and then up at Quintus. He rested back on his palms. “Possibly a water spirit, perhaps a Caoineag that will do the will of the master. That is just a presumption, and I haven’t seen such a thing since I was a toddler. I thought I’d dreamed it then. Porcius is very lucky.”

The thickset man climbed off Severus as the man lay still at last. “I feel lucky.”

“Caoineag?” Quintus glared Porcius’ way for a moment and then returned his gaze to Rufus. “Will the water spirit carry on? Is it gone with Severus life?”

“I cannot say. I’m not a worker of magicks, but I know the lore.”

“Stop your damn smiling,” Quintus seethed, reached out and grabbed Rufus’ hair and slapped him across the face. That move worked. Rufus stopped smiling. “I’d like to stomp your damned fool face inside out.”

Porcius stepped up by Quintus. “The kid knows the lore of the area. Don’t kill him, sir. We don’t know what lies in wait for us beyond.”

“Fat lot of good that did us just now,” Quintus retorted, releasing the boy again. “At least we might know the name of the damn things that killed a soldier, huh? Caoineag. That’s just damn wonderful.” He stared at Porcius for a few moments, and said, “Promise me this minute that if I’m killed by some nameless horror, you’ll throttle this accursed Celt whelp and not let him laugh at my body. Savvy?”

“Will do,” Porcius promised in a studious voice as

Quintus walked around Severus body along with the rest of the men, cautiously easing toward the entrance of the cavern.

Rufus looked up at Porcius, who held out his right hand. The boy grasped it and was lifted back to his feet.

"Fetch me my sword and shield," Porcius said gently, and turned his head up to look at the night. His body trembled as the boy ran to get his weapons. He then looked at his hand where the water had flowed, alive, ready to kill him, full of spirit. That was blind luck Severus bought it, he mused. If that had been him, he'd not have been able to fight, just lay there and die like a drown puppy. That was no way for a Spartan to perish.

When he returned, Rufus asked, "What troubles you, sir?"

Porcius shrugged and opened his eyes, then cocked his head. He undid his helm strap and pulled it free. "I was someplace else for a moment. Can you hear that?"

Rufus winked as he gave him his implements. "The death on the wind? Yes. I hear it. Your ear is more in tune since . . . " He stopped and looked at the Roman group surrounding the cavern, looking in the distance beyond the forest as well.

"Kid, watch that tongue." Porcius pulled his shield over his arm and winked back at him. "You can still get me stuff and serve August with no tongue in your asinine mouth."

Rufus made a bow that truly mocked Porcius, but the soldier didn't make a note of it by striking him. He understood the Celt no longer content in his simple service and would be dead very soon, either by the hand of Quintus, the edict of Malitus, or dessert for the beastmen. Rufus wasn't special, Porcius ruminated hotly. Thousands of Celt boys had been murdered in the past few centuries by Roman swords.

"What is it?" Porcius wondered as the small crowd of soldiers parted to let him nearer to the opening. He saw the twins move Severus over to one side and put coins on his eyes. He figured that not just an act to pay the ferryman to the realms of death beyond, but stop by buzzards from picking at the eyes first.

Quintus knelt on a single knee, peering into the opening. "I'm not sure I want to know." He didn't turn his head as he ordered, "Bring up the Celt." Rufus slowly walked to Porcius' side and Quintus faced him. "What's down there?"

"The netherworld of the beastmen," Rufus said flatly.

Porcius had to laugh. Once. "You jestin' me, kid?"

"You asked."

Whispering, Porcius replied, "So I did."

Rufus said, "There's a passage down there to where they come from, beyond night, beyond earth, beyond all of your dreams."

The Romans all exchanged looks of confusion until Decimus deadpanned, "Isn't he suddenly helpful?"

"Yeah," Porcius grunted. "A treat for an afternoon and evening, he is."

Rufus stated, "I've heard this is where it is." His voice fell matter-of-factly and Porcius waited for a moment, figuring Quintus would strike the Celt anew. But he didn't.

Quintus stood and stated, "Many lands have scary tales about what lurked in caves or in tunnels under the Earth itself. Many say it is the little folk or giant worms. I've seen no such evidence beyond the nightmares of savages, but this, here, I've seen the giant things and know better."

Porcius asked, "Folks know this place is here, kinda hidden, and leave it be?"

Shrugging, Rufus replied, "Wouldn't you?"

"You got me there, kid." Porcius offered. "We ought to fill it in. Have every damned soul in the Legion grab a shovel and cover this opening up for all time."

Quintus turned to him. "What?"

"It'd take a thousand or more hands, but we should all bury the damn entrance. No use fighting those things and dying."

Quintus looked at the aperture. He thought on that an extensive while. "That might not be a bad idea, Porcius."

"Glad to hear you say it," Porcius coughed and peered in the hole with him. "I don't fancy fighting them all."

One of the men put forth, "Surely there is another entrance, not just one into that damned hole?"

Quintus and Porcius swapped a look, but the Spartan spoke first. "August might be walking into the ass end of it. Wouldn't that be the crap?"

"Wonderful," Quintus muttered. "I'd like to see down in there, though."

The men stepped back, shocked, but Porcius spoke up. "Seriously, sir? Doesn't the trap of the wizard here that slew our brother soldier convince you not to do that?"

"It was meant to scare us," Quintus sniffed, staring into the tunnel.

Porcius eyed the man with spacious eyes and said, "It worked, sir."

"If Drust wanted us dead, wouldn't he have loosed a bigger version of the buggerman, as you called it, some demon or whatever, than just this simple water spirit?"

"Perhaps he only toys with us in the act to kill one of us to make the rest run down there for revenge."

"Revenge? Is that all that motivates men?" Quintus rubbed his chin.

He faced Porcius. "You and the kid, come along with me. The rest of you guard our rear exit. We will venture down a little ways."

"And then?" Porcius asked as Rufus joined him.

Quintus smiled with earnest before he turned to lead the way into the hole. "Then we run like drunken fools at Saturnalia."

It was in the night when a new attack came to the Legion, and when it did, it came from a wholly unexpected direction. Under Malitus and Ralta's orders, the Romans were prepared to stand against the Picts and the bulk of their attention was focused in the direction of the seemingly unending horde of the savages that continued to grow before them in the valley's edge.

Mathew was in command of the squad watching over the Legion's horses for the night. The animals had been tied far back and away from the 9th's forward lines, behind the places where those who could sleep, and others sat about raging fires, talking and hiding their fear of the day to come. The horses had been acting strangely as if the trepidation of the men in the makeshift camp infected them deep inside as well.

When the first of the animals' death cries echoed in the night, Mathew had thought the Picts had somehow maneuvered a few squads around the Roman camp to strike at them from the rear. Such a thing fit with his vision of terrible Pict tactics. A group rushed to secure the many horses, expecting to be facing men with axes and spears, only to find themselves bearing down upon dozens of hair-covered monsters.

"Mishce, warn the others! Everyone else, spread out and kill as many as you can," he ordered at the top of his lungs. "We must save the horses." Inwardly, he laughed darkly at those words. These beasts were smaller than those he had seen in the previous clash. They were closer to man-sized but a single glance at the thick muscles rippling under the hair that hid their flesh told him the things would be far from easy prey.

Thank the gods, most of the monsters broke, disappearing into the trees, as he raised the alarm. Most, but not all. Many stood ready to meet the squads under his command head on.

The Romans and beasts met in a storm of slicing swords and bone crushing fists. One soldier took a punch to his face that left it not much more than a smear upon the front of his head. Another who had leapt forward, thrusting his blade at one of the monsters, got caught and flung through the night like a child's discarded toy. His body bounced from a nearby tree with a sickening crackle only to soon lay still, a crumpled mass upon the ground.

Mathew didn't let those horrors slow him, though. His sword dug deep into one of the beasts' shoulders, cutting meat loose from bone with a sickening squelch.

He recoiled rapidly from the forceful fist that swept downward at him as he readied his sword once more. His next swing created a slit across the stomach of the beastman that stood before him. Its entrails erupted from the opening with explosive force, strands of intestines unfolding into snakes that piled themselves at the monster's feet. The beast's eyes gaped as Mathew brought up his sword into the bottom of its chin, pinning its mouth closed at an angle, before entering up into its brain.

Mathew yanked at his blade but it was stuck inside the monster, wedged between bones, and refused to be pulled free. Cursing, Mathew let it go. Not far from where he stood lay the corpse of a Roman not as lucky as he was. He flung himself towards the fallen man, scooping up his dropped gladius. Even as Mathew did so, another of the monsters was on a B-line for him. It plowed into him with such force that it knocked Mathew from his feet and sent him rolling through the grass. The breath left his lungs in a single heave. As he fought to get to it back, the beast closed in. Its golden eyes burned with a feral madness driven by hunger and frenzy.

Noticing that most of the men of his immediate squads lay dead, Mathew made a promise to himself that he would join them soon, not as a coward but as a Legionnaire. With a yell, he launched himself to his feet, sword in hand. He swung the blade in a wide arc in front of him. Its metal met bone as he severed the hand that the beast had been stretching out towards him. A fountain of blood pumped from the jagged end of its arm where its hand was half a moment before. Mathew pressed his advantage, closing on the thing, and put his full weight upon his blade, sinking it deep into the monster's heart, and driving its body over to the ground.

The familiar sound of singing bowstrings reached his eyes through the chaos of the battle. A group of the 9th's archers had joined the fray. Another beast that lumbered in his direction stopped as three arrows buried themselves in its chest. It looked down at their still vibrating shafts in shock and horror before blood began to bubble from its mouth. It gave Mathew a final sneer before it toppled face forward to move no more.

The arrival of the archers broke the courage of even the bravest of the smaller beasts. The monsters fled back into the darkness from whence they came. His breath came in ragged gasps of exhaustion, and pain from the bruise already forming on his skin, Mathew watched them go, relieved and thankful to still be alive.

He looked to the sky, at the full moon, and wondered why the gods would play such games with them. All his life he'd giggled at the idea of a pantheon of gods up in the sky, drawing lots over the affairs of men. That seemed puerile to him. It still did. But the idea that a god—or gods—created man and these monsters to fight for some mysterious aim, didn't fill him with gladness. However, he pondered, he may soon find out what lurked beyond that curtain of night, and which god was factual, if any at all. That idea scared him as well.

With only hours to go before dawn, and the likelihood of a full out attack by the Picts imminent, the skirmish with the beasts couldn't have come at a worst time. It took a lot of effort for Ralta to put on a smile for the poor youth who led the rear squads to meet the creatures. Truth be told, the youth had done a fantastic job of handling the matter. If not for his quick actions, the Legion might have lost more horses and been undone. Mathew had earned more praise than Ralta had time to give him, but such was life in the military. Nonetheless, Ralta made a mental note to keep the lad in mind for promotion, assuming the both of them survived the next day.

Ralta doubled the rear guard, assigning a good number of archers and slingers to it before returning to where Malitus awaited him.

"What was all that about?" Malitus asked, staring into the darkness and the forests like he could really see what went on within.

"No idea," Ralta shrugged. "The beasts that were killed were all young ones. Could be they were just hungry, and the horses—all tied up in masses like that—were just too tempting a meal to be ignored."

"A youthful rag?"

"Perhaps."

"Ralta, you assign human traits to beasts of the field. Stop that."

"I'll try."

"Or perhaps this was a test." Malitus frowned, sipping a bit of wine, but taking a very tiny drink, trying not to show anyone he was getting drunk to calm his nerves. "It may be that their elders used them as an assessment on us, to see if we remain capable of posing a threat to them despite our heavy losses."

"Now who gives them human qualities?"

Ralta shrugged again. "We can't fight the Picts and those monsters."

"No," Malitus agreed and took a deeper draw on the flask, "But we must."

"I fear so."

"May the gods have mercy upon us come the morning."

Ralta said, "Choose your favorite god and get cozy, sir. You may get to meet them soon."

The General sighed loud and glared at him. "You are the first ray of sunshine this day."

"I try, sir."

Tancorix understood terror, in this world and the one she came from. Although that time was long ago, she understood fear and war. These factors didn't change, thus the world didn't seem too different for her at that moment. The army of Pictdom, their armor, weapons and even their gods didn't match, but they still had the same blood.

When, from out of the night, the group of short hairy beasts ran toward them on the great plain, she thought the new life to be a short one, as even the horses rebelled.

Weaver couldn't react a spell fast enough to protect them from the beast. The creatures ran right past them, and relief spread over her. They exchanged confused looks, but pressed on to rejoin the body of the Pict confederation.

The words of Weaver kept bouncing back on her, and while her initial desire to strike the wizard woman down ran scorching in her veins, she also understood

Weaver to be correct. What power that aging woman must have to be able to reach out across the centuries and pull her to this time. The Queen didn't understand it in full, but did remember her being pulled by her hands in the netherworld, and being cradled like a baby, swimming through a thick mass like water until she returned to the realm of sunlight out of the darkness.

Another thing about Weaver concerned Tancorix, and that was the wizardess' choice in apprentices. Ragala showed her little respect and mouthed off too often. The Queen struggled to understand why Weaver kept her around. Perhaps it was a family obligation or the suggestion of another. From what she saw, though, Weaver took orders from no one in any of Pictdom and all the others of the woods bowed to her, save for Drust.

She heard Weaver's apprentice ask where the beasts were going that scampered past them in the night.

"Back to the bowels of the earth, or to run off the edge of it," Weaver snapped as their horses thundered towards the edge of the great forest.

That mental image made Tancorix want to smile, but she buried the feeling deep. Soon, she could be herself with these folk and they would respect her, not just as a novelty or a supernatural event. There were things she had to do, things she had to find leftover from her ancient time that truly had to endure until that moment. Once she found the tree of life again, things would really change for all of Britannia, as they called the Isle now.

Within a few minutes they stopped, hearing chaos on the wind.

Tancorix wore a panicked look.

Weaver nodded and waved her right arm to keep following her around the edge of the forest. "The young beasts attack the Romans."

Ragala started to applaud over and over, but soon stopped when Weaver's look soured at her.

Tancorix smiled. "Good on them then."

Weaver declared, "Drust must be having a lark in this night after all. Let's hope they eat a few of the faster ones."

When they rode about the edge of the forest, the moonlight showed the Pict pickets, waiting for them and waving them in closer. As they went about the border to the open plain, the Queen saw the encampments of the Pict tribes spreading out as far as she could see. Like flies on rotten meat, the Picts infested the land, hugged the forest and were tough to count.

Then she smiled. This was very good.

Chapter XII

August awoke clutching fistfuls of grass. It felt good being where grass grew tall and wild. His heart thumped fast, as he thought himself free, dragged from the cave of the beastmen and ready to run wild again. He looked up, pining for the oaks of the area of Caledonia where they had invaded, but instead saw tall fir trees, some with fire dripping from the branches.

This reality he perceived couldn't be so. Sadness held him tight and poured across his body, as thick as honey. He thought himself dead with . . . but no . . . this was not to be. Shouldn't heaven look like home? Just by the trees, the time of year of his vision, more closer to full harvest like September not the end of July . . . and the river basin of Ems, which can only be found in Germania in the Teutoburg forest.

Yes, the Romans lost three Legions at that famous battle in Teutoburg forest, and the pitch falling from the fir trees dropped as leftovers from a volley of flaming missiles. However, August couldn't recall this event for real, as he'd been born decades later. There were tales he heard of his great grandsire standing with the rest of the tribes to hand the Romans such a crushing defeat. Granted, he'd played out the scene a hundred times in his head as a child. And yet, here he was, holding the grass in his homeland, at a battle he'd never seen.

"Three full Legions," he grunted to no one. "How did a bunch of muddy barbarians defeat three Legions?"

The story, well told, declared how a confederation of tribes pulled off the mean feat. The Bructeri tribe stood by those of the Chauci and the Chatti alike. Any differences between the Cherusci, Marsi, and his own folk, the Sicambri of the Rhine had been put aside. From a child on, he'd heard the yarns of how they fought for so long and crushed the Romans. This fact, even if the Romans kept coming back, provided hope to all that the disease of Rome could be crushed. The tales seemed illogical once he'd been educated to the ways of Roman warfare, but then again, he chose to think that his blood rose to the task and did what few could do.

August rolled over, saw the skies of Germania overhead, and wept, for they faded away in moments. He'd seen the power of Rome then up close, and how they operated far from his homeland. Rome's war desires ran like a fine mechanism, not flesh and blood. Sometimes, flesh proved well enough, his father had instructed him when showing him the proper way to throw a punch. When he blinked again, the flickering golden lights on the cave walls covered in green lines gave his heart more reason to race. Nevertheless, August had resigned himself to die here in Britannia, under the earth and this reality slapped own his dream of the forest back home.

"Wake up," August heard in Latin, as well as Greek,

and Celtic verbiage. The voice was male and youthful. He thought of young Rufus, at first. He sat up on his elbows in the cave, trying not to be so focused on the domed ceiling full of jagged spikes. He faced the speaker with a sigh. This was a child, a bit younger than Rufus, but not Celtic. This boy had darker hair, so orange it shown flecks of black in it, a strange combination, but the green eyes showed him a Pict. The singlet piece tunic he wore confused August, as it wasn't a normal cloth he'd ever seen, but took it as a rank or status to wear such a well sewn garment.

"I'm awake," August assured him as the scent of the beastmen overwhelmed him. Their raw, earthy, fecal odor permeated the large chamber cupped with the stench of rotten flesh. He thought himself far from the place where they'd first peered inside. He looked to his left or right and saw none of his men, but a few of the gray furred creatures lingered in their living areas not far away. Here this boy stood, unafraid, speaking loud.

"Who are you, kid?"

Eyebrow raised, the child replied, "I am Gonar, apprentice to the high priest and master of all the wood, Drust."

"Good for you." August groaned as he tried to get to his knees, his body full of aches and devoid of weapons. "How is it I'm still alive?"

"My master wishes it, for now."

"Wonderful, Your master around?"

Gonar nodded. "He prepares for the Lammas festival and the great battle to come soon."

"I get to miss that, huh?"

"That's not for me to say."

August looked about at the beasts, many sleeping, but a few awake, eating hunks of human limbs. He nearly gagged. “How is it they don’t eat you or me?”

“They honor my master for now. They do as they must.”

“For now, aye? That doesn’t sound really comforting.” August stood, wobbled, but then planted his feet firm. He noted the child, and how fearless he appeared to be, not flinching as the flesh eating went on within an arm’s reach.

Gonar turned and said, “Come along. I shall show you a wonder.”

They walked about twenty yards in the huge cavern and August saw the glow of a towering shape sporting glowing orbs of light. The one dark furred creature resided at the base of the tree-like shape, laid out, snoring. It reminded August of dogs he’d seen slumber near a burning hearth. Whose pet was this?

They stopped and August asked, “And that is?”

“Adelaido, king of these beastmen”

“He doesn’t look so royal.”

Gonar shrugged. “He’s drunk.”

“On what?”

Gonar looked at him keenly. “Human meat and trying to copulate with the Pict women from the Rutland village.”

“That’s pretty terrible.”

Gonar agreed with a nod. “Yes, precisely so.”

August reached out and turned the boy around. “So this is all right to you? Your own people used as meat and whores? Worse, killed in the process?”

No emotion in his face, nor did he move away, Gonar replied, “You think me a simpleton? Of course this is inhuman. Not even barbarians, as you call them, would condone such acts among their own men. A man caught in perversion is thrown into a bog, a great stone tied to his back. No, but don't preach to me, man of Germania that bows to Rome, of what is right to do under the threat of invasion or death itself."

August's look intensified. "How can you know that?"

"I'm a wizard's apprentice. You should see me do sleight of hand with a coin."

August wanted to backhand the child, and was certain the kid would've taken it and smiled, but the form of Drust came into view from about the tree of glowing balls.

"We meet at last, man of Germania," Drust said, but he looked up at the tree of light, as if he spoke to it and not August.

"You don't know me at all," August said as they came closer to the big tree and Drust. "Nor do I you, really."

"But you are mistaken," Drust replied as the boy walked over and stood by his right side. He looked at August and the light of the swirling orbs danced on the side of his face. "I have seen your dreams in the vast ether-realm, smelled your true courage on the wind, and yes, beheld you from afar. I know you are not like them, like the Spartan who plays games in the spirit realm with the arisen Queen Tancorix. I know what you feel and that who you pray to is quite contrary to what your Roman lords love, no?"

"So what does any of that matter? You and these things are out to kill us."

Drust smirked. "But we all know this. I see from

your dreams you recalled a time when your peoples did the same thing to the Romans."

August trembled, afraid that the wizard had indeed looked inside his dreams, or caused them. "Why am I alive?"

"Rufus, the boy that is your body servant, he spoke highly of you."

"Yes?"

"I read it in his mind, even if he despises you for being a slave to Rome."

"I see." He thought about that and it made sense, Rufus really hating him. He'd have to live with that uncomfortable fact, but it might be a short time. "Well, now, if I see him in the next world, I'll thank him."

Drust shook his head. "No need." He turned and from one of the tunnels walked Rufus, his face listless, but soon breaking and running for August. He embraced his master and choked back a few tears as they separated.

"What are you doing here?" August asked, his hands on the boy's shoulders, then gently clasping his hair.

Rufus turned and looked back the way he came. In a moment, August understood, as he saw Quintus, Porcius, and the twins step into the light.

Drust looked up at the tree, and so did the rest of them. "Now, gentlemen, what shall we talk about?"

"Riders!" one of the sentries shouted as Ralta rushed forward at his cry. The battle hardened, giant of a man looked out passed the edge of the Roman lines to see them coming. He could tell at a glance they were merely the pickets he'd ordered out returning. Yet, they were not alone. A huge man, bounced and grunted along the rough ground, dragged behind one of the Roman horses on a thick rope.

The Roman line parted to allow the riders entrance. The battered man they had brought with them was a Pict warrior, denoted by his size, orange hair, tattoos and foul smell.

"Sir," the commanding officer of the pickets addressed Ralta. "We found this one here snooping around at the border of the forest."

"Did you now?" Ralta yawed and looked him over, bored.

"We decided to bring him in for questioning."

Ralta didn't know whether to laugh or cry at the words of the young officer. It was good he showed such initiative but utterly pointless to take a prisoner for questioning now. The Picts were not far, and gathered for the coming assault. There was likely little this man could tell them that they couldn't figure out themselves.

Giving the young officer a quick, vague nod, Ralta watched as the riders dismounted. The Pict warrior, though alive, lay in rough shape. Entire patches of his flesh had been scraped away. Blood smeared rags were all he wore for clothing. Even with the best medical care the Legion could offer, Ralta gave the man a day or two at best. Still, the Pict warrior's eyes burned fierce, if very pained, as they met Ralta's. His hands were bound up fast, but the rope that had pulled him now lay limp, discarded on the ground.

When Ralta made no move to approach the man and question him, those gathered around the Pict began to taunt him. Some poked at him with their swords, some drawing blood as they nicked his already heavily injured body. Another used the butt of his spear to shove the Pict around. Others threw small rocks until one brave soldier walked straight up to the Pict, shoving him back into the dirt. Laughter abounded, but it was short lived.

The Pict grabbed the soldier's ankle and jerked. The soldier fell hard onto the ground and screamed as the savage rolled on top of him. The Pict's teeth tore at the soldier's throat, working upon it like a crazed wolf. Blood spurted out in a fount from the soldier's neck as the Pict reared his head back in victory, paying no attention to the geyser of red that washed over his chin and cheeks.

The Pict's eyes were feral then. Ralta could see the man was lost in blood borne fury. The time for games had ended. A group of his men closed in on the Pict, kicking his battered body even as he clawed and bit at their legs.

"Enough!" Ralta ordered as he shoved his way through his men, drawing his sword. "This gains us nothing and has lost us a man."

Ralta plunged his sword deep into the Pict's heart. The Pict warrior's hands closed around the blade of Ralta's sword, its metal sinking into them and releasing fresh rivulets of blood. The Pict gave a final growl as his eyes rolled upwards to show only whites and his body flopped, unmoving, to rest at Ralta's feet.

Pulling his blade free of the dead Pict, Ralta knelt and wiped it clean on the grass. As he did so, the men around him were silent. Ralta understood this sudden quiet as fear of his anger, but his own silence stemmed from the horrors his supposedly civilized peers were capable of in times of war. He had seen it all before on many fields, in many lands. It was one thing to kill in service to the emperor and an entirely different thing to vent your own fears on a helpless man, savage or not. The whole affair had left a bad taste in Ralta's mouth but such was the way of the world.

"One could only hope for a better tomorrow."

The men looked to each other, unsure of what he meant, but stayed at attention.

As Ralta rose, Malitus walked into view, the crowd parting before him as he came. "Ralta?" he asked seeing the giant's sour expression. "Trouble?"

Ralta shook his head. "No, sir. Just cleaning up a mess that happened upon us. It has been a strange night."

"I see that," Malitus smiled, eyes wide at the body at their feet. "Was he a messenger?"

Again, Ralta shook his head in the negative. "A scout or a spy perhaps for that dearth of savages over the way. Either way, he's been dealt with."

"I think it's past time we spoke with these Picts and told them that the 9th will not surrender without a fight. Choose two men, good ones, and send them to the Picts under a sign of peace. There's no harm in trying to warn them off before things go in the pot and if this Queen of theirs will agree to an audience, so much the better for us all."

No harm to you, Ralta thought, but answered, "Yes, my General. I'll do so at once."

Malitus yawned, stretching his arms. "I think I'll catch a quick rest before things get truly interesting. It is a beautiful morning, though."

Ralta stared after the General as he disappeared through the crowd, heading back to the center of the camp. While he slept, Ralta would be busy deciding which two men to send, possibly, into the cold, cruel arms of death. He wished to go himself, truly, as he'd love to talk to the Queen of the Picts. Ralta understood he'd probably not return if he did so, though. The men reacted to the smile he couldn't curb, and took on unease steps in their stances. He grew somber, not wanting them to be assailed by any more uncertainties.

He felt the war coming, that the Picts wouldn't listen to reason and just disperse. They understood the Legion would keep going up into their lands and divide their world in half . . . then into smaller sections. No, they would fight, not go home and wait for servitude.

In his mind's eye, Ralta wanted that forest set to fire with pitch and a sign that they should run. Perhaps they'd listen, but his hopes were in vain, he figured. Though the closed ranks of the army would pinwheel their way through and army of barbarians, Ralta didn't like the other factor on the battlefield, that of the beastmen lurking nearby.

Once morning broke, Tancorix and Weaver did as the other Picts did. They ate and laughed, telling funny tales and mostly listening to those from the chiefs of the tribes. Some came from far away, from the isles of the northern seas, many with young men spoiling for a fight to prove their manhood.

Ragala sat silent, so much so Weaver muttered, "What has your tongue this morn? Usually, you wag it too much."

The girl whispered, "To make such impractical merriment in the face of war and such horrors, how can this be right?"

Weaver gave a soft chuckle, but a great Pict war chief, his hair so think his mouth couldn't be discerned, laughed loud. All fell silent as the birds sang overhead.

"We walk side by side with death, every day, girl," the Pict war chief thundered, slapping his grimy right fist against his heart. "Death is a part of life."

One of his soldiers, another thuggish man sporting a shock of orange hair, said, "Yeah, it is, the last part!"

They all smiled and many laughed at the loud words.

The chief stared at Ragala intently. "Be at peace, wee lass. There is no such thing as eternal death, girl. Life goes on, in another form."

Ragala retorted, "How can you know that for sure?"

The chief grinned, showing a mouthful of darkened teeth. "My grandsire Alethea told me so, and she wouldn't lie." Again, laughter rippled in the ranks and the chief finally said, "The testimony of my senses tells me life goes on and on. I look to the wonderful sky, the eternal bed of stars the gods paint their magicks on, and see no end to it. I feel the earth under my feet and bow to kiss it warmly. It is good to be alive. Yes, it truly is, wee lass. It is good to be here this day and good to die." The men all grunted their approval loud and so did the women in the area. "But if we can crush the rotten Romans, that's all the better, huh?"

As they all roared with approval, Ragala shouted out something she had to repeat as the noise died down. "What of the beastmen?"

The war chief upended a skin of wine and then let the red juice trickle from his beard, giving indication where his maw did reside. "What about 'em?"

"How can you battle them?"

The chief winked. "When one doesn't fear death, that helps out quite a lot, but they don't scare me in the slightest."

Hands fists, Ragala demanded, "Why?"

The chief drank again and spat. "They can die, little girl. Everything can die." His raw countenance suddenly took on a twisted facade of humor as he glanced toward Tancorix and Weaver. "Accept for that Queen of ours over there and a few of the kindly wizards of the woods, yeah, everything can die in the flesh. Even the great goddess bested our risen Queen once, so long ago, if one believes bar songs and fables of the campfires."

Again, loud howls of laughter rocked the green glade and they all settled in to finish eating. Slobbering and chomping replacing laughs fast, but smiles still abounded as they ate heartily of a fortifying breakfast.

Tancorix whispered to Weaver, "Who is that one? The biggest man who spoke?"

Weaver never looked up from munching berries and replied, "Taloric. He's a true warrior, but anyone can see that."

"Agreed."

"The big man who shadows him and mimics his every move? That'd be Mosnar, nephew of Taloric."

"Do they all follow him?"

Weaver shook her head slightly, but still didn't look up. "The tribe of the Caereni certainly do. They are from the western highland and the north far to the seas. Good fighter for the leader of sheepherders. Mosnar is his muscle if he decides not to use his own. He's built like a tree trunk and I doubt any fear runs in his veins."

Tancorix finished eating and walked out into the open meadow where thousands of Picts reclined, eating. Weaver and her apprentice soon followed her. They walked a bit away from them in the open tall grasses.

Weaver asked her, "Something on your mind, my Queen?"

Tancorix eyes flickered, wondering about her use of that word. "You said they all don't fight for Taloric?"

"Gods, no, my Queen. Most tribes hate each other, but they hate Rome and their tentacles a great deal more."

"Then for me?"

Weaver nodded. "You're a legend and from another place, back in their own gloomy history. Many saw your resurrection and the story traveled far. The tribes understood my magicks and I had a great audience to do my magick. Many told of the ceremony and your emergence from the egg on the altar near Rutland town."

"It didn't bother you to be watched so as this happened?"

Weaver snorted quietly. "Men play like little boys not being able to piddle when another is near. I don't care who watches me rip this reality in half."

"So, they believe I am myself and will follow me?"

"Yes. They want the Romans dead too and a united land here would be a good thing. Look good and keep your breasts up when you walk by them all. They know who you are and where you came from. The fact that you live gives them reason to fight. They hear of magicks and some have seen such acts of simple enchantment, but you, huh, you are the embodiment of hope through my wizardry. You make them feel invincible."

"These tribes, they are not as my people in the past."

Weaver scoffed. "Of course not. Your time was thousands of years ago before the great deluge. No, these all are different, some carry standards, like the Taexali tribesmen who are taken with themselves and their great town of Devana. They are no better or worse than their neighbors, the Vacomagi that camp back by the trees there."

"Why do they camp farther away?"

Weaver shrugged. "I'm not sure, to be honest. Perhaps they are not as impressed with you as the others. I have visited their towns of Tamia and Tuesis in the past. They do great brick work and are strong as oxen. If you can see, their spears are as thick as a man's foreman. One of those will go through a man or beastman"

"And the rest?" Tancorix waved across the plain at so many divisions in tribes, but all similar in appearance and clothing.

"The Carnonacae, the Cornovii, the Creones and the Venicones, those bastards will fight to the end. They look for a reason to kill. They are half mad once the blood scent gets on them. They hunt well, especially the Venicones."

"Do any lack courage?"

"No. All are good fighters, but some are less

experienced in great, grand warfare like what is to come. The Decantae are sort of inbreds with tribes from afar, but are want to prove their manhood to overcome such a title. The Lugi are few and their women folks a bit hairier than the rest, but they fight better than their men."

"Why are they so hairy?"

Weaver shrugged. "They just are. I don't know the jests of the gods. The Smertae, my tribe, are a good folk, but what else would I say of them? They are not as known in the world as the Caledonii, but those bastards are mostly Celts anyway, or that is the thought."

"I see."

Weaver took a drink and nodded hard. "They will fight for you, my Queen. We will crush the Romans."

"I enjoy your confidence."

"Good, see that you share it, or at least fake it in front of them."

Tancorix wondered, "And what about the beastmen?"

Weaver looked back across the plain at the great forest as if she could spy Drust out there beyond the woods. "That is another matter."

"Do you understand why Drust has brought them here?"

"His line was that he brought them forth from the inner earth to destroy the Roman invaders of Pictland."

Tancorix looked at her sideways. "You don't accept that readily, correct?"

"Correct. I know Drust very well. I know what he's really after in life, but that's always unattainable."

"And that is?"

Weaver sighed loud and spread her arms out and looked up as if to embrace the heavens. "Immortality. Piss on the Romans."

"One cannot live forever," Tancorix nodded, looking at her own hands.

Weaver dropped her arms but kept looking up. "It's a terrible thing when one has lived longer than all living men, for centuries and then, one starts to die having never found the answer to immortality."

"Even I know this flesh is all I have and someday, I must die."

"Many died so that you may live. Not many could live with themselves after what I have done. However, the weak and the deformed have served their purpose." Weaver looked at her. "Yes. And some are not happy that they have to die. At all."

"You said Drust is dying?"

Weaver mocked, "We're all dying, my Queen, since the day we are born." The wizardess waved her off. "I must pray and sacrifice for the coming fight."

"When will we come to war?"

"Soon."

"It is exciting, no?"

Weaver didn't look at her. "Not specially. My lust runs in a different way than that of war. You can kill a man but once."

Flavius sat on his behind outside the door of the Fogou. He couldn't stop shaking no matter what he covered himself in or how much he hugged himself. His guts were empty, all voided, either by gagging or releasing naturally from below. He felt like a coward.

"I'm true politician material, father," he said to no one for all the men with him were dead or left in the tunnels of the earth.

August, his friend, got dragged back into the chamber by the monsters, and two of the soldiers with them died trying to stop it.

Flavius watched. He couldn't raise his sword or shield. He just looked on as they all disappeared from his sight. He couldn't bring himself to do anything as men he knew were turned inside out by the Greymen. Though he didn't hear August cry out, he assumed him dead as well at their touch. The powerful man from Germania constantly gave him confidence that tomorrow would always rise. Now, Flavius felt so alone and afraid, a world away from everything he grew up to love. He'd fled and backed away, escaping with his life, such as it was.

Eyes shut tight, he saw the others run before he did. They all ran down the tunnel toward the place of bones. Flavius felt a little forgiveness in that he ran last, but this soon dissipated when they ran into the group of younger beast men in the tunnel. All of the men died, but killed the creatures, youthful as they were so small. He helped in that, but alone survived.

Not impressed with his showing as a soldier or a man, Flavius slowly put his clothes back on and tried to straighten himself up. He didn't see the Legion in the daylight by Rutland and didn't expect to, but walked out to the rough path that passed for a road out of the town. He wondered where the populace was, still, and doubted they'd ever return.

He followed the path of the Legion, clearly leaving a trail as they marched and wheeled their siege artillery farther north. Flavius walked in the open down the middle of the road, but suddenly felt afraid. He then went to one side of the road more, following the ruts in the ground, but then he eyed the forest. He stepped back into the middle of the road. The image of a long arm swiping out and slapping his head off wouldn't leave his mind. He'd loathe it if he were walking along and suddenly wandered into the afterlife, greeted by his grandsire and others laughing that he didn't know how he arrived there. Then again, he thought, it could be worse than that. The beasts would hit him low and maim him up bad, and eat him slowly for a week.

"I don't want to die here, I don't," Flavius said to the air. He thought of home, of the warmth of Naples, and how golden the sun looked there . . . not streaks of white light as in these dreaded muddy isles. "Gods, help me find my way on to my home." He stopped for a moment, looked back south the way they all came, and pondered returning that way. Running like mad until he collapsed sounded really fine at first. If he did and survived by some jest of the gods, and the Legion returned from Caledonia, he'd be found out . . . then executed as a traitor. He swallowed hard and turned to the north, knowing nothing good lay there.

Truly at a crossroads in his life, Flavius wept. He then knelt down and got sick again, but nothing came out.

An hour after Ralta dispatched the two men to ride to where the Picts encamped beyond the forest, they returned. Well, their horses did. Though diplomacy could work, Ralta usually used it via his men sent out to get info on his enemy. The bodies of the men were tied onto the backs of the horses. The heads of the riders were gone and blood caked their shoulders and down the front of their armor. Ralta met the two horses personally and led them into the Roman lines. He cut the corpses loose and they fell from the animals.

"Well, you have given me great information on our enemy after all. This is very clear. Oh Queen," Ralta lamented loudly. "Talking to you would've been a delight, but truly, it wouldn't be worth such a fate."

Only then did Ralta and those around him gathering in notice the dead men's armor had been removed and put back on incorrectly. He removed the men's armor chest plates to see stitches sewn into the flesh of their stomachs, not quite sealing up the heads inside of their body cavities. One man's nose poked out just above where his belly button should have been, the long threads crossing his nostrils like a bow.

"By the gods," Ralta yelled and leaped to his feet, the host of men drawing back as well. "What sort of monster does something like this?"

None of the soldiers around him appeared to have an answer though several did take a knee to vomit up their last meal.

"Get the General," Ralta commanded, hands turning to fists and his look of hot anger not hidden to anyone.

Minutes later, Malitus stood with him, staring

down at the butchered corpses of those chosen to be his representatives.

"I . . . I didn't realize they would . . . " Malitus started to apologize.

"Leave it be, sir," Ralta warned, his revulsion and anger leveling out. "Not all of the experience in the world or learnings from the scrolls of wise men can prepare a civilized man for such barbarity in its natural state."

"What swine."

"I ask only that you see now that there will be no talking with those savages out there. None at all."

"I concur."

"They are as much animals as the beastmen. What rational mind decides that this is the answer to any question? What sort of man or even female could conceive of such a terrible thing?"

Malitus continued to stare at the corpses. "Are they?"

"Yes," Ralta said in almost a whisper. "The head of each man is *inside* the bowels of the other. That head belongs to the other man."

"Mithras . . . " a soldier nearby called on his deity as he heard the words and suddenly comprehended the savageness of the act.

Ralta turned to the men and pointed at the bodies. "Take a good look. This is the fate of a man who flinches or finds himself a coward on this day. You think the beastmen eating you is a bad thing? Look at the kindness of Pictdom. They are all about souls being in the head. This is probably some joke or domination game they play at."

Malitus made a sick noise, covering his mouth with

his right hand. He shook off his queasiness like the veteran he was though. "It is done then."

"Yes, it is. But the greater play awaits, sir."

"Our only answer to those savages now can be *our* blades inside them."

"A fate too kind for them, sir." Ralta frowned.

"Agreed."

"But in this less than perfect world, I'll settle for it."

Malitus upended his flask but found it empty. He cursed and then said, "Indeed."

Chapter XIII

Porcius stood not far from Quintus and the twins, still stunned from their entry into the underworld they currently inhabited. He remembered taking the point after Severus' death, going down with Quintus at his back into the cavern. His mind reeled at seeing the two reptiles behind stone bars. He shivered at that memory. He'd seen crazy animals from the African continent, but those things they left behind on their way down were incomprehensible. Like the beastmen, those were something spewed from the doors of nightmares or the realms of real demons. He did note the five sided star on each set of bars, and recognized that symbol as one used by the tribes in Britannia. What perplexed him was the crooked cross over the pentagram, and what that power implied. Some symbols were older than man, or things dealt with my ones not from here, be they gods, devils or men of a different epoch.

But they'd had little time to ponder these things or sights, nor see farther into the inner chamber when the host of youthful beastmen were set on them, coming down the ramp and subduing them, killing all in the party, save for Quintus, Rufus, the twins and himself.

He recalled the fight and being brained by one of the youthful beastmen just as he slew one of the smaller creatures. True, he'd thought himself dead then as he fell, and since it all happened through his eyes as a slowed down version of reality, Porcius figured his days were done.

He then soon enjoyed the bleary dreams of an eternal bathhouse full of naked women that swirled in his mind. Nonetheless, these wonderful images soon busted apart and a more painful actuality slammed into his mind. Drust and his little apprentice woke them up and said they had a friend of theirs to see them. Angry that he may have to die more than once, Porcius arose, head throbbing and body aching. He was very cheerful, in a way, to see it was August, though it meant the German was just as screwed as the rest of them.

"August!" Porcius called out and jogged over to him, giving him an embrace, not caring for the looks Drust imparted at his actions.

"Happy to see me?" August half laughed, eyes still on the glowing orbs of the mock tree near him. "We all get to perish together? What a grand time it will be after all!"

Porcius chuckled, unsure what to think. "As it should be."

Quintus' jaw tightened as he walked to the men and turned to Drust. "All right, you have us. What is this now? What are these things hereabouts and why have you done this?"

Drust walked near to the glowing fake tree, the dancing lights across his face showed every bit of his age. Like a cut down tree, the lines in his face betrayed him as an ancient oak, full of supplementary lines and more ridges than one might think possible.

"Lammas is upon me." He then let his breath go and muttered, "Us."

August looked at Porcius and then Drust. "I've heard of it."

Drust's manner tightened. "From the lips of a starving slave or a tortured prisoner? Isn't that the way Romans learn from their new subjects?"

"You generalize, but . . . " August's voice hesitated.

Drust smirked, but still looked at the tree. "Aren't you entertaining? You know what bastards the Romans are, German."

Quintus stepped forward, flanked by the twins. "Watch your tongue, August."

Face to face with Quintus, August replied, "Or what? You'll have me flogged?" His manner hardened as he leered at Quintus. "Go ahead, call on your men to have me beaten into submission like a good servant. I'll wait right here for them to get me. You have bigger problems, sir, like living another minute."

Quintus' look drilled into August's face, but he made no further move or speak.

Porcius asked, "What of Lammas? That's important to you, isn't it Drust?"

The ancient man slowly turned and looked at them. His features nearly blotted out by the glow behind him. "You are somewhat wise, if a glutton, Spartan. Life is important and days of the year, precious to our group and folk."

August said, "You don't mean the Picts, do you? You speak of your druid cast."

Drust sighed and his humor faded away. "Druid.

That is a word you filthy men in armor use to describe what they don't understand. There are few in our assemblage these days, but we guide all those around, and yes, the Picts are our folk of this region. Rufus knows our cousins in the low lands, even if they are just Celts."

Rufus put his head down and said nothing.

Porcius glanced at Rufus, but noted Drust's apprentice staring at the tree. "What does Lammas and your kindred have to do with these monsters?"

Stepping up to face Drust head on, August asked, "Did you bring them here, bring them forth from the earth?"

Drust's moderate politeness faded away. "Like seeds planted in the dirt? Fascinating idea, but not quite so."

Quintus stepped closer, accusing Drust, "And you have no problem feeding your own kind and kindred to these things? What sort of religious leader are you?"

Drust's look at Quintus hardened. "Sacrifices are made in war, Roman. You know this more than most do, or is it you care less than the others? How many innocents or regular folk have fallen down dead under the heel of Rome in the name of your great progress or the whim of a mad emperor? How many poor people or their children have been killed or made a part of your war machine in the name of advancing civilization?"

Quintus raised his right hand, but then lowered it. Porcius figured him unwilling to strike the aged druid in this realm of beastmen.

Drust stared at Quintus a long time. "You want to kill me, don't you?"

"Your grasp of the obvious is great indeed."

"I'll pass on soon, but not by your hand. It is the natural stem of life, death, you know? We can try to put it off and can, but all things die. The spirit and soul, though, live on, forever, either here or beyond night in the realms of light."

Left foot stamping, Quintus scoffed. "I don't care to debate religion with you, woodsman. Who are you to preach to me about anything much?"

August stepped up to Drust, and the apprentice Gonar stood between them. "But why? What's the thing with these dirty beasts even for? You have an army of a hundred thousand Picts out there, the running scouts estimate, why use these creatures on us? Insurance? To get a rise out of us? And at the cost of your own folk?"

Drust focused on August. "Another wise man amongst the fools. Yes, indeed, but the creatures serve my purpose." His mouth barely moved as Drust said, "It's all about blood."

"Blood?" August nearly spat back.

After he stepped back from them a little, Drust replied, "Yes, all about blood. Even that new religion you pray to is based on blood sacrifice, German, so it is not uncommon."

Quintus stared at August, not understanding clearly by his dumbfounded look, but he soon glared back at Drust.

"Blood is life and without it, death," Drust explained, eyes closed. "With enough of it, even the gods are happy." Eyes flickering open, Drust walked about the glowing tree. "It's all about blood, all faiths of this planet, you see. That's what is going on in the eternal battle of light and dark that rages beyond night itself."

Porcius' eyes narrowed at Drust. "You need blood?"

He didn't answer and the twins exchanged a look.

Porcius added, "A lot of it?"

"Yes," Drust hissed, his face again illuminated by the tree, his right hand reaching down to caress the hairy cranium of Adelaido who rolled on his side and balled up his body like a fist, not seeming to be aware of any words spoken.

August asked the question Porcius was going to. "What for?"

"For life," Drust said, eyes glowing near to unadulterated white in the bizarre light.

The whole of Pictdom gathered about Weaver on the opposite side of the valley. Back into the trees of the opposite forest, she stood by a semi-circle indentation in the tree line. She glanced behind her at the small stone slab set atop two tiny rocks. The crowd grew silent as she pulled up the sleeve of her left arm and pulled a torque from her bicep. She held this swirled torque of iron high for all to see and chanted out words. She kissed the object wetly, leaving much salvia, wiped the torque on her forehead, slapped it to her heart like a sucker punch, licked the side of it again and cast it into the semi-circle of open space.

When she threw the object, all of the Picts took a knee and quite a few gasped.

Her hands then held high, she chanted again.

From out of the woods came Ragala and Tancorix.

Though the Queen walked with her hands on her hips, the girl Ragala carried a bloody mass in each hand. The girl stood by her mistress as Weaver chanted on. She dropped her hands and reached down, taking their bloody objects from the girl. She turned, faced the crowd and held up her hands.

The Picts bowed their heads, for the most part, but many peeked. They'd all heard what she held that morning . . . the hearts of the two men from the Roman delegation up to the sky.

Weaver cried loud. Soon, she turned and walked into the edge of the woods. With a groan, she knelt by the stone altar. Weaver put down the hearts and leveled her bloody hands flat over them. After a few moments of speaking and clicking her tongue to her teeth, Weaver dropped her palms to the hearts, clutched them up tight in her grip and pushed them over close, nearly bumping them together.

"Arise, tribes of Pictdom," she hissed, not seeming to care of any heard her, but her voice echoed out of the woods so loud quite a few standing took a step back. They all looked about, unable to understand how her voice came out so thunderous and rolled across the dell. "We will march on this morning, thousands of hearts, but one beat." She then dashed the hearts together, causing her apprentice to jump and Tancorix to step backwards out of the grove. Her hands ground the hearts collectively and she pulled her digits back from the mess on the altar. Weaver slashed at the hearts like she chopped them with the side of her hands, but never touched them. Smoke arose from the altar all about where the hearts touched stone. "From the smoke of this altar, humble and simple, bless us to stop the hearts of all Romans, here and forevermore across the earth, all the days of our lives."

She stood and stepped aside, the folds of her robe showing any close enough to see that the combined heart was afire.

The Picts moaned as one and uttered the name of their goddess, "Roan!"

Tancorix's face twitched at the invoking of the goddess and stepped forward to say, "Rise and take up your arms, tribes of Pictdom. We shall go forth and slay them all to the last man."

"Shall we?" a male voice called out, breaking the eerie silence.

Weaver's jaw dropped and Tancorix blinked hard, surprised.

The crowd stood again, and from the countless ranks of Picts came Mosnar, the stout, thuggish warrior, long hair waving in the breeze. "You will lead us, aye? The one the goddess Roan cast in the flames of Hell?"

Tancorix, hands still on her hips, looked down on Mosnar from her elevated position by the trees. "Yes. That's why you called me back from across the centuries."

"Yeah," Mosnar snapped her off. "I've heard that whole story. We've all heard it. Most of us saw you arise from the dead at that ceremony, pop out of that egg as a young girl. Are you worth the colts sacrificed for you? That doesn't mean you can fight your way out of a dung heap."

Hand dropping to her sides, Tancorix replied, "I'll take on any man you offer."

Taloric stepped out from the crowd to stand with

Mosnar and the gasps reechoed about the group. "I concur with my nephew, Queen," he said sarcastically, but no menace lurked in his words. "I'd like to see who I'm going to fight and die for."

Tancorix looked to Weaver, who betrayed no emotion as she wiped her hands off on a cloth already bloody from Ragala cleaning her hands.

"Form a circle," Tancorix commanded. "I assume this is still done?"

Taloric nodded quickly, slapped Mosnar on the back and stepped back into the ranks of his looming tribesmen.

Tancorix stepped into the circle of Picts. Across from her, Mosnar entered as well to the sounds of many a grunt in the multitude. She would soon wipe the smug sneer of contempt from his face, Tancorix thought.

Ragala whispered, "We have no time for this!"

Unconcerned, Weaver kept wiping her hands. "There's always time for one on combat, girl. Shut your mouth and learn for once."

The brute of a man advanced upon her slowly, egged on by those about them desperate to see what happened next. His movements were unhurried and filled with confidence. Though he wore boots fashioned out of deer hides with souls well worn, he wore little armor, save for a bronze piece covering his manhood and a stolen Roman chest-plate that didn't fit his barrel chest well. His dagger remained sheathed upon his hip for he must have felt no need for it.

Their eyes met, each waiting on the other to make the first move.

With the reflexes of a feral cat, Tancorix dived at

Mosnar's legs, but he slapped the top of her head, driving her mound of red hair into the grass. This move earned the guffaws and sarcastic applause of the Picts belonging to his tribe and the uneasy murmurings of most of the rest watching. She recovered quickly, surprised that Mosnar didn't take the opportunity to kick her in the ribs when she lay prone for a moment. *No, the big fool*, she thought, *he toys with me like a feline and a wounded mouse.*

Tancorix circled him and tried to be patient.

Finally, Mosnar came forward, with a shriek, his arms extended, making a grab for her. Smoothly with an uncanny grace, she slid between those great arms, thrusting her open palm outward to connect with his chin. The blow knocked his head back as Mosnar grunted, spitting a few blackened teeth. Tancorix allowed him no time to recover. She ducked low, one of her long legs snaking beneath his lumbering feet to sweep them from under him. Mosnar cried out as he toppled hard to the earth, more out of shock at the maneuver than in pain.

The crowd took a breath, but many clapped and cheered the stunning move. Quite a few people up front took a knee so more could see to the back. All throughout the crowd many whispered and hissed, telling those farther back what happened and so on until the talk sounded like a lurid halo of wasps in the meadow.

First blood was hers as Tancorix allowed Mosnar to return to his feet. His smugness was gone. Anger flushed his cheeks as he wiped blood from his split lip with the back of his right hand. Tancorix felt his eyes gauging her as Mosnar hesitated, taking the time to consider his next attack. Still, his dagger remained in its sheath. Not so with her own. Tancorix gripped the handle of her dagger tightly, readying it.

Round and around she stalked him, jabbing the blade forward, but not once arriving close to his flesh. She tested Mosnar's reflexes, but felt he held back and didn't offer much in the way of revelation. Even that big Mosnar realized she tested him.

Mosnar growled through his shattered teeth. "If that's the best you got little Queen, you're going back to the land of the dead."

"Come and make good your boast," she laughed, eyes afire and on him.

"Is it true the legend Gorias La Gaul ate you for supper?" He smiled his bloody grin and many in the crowd clapped, having heard such a tale. "That your soul was contained within him for all of his life after that?"

Eyes unblinking, still moving around him, Tancorix said, "Gorias didn't . . . well, in death that is . . . no one lives forever . . . "

Tired of her talking, Mosnar charged at her once more. She stepped forward, her right foot flashing upwards in a round house kick towards his throat. Mosnar caught her by the ankle, smiling. Tancorix returned his smile, slashing the wrist of the hand that clutched her ankle. Blood flew as her blade tore his flesh. Mosnar shrieked and let go, trying to back away, amazed at her bend and dexterity to pull off that shot. The dagger went through his leather wrapped wrist guard, but he was glad to show all that the veins of this wrist were intact.

Taloric sighed loudly, but shook his head. He never

entered the circle. His tribe raised their voices, cheering on their man.

Weaver looked on, no emotion, arms still folded, watching.

Tancorix soon was on Mosnar, though. In a wild, frenzied dance, she moved about him, her blade spinning in her fingers for a moment, then clutched tight, raking and stabbing until her circle about her opponent went complete. The Queen stood before him just as she had only a moment before. Blood dripped and flowed from a half dozen minor wounds covering his stout frame. Tancorix met his eyes and saw that she had made a mistake. Tancorix had underestimated the burly warrior and was about to pay dearly for it, she thought. Mosnar's speed matched her own, allowing her no time to dodge as he came out of his shell and leapt. His fist struck the side of her skull as he lunged out at her in desperation. The brightness of pain blinded Tancorix as she reeled from Mosnar's blow. Her lungs emptied themselves of all air as the Pict warrior followed up that move with a fist that rammed into her midsection with such force, she crumpled over.

Fool, she cursed herself, fighting through the pain as she gasped for air. If she didn't act fast, all was lost. Mosnar stood above her and his right foot came driving downward at her head. She barely rolled away in time to escape having her skull fractured or worse.

The Picts all roared in cheers, loving the action and display.

Weaver watched still, arms folded under her bosom, no emotion on her face. She breathed very slowly as if timing something out. Her apprentice glared at her as if she should help the Queen, but Weaver didn't acknowledge the girl whatsoever.

As Tancorix sprang to her feet, Mosnar was ready for her. His backhanded slap jerked her head to the left, sending a spray of red from Tancorix's mouth as the flesh of her lips met teeth. Before she could recover, he had her enveloped. His thick arms wrapped around Tancorix's lithe body, lifting her from the ground. Tancorix's feet kicked fiercely as she struggled to break the brutal hold. His arms tightened, smothering her against his chest and threatening to break the Queen's spine. Mosnar's head snapped forward into her own, stunning her with the head-butt. Tancorix's vision suddenly came edged with darkness but she refused to allow it to claim her.

Mosnar laughed, saying, "The immortal Queen of the Picts? My hairy, aching ass." More of the men laughed along with him and several voiced their displeasure at the display. "No man would be allowed to best you? Is that why the baby goddess Roan beat you? Isn't that what the drunken men of the bars say, hugging their harps close rather than a woman?" Mosnar giggled. "I'll send my ten-year-old next time, you hear me Queen? He handles my light work."

Those words roared in her mind, and she understood that eternity drew near. Tancorix gritted her bloody teeth for all she could think on was that she couldn't come back across the shades of night to die like this.

The hand that still clutched her dagger twisted about and tried to stab upwards, but the weapon didn't find a home. Mosnar effectively pinned her arms down as he grappled her in close, figuring her knife would be a factor. Not beaten yet, she slithered a little and thrust her backside against his manhood. He shook a little, not ready for such a sensation, and Mosnar's grip slackened, just a little. That slight bit, that bare fraction of an inch was all she needed to strike.

She thrust up fast, burying the blade to the hilt in Mosnar's arm pit. His wail was like that of a wounded cat's as he released her, stumbling backwards.

As the crowd took a step back, many fell down in the rear guard, but Taloric and many warriors hemmed the circle still, unmoved, but openly frowning at this turn.

Tancorix landed on her feet, coming fully upright, sucking wind into her bloody lips. "I am Queen," she shouted. "Forever!"

Mosnar drew his knife at last.

She advanced, kicking away his dagger as it came out in a move that made all but Weaver gasp loud. The knife flipped to the grass and she attacked anew, diving like a child leaping into a deep river for a pleasant swim. After she slammed her head into his chin, she straddled his waist. Tancorix's dagger slashed Mosnar's throat open from one side to the other in a single motion. An explosion of blood gushed forth, spraying into the air, as a continuing stream of it poured over Mosnar's chest and hers, drenching them in red.

The man's eyes bugged as he stared at her in his final moments. His hands rose in attempt to stop the river of blood ushering forth from his mangled throat. The gesture was, of course, in vain. Mosnar dropped to one knee before her, kneeling.

"So, you bow to me now?" Tancorix shouted into

his face as she wiped his blood from her breasts and licked it off her fingers some like tasting sweets. “Too late.”

With all that was left of his strength, he made a final attempt to grab her. Tancorix easily avoided it. Finally, the man collapsed, falling forward, and moved no more.

Another cheer arose from the circle around them. “Tancorix! Tancorix!” came the chant that washed over them all and surely floated out to any within earshot.

Her smile broad and crimson as Taloric boomed his voice above the cheer, “So it done! Let all praise our eternal queen, Tancorix! Only she can guide our people!”

She looked at Weaver, whose lips quivered a little, almost as if she was speaking. An eyebrow raised at the wizardess, Tancorix blinked.

Weaver dropped her arms and then applauded her queen in din of cheers. Very politely.

As noon drew near, a series of tables made a rectangular base for the maps Ralta spread out. General Malitus and the other commanders of the divisions and auxiliaries gathered in as close as they could. The tent had been opened by the men so that Ralta could gaze out at the vast plain and the forest beyond.

“General, here is my plan of attack,” Ralta pointed at the maps and then gestured his hand up at the view before them.

Malitus looked down and up several times as he read it out, nodding, confirming everything looked correct.

Ralta said, "Our scouts have mapped this area out and it is fine with olden territory maps we did on scouts sent long ago. This great forest here isn't very thick, just high, like the gods seeded a natural wall to guard the vast valley beyond."

"That valley is like this one?" Malitus asked, fingers drumming on the map.

"Almost exactly, save for the end beyond turns up slightly and meets a great timberline that goes on for many more miles."

"I see."

"We can navigate around this first line here easily to the west and then swing about to properly engage the enemy's force. If they draw back into that huge forest there, well, we will not be fighting them at all today."

"You mean to have this fight now?"

Ralta nodded. "I tire of this insipid game and we'd be done with these Picts. Once we bloody their nose, their confederation will break and we'll walk through them. I have every confidence that is how this will play out."

"And what of the beastmen?"

Ralta looked up at the first. "Yes, what of them? It's a pity Quintus and August never returned as I'd like to know what we are dealing with."

Malitus frowned. "There's no way to know if they found anything, but their absence is troubling. The lines could use them."

Ralta's face, blank and stern, didn't betray he felt this way also. "They have others ready to fill their places—such is the way of the Legion."

"Indeed."

"If the creatures attack, they will do so from the trees. Our artillery will be focused on that direction, hoping to take them down as best they can should they attack. Setting these trees to light first will at best, flush out the Picts watching from there."

"Understood."

Ralta swept his hand on the map in a chopping motion, pointing to various units. "United, we shall cut into them. We'll assemble and let them come to us. I think they will be spoiling for a fight before sundown."

Malitus looked up at him. "Why do you say that?"

"Because Lammas is near, a holiday for them. I'm sure they will want to be bare assed and drunk by midnight."

Laughter chattered among the officers as the General nodded.

Ralta yawned. "There's the chance they won't want to engage us at all."

"True," Malitus agreed.

"But I have a feeling, call it a sensation or an inkling they are going to attack."

Malitus smiled. "What magic is this of you?"

"No magic, sir, just a hunch, shall we call it?"

The General walked to the edge of the tent and Ralta joined him. Their eyes scanned the forest and the units assembling. "Your magical hunches tell you anything about the beasts? They have to be out there still."

Ralta paused, thought a few seconds and answered, "I wish I could tell you something positive. They are not just dumb beasts, I would reckon, or they'd have kept at us. I don't comprehend it exactly, their desires or wants."

"Do you feel a greater force than us is moving this into place?"

Ralta raised an eyebrow at him and wore an incredulous look. "Like the gods themselves are at play here today?"

Malitus didn't look at him. "Yes. I feel suddenly insignificant."

"Nonsense. Please, stop such talk, sir. I think this is all chance, not a jest of the gods, if there even are any."

"You don't believe in any gods?"

Ralta shrugged. "Who can say for certain? It's not impossible, sir, but that they care if we kill a slew of barbarians or not is beyond silly. Seriously, what stake could the gods have in such a thing? Or the beasts? Why would they care?"

"The ideas of good and evil are not new."

Ralta smiled. "And we are evil because we push the border of Rome further north? Are we evil because we bring roads, water and sanitation to these mongrels? So be it then. I don't know if a dark force lurks getting randy over our evil acts, and I mean that in pure jest. But if there is such a thing, I like our odds of victory."

"Oh?"

"Yes. The darkness from beyond night itself wishes bad things, don't you know?" Ralta smiled. "Then we shall crush them and their hairy pets. This time, we will be ready and will be coming for them. I do so detest being the southbound end of a northbound female dog."

Flavius watched the 9th Legion from his position in the thick woods that stood between the sprawling plain and Rutland behind. He kept repeating his speech to himself, trying to rehearse what exactly to say to Malitus and Ralta as to what happened in the tunnel. Eyes closed, he tried to think of their reaction to being the sole survivor of the group, to being the man that who lived and to the revelation of what lay below.

Checking himself, he looked the part of a player in the drama. Blood stained his clothes and armor. He'd searched himself for a wound before, making sure none of it was his. Flavius remembered a cavalry commander, the one before August ascended to leader named Aulus. That man, a Syrian from so far away, had a great sense of humor and rode a horse like he'd been born atop one. Aulus perished because he'd knicked his heel in a minor skirmish with some rogue Celts and refused any treatment before a long ride back to the fort. When the troop arrived, Aulus was laughing, joking even, as he climbed out of the saddle and dropped dead. Flavius held no desire to bleed to death accidentally, unaware of an injury.

He backed to a tree, again redoing his story again, Flavius felt himself ready to recite it . . . and then sank to his behind. Tears flooded down his sweaty face and his nerve wavered. Flavius covered his eyes with his hands and wept like a scrounged child hiding in a thicket. At first, Flavius wondered why his body wouldn't respond suitably, why he couldn't arise and join the group. Frankly, he understood the reason all too well.

"You're all going to die," he mumbled, then dropped his hands to his knees, turning his head to where his brothers gathered. Oh, perhaps they'd come through as Romans usually did, even against such an impossible Pict force that swarmed out there someplace . . . but with the monsters also around, Flavius had no faith in their ability to survive. If he ran out there to join them, no matter their verdict on him, he'd die right alongside them.

He saw the Legion getting into formation. They were marching and not to the south. They were going farther into Caledonia.

Hands back over his face for several minutes, Flavius tried to pray and couldn't get the words correct. He wanted the darkness to swallow him up and for this all to be a dream. He wanted the gods to save them all, but wanted them to save him alone even more.

They will expect me to fight with them, he thought over and over again. *They will expect me to die there with them if need be.*

Flavius swallowed hard and felt the need to get violently ill, but he ran empty. For the first time since leaving the tunnel, though, he felt thirsty and hungry. The Legion would have provisions and get him straight, he understood that. Then again, the Fogou had many supplies, too.

No, he couldn't do it. Flavius understood that this was true betrayal of the Legion and Rome, that his career would be ruined. But then again, he reasoned, no one knew it but himself. He dropped his hands, smiling, understanding that there were no survivors to tell how he ran nor of him not joining in with them now.

He turned his head south, as if his mind could

transport his flesh there in an instant, to a safe haven, back to the barracks and meager troops left behind at their starting point.

His heart sank again, knowing that when the Legion marched home, any who survived, he'd be discovered as a traitor. That kept returning to his mind and Flavius shook. He wanted to go back to Rome, but not in chains. Betraying the Legion wouldn't get him a trip home, he figured, but if he were lucky, the cross. Days dying on those poles or a tree, he mused. How ironic. No, citizens usually could get beheaded, but commanders could be cruel.

In this forest, he felt so safe which was odd, considering how many monsters lurked about the countryside.

He watched the Legion start to gather up and get ready. In many ways, his body thrilled at the thought of that march, of the action to come, but his will soon dried up and he sank back.

Flavius couldn't make himself rise up and join his brothers.

Chapter XIV

Porcius shook his head and then glared at Drust. "Blood for life? You are a madman who needs to get out of the caves and trees more."

August looked at Porcius, bleary headed over the words spoken by the wizard, then back to the druid. "It is crazy talk, Drust."

Not looking at him, Drust said, "You think I created the idea of blood sacrifice and gifts from the gods because of it? You are not paying attention to many of your own religious ideals and teachings. It's all about blood. I wonder why it appeases the gods. Aye?"

Quintus held up his hand to August's chest. "Wait, he says he needs so much blood, and that he didn't disagree when you said his Pict folks could overrun us. But needs these monsters for . . . what? More bloodshed? On his own folks? But what for?"

Porcius looked at the lounging beastmen and their King, practically a kitten in the hands of Drust. "Your magick keeps them at bay."

Durst turned, eyebrow raised and eyed Porcius. "Brilliant, Spartan. If I had a bag of candies, I'd give them all to you."

Stepping back as if to strike him, but the settling in

again to where he stood, Porcius said, "You have a plan, something lurks beyond all this."

August's head turned and he looked across the great chamber over toward the lip that led to the narrow tunnel they came out of before. "Magick holds them at bay . . . " he mumbled. " . . . the damned tiny dragons . . . "

Quintus looked up at the tree. "And what is this?"

"A tree of life, full of balls of dragonfire," Drust answered simply. "What? You look as if you do not believe me. You asked and I answered."

Quintus nodded. "This is your reward for it all? Dragonfire, whatever that is?"

Drust smiled at him. "You are bordering on daft, Roman. Dragonfire is like liquid flame, rolls and eats all in its way as it must. A spark of it can consume a human body. Imagine what a ball of it can do to an army?"

"Your recompense?" Quintus fumed. "This cannot be all of it. Reach out and grab for you have it already. You are waiting for something."

Drust frowned. "Don't be a dolt. You think I bartered with these creatures for such an exquisite accolade? You think my magick didn't know where this celestial tree was? You take me for a donkey indeed, you dolt?"

August turned in a circle and suddenly reached over and grabbed Gonar by the shoulder with his left hand. August's right hand pulled the tiny blade from the apprentice's belt. The Roman from Germania ran for the lip.

None of the other Romans joined him and Quintus called for him to stop.

Drust chatted and roared in his throat.

Two beastmen awoke and shook their heads. In a moment, they were after August in his path heading to the tunnel.

But he didn't leap into the gap there. August stopped at the mouth of the cave and turned about quick, facing all that watched him. He took the pommel of the blade and smashed it into the symbol on the stone bars of the cages keeping the dragon-like beast inside. He smashed again and again to no avail, then crossed the way and tried to break the other seal just as the growling beastmen grabbed a hold of August.

Drust shouted, "Don't kill him."

They didn't, but disarmed him and dragged him, cursing and kicking, back to the tree area. Once they threw him on the stone floor by the others he groaned loud, rolling over very slow, in pain, they stepped back several yards.

Drust regarded him only to say, "You swear salty for a man who believes deeply in the White Christ."

"I'm a Roman soldier," August reminded him as he rolled over. "I happen to know all the curse words."

While Porcius and the twins knelt by August, Quintus challenged Drust, asking, "Why tell us this? I'm sure we are about to die or be eaten by these animals."

"I'm not going to kill you," Drust sighed, his long hair shaking side to side a little. "Such is the way of a scared girl, aye? You would be dead already if I wanted to kill you. That's the appetite of a Roman, hmm? Kill them all and build fences? Shut up your fool mouth and open your foolish mind. I'm going to enlighten you."

"What?" Quintus stammered, his anger going in many directions.

"It is Lammas, a high holiday for us from all time we know." Drust stepped a bit away from them, both arms up high when he said *Lammas*, but he dropped them soon after. "Today, this very evening, I'll have my vital sacrifice and you will all go out and be a part of it willingly. My hands won't get wet with your blood a single drop."

Porcius said under his breath, "That's big of ya."

Drust continued. "But I want to you to go into eternity knowing reality. When you face your god, gods or the chasm of hell itself, I want you to know."

Drust reached down and caressed the head of Adelaido and then drew back. He spread his arms, fingers fluttering, and started to chant.

Soon, their eyes closed, and they could see a different reality, a vivid life they viewed events from afar, like in a dream, guided by the voice of Drust.

The march of time goes where it must, and the footprints of the Greymen go as well, be they gray or dark of hue.

Adelaido was the King, largest, strongest, deadliest of the beasts. His lifespan ran so long and his memory longer than any of his brothers. Among his kind, history was passed from one generation to the next just as human kind, too, remember what had gone before. Even he, however, did not know the true origin of his race. Once, the whole of the world, all its lands, across the waters and beyond, belonged to his kind. They were the rulers and masters of all things beneath the rays of the sun. They had watched humanity emerge from its gardens, cast out into the world. They had watched the poor, weak, and near hairless race grow.

And grow quickly it had. In a matter of generations to Adelaide's race, the human had grown to outnumber them. In ages long past, the Greymen walked free, not in conflict with man any more than a panther or an elephant. As man started to leave caves and knit branches together to live in, the Greymen moved farther away, but there was no conflict. When man began to put one brick upon another and commune with what they thought were gods, conflict arose. Man grew in knowledge, thinking himself superior to all creations and children of the earth, thus, he saw the Greyman as a beast, not an equal.

The shamans warned against interfering with the lesser, "hairless" ones, as the humans were come to be known to them. Their explosion of growth was left unchecked as Adelaido's people withdrew from lands they had previously ruled.

Though ever pressed by the warriors, the shamans would not relent in their warnings not to engage the hairless ones. And so it went, that the great beasts gave up more and more of the world. They hid in the deepest forests and moved their civilization underground into caves and the sides of the very mountains themselves. When man created the fence and called it civilization, the Greyman left him to that and went further into the forest, and back into the bowels of the earth.

Many times the warriors turned against their

own in attempts to break out from under the yoke of the shamans' decrees. Many died in those great civil wars but never once did those who sought the blood of the humans triumph. The tribes and kingdoms of the beasts became scattered and cut off from one another. Though they could feel each other their blood and emotions, they were separated. Broken in such a way, the beasts could never hope to eradicate the hairless ones as they might have in the beginning.

The greatest of their cities rested in the sky-touching mountains of the land the hairless ones called Asia, surrounded by snow, and nearly unreachable by those outside. Then, by chance more than anything else, that city was discovered. Men came in unimaginable numbers against it. Men who feared them. Men who hated them for their appearance and ways. Men who did not understand nature and its subtleties. The city fell and with it the most holy of the shamans. The psychic tremors of that horrid massacre were felt around the globe. Though most of the scattered tribes merely mourned the loss of the heart of their race, Adelaido's was not content with tears and grief. They and a handful of other tribes decided that blood would be answered by blood.

They renounced their peaceful ways and became the monsters the hairless ones believed them to be. With their great strength and power, the humans were near powerless against them. Most of the tribes like Adelaido's contented themselves with holding the ground they had, killing any foolish enough to venture into it.

For Adelaido's kin though, this was not enough.

They declared war upon the hairless ones and moved about the land, wiping out all of the humans they came across. As their numbers dwindled, the great kings of the fiercer tribes realized they could not match the humans. Even if they slew dozens for each warrior they lost, a war of attrition was impossible and would ultimately be lost. At last, they, too, withdrew from the new world of man. They licked their wounds, and when their strength returned, ventured forth once more to kill and ravage.

And so this cycle continued and continues still. The time came for Adelaido to lead those who were his into the never ending war only this time, a human was waiting for them. Adelaido's kind knew of magic. Their own shamans had worked wonders with nature.

This man presented himself as a friend and made promises of his own magicks that Adelaido could not dismiss out of hand. An alliance was formed, be it a temporary one, between the beasts and man. Adelaido cared not who he and his killed of the humans so long as they killed and the guidance of the one called Durst provided them with an ample amount of human flesh to eat and bones to gnaw on.

When this land was consumed, Durst along with it in the end, they would move on to ravage more until they could do so no longer and were driven once again into retreat beneath rocks of the earth and the shadows of the forests that remained untouched by the hairless ones.

This was their desire, hidden in the folds of the King's mind, a sight easily accessed by the magick fingers of Drust.

The great line of Adelaido stretched from here, in this hairy thing at the foot of a tree of fire, into the distant past. He is that creature, the same one, his mind and flesh for all time, renewed by the passing of their meager consciousness. Not full of souls and spirits like humans, the Greymen passed on to the next generation, to a new beast man formed of their loins. When the time was right, when the ages were done for Adelaido, he forced his self into another and thus, continued on.

The King fathered many a child, in the past, and thus, had a ready vessel for his next life. Adelaido would be eternal for all time, his shamans be damned.

The King of the Greymen gripped his son by the head, and the child submitted as the King vomited his self into him, in a clear stream not unlike a heaving bile, pouring into the pores and mouth of the child, and in time, when Adelaido heart ceased, the pup became the King. The eternal essence that was Adelaido returned, his energy, his ways, into the new child.

But here, alas, lays the King of the beastman, the last of his line, dying, and longing to pass himself into the ready self of another. Why did the King make a bargain with Drust? Look closer at the King.

Adelaido had been mutilated. He bore no stones to be able to father another. Did you notice all Greymen were gray here not black in fur? Adelaido has no children, not this one, and his vain attempts to breed one with his own child or human folk fell short.

Promises on the wind to the King that if he and his kind complied that all past glories would be realized again. Drust made the bargain, knowing the appropriate vessel was needed. But it couldn't be common human, as much as the beast tried to create one. This individual had to be unique, and out of the ordinary, one constructed not as most creatures are, or, as most humans are.

Tancorix, Queen of the Picts, knitted together by the magicks of Weaver, from the blood and flesh of many donors, would be mated to the spirit of Adelaido and produce the offspring of their kind. She would be blissfully unaware of her real destiny, fostered by Weaver after once the war on the Romans was won, or why she'd been called forth for real. Yes, she'd unite the tribes, but would they really want to be ruled by an egomaniac from the antediluvian era? Unlikely.

Thus, the song of Adelaido draws to a close. Once the battle is met and the slaughter ends, Tancorix will be used as a vessel for the king and the desires of Drust.

Porcius shook his head, free of the vision, his heart ready to explode at the fate of Tancorix, divined by her own priests. Weaver, the wizardess from the north, who seemed in conflict with Drust . . . but was she at all? Had they created this grand ruse on them? They needed the beasts and a confederation of Picts . . . to destroy the Romans?

Blood. Drust needed blood. And a lot of it. Why?

Lammas. He needed a huge amount of blood. A massive . . . sacrifice. To whom? For what?

For life, he'd said.

For whom? Not for the beastman King . . .

And when they awoke, they were alone. No Drust, no apprentice, no beastman, not even the snoring King.

August sprang up and called out their names, as they were so few. "Quintus, sir! Porcius, Crispinus, Decimus, Rufus! They are all gone!"

All stood in time and looked about the vast subterranean area. Indeed, like he said aloud, they had been left.

Quintus shook his head. "Mummery and tricks, something about these wood worshipers, they make me sick." He slapped Rufus across the back of his head and turned to see Porcius holding up a gladius. "What?"

"They are all right there, sir, our weapons," Porcius pointed at the small pile of items on the floor. The twins already were there, reclaiming their bows as Porcius said, "It's like they wanted us to find them here now."

Quintus and August joined them. "Perhaps they did indeed." Quintus said quietly, thinking it all over. "I do think they want us to die."

August started to say, "They don't give a damn, sir . . . "

Quintus eyes snapped up and drilled into August. "You! German and lover of the Christ. Don't think I've forgotten about you. What a deceiver you are."

August eyes turned cold. "I hope you never do, Quintus Pilate, until your dying day, no matter how soon that might be, *sir*."

Both men took up their swords and helmets again. There hung a few moments where each man thought the fight between them would commence, but they carried on with the others there instead. Quintus pointed with his shield beyond where August had been. "We came in over there. Let us make our escape."

Crispinus pointed at the glowing tree with his bow. "Something is wrong. I think there are a few of those balls of light missing."

Porcius scanned the tree. "That may be." He reached out and touched one of the globs of churning flame. "Strange. I wonder if I could break it with my sword."

Quintus cussed him and then said, "Don't bloody find out, fool. Dragonfire they said it was?"

"Yeah," Porcius answered, mesmerized by the globes for a moment.

"Even if that is a lie, we don't know what magick lurks here in these caves." Quintus turned to the exit. "I do know the creatures are gone, so let us be as well."

August turned to Rufus, who stared up at the glowing tree. "Come along, Rufus."

Rufus bowed his head and didn't move but a single step.

Quintus laughed. "So sad that your kindred left you behind to die alongside us? Stupid boy. They think you a dog, too."

As they turned to go, August went over and put his hand on Rufus' shoulder. "Come along, this is almost finished."

His eyes focused on August's face, he said, "I know."

Weaver walked with Ragala through the middle of the lines of Pict warriors. She heard the cries of Queen Tancorix as she rode down the lines of the tribes of all Pictdom. Weaver, her apprentice and a few warriors carrying wood planks, emerged from the lines to see the Queen. There she rode, bare-assed and bareback on the roan horse, long red locks flying as she entreated the gods to help them. A few Picts exchanged glances, not knowing the gods she referred to, but the sight of Weaver made them all firm up their guile again. Most of the crowd was insane with bloodlust, all with her and ready to die and better yet, fight.

Thousands of Picts sat on horseback, flanking in the masses of fighters in the middle of the giant confederation of troops. Unlike their opponents, male and female fought side by side and shouted curses at the Romans across the meadows. Some had even learned Latin words and phrases in Greek so the Romans could understand their curses.

She watched the Queen and suppressed the desire to shake her head at the tresses of red flying in the air. Her own mass of flowing hair, naturally curly still at her advanced age, had been painted by time with gray and tips of white, but under all of it lurked a dull red, so badly faded by the cruel march of time in her flesh. She looked at her apprentice, the snarky Ragala, and thought she'd kill many to be that young again.

A deep breath entered her bosom and her body felt very warm as the warriors set down the planks and made her an altar.

Knowingly, Ragala whispered, "Lammas is here, mistress."

Not looking down, but focused on the sky above,

so clear and perfect this afternoon, Weaver replied, "Indeed, child. It will be the last Lammas for many of us today. That is not a bad thing, far from it."

"We all shall fight?" Ragala asked, her face glowing, ready to join the Great War at the smallest of words.

Weaver grimaced down at her. "I want the eyes of that General, girl. You will bring them to me. You hear me?"

Ragala nodded and knelt by the altar, watching the warriors bring forward the prancing white horse, so perfect. The girl smiled at the spring in its step.

Tancorix relaxed her entreatments down the line and Weaver raised her arms. She closed her eyes and called on their secret god Roan to aide them. Most all grew silent down the way and focused on her, several shushing their children to listen to the wizard woman.

"Lugh, eternal father god of our folk, send forth your shining spears into the hearts of the invaders! Let us today taste their blood through the ground this day, and let that same sacrifice reward your true children of this earth!"

The mass of Pictdom moaned the name "LUGH" sounding like a colossal cattle call, or an erotic moan.

"Roan, goddess, ride with his this day and destroy our enemy seven fold as you took out the marked one of the eternal creator!"

The crowd grunted "ROAN" loud.

Once this prayer to the gods had died down, Taloric stepped forward to raise his kilt and taunt the Romans. The sudden invocation of proper silence for their god's ears was shattered fast by vulgar jeers as the rest of the men and many of the women brandished their genitals at the Romans. Freely, many waved it all and cursed more salty than before.

The horse stood by the wooden altar and Weaver held out her right hand.

Ragala drew out the short sword on her hip and gave it to her mistress.

Weaver kissed the blade and said, "This is the day the god Lugh has made. Let us rejoice and be exceeding glad in it."

Ralta sighed as Malitus walked up to him at the first of the Roman lines.

"Well?"

Ralta replied with a wave at the barbarian ranks across the way, "They refuse to come out and acknowledge our demonstration of power, so the division and cavalry we sent out are coming back. It is our right to claim a moral victory here as they have done nothing to show us their hand, aside from their Queen riding naked down the lines."

The General looked on the shields of thousands of soldiers. "I'm glad to see we've kept a tight lip on that regard."

"The time for cat calls will be another day," Ralta cleared his throat and peered across the enemy line. "She is quite a fetching Queen, though I say, however she rides roughly well on that horse, naked and all, sir."

"That isn't our concern. If she is captured alive . . . "

Ralta looked to the heavens. "Please do not promise me her as a rape delight, sir. That is beneath me." When the soldiers around him gave a slight giggle he winked at the entreat *beneath him*, making them think he'd indeed cover the Queen of the Picts if captured. However, he had no plans to take her humanity that way.

"War can be Hades, Ralta," Malitus said dryly.

"Dear me, I see their priestess or wizard woman is out to make a show."

All focused on the curly haired wizardess as she entreated the gods, and then took a blade to a perfect white mare, spilling its guts onto a small wooden altar.

The disgust of many of the troops riddled the air and the General cursed them well before saying, "Damned barbarians indeed. They aren't bright enough to see this is a waste of time and good horseflesh?"

Ralta said, "I hear when they make a new monarch, they boil the guts of such an unblemished horse in water and baptize the King or Queen in the juices."

Malitus turned a shade of green as he took in the words. "I want that woman dead, you hear me? Dead. That wizardess? I will give a great reward to the one who slays her and brings me her head. I want to see her dead."

"Your love of horses astounds me," Ralta needled the General.

Malitus snapped his head about to face him. "These savages are what the emperor wants brought to heel. We shall kill every one of them. It can be done."

Ralta nodded. "I am sure of it, sir. We will hit the center of their force and pinwheel quickly our way like in the battles of old. The fools over there, for all of their might and numbers, will fold in time under the tactic."

"Good."

Many of the men chuckled and the General frowned, as he saw what Ralta did.

"Dear me, they are a proud lot. Look at that display of class and breeding, sir."

Many of the soldiers gave jaded applause to the display of sexual organs flapping out across the way.

"We'll best them that way, too," Malitus promised, teeth soon grinding.

Ralta sighed, waving a friendly hand at them that taunted them like he were passing on a summer afternoon. "What of their Queen? The bareback girl covered in tattoos?"

Malitus shrugged. "Take her alive and have her ravaged for a week before we burn her alive. If we can't take her alive, well, just ravage her for a day then."

The men nearby giggled at the joke.

Ralta turned and raised his arm, soon to let it drop. It was time to form up and be ready to fight the barbarian Picts.

The infantry fell out in triple battle order steadily, the Hastati troops in the first line up, ten groups of one hundred and twenty spearmen, a thousand two hundred in all. The second line, the Principes, equal in number to the Hastati, formed next. This formation took on the checkered quincunx formation behind the others many yards. Next formed the Triarii, ten groups of sixty men, setting up six hundred in formation behind the two forward lines. These men carried longer shields and wore more armor. These were the oldest, wealthiest soldiers, and not used to overt battle.

Ralta spoke the line none wanted to hear about, "If it comes down to the Triarii . . . " but never finished. It was understood if these men had to fight long it was a war to the bitter end.

Thousands of soldiers of the Velites came up to

their groups, these poor soldiers, none armored but sporting weapons, attached to each portion of the three lines ahead as the extra force to deflect all else that got by them.

But before they marched, the artillery started to load up the pitch and it was struck to fire. Their war ballads, hummed low, were full of fire, too.

General Malitus ordered, "Soften them up well with the artillery and let the archers fill them with arrows. Let's see if the long bowmen can test that armor or guile of theirs."

Ralta nodded, knowing many of the Picts die wore no armor or clothing, seeing it as unmanly to do so.

"We are as one," the General called out. "I fear not the beasts, either, for we stand as men at the ready, not surprised as before." He secured his strap and shouted, joined by all men on the plain for Rome.

Flavius had fallen asleep in the murky woods, a fact he damned himself for immediately upon waking. "One of those things . . . " he started to say, be thought himself a fool as no one was there to hear his words.

Would anyone? He felt utterly alone, the coward he'd became, and now that the troop movements had made him awake, he felt all the worse. He recalled the words of an old singer in a tavern, saying a story on how a sleeping band were killed in the night by a dragon, and woke up in Hell not knowing how they got there. Yes, indeed, one of the beastmen could've made playful work of him, crushing his skull in fast and no more thoughts would ruin his day.

Flavius did look on the field banishing the images

of waking up in true paradise, only to be cast out elsewhere when the nearest goddess with huge breasts read his deeds. The deed list ran fine until this act, one that made the gods give him looks of pity and ultimately, to send in the guards to cast him into eternal fire.

Hands over his face, he tried to laugh at his visions. Many faiths didn't teach of such an ending but he'd read too much. Straying from one belief confused him and now he feared gods he didn't even believe in much. But worries on what lay beyond death weren't his prime concern. Still breathing once this day finished was, frankly. He'd worry on facing gods or God in due course.

Something in him kept telling him not to join his brothers on the field. All things in his training screamed at Flavius to go on, get out there, take up arms, and fight. But his logical mind, and the words of his old professor, Nerva, rebounded in his head. Nerva taught them logic, intelligence and other Greek things some in Rome thought trifling, but not unhealthy to know. Nerva had dropped lines about dying well, but not foolishly. The tale of the 300 Spartans was famous among all fighting men, not just Porcius, and their loins burned to be that brave in the face of greater odds.

Across the other side of the valley Flavius had glimpses of a giant orange mass, Picts more than he could ever count . . . and then his eyes looked down the tree line and saw what the Romans couldn't see yet . . . hundreds and hundreds of beastmen ready to broadside the Legion. He wondered if even the fabled 300 would've called it a day in such a situation.

Again, slinking down on a tree, feeling like the worthless coward he'd became, Flavius wept and wondered if the life he fled to was worth living, if the burden of this all could be erased. He shook his head, Nerva's words holding him up, that as long as one drew breath, life could matter. He could do himself and Rome no good dead.

So, again, Flavius watched as the army prepare to advance on the Picts. He turned his eyes to the sky and saw two ravens circle. His heart sank further.

The Romans fought not just against Picts or creatures, but the magicks afoot of these savages. How could they survive?

How would he ever survive in that fight? How would he ever survive once it was done?

In light of the later afternoon, the beastmen all fell out into the valley. They formed not perfect ranks or groups, but assembled their numbers completely. Adelaido stood ahead of them in the center, and turned to give Drust a look.

Drust carried a bag up from the darkness. He didn't give the leader of the creatures any sort of expression or signal.

Gonar stood before the mass of the beastmen. The youth, though, was at work, assembling a simple flat plank of wood over two heavy blocks. The makeshift table became a natural altar when Drust pulled two wretched red objects from a bag on the ground. He held aloft these objects, hearts, and crushed them together, chanting words. Gonar stepped back as two ravens fluttered down from the sky. A few of the

Greymen stepped forward, wanting to swipe at such things, but their King growled to keep them back.

The ravens landed on either side of the wooden altar and looked up at Drust. Their black eyes blinked in perfect rhythm with each other.

He offered his forearms and each bird flapped a bit and landed on him.

"Go now, Hugdin and Mundin, be my eyes and guides in this war and sacrifice. Be my arms of thought and mind." He raised his arms and the huge birds fluttered into the sky, crying out as they ascended high and made a circle before moving to the west. Drust closed his eyes, smiled and then looked down at Gonar.

A single tear escaped the eye of Gonar. "Is the day here, master?"

"Lammas has arrived, the first harvest festival for us. Lughnasadh as we say is here at long last. Lugh of the shining spear looks down upon us well." He then leaned down, bloody hands on the boy's shoulders, and said into Gonar's heed without moving his lips, "On you and I. Today, we are together."

"I'm afraid, master," Gonar confessed, tears springing to his eyes in full.

Drust wiped the tear of the boy from each eye with his thumbs and then tasted them. Smears of blood were under the boy's eyes like war paint. He looked across the valley and could hear the Roman army assembling. "So am I." Drust looked back down at the boy and winked. "Fear is human so we are not quite gods, are we?"

"No, master, not quite."

Drust then said gravely, "Not yet." He leered at the

King of the beastman and nodded. "Let the blood of the Romans fill the grass of our land. Let the earth feed from it and give blessings to its proper children."

Gonar asked, "Once this day is done with, will all recall this event of war as one to never be forgotten?"

Drust coughed and watched the mass of hairy things start to grow anxious and take steps out of order. "On the contrary, son, no one will ever know this day happened, not clearly. But that is good. Only flesh longs for memory or lauds. The earth will remember and the wood, well, the wood knows."

The creatures grunted as one then started to move to the west.

Chapter XV

Taloric beat his chest with his fist and then extended both arms over his head, continuing the loud yell he'd authored long before. After a half minute, though, he dropped his arms pulled his sword from the ground where he'd shoved it to rest before. He yelled the shout not at the Romans but at the rest of his tribe, asking them if they were ready. They all answered in the affirmative, punctuated by rowdy sounds from deep in their guts. His eyes, untamed and wide, turned to Weaver. His words were near to buried in the frenzy of the Pict multitudes, all shouting.

"We shall take it to them!"

Weaver's eyes remained steadily on the Roman divisions as they slowly advanced out into the grassy valley. Her arms, down in front of her by the remains of the white horse, stayed steady, not quivering as those of her apprentice did as Ragala tried to hold them still at her sides. Weaver gave Ragala a slow glance, then returned her gaze up to the Roman lines, all starting to move like a wall of metal and redness buried under armor in the sun.

"Wait," was all she said as her look fixed in and her face gave no emotion.

Tancorix, still on horseback, looked as shocked in her face as Taloric was crazed in his. Mouth open, spear in hand, horse dancing, she searched for the words to yell.

Taloric looked at his Queen and then at Weaver, then back to Tancorix.

The Queen jabbed her spear at the sky like she could pierce it if she stabbed hard enough. She then demanded, “What do we wait for?”

Emotionless, her hands full of horse entrails, Weaver said, “You will know.”

Once the beastmen departed, leaving Drust and Gonar alone, the old man turned his back to the coming battle. With true purpose in his steps, trite and fast, Drust walked to the tree line of the forest. He looked in the woods like the lost man in a crowd, searching for an old friend, for Drust smiled when he discovered what his eyes longed for.

Gonar stayed behind his master a little ways, and then picked up the bag Drust had dropped by the altar before. The boy watched his master walk to an ugly tree. The tree, half dead, split in half, and bent to the waiting ground, shrugging like a body killed and curled up cumbersomely. The old man undid his robe and let it drop to the earth. Though impossibly old, Drust’s body looked as lean as a man in his twenties, Gonar thought, but he’d seen him naked before. Many doubted the true age of master Drust, that he couldn’t possibly be centuries old, mainly due to one’s logical mind. If one listened to the tales of one’s grandparents, they all knew Drust . . . and Weaver for that matter, and so did their grandsires. That Drust looked so old in the face and hair, yet possessed such a youthful frame, that oft confused Gonar, but spending so much time with his master, he understood him truly what he claimed to be.

Drust then turned about and lay down on the ruined tree, the shape not unlike a reclining chair or cupped hand once the old man used it as such. Drust lay back, eyes blinking many times up at the trees leaning overhead, and curled each hand under an outstretched branch under each arm. He let out a deep breath and it shuddered leaving him. That almost sounded like a weak or fearful exhale to Gonar, but he'd not soon impart such a theory.

Gonar joined his master and made to show of the state of Drust not much of any emotion. They both understood what was about to happen. The boy then reached unto the bag.

"It has all fallen into place," Drust muttered. "All is as I have designed."

"Yes master."

"Brilliant?"

Gonar smiled, but it faded away fast. "Yes, master. You are never wrong."

"I'd not say that, but I have cultivated this well into place."

"Yes master."

Drust gripped the edges of the branches until his knuckles went white. "Crucify me. Let us be done with it."

With a nod, Gonar held up the hammer and nails from the bag. With no more words, he went to work on his master.

"Sir," the communal shout came from the members of the veteran squads clustered around Malitus. "The beastmen approach from the east!"

His head turned toward the creatures that walked toward his lines. No emotion of concern touched his face and he didn't even mete out an admonishment or impart a dirty look to those who panicked at the sight. He showed no fear, rigid as a rail, and thus, the others soon calmed at his resolve. Such is the meddle of a true leader.

Blithely, he said, "They're not running."

"Why is this?" one of the troopers shouted then tried to stifle his tone.

"Just walking toward us like they are on a fine stroll," Malitus observed and feigned a yawn. "Ready for you this time." The General nodded to Ralta who shouted out the command for the army to shift to the right.

Artillery pieces ready to light up the Picts turned to the beastmen. The soldiers in front maneuvered to the right flank and came near to locking shields. There was no hesitation in the line, their numbers held true and straight on they went. They kept marching, the army shifting to the east, not the Picts in the north.

Ralta mounted up and rode to the brink of one of the marching columns to get a clear look in the afternoon's light. He adjusted his helm and turned to the rest of the divisions behind him. His eyes gleaming, Ralta couldn't help but smile in the face of such a sight.

"Sir?" one of the centurions asked of his jovial face. "What is it? Good news?"

"They bring us presents. I am astonished. This should be interesting indeed." He turned and raised his arm, knowing the artillery would fire on his signal. He growled under his breath, "You should have stayed in the ground, monsters."

Nonetheless, Ralta ire lessened when he focused on the lone dark haired monster leading the Greymen. Though the distance too great to tell for certain, Ralta thought the thing to be staring right at him. Ready to fight, ready to slay and ready to die, Ralta jutted out his chin, as if he welcomed a man to join him at the bar for a round of drinks.

"King," Ralta spat at the idea of the one leading the beastmen. "I'll show you the way to hail Caesar, with the sound of your heart beating its last."

In the clutches of the beastman King, like a half dozen others near him, rested a clear globe with a swirling light inside it.

August commended Porcius for finding the way out of the cavern.

"There are a hundred tunnels leading lower down into the earth," Porcius promised as they stopped near the entrance up the long stone ramp incline. They caught their breath and observed the identical twin dragon-like things imprisoned by the stone bars. "I reckon that's where the beastmen all come from, down in the earth."

Once they caught their wind, they all went past the creatures, though Quintus pausing to look at them again.

August said, "Not so pretty, aye?"

Quintus jogged after him. "What are they for? Why are they there?"

August shouted back, "It's not our concern."

"They must be for something," Quintus reasoned. "It is like they are guardians of the entrance. But there we go, right on past them at liberty."

August figured that this statement was true after a fashion, but he had bigger concerns as they broke to the sunlight.

The twins had gone on before them and pointed at the panorama of war that stretched out before their eyes. "Our brothers are assembled to fight them." Decimus exclaimed, hopping up and down fast. "Let us go to be with them as one." His brother nodded at his words and raised his bow. They didn't wait for anyone else, the twins ran off in the distance wake of the beastmen, who were clearly ahead of them. The brothers veered off to the left, hugging the tree line, trying to sneak about the mass army of creatures to rejoin their own military.

The rest exited the cavern and turned to their right to see Drust reclined back on a ruined old tree. In the sunlight, they could all perceive the points of nails protruding out through his wrists that were wrapped about gnarled branches . . . his feet nailed together on the roots . . . his apprentice nearby, eyes closed, facing the coming war.

"What craziness is that?" Quintus eyed Porcius and August. "Forget these freaks. Let us follow the twins."

As the two started out, August stopped, turned, took a knee and put his hands on Rufus' shoulders. "Go. Please go on. Now. I set you free." He touched the delicate chain on the boy's neck but did not remove it.

The boy blinked and tears ran down his face.

August let a tear escape as well. "It was never right for me to own you, or anyone. Go free. Go back to the free ones of your folk, or live in the woods like an animal if you so choose. I don't care what you do now, boy. I set you free." He stood quickly, turned his back and said, "I never want to set eyes on you again. If I do, on that day, you shall surely die."

As August started to follow the others, Rufus whimpered, "You won't see me again, master . . . August."

The soldiers jogged out of sight and a roar came up from the beastmen towards the Legion as if they had but one throat.

Rufus turned his back to the great noise. He faced Drust and Gonar.

Drust's head came away from the tree and he opened his eyes, but Rufus saw only whites. He shook at that face and the eyes, that clearly saw more than just him.

Rufus nodded and jogged back into the cave entrance.

Ralta's mount danced back as the beastmen roared. He gripped his reins and dug in his heels, trying to keep the mount in line.

The soldiers in front of Ralta took a tentative pause but kept marching forward.

But the dark one of the beasts, he took the globe of fire in his palms and held it down between his legs much lower than before. With an incredible move, his body contorted and he slung it far into the air. The glowing globe flew high, mounted up through the air like a mortar released from a sling. The radiant sphere went on over the first divisions, passing high above the head of Ralta and even the second line into the ring of veterans beyond.

And fell.

The globe exploded into an immense heap of flame that only rose up a few yards, but rolled out like water in every direction, gaining in volume as it moved away from the impact point. For a hundred yards square, the flame rolled on out like raging lava from a volcano, destroying the grass, converting it to a lime green ash and grabbing each soldier it found in an embrace. The men, enveloped quick like a thick orange colored water poured up their bodies heading for the sky, but this fluid consumed and baked them where they stood. Their skin sizzled, turned porous and peeled back in several layers in a moment's time, quickly giving way to muscle, then bone. These skeletons of flaming bones cloaked in armor staggered on, then fell, with no fanfare.

The air about the burning waves hissed like a thousand vipers were present. When the soldiers tumbled to the ground, their empty sockets couldn't see the earth itself turned a sponge tight crisp surface.

The Greymen released their volleys in turn, only a half dozen shots of the globes full of living fire went out and into the Roman lines, but each one struck another section of the tight wound Legion. Each time the result came out the same, a flame unlike the dirty pitch projectiles burned up hundreds of soldiers and put great gaps in their well laid out forces.

Then, the beastmen attacked.

The forward ranks of the Roman Legion no longer stood in a measured line, all near to interlocked. The balls of fire scrambled the cohesive unit and they pulled back, confused, unsure what they faced and not wanting to be doused in this odd fire. In utter disarray, they didn't dare retreat, but were flummoxed over what to do next. They were men of Rome, hardened veterans every one, but none of them had ever faced anything like the magic the Greymen had unleashed upon them in the strange fire. Men, their bodies ablaze, rolled about trying extinguish fires that wouldn't die, but this motion didn't last long as the fire ate them in moments. The smell of their charring flesh filled the air as their screams rang out, however brief.

Ralta slid off his horse and sprang into action, barking orders as the lines of fire slowly came to a halt. The animal was far too panicked by the flames to be of any use anyway. All around him, horses were tossing their riders from their backs and running wildly, trying to escape the beasts that were barreling towards the Roman lines. One horse, kissed just a bit by the mystical flame, ran quite a long way on three legs before staggering to the earth.

"The fire doesn't burn forever," Ralta shouted at them with force. "Reform and seize up!" His eyes at the oncoming wave of hairy beastmen, he looked for his support troopers. "Archers! Fire!" Ralta bellowed, "Everyone else form up, damn your eyes! Form up fast all of you and hold! It's do this strong or die time, lads!"

Roman archers all leveled their weapons at the

coming mass of beastmen. While most tried to aim, the chance to hit a target ran good for there were so many and they moved very close together. The volley from their bows and the subsequent second shot of bolts at the charging beastmen flew true on, slamming home into the monster's hair bodies. The arrows held no pattern, not favoring head shots or chests, in fact, many lodged in arms and legs, making the running motions of the bleeding Greymen rather comical if not in the middle of a bloodbath.

Ralta couldn't spot a single beast falling beneath that first volley, but the second sent a few down, tripping up the others that ran too close behind. The archer corps fired off two more rounds from their quivers before the beasts closed in on the unit.

The volleys had better effect than the first few, but it didn't deter the attack. The bolts in their bodies only angered the beasts and drove them on. With the latter volleys dozens of the beasts met their deaths. Archers then broke ranks and picked targets, concentrating their fire on the closest of the beasts turning at them. For each monster that died outright from the heavy Roman bowmen, more staggered wounded badly, whether from blood loss or the sheer number of arrows sunk into their bodies. With each step the blood painted the gray fur of the monsters and the wounds took a toll upon them. All of their frenzy couldn't compensate a heart hungry for blood.

Those who had short spears let them fly at the wall of beastmen. Ralta watched a spear sink into the chest of one of the monsters. Blood gushed from the wound right on cue, but the beast refused to fall. It snapped the spear's shaft, leaving the weapon's head buried in its ribs, and continued forward with a pained, furious roar.

Ralta yelled a final series of orders at the men around him and then he had no time to focus on anything other than his own survival. Two of the beasts closed on him fast.

"For Rome," he shouted, moving forward to meet them.

The first beast lashed out at him with one of its massive fists. Ralta brought up his shield, blocking the blow. His shield broke, splitting down the middle from the force of the impact. He reeled backwards, his arm arching though by the graces of the gods not broken. Casting his shattered shield aside, he steadied himself. The overconfident beast must have assumed its blow had removed him from action. It paid dearly for that mistake as Ralta's blade slashed a two-foot-long gash up the length of the beast's arm as it tried to continue on pass him. Blood splattered over Ralta as he pressed the advantage of surprise he had lucked into. His sword opened the beast's flesh twice more, first leaving a trail of blood upwards over the beast's chest as it turned and then again on its back swing. The beast was beyond anything but animal rage now. It gave no thought to protecting itself as it lunged at Ralta.

Ralta propelled his sword forward, bracing it with all his strength. Its tip parted two of the beast's ribs and plunged into the giant's heart.

Ralta let go of the blade, knowing he'd never yank it free in time to face the other beast that was upon him with it wedged as it was in the body of the first. Ralta ducked the hair covered fist that came at his head and shoulder rolled on the ground towards the corpse of a fallen Roman. The man's headless body rested in a pool of its own blood that continued to pump out slow of the jagged and torn stump of its neck. Ralta's hand closed around the hilt of the dead man's sword that lay in the congealing blood. He brought it up and around. With a loud thunk it made contact with the beast's hand that had been reaching out to grab him. The beastman jerked its wounded hand back as Ralta finished his roll, coming up onto his feet in front of the monster. The eyes of man and beast met up firmly. Ralta watched the storm of hate and fury raging in the beast's desolate eyes as it stared at him, cradling its wounded hand that dripped crimson badly.

All around them, the battle raged on. One Roman howled as a beast lifted him from the ground in a hug that crushed his ribs and snapped his spine. Another soldier charged one of the beasts, driving his sword to its hilt into the thing's gut. The wounded beast's hand closed around the soldier's throat as blood erupted from his mouth like an explosion of vomit. The Greyman released the soldier's corpse, yanking the blade free of its stomach. Trails of intestines poured out as the blade exited. The beast looked down at its own innards as if confused by the fact that a mere man had hurt it so. Flinging the sword away, the beastman fought in vain to ram its insides back into itself as blood soaked the hair of its frantically working hands.

A Roman soldier, his sword gone from his grip, fought a beast that towered above him, using his broken shield as a weapon. He raised the remaining piece of his shield over his head and brought it down onto the beast's right knee as he fell with the blow, adding the weight of his body to his strength. The piece of shield drove into the monster's knee. The noise of splintering bone preceded the beast's collapse. It toppled over to the ground near the soldier who fought to tear his dagger from the sheath it rested in upon his belt. His moves went too late though. The wounded monster caught him by the arm, jerking him to it. The beast's mouth opened wide and then closed as its teeth crunched into the soldier's skull. The man's body flopped and jerked about as the beast held it close and continued to chew deeper into his brain.

Mathew tried to rally several of the men into forming a square of interlocked shields, but failed. A fresh wave of the gray creatures came up from the rear of their group and swept over the Romans as they tried to structure up. Heavy fists, like great sledgehammers, broke bones and sent men to flying. Quickly, Mathew dodged a fist aimed at his helmeted head and countered by ramming the blade of his sword into the soft flesh of the attacking creature's armpit. He gave the blade a sharp twist before pulling it free. The beastman reeled, retreating a few steps, as rivers of scarlet flowed down its side. Attacking again, Mathew swung at it but even wounded the thing managed to bring up its other arm to block the strike. Swinging wild, Mathew's blade shaved a chunk of skin and muscle from the arm that blocked it from the beast's neck, wounding the monster further. The beast released a sound like the whimpering of a dog as Mathew pressed forward again. This time, his gladius found its target, opening the creature's throat from one side to the other. With a thud that seemed to echo in

Mathew's ears, the beast fell, almost hugging the earth in one flat fall.

Before the body even hit the bloody ground, Mathew scanned the battlefield for another of the things to dance with. He spotted his leader Ralta, not far away, engaged with a monster of his own. Mathew sprinted towards Ralta through the chaos of the battle, his desire to aide his leader in the front of his mind.

With gritted teeth Ralta strained to free his blade from the fallen beast's hand. The monster had caught his sword by its blade and refused to let go despite the blood that drenched the hand clamped around it. Ralta barely avoided the thing's other hand as it made a grab for him. Holding fast to the hilt of his sword with one hand, Ralta used his other to draw his dagger. Once the knife sprang free from his belt, he released his hold on the sword. The sudden surrender of the weapon the two fought over unbalanced the monster. It jerked back as Ralta jumped forward *onto* it. Ralta's fingers closed in the hairs of the beast's shoulder and he used that hold to pull himself upward in his movement. His dagger entered the side of the beast's throat with a wet squelching sound. The beast's eyes went wide as it realized it had just died. Ralta leaped off of the giant as its body toppled forward, landing in front of a startled Mathew who had apparently been coming to his aid.

Mathew opened his mouth as if to say something but only blood flowed out, running over his chin. Ralta watched Mathew's eyes glance downward to see the red soaked hair of the hand that emerged from his chest. Suddenly Mathew yanked from the ground and sent sailing through the air as the beast that had slain him shook his body free of its arm.

The monster that had slain the soldier was no ordinary beast. It was their dark King and Ralta found himself face to face with it. The hairs on the back of his neck stood up, reacting to the primal fear that not even Ralta's veteran hardness could completely overcome. The King of the beasts drew itself up to its full height, towering over Ralta, as he backed away from it. All his life, Ralta had trusted in whatever weapon he held in his hands. Now in this moment, the sword he clutched seemed a puny and powerless thing before the might of the creature that advanced upon him. There was no hurry to its pace. The King of the beastmen didn't roar or even part its lips in a snarl. It simply marched towards him, sure of itself and its power.

Ralta took a final look at the battle around them. His men, though many had fallen, were holding their own as best they could on the monsters, pushing them backwards. They were hurting the beastmen and making them bleed for each Roman life the monsters claimed. Ralta felt hope at that moment, that they would indeed break the back of the monsters and see tomorrow. The 9th Legion would see no end this day and he took pride in the fact the ones who fell would die as men of Rome, fighting on to the very last breath they had. In the distance, though, he could hear the roar of the Pict army calling on their god, Lugh or someone else he couldn't identify. Suddenly, his hope dissipated.

A part of Ralta wanted desperately to run, turn his back to the monster, and let his legs carry him away from this madness. It shamed him and that embarrassment became anger.

"For Rome," he cried and raced at the King of the beasts. His blade arced over his head and came downward at the King.

The creature effortlessly knocked the blow aside, skillfully or luckily using the flat of his hand to perfectly impact on the flat of Ralta's sword. This shot sent Ralta's sword bouncing to land somewhere far away in the grass of the field they fought upon.

Shaken to his core from the beast's rough parry of his attack, Ralta barely saw the massive hand that slapped him in the next volley. Something changed with his hearing. The sounds he heard were muffled and the world spun around him until his head finally stopped rolling and his eyes focused just enough for him to see his headless body spraying blood from the stub of its neck collapsing at the feet of the King of the beasts.

The oldest company of grizzled veterans of the Legion pulled their shields close and prepared to join the insane battle. Though shielded from the battle for the most part, these men fell out into formation about the General, fearless.

The crazed confrontation with the creatures looked like nonsense to Malitus, who hung back with these veterans. He almost casually turned to be reassured that the auxiliaries were ready. He sent orders down the chain of command for the artillery to readjust then to get the auxiliary troops to swing out on each side of the massive fight, like pinchers, and attack at the edges. They'd have fired already when the beastmen appeared then, but the strange balls of fire they threw confused the numbers of their men in front of them.

The artillery released their initial volleys throwing a rain of burning pitch across the back half of the beastman army, inadvertently cutting off their escape and pinning their numbers to the Romans. Another round of missiles from the catapults, rocks and more, launched against the main body of the beastmen, further scattering their numbers. Many in line took their shots and the giant shafts released from lower artillery pieces nailed dozens of the beasts outright. Mindful of other threats, they quickly reloaded and kept at the ready. When the battle turned on their men, they hesitated, unable to fire at their own men.

The dearth of the troops in retreat to find a spot to reform, the veteran core fell out, standing at the ready and waited for their signal to envelop the conflict or broadside it.

As the troops slinked away, reassembling as best they could, the veteran forces prepared to spearhead into the middle of the fray.

That's when the Picts let out their war cry.

Many fighting, many charging, even the dying stopped to listen as the crazed shout came up from the distant valley. When the Picts began their charge, Malitus broke off the veteran advance before it began and ordered them to swing about and hit the Picts. He also ordered the artillery to go back to their original aiming point, but it was too late for that. Many had reloaded and fired again at a few of the beastmen moving toward open territory. While these creatures were hit full on by the pitch loads, and ran aflame away until they collapsed, the reloading and re-aiming process would take a little time. The Roman's didn't have much time.

The Picts had swung about, tens of thousands of them in a curling loop to the west, flooding the artillery lines and flowing over the war machines like fresh blood down a forehead.

Several in the artillery ranks and a few of the surgeons broke and ran back south down the way they'd marched. Hundreds of Picts pursued them, throwing stone axes and blowing darts at their backsides. All those that stayed to rearm or re-aim their pieces died where they stood, crushed by a group using heavy war hammers. After the first few Romans were pinned to their artillery pieces by the hammers, their legs or pelvis' bones crushed to the machines, the Picts started a lurid game of it . . . who could smash a soldier in place and not kill him outright. Their game drew much mirth from the crew there, mostly a younger brand of the Picts, but as most teens will do, a few dozen at a time or in this particular case, several thousand, it got out of hand. First, they started a rag of riding past and cutting off an ear of a pinning Roman. Then, it escalated into riding by lopping off a head to see of a Pict on the ground holding a broadsword could swing and strike the airborne head. Soon, the Picts were roused from their game by their superiors, who, while laughing themselves, told them to finish them and rejoin the ranks of the great force.

Malitus joined the veteran group as they stood and waded, shield to shield, into the wild Pict force. The barbarians fought crazy with these vets, but stupid, many dying for no reason other than glory seeking. These savages had no experience in war, and many waded in with both hands over their heads holding their swords. The Romans where glad to supply a means for their deaths. However, Malitus felt terror as the endless field of orange hair spread out before him. So many fell as they fought badly, but the sheer numbers came near to bailing out the sea with a chamber pot.

Several of the Picts rode in on horseback to them then, hundreds of men swinging long cudgels and a crazy bare-assed woman, stabbing with wicked lances and chopping with great axes. One big fool sported a war hammer that looked comical until it drove a Legionaries' helmet down in-between his shoulder blades.

Malitus fought on and the field of battle shifted, the press of The Picts force pushing back their shield wall. He looked up to see the sky dim as a rain of arrows dropped on the men. They maneuvered to the turtle position, but their small groups of turtles felt the feet of ten thousand Picts on them and collapsed their shelters. Chaos reigned on the battlefield and Malitus found himself running like mad with no destination.

Drust groaned on the tree as the blood ran from his limbs. "I feel them, Gonar," he croaked. "I feel them close."

"Yes master."

"Every life lost, every soul as it leaves the body, every drop of blood on the earth itself." Eyes closed, his body seethed. "I feel them all."

"Is it time yet?" Gonar asked, hands shaking so much he held them together tight.

After he cleared his throat, Drust's voice still came

out trembling as he asked, "Do you remember our first meeting?"

His hip leaning on the aged tree roots that looped up, Gonar said, "You ask me so that you can tell me, my master, but I have heard the tale of being brought to you so many times, it's almost like I can recall it."

His cracked lips parted and a parched tongue stuck out a little before saying, "Tell me."

Gonar looked to the sky, the din of battle and the howls the dying in the distance not bothering him as he spoke. "Sometimes, I remember it one way, and others, very different. I can recall seeing you so long ago, like in a dream, like I emerged from a river, eyes full of water and there you were, looking down on me. You looked just as you do now, not a hair different. That memory stays with me but it isn't possible that it can be real."

Drust croaked again, "Why is that?"

"Because my grandsire Relle carried me, putting you in my arms in the wondrous stone circle at Callanish when I was but a few months old. There's no way I could recall that moment, but I've heard of that day, on Lammas, for all of my life."

"You've seen so much with me, little one, why is it you cannot believe your clear memory of that day?"

Gonar blinked and a tear ran down his face. He quickly wiped it away but his master made no note of it. "I remember other days stronger."

"But I ask you, why?"

Gonar closed his eyes shut tight. "To remind me of my duty."

"That you are truly mine, indeed, even before you were able to walk to that circle and take my hand?"

"Yes, master."

His breathing labored, Drust said, "You are mine, Gonar. You always have been."

"I understand."

"But don't weep for this life of yours. You understand what will be."

"Yes, I do."

"But you are afraid?"

"Of course. I can feel your fear, too, master."

Drust's face twisted a little and he kept shaking in his crucifixion to the tree. "Of course I am. I face a thing not very easy. Can you feel it, too?"

Gonar nodded, his hands extended out to show all of his fingers to be trembling. "I feel like rain pelts me, master. I feel the tiny pushes of all of them as they bounce off your spirit." Eyes very tight, more tears ran down Gonar's face.

"All of their souls, they feel like a punch in the groin to me, but one all over my body. I need them and they sink in. You are mine. You feel their kiss as well."

"They are starting to hurt. It's going to hurt bad, isn't it?"

"Your learning will soon expand out beyond all things you could ever dream of, son. Things you may not want to face, but yet, they are."

Eyes open, he looked to the distant battle. "So many dying."

"Yes, and I find that very good."

"It is going to get worse, too."

Drust lifted his head a little, his mane of hair matted on the tree. "I find that very great indeed. It is all going as I premeditated. There is but one thing left to do before I leave."

"Is it time, master?"

Durst choked with a quivering head, "Yes. Climb on."

"You don't ask if I am ready, for . . . "

"And why don't I ask such a thing?"

Head down, Gonar replied, "Flesh questions. Wood knows."

"Indeed, now climb on."

Gonar took many breaths as he dropped his tunic and stepped up onto his master's body, straddling him.

"I am sorry that I do have a question."

"One last one, my son."

"This is going to hurt, isn't it?"

"Quite a lot," Drust said, a half chuckle in his voice. "But birth is always painful."

Chapter XVI

Rufus looked deep into the globe between his knees and breathed on the clear surface. A slight mist of flame bubbled on the interior at his breath. He drummed both sets of his fingers on the sphere. The fire within the globe snapped out, touching to his fingertips, like it wanted to kiss his flesh. He took his hands back, wary of Drust's warnings to be careful and not stare into the globe too deeply and for very long. His mind swirled at the implications of the orbs, that they were from a fabled tree that held dragon-fire somewhere on the Isles . . . a tree he'd really seen below the ground. Somehow, this flame came culled from an actual dragon thousands of years before. His mouth dry, he thought on other childhood fables and that they also may just be reality. One like Drust, the eternal wise man of the oaks, who was immortal. Rufus shook his head fast as if to let the reality of those fables slide from his exhausted mind.

He didn't watch any of the war, nor could he hear any of it from the position he sat, deep in the cavern of the beastmen, at the confluence that led into the narrow tunnel of bones. He sat just out of eyeshot of the writhing twin creatures behind the stone bars. His mind reeled as he studied the creatures and then looked away. In many a night time fable, he'd heard tales of creatures like these, called Uilepheists.

"But you are real, no?" he looked up and whispered to the creatures that leered at him through the strange bars. "You are conjured from master Drust?"

Neither of the Uilepheist creatures spoke to him, but their eyes, so reptilian and distant, did follow his every move. He felt they didn't seek to understand him, but to simply eat him. But that was the way of dumb beasts, no? One couldn't really control those things in nature that were meant to be wild, not for long, not with spells or stone bars. Not forever.

His eyes moved down from the tiny dragons and traced the symbols on either side of the walls. These mystic symbols that were locked over the pentagrams fixing the bars made his mind reel and heart beat faster. Rufus' hands shook sometimes and he almost put them back on the globe to steady them outright. He looked down the tunnel into the great chamber of the beastmen and waited.

Rufus felt happy to be alone and that solitude hadn't bothered him in the past. The woods and the caves never had made him afraid as a child or afterwards. He used to dream of being a man of the oaks, a wise man of the wood, living in communion with the gods of the forests.

His mouth went sour after a brief bit of happiness. The gods of the forest didn't care much for the Celts or Picts, he figured, else wise they'd have done more to stop these red breasted, perfumed pricks from afar. This violence on the field of battle, this great slaughter, wasn't a program of the gods to help them be free. His freedom, if he really got any of it, would be a byproduct of what it was really about. No, this wasn't about the gods or goddesses and their mercy. This was about master Drust and his mate, and their selfish desires. All the rest, them, the Romans and the beasts, were just stepping stones to reach over a creek. A creek in his mind that ran with blood.

August, Porcius, Quintus and the twins swiftly navigated the edge of the forest to avoid the mass of creatures attacking. Granted, the idea of fleeing into the trees slapped August a few times, but he felt drawn into the battle like a foot sinking into the mud.

Bursts of flame painted the field and over a thousand Romans lay dead or dying. The creatures attacked all over in the forward ranks of the Legion, and the ordered lines broke across the valley.

Just before they reached a point to enter the fray, Quintus pointed to the north with his gladius. The orange mass of Pict humanity seemed to flatten out on the opposite edge of the forest and began to sweep towards them.

Quintus raged and ordered them in, seeing a rear guard still formed and getting ready to hold in lines against the Picts.

As they ran fast into the field of battle, the Picts let go a great war cry and ran forward at a rapid pace.

August entered the fight, stabbing the nearest Greyman and swinging his shield hard, maiming many other creatures as he ran past, trying to get to a section of the gutted army where the shield walls still looked to mean something. Somewhere in the mix, he lost sight of Porcius. The big Greek ran toward the Picts like he knew where he was going.

The call of the god *Lugh* echoed over their heads and the earth shook as a force of so many thousands Picts thundered toward the turned flank of the Legion. He'd never seen so many people, but heard tales of such masses of barbarians. August waved off the twins as he saw the mass of humanity flood about the artillery section of the Legion, many dying in the press of flesh, but swallowing the Roman soldiers up fast.

Soon, utter chaos reigned as Romans ran everywhere, the creatures mingling with the Picts, who flowed through, like ants in a dispelled mound.

In the crazed fray, August saw a Roman stop and face him, staring eyes full of bloodlust.

Quintus.

Weaver swept her arms about, the curved farming sickles in each hand, removing the throat of a Roman soldier who'd been knocked to his knees. He gasped loud, a sucking wind from within his body pulling air in one last time. She moved on, seeing one of the Greymen on his all fours, two Pict warriors hacking at him like he was a tree trunk with their axes. She went on past, kneeling once to hamstring a soldier and then castrate a Greyman in the next moment. Her back pressed and flowed with hundreds about her, and she swam in the complex surge of bodies, mostly her own folk pushing against many Romans and a few beasts.

She felt every one of them die, though, like a finger jab to the back or gut. Her spells weren't broken because of the rush of the war over her position. Every life, every soul, every damnation Weaver felt course into the mystic funnel she'd created in the ether-world. The souls and spirits that poured over her came to make her feel so full, like after a feast of venison and roots.

A gush of blood splashed across her face and Weaver didn't flinch, her focus riveted on the sensations dropping on her spirit. *The time had to come soon*, she thought desperately, and looked for Ragala. The girl's head bobbed in the distance and came closer in the din of battle.

When the figure of General Malitus staggered into her view, Weaver smiled. The man, not beyond his years, but one having seen better days, set his feet and glared into her face, his chest heaved . . . a chest devoid of his breastplate armor. Malitus held no shield, one of his leggings had been ripped off and blood spattered his underclothes. His helm strap dangled, but his cover remained as Weaver stepped up. He still gripped his crimson gladius.

"You," he growled, eyes set on her, a person he'd not really ever seen clearly, but was obviously well aware of her presence in the Picts.

"Mihi?" she taunted him sweetly in Latin, lips parted, blood from an unknown source running into her teeth.

He jumped over a fallen Pict warrior and swung his gladius, meaning to slice into her bosoms from her torso, but she countered with the sickle in her left hand. This move, though blocked, broke her implement in half with ease. She just swept the shot away, and grinned her bloody smile at him, unconcerned.

Weaver went to cut him low with her right sickle and he easily parried the shot away. The General turned the gladius over, shoving it straight into her belly. Near face to face, their eyes locked.

Malitus grinned. "Welcome to Rome."

Weaver's mouth opened wide as did her eyes. Her hand dropped the sickle. Both hands gripped The General's shoulders as he drove the blade through her body.

She smiled again.

His grin faded.

Weaver said with happiness in her voice, "*Vos enim mori . . .*"

He pulled back from her touch, twisting the blade as he did so. "Oh, I'm about to die, aye?" He turned the blade over, ripping loose a huge section of Weaver's intestines out as he did so. She staggered but didn't fall. He laughed and stomped a section of the guts down fast to the grass. As he watched her go slowly to her knees, he snapped, "There are some guts for a spell, you rotten witch! Prophesy to me now! Prophesy!"

Her eyes squinted shut; she shook badly. Weaver muttered, "*Vos enim mori . . .*"

Suddenly the look on Malitus face changed. His mouth widened and he gagged, at the same moment a sword tip popped through his midsection, just below where his sternum stopped. On that blade, a loop of his guts shook.

Weaver reached out and grasped the gory bit of flesh and pulled it close to her own intestines on the grass. Her legs quaking, she struggled to stay up on her knees, trying to breathe, but unable to stop smiling.

Malitus turned, his steps wavering, blade still through him to face his killer.

Little Ragala looked up into his face, smiling through bloody lips as well. Her hair a tangle, half ripped loose from her scalp, nose broken, but otherwise all right, the girl smiled.

Weaver fell to her back, gasping, but laughing as well.

Malitus fell to his knees, looking down at his stomach and then at the girl, who cracked her knuckles and pulled two tiny daggers from her waist belt. She stabbed both knives into his skull and delved them into his eye sockets. His hands to her wrists for a moment, they soon fell away as he gasped, agony whiplashing through his frame.

Ragala stepped off the prone body to the Roman General and walked to Weaver like a war wasn't going on around them. She put her twin blades away and stood astride the body of her mistress, staring into the sky. She held out her hands, showing the eyeball in each palm and fingers gripped lightly.

Weaver held out her hands as she gasped, "*Vos enim mori . . .* "

The girl nodded as she reached down to claps hands with her mistress. "I know, I know. He's gone."

Weaver pointed to her own eyes.

Ragala went to place the eyeballs on her mistress's face.

Weaver said, "I wasn't talking to him."

The wizardess' hands gripped the two daggers of her apprentice from the belt holsters and stabbed the girl in the sides, causing a scream so loud that it pierced the din of war. Ragala's mouth froze open in shock as her scream faded. She fell forward slowly into Weavers embrace and felt the blades delve into her back.

Arms about the dying girl, Weaver's voice groaned loud, and those nearby stepped away from the strange happening.

Weaver heard the voice of a woman, perhaps even Tancorix, exclaim that the bodies were glowing and melting like dying embers. The wizardess' ears popped and Weaver heard the in rush of air like when one emerges from a lake swimming. There was a great deal of pain, her very being felt stabbed and crushed a hundred times.

But soon, Weaver felt no pain whatsoever. In fact, she felt incredible, better than she had in decades.

When she stood, she looked at the others on the field of battle and they gaped, open mouthed at her appearance. A few dropped down and prayed. Many more ran away.

Weaver stepped away from the body of General Malitus and stretched her arms to heaven.

Ragala was nowhere to be seen.

Porcius crawled from beneath the mound of limbs and flesh that he'd been swept off with when the beastmen ran back for their grim cavern. He scuttled for a very long way and then sat on his backside, looking at the great battlefield and the death all about him. Porcius couldn't see any more Romans but plenty of Picts as they pushed the beastmen away and then headed south, after any Romans who fled, presumably.

When the roan horse holding Queen Tancorix

trotted up to him, he smiled, but couldn't muster the strength to laugh.

"So, Spartan," Tancorix said loudly. "You have survived the war."

He held out his hands and gave himself sarcastic applause. "For what that is worth. I think I'm bleeding from everywhere, but not cut deep."

"I had hoped you would, that is very true. You are a fine warrior," she said and climbed down from her horse.

Porcius breathed deep, feeling a number of wounds wheeze out blood and aches abound. His lungs shuddered deep in his chest and he couldn't quite clear them out. His chest ached and ribs moved by themselves. He cursed himself, a mass of broken bones and cuts

Tancorix pulled down a bow from her mount and then reached behind her head and took an arrow from a quiver. "I used to be an excellent shot, you know, thousands of years ago."

Eyes on her, understanding all at last, Porcius smiled. "Who can say? I bet you aren't skilled enough to get it through my heart with one shot."

She notched the arrow.

Porcius lay down, his back to the earth.

Tancorix straddled him. "On your elbows, Spartan," the Queen ordered. "I'd not do this to one such as you on your back."

Up to his elbows, Porcius asked, "There. Now, are you going to nag me to death or send me to my ancestors? I'm very tired."

She let the arrow fly. The thrum of the bow strung echoed on the quieting field and the missile pierced through Porcius chest to exit out his back, mostly. He stayed aloft on his elbows and grimaced at the pain.

"Damn," he said, softly. "I hoped that would be faster." He then laughed and his head lolled back on his neck. His helm fell off, but he didn't flatten out. Porcius stayed on his elbows, grinning up at the clear afternoon sky as his eyes saw their last. He did, though, hear Queen Tancorix mock him in Latin as he departed.

"*Sic semper tyrannis.*"

August easily bested a few Picts in hand to hand, as they had no style to fight with a sword, other than hack and slash. Each one fell for his tactic of suckering them in close and back swipe to cut their thighs out.

Walls of beastmen clashed with the Romans, but many of them stumbled back at the flood of the Picts.

Down to a knee, August avoided one wave of creatures and humanity, but caught sight of the twin brothers Crispinus and Decimus, not aiming their bows at the creatures or Picts . . . but each other. They counted out a sequence and fired, each shooting an arrow through the eye and brain of his brother simultaneously. Their bodies fell fast, but were soon ripped asunder by the creatures, but they were dead before it happened.

August felt the pommel of a sword crash into his helmet. The shot sent him to the ground and he slid on the bloody grass. That slide was all that saved him from the falling sword of Quintus. Again, he pulled the sword up and stabbed at August. Rolling, August avoided death and swiped his ankle, leg whipping

Quintus to the ground. On his all fours, he scampered forward, head thrusting into Quintus' gut as he rolled over, sending his commander to his back.

Quintus swung his left arm up, dagger gripped tight, and stabbed the blade into August's chest plate armor. The knife didn't enter flesh, but felt like a punch all the same.

August maneuvered over Quintus' legs and brought his sword up to bear. Both men to their knees, they exchanged a few sword thrusts, but didn't land a shot. August moved back, got to his feet just as Quintus charged him, crazed slashing.

Something filthy about his Germanic heritage on the wind, but August grabbed Quintus over his back as he tackled him. Again, he felt the dagger of Quintus, probing his armor, going for a soft spot. He felt a sharp pain by his kidneys, but suddenly Quintus was off him. August again defended with his sword, but saw that this wasn't necessary any longer. A group of Greymen stood by them, five holding Quintus like a doll. The five, four with a limb and one with a head, pulled back. Quintus barely cried out as he was ripped apart, not as clean as the original thought of the act, if there truly could have been one. In fact, while both arms and head came loose, painting their Greymen in geysers of blood, the legs stayed on, but he wrenched apart in the midsection, elongating his spine and guts into the open air of Caledonia like a wishbone.

August turned about to run and felt the earth come up to meet him from behind. No, nothing struck him save for a tide of huge feet trampling him down. These feet soon left him and were replaced by smaller ones, those of men, some wearing crude deer skin covering, others sandals but mostly, calloused bare feet. He tried to breathe and couldn't, but in a minute looked up and saw the mass of beastmen moving away and the rear side of the Pict army flooding after them. The monsters headed back to the cavern from hence they originated.

August still couldn't breathe and his body ached so much, but soon felt so cold. The din of battle faded out of his ears and he tried to rise, but couldn't. A high pitched ringing filled his ears, and then he felt a hand in his, pulling him away from the ground. The world washed-out away and the afternoon light suddenly became impossible to see through. The hand in his, so warm, lifted him up and he felt all of his pain depart away.

A voice said from all about him, "*Well done, good and faithful servant; August Wolf Arminius, you have been faithful over a few things. I will make you ruler over many things. Enter into the joy of your master. Forever.*"

Eyes closed tight, Rufus dreamed of his homeland, a merry place of his childhood, but a dreamy one for certain. In his youth, there had always been Romans. Tales for elders told of a time long ago when there were no such people in the Isle and the Britons ran free. He liked that idea, even if it were a fantasy. It felt good. Smelled good too, like baking bread and the morning wind over the forests after a heavy rain.

A terrible scent and loud growls roused him from his light slumber. Panic gripped his body as Rufus thought he'd slept on past his hour of action. The growls though were far enough away so his terror subsided. He'd been seen, though.

Rufus got to his feet and stared at the influx of beastmen to the huge chamber. Many bled and all were angry at the chaos in the world above. They pushed each other, angry to have been suddenly found themselves there. A beastman with bloody white fur pushed off his brothers and even bit into the cheek of one of them. Suddenly, all of them seized the bloodiest of their brothers, screaming "Minh!" over and over before they ripped him to pieces.

Then they looked at Rufus.

He didn't shout, didn't threaten, none of that. Rufus just smashed the globe into the archaic symbol on his left and the smashed it to his right as Drust had told him to do. His zigzag motion drew the view of many of the creatures so full of ire.

The substance holding the flame within adhered to the pentagram and stretched across the opening. Rufus stepped way back as the fire exploded, bursting beyond his place, hiding all out in the great cave away from his sight for a moment. But his flame sphere spun in circles where he'd just stood, consuming a few feet of stone on either side, and causing the ground all about them to shake. Rufus turned and ran as he heard the howls of the Uilepheist creatures. When he turned from the narrow shaft to look back, a great avalanche of stones started to cover the opening to the tunnels, but he saw the Uilepheist dragons squirm out from their prisons, screeching as they slithered out into the chamber of the beastmen, following the wave of rolling dragon-fire.

He didn't see what happened next to any of them, but his ears testified to a screaming tone from the beastmen he'd not heard before, not even on the battlefield in the distance. He paused a few times, wanting to make sure it all went down, but his crazed curiosity went away and Rufus ran. Within a few moments, his ears were spared the loud screams in the chamber as the rocks and dirt sealed the chamber away forever from him.

Rufus ran in the dim tunnel, stumbled in the piles of bones and then struggled to climb onto the lip of the ledge along the tunnel. He walked sideways, sliding down the way until he reached the other tunnel openings.

He thought to go south and just run away from it all, but his inquisitiveness led him up and out into the Fogou of Rutland. Soon, he then slipped into the forest and jogged, dodging the trees and making his way to the scene of the battle.

His eyes drank in the great massacre on the battlefield and he saw the wave of all Pictdom driving all survivors in the open to their utter doom.

Rufus walked out into the open as the Picts chased down many on horseback and speared them and their horseflesh alike. Rufus watched and was spotted by the Picts.

He ripped off the tiny chain of his neck. Rufus pulled off his sleeveless tunic. He then undid his kilt and threw it against the ground.

The Pict warriors gave him a cheer as Rufus walked off to the south-west, naked, into the trees.

Gonar lifted his head from the tree and saw afternoon sky fill with projectiles. The flaming balls of pitch dropped onto the field not far from where he and his master had reclined on the tree. The Greymen ran like mad, heading their way. None came for the forest area where Gonar was, but headed into the mouth of the cavern.

The flames rained down like hell fell from the sky, but when Gonar closed his eyes, he felt a sudden rush, as he saw through the eyes of the ravens flying overhead. His chest pounded as he saw the Picts manned the artillery pieces of the Romans, and turned them on the fleeing beastmen. After that volley came a huge bulk of barbaric humanity, the whole of Pictdom on the field, chasing, crushing and killing all that was in their path.

Gonar could see their feral Queen, Tancorix, her horse swiped from her bare ass by a vicious beastman who was soon hacked to bits by a dozen Pict warriors with swords. A few of those swords broke as they hacked, but flying debris didn't stop the barbarians. Tancorix came up on her feet, fighting, joining in the fray with a blade, blooded by the battle. She emerged, newly baptized in red along with that huge man, Taloric. They laughed together and went to finishing off the Romans and then, chasing the beastmen back.

While many of the Greymen went into the earth again, the great dark haired one, Adelaido, stopped short of the mouth of the cave, seeing Gonar by the woods. His dark eyes glared at Gonar, his lips peeled back in a rage as many of his brothers pushed past him to get into the cavern.

Gonar stepped off the tree, and the King of the beastmen's head tilted. Eyes blinking at him several times, Gonar figured that deep in that animal mind, Adelaido understood a great many things. Clearly, he could see the Picts had no allegiance to his hairy folk from the earth's innards and had turned on them in the heat of battle, treating them as worse than savages. He comprehended master Drust had used him, somehow, but couldn't quite understand it all.

Gonar felt positive his own appearance riled up mystery in the mind of Adelaido. When Gonar shrugged off his master's nailed hands, letting the spikes pull from his own belly . . . and clearly seal back up in the light of the flickering artillery deposits, he figured that animal King smelled magicks in the air. Still, more Greymen pushed past him and Gonar guessed the King wanted to run over and slay him. Could he? Would he try? He waited for the attack, but did not seek it. Like his master before him, he listened, he waited. Wood listened, wood waited. Wood knew.

The roar of the huge force of Picts neared and Adelaido moved into the mouth of the cave with great haste, looking at Gonar and then at the oncoming rush of wild humanity. These Picts started to run slower, they too seeing Gonar and what he did next.

He reached back and took up the long white tresses of his master, now stained with blood. Gonar moved them over his head like a hood, the dented face of his master, fibrous, willowy and curled inward to form a perfect skull cap, as if all his bones were no more. The exhausted husk of Drust's body slid over Gonar's close, pulled about himself like a robe. Gonar then laughed, a cackle that made the Picts stop and drop to their knees and one that forced the King of the beastmen to back up from the mouth of the cavern, unsure of what he saw.

Slowly, Gonar started to walk toward the mouth of

the cave. He stopped, turned to the horde of Picts and waved once with his right hand. The motion wasn't the gesture of a silly boy or a taunt. No, he beaconed one of the Picts to come to him, someone specific.

From out of the mass of humanity emerged a small girl, barely thirteen to look at her, but naked, pale and sporting a mane of curly red locks that draped her bloody body. She walked up to Gonar quite casually before the army of barbarians, and looked him in the eyes. A grim silence spread over the Picts, punctuated only by the cries of the dying far off behind them.

Gonar reached out and took her left hand. They turned, together, and walked toward the mouth of the cave. The King had long since run down into the earth, but they pressed on, very indifferently. Hand in hand, they stepped into the edge of the cavern and peered inside. Far down into the tunnel that led to the great chambers, they saw Adelaido watching them . . . .

The children stopped by the stone bars of the cave's mouth. Gonar reached out with his left hand and touched the pentagram and rune that held the Uilepheist creature within.

He nodded to her and said, "Weaver, likewise."

The young Weaver reached out with her right hand and touched the other pentagram. Together they pushed and called upon Lugh and Roan at once. A corona of light enveloped the two youths.

The beastmen down below and the Picts watching behind drew back.

Still holding hands and glowing a little all over, the two youths moved back up the tunnel several steps.

Stone crashed outwards as the twin Uilepheist creatures burst forth, the ground and cave shaking.

They let out a high pitched howl suddenly repeated deep in the chamber. Many that day will tell of that echo, but others drew bigger tales, that other Uilepheist creatures lurked down the bowels of the earth and were set at the beastmen in that direction. They could all hear a scream from down inside and felt the earth move again.

Gonar and Weaver emerged from the cave mouth just as it collapsed inward. After a few moments the Picts arose and cheered, chanting the names of their two gods, their people and then, their wizards. While simple barbarians, they weren't fools. They saw their enemies vanquished and the two wizards that guided them born again.

Once they quieted to a degree, Gonar announced to them, "Lammas is here, my brothers and sisters. Let the feast begin!"

Again, the cheers broke out and they all started to leave the place.

Gonar undid the skin of Drust and let it fall away to the ground. Again, he took up Weaver's hand and squeezed it as they walked.

She looked into his eyes and smiled.

Her hand felt so warm to Gonar, soft and supple, like the caress of a newborn.

Gonar said, "All for you."

Weaver smirked. "All for us, Drust."

Gonar winked. "Forever."

Epilogue

"There's one alive over here," came the words into the ears of the prone Roman soldier, his body in the mud and brush at the edge of the forest.

Hoof beats rang out loud in his ears. The horses and men speaking were very close. The soldier heard a voice command with force. "Turn him over for me and tell them to stop trying to put out the fires of Eboracum. May as well let it all burn down."

"Yes, sir."

"Bloody Picts, they ravaged and burnt it beyond our ability to recover."

Hands flipped the horizontal soldier over. "Yes, he's breathing, sir. First one we've found in the territory."

The hoof beats stopped nearby, but the eyes of the soldier didn't open. "By the gods, look at him, covered in blood and filth, his shield broken and no sword."

Many hands shook him. "Come on, soldier."

A voice commanded, "State your name and rank, soldier."

Eyes blinked, and the parched mouth opened, but gave no sound.

The officer on horseback ordered, "Give him wine. Loosen that tongue up for us."

"I bet he has some tale to tell," one of the other soldiers stated.

Once he sat up, cradled by two Roman soldiers, and wine had washed the man's gullet, he sputtered, "I am Flavius Varius, fourth Tribuni Augusticlavii to the 9th Legion of Rome."

The man on horseman chuckled. "That's quite a name for a man barely alive and covered in blood, excrement, and scars."

"What?" one of the soldiers questioned, but still fed Flavius wine.

The soldier nodded. "Yes. That means *golden haired life*. Well, you lived through whatever happened here, sir." The man saluted him, being a centurion, Flavius did outrank him. "What of the 9th?"

Flavius sat up more set to his buttocks on his own and looked around. He then nearly leaped off the ground in a start. Then men held him down until he relaxed.

"Easy, sir, you've had a terrible fright."

Flavius hissed, "It was monsters . . . "

The centurion asked, "Monsters? The Picts you mean?"

Reality crashed in on his mind, or at least, the present reality he chose to accept.

Flavius swallowed more wine and looked about, recognizing the hills around what used to be the Roman fort city of Eboracum. "Picts . . . so many . . . "

"Yes, but they've all gone back north now."

"North?" Flavius gagged. "Good . . . good . . . "

"Sir, monsters?"

Eyes shut for a while, Flavius breathed deep. "Monstrous, I mean . . . just terrible . . . what the barbarians can do . . . "

"Yes," the centurion agreed. "They are pure savages on ice, sir. We'll get you cleaned up fine and healed up well again."

What a preposterous thing if he told of the creatures, inane monsters no one had ever seen before really. He'd be taken for war mad and a laughing stock if he told the truth. Flavius thought of all his friends, of the men he left behind and how they all must've died under the feet of these beasts. But where were they?

"Where are the rest?" Flavius wondered as they pulled him up to his feet. "Where are my brothers? Where is the Legion?"

"From the patrols up north and all we can see, you are the only one alive."

Flavius blinked. "The last one? How can this be? We were so many against . . . monstrous . . . peoples . . . all around . . . "

The centurion nodded. "The sole survivor, sir."

"Gods . . . " Flavius gasped. Could he really be the only one left?

One of the men offered, "Whatever gods you pray to, I want to know. They did a great job saving your behind, sir."

"I guess so . . . yes . . . praises . . . " but his voice trailed off but he sucked down more wine, choking a little but smiling to the men, who returned his good look in humor. He tried to name a god, to throw out a random deity he would put in a hug for this great blessing, but he couldn't recall the name of any at that moment. Not a single one.

"The last one, harsh indeed," the centurion said. "That'll make some story to the people back home."

"Yes, I suppose so . . . "

" . . . and on the Senate floor."

"It will, won't it?" Flavius croaked as they steadied him on his feet.

"Easy men," the centurion smiled. "Don't drop that man one bit. You might be handling a future Senator or even better."

They bore Flavius to a tent far away and out of the smoky ejecta from the falling fort. They left the flaps open to the great tent. An attendant slave brought basins and towels. He bathed him thoroughly and a doctor arrived to study him, bind over his wounds well and then let the slave clothe Flavius' aching body gently.

Flavius lay down for a bit, but his body couldn't adjust to the comfort of the simple cot, so he sat up and looked into the woods at the mists of the morning.

He saw two figures there in that cloudy morn. His heart leapt at first, thinking a charge of Picts about to overrun him and his survival from the insane war was all for naught. In a moment, he calmed, for they were just children. He sighed, but a bit of panic remained. The children were not Romans and didn't run away nor fade away like a dream.

The boy was very tall for a youth probably just reaching his teens, his forehead broad and hair long to his shoulders . . . but colored gray.

Savages, Flavius smiled a little. Who could figure them?

The girl beside the boy, certainly the same age, barely a teen, her flowing reddish locks naturally curly and spilling over her shoulders, had skin so pale it shown ivory in the morning light. When the other soldiers spotted these two in the woods, they shouted at them to come out. The two disobeyed. They turned to go, but smiled. They took each other's hands and faded back into the woods.

Flavius lay down and took many breaths, trying to convince himself that the boy didn't look exactly like a younger version of the great druid master Drust.

Coda

"Thereupon, having reformed the army of the Rhine in regal manner, he set out for Britain where he put many things straight and was the first to build a wall, eighty miles in length, by which Romans and barbarians should be divided."

In the year 122 A.D. emperor Hadrian visited the Isle of Britannia and ordered the building of a wall eighty miles long. The stated reason given in *Scriptores Historiae Augustae* was to separate the Roman empire from the barbarians of the north. That was it. Unlike most frontiers, this wall, with its many forts along it, would tend the border and allow access to only ones they wanted to the empire. While that came as an official reason, defense was the clearer one put to the senate. However, as many observed firsthand, the wall sat in rather strange locations for a good defense, and cavalry units serving in forts there would have no real point, save for patrols.

Men of the II Augustus, VI Victrix and XX Valeria Victrix Legions, built the wall over the next six years, along with help from soldiers of the British fleet. These forts were never manned by any Legion, but by auxiliary forces alone.

There are a great many theories on the fate of the 9th Roman Legion. Many think it vanished in the mists of Caledonia, others that it was disbanded, but it is not mentioned again in history after 120 AD.

The conventional theory is that the Ninth fell in a conflict on Britain's northern boundary against the native Picts or rogue Celts. The distinguished 19th century German classicist Theodor Mommsen stated that, " . . . under Hadrian there was a terrible catastrophe here, apparently an attack on the fortress of Eboracum (York) and the annihilation of the Legion stationed there, the very same Ninth that had fought so unluckily in the Boudican revolt." Mommsen quoted Roman historian Marcus Cornelius Fronto, from the 160s AD, who said to emperor Marcus Aurelius: "Indeed, when your grandfather Hadrian held imperial power, what great numbers of soldiers were killed by the Jews, what great numbers by the Britons." It is plausible that Hadrian's wall was a response to a military catastrophe.

However, inscriptions later have added some credence that more than one senior officers, possibly deputy commanders of the Ninth in 120, lived on for several decades to lead renowned political careers, the Mommsen theory has fell out of favor with various academics.

. . . And on the Scottish mountain of Ben MacDhui, hundreds of miles from the wall, tales are told of a giant, humanoid beast, the *Am Fear Liath More*, or, The Big Grey Man. Many believe that this isn't just a flesh and blood beast, but a phantom, spirit, or possibly a gateway between world hidden in the magical lands of the highlands.

About the Authors

Eric S Brown is the author of numerous book series including the Bigfoot War series, the Kaiju Apocalypse series (with Jason Cordova), the Crypto-Squad series (with Jason Brannon), the Homeworld series (with Tony Faville and Jason Cordova), the Jack Bunny Bam series, and the A Pack of Wolves series. Some of his stand alone books include *War of the Worlds* plus *Blood Guts and Zombies, World War of the Dead, Last Stand in a Dead Land, Sasquatch Lake, Kaiju Armageddon, Megalodon, Megalodon Apocalypse, Kraken, Alien Battalion, The Last Fleet, and From the Snow They Came* to name only a few. His short fiction has been published hundreds of times in the small press in beyond including markets like the *Onward Drake and Black Tide* Rising anthologies from Baen Books, the Grantville Gazette, the SNAFU Military horror anthology series, and Walmart World magazine. He has done the novelizations for such films as *Boggy Creek: The Legend is True* (Studio 3 Entertainment) and *The Bloody Rage of Bigfoot* (Great Lake films). The first book of his Bigfoot War series was adapted into a feature film by Origin releasing in 2014. *Werewolf Massacre at Hell's Gate* was the second of his books to be adapted into film in 2015. Major Japanese publisher, Takeshobo, recently bought the reprint rights to his Kaiju Apocalypse series (with Jason Cordova) and it is slated for 2018 release in Japan. Ring of Fire Press will be releasing a collected edition of his Monster Society stories (set in the New York Times Best-selling world of Eric Flint's 1632) later this year. In addition to his fiction, Eric also writes an award-winning comic book news column entitled "Comics in a Flash." Eric lives in North Carolina with his wife and two children where he continues to write tales of the hungry dead, blazing guns, and the things that lurk in the woods.

Award winning author **Steven L. Shrewsbury** lives and works in Central Illinois. He writes hardcore sword & sorcery and horror novels. Twenty of his novels have been published, including *Born of Swords*, *Within*, *Overkill*, *Philistine*, *Hell Billy*, *Thrall*, *Blood & Cell*, *Stronger Than Death*, *Hawg*, *Tormentor* and *Godforsaken*. His horror/western series includes *Bad Magick*, *Last Man Screaming* and the forthcoming *Mojo Hand*. He has collaborated with Brian Keene on the two works *King of the Bastards* and *Throne of the Bastards* and Peter Welmerink on the Viking saga *Bedlam Unleashed*. A big fan of books, history, guns, the occult, religion and sports, he tries to seek out brightness in the world, wherever it may hide.

The end?

Not quite . . .

Dive into more Tales from the Darkest Depths:

Novels:

The Third Twin: A Dark Psychological Thriller by Darren Speegle
Aletheia: A Supernatural Thriller by J.S. Breukelaar
Beatrice Beecham's Cryptic Crypt: A Supernatural Adventure/Mystery Novel by Dave Jeffery
Where the Dead Go to Die by Mark Allan Gunnells and Aaron Dries
*Sarah Killian: Serial Killer (For Hire!)*by Mark Sheldon
The Final Cut by Jasper Bark
Blackwater Val by William Gorman
Pretty Little Dead Girls: A Novel of Murder and Whimsy by Mercedes M. Yardley
Nameless: The Darkness Comes by Mercedes M. Yardley

Novellas:

Quiet Places: A Novella of Cosmic Folk Horror by Jasper Bark
The Final Reconciliation by Todd Keisling
Run to Ground by Jasper Bark
Devourer of Souls by Kevin Lucia
Apocalyptic Montessa and Nuclear Lulu: A Tale of Atomic Love by Mercedes M. Yardley
Wind Chill by Patrick Rutigliano

Little Dead Red by Mercedes M. Yardley
Sleeper(s) by Paul Kane
Stuck On You by Jasper Bark

Anthologies:
Tales from The Lake Vol.4: The Horror Anthology, edited by Ben Eads
Behold! Oddities, Curiosities and Undefinable Wonders, edited by Doug Murano
Twice Upon an Apocalypse: Lovecraftian Fairy Tales, edited by Rachel Kenley and Scott T. Goudsward
Tales from The Lake Vol.3, edited by Monique Snyman
Gutted: Beautiful Horror Stories, edited by Doug Murano and D. Alexander Ward
Tales from The Lake Vol.2, edited by Joe Mynhardt, Emma Audsley, and RJ Cavender
Children of the Grave
The Outsiders
Tales from The Lake Vol.1, edited by Joe Mynhardt
Fear the Reaper, edited by Joe Mynhardt
For the Night is Dark, edited by Ross Warren

Short story collections:
Ugly Little Things: Collected Horrors by Todd Keisling
Whispered Echoes by Paul F. Olson
Embers: A Collection of Dark Fiction by Kenneth W. Cain
Visions of the Mutant Rain Forest, by Bruce Boston and Robert Frazier
Tribulations by Richard Thomas
Eidolon Avenue: The First Feast by Jonathan Winn
Flowers in a Dumpster by Mark Allan Gunnells

The Dark at the End of the Tunnel by Taylor Grant
Through a Mirror, Darkly by Kevin Lucia
Things Slip Through by Kevin Lucia
Where You Live by Gary McMahon
Tricks, Mischief and Mayhem by Daniel I. Russell
Samurai and Other Stories by William Meikle
Stuck On You and Other Prime Cuts by Jasper Bark

Poetry collections:

Brief Encounters with My Third Eye by Bruce Boston
No Mercy: Dark Poems by Alessandro Manzetti
Eden Underground: Poetry of Darkness by Alessandro Manzetti

If you've ever thought of becoming an author, we'd also like to recommend these non-fiction titles:

Where Nightmares Come From: The Art of Storytelling in the Horror Genre, edited by Joe Mynhardt and Eugene Johnson
Horror 101: The Way Forward, edited by Joe Mynhardt and Emma Audsley
Horror 201: The Silver Scream Vol.1 and *Vol.2*, edited by Joe Mynhardt and Emma Audsley
Modern Mythmakers: 35 interviews with Horror and Science Fiction Writers and Filmmakers by Michael McCarty
Writers On Writing: An Author's Guide Volumes 1,2,3, and 4, edited by Joe Mynhardt. Now also available in a Kindle and paperback omnibus.

Or check out other Crystal Lake Publishing books for more Tales from the Darkest Depths.

Hi, readers. It makes our day to know you reached the end of our book. Thank you so much. This is why we do what we do every single day.

Whether you found the book good or great, we'd love to hear what you thought. Please take a moment to leave a review on Amazon, Goodreads, or anywhere else readers visit. Reviews go a long way to helping a book sell, and will help us to continue publishing quality books. You can also share a photo of yourself holding this book with the hashtag #IGotMyCLPBook!

Thank you again for taking the time to journey with Crystal Lake Publishing.

We are also on . . .

Website:
www.crystallakepub.com

Be sure to sign up for our newsletter and receive two free eBooks: http://eepurl.com/xfuKP

Books:
http://www.crystallakepub.com/book-table/

Twitter:
https://twitter.com/crystallakepub

Facebook:
https://www.facebook.com/Crystallakepublishing/
https://www.facebook.com/Talesfromthelake/
https://www.facebook.com/WritersOnWritingSeries/

Pinterest:
https://za.pinterest.com/crystallakepub/

Instagram:
https://www.instagram.com/crystal_lake_publishing/

Patreon:
https://www.patreon.com/CLP

YouTube:
https://www.youtube.com/c/CrystalLakePublishing

We'd love to hear from you.

Or check out other Crystal Lake Publishing books for your Dark Fiction, Horror, Suspense, and Thriller needs.

With unmatched success since 2012, Crystal Lake Publishing has quickly become one of the world's leading indie publishers of Mystery, Thriller, and Suspense books with a Dark Fiction edge.

Crystal Lake Publishing puts integrity, honor and respect at the forefront of our operations.

We strive for each book and outreach program that's launched to not only entertain and touch or comment on issues that affect our readers, but also to strengthen and support the Dark Fiction field and its authors.

Not only do we publish authors who are legends in the field and as hardworking as us, but we look for men and women who care about their readers and fellow human beings. We only publish the very best Dark Fiction, and look forward to launching many new careers.

We strive to know each and every one of our readers, while building personal relationships with our authors, reviewers, bloggers, pod-casters, bookstores and libraries.

Crystal Lake Publishing is and will always be a beacon of what passion and dedication, combined with overwhelming teamwork and respect, can accomplish: Unique fiction you can't find anywhere else.

We do not just publish books, we present you worlds within your world, doors within your mind, from talented authors who sacrifice so much for a moment of your time.

This is what we believe in. What we stand for. This will be our legacy.

Welcome to Crystal Lake Publishing—Tales from the Darkest Depths

CPSIA information can be obtained
at www.ICGtesting.com
Printed in the USA
LVHW01s1516190218
567133LV00012B/838/P